GIRLS ON FIRE

ROBIN WASSERMAN

ABACUS

First published in the United States in 2016 by Harper
First published in Great Britain in 2016 by Little, Brown
This paperback edition first published in 2017 by Abacus

1 3 4 5 7 9 10 8 6 4 2

A CIP catalogue record for this book
is available from the British Library.

ISBN 978-0-349-14131-2

Printed and bound in Great Britain by
Clays Ltd, St Ives plc

Papers used by Abacus are from well-managed forests
and other responsible sources.

MIX
Paper from
responsible sources
FSC
www.fsc.org   FSC® C104740

Abacus
An imprint of
Little, Brown Book Group
Carmelite House
50 Victoria Embankment
London EC4Y 0DZ

An Hachette UK Company
www.hachette.co.uk

www.littlebrown.co.uk

Robin Wasserman is a graduate of Harvard University and the author of several successful novels for young adults. Her writing has appeared in the *Los Angeles Review of Books*, *Tin House*, the *New York Times*, on theatlantic.com and elsewhere. A recent recipient of a MacDowell fellowship, she lives in Brooklyn, New York. *Girls on Fire* is her first novel for adults.

'Like lightning in a bottle, Robin Wasserman's *Girls on Fire* captures girlhood friendship in all its shattering intensity. Seldom do you find a novel that so transports you to the dark, febrile terrain of adolescence, when intimacy and connection can turn on a dime to something far more dangerous. A captivating, terrifying novel, and one you won't forget'
Megan Abbott

'Flicking between points of view, Wasserman is even in her storytelling, sustaining her narrative by slowly revealing the dangerous secrets Lacey is keeping. Wasserman writes with immense energy. As a portrait of a coming-of-age, obsessive female friendship, the novel is captivating' *Sunday Times*

'The tumultuous emotional extremes of adolescence are vividly conjured up in this brooding tale ... This creepy tale is powerful and haunting' *Sunday Mirror*

'A deep, dark vision of the dangers of girlhood emerges from this captivating novel' *Stylist*

'Electrifying story about two teenage girls and a mystery suicide' *Heat*, Our Top Five Reads

'One of the most gripping reads of the year. Heady, atmospheric and thrilling, you'll be turning the pages long after you'd planned on putting the book down. And it is well worth staying up for' *Irish News*

'Part murder mystery, part love story, this page-turner explores the dark side of the all-consuming friendship between a wide-eyed good girl and a grunge-worshipping rebel' *Cosmopolitan*

'A gripping coming-of-age story with a difference' Natasha Harding, *Sun*

'A book so wonderful, so terrible, so nightmarishly compelling that I hardly knew what to say when I finished reading it. Wasserman has wrapped up a love story inside a murder mystery, a promise and a testament inside a confession – and has a title ever been truer? The reader comes away singed' Kelly Link

'Like a mini *Thelma and Louise* as directed by David Lynch ... Dark, disturbing and utterly fresh, this is a story to pick up and not put down' *Stylist*, The Most Addictive Thrillers of 2016

For my father, who believed that I could.

In the Age of Gold,
Free from winters cold:
Youth and maiden bright,
To the holy light,
Naked in the sunny beams delight.

—WILLIAM BLAKE

Queen of lies, every day, in my heart.

—KURT COBAIN

GIRLS
ON
FIRE

TODAY

See them in their golden hour, a flood of girls high on the ecstasy of the final bell, tumbling onto the city bus, all gawky limbs and Wonderbra cleavage, chewed nails picking at eruptive zits, lips nibbling and eyes scrunching in a doomed attempt not to cry. Girls with plaid skirts tugged unfathomably high above the knee, girls seizing the motion of the bus to throw themselves bodily into their objects of affection, *Oops, sorry, guy, didn't mean to shove my boob in your face, was that a phone in your pocket or are you just happy to see me.*

Try not to see them, I dare you. Girls, everywhere. Leaning against storefronts, trying so hard to look effortless as they dangle cigarettes and exhale clouds of smoke; tapping phones while shrieking about how *Mom is a such a bitch.* Girls hitching up skirts by the liquor store, hoping for a handle of vodka if they show enough leg; girls in the makeup aisle, gazing helplessly at the nail polish display like they can hear you silently cheering them on, willing them to scoop those cherry reds into a bag, to succumb to temptation and expectation, to *give in.*

Give in: Pick a pair of them, lost in each other, a matched set like a vision out of the past. Nobody special, two nobodies. Except that together, they're radioactive; together, they glow. Nestled into a seat in the back of the bus, arms tangled, foreheads kissing.

Long for the way they drown in each other.

Follow them off the bus and onto the beach, as the one in charge—there's always one in charge—shakes her curls free. Her makeup is expertly applied, her beet lips excessively large, kissable. The other girl wears no makeup at all, and her hair, bone straight and dyed platinum, flaps in the ocean breeze. Watch them lick soft-serve, pink tongues flicking spiraled cream. Watch them turn cartwheels in the surf, watch them slurp Dorito dust from sticky fingers, watch them split a pair of earbuds and stare up at the clouds, their secret soundtrack carving shapes in the sky.

Try to hold yourself back from rising over them, casting them in aging shadow, warning of millennial futures, the end of days, days like this, warning them to taste each sugary minute, to hold on tight.

Hold back, because you know girls; girls don't listen. Better, maybe, to knock them out, drag them into the sea. Let this perfect moment be the last, say, *Go out on a high note, girls*, and push them into the tide. Let them drift off the edge of the earth.

Impossible not to see them, not to remember what it was like, when it was like that. To sit there, shivering, as the sun dips toward the horizon and the wind blows cold over the waves, as the sky blazes red and darkness gathers around the girls, neither of them knowing how little time they have left before the fire goes out.

Remember how good it felt to burn.

US

November 1991–March 1992

DEX

Before Lacey

They finally found the body on a Sunday night, sometime between *60 Minutes* and *Married with Children*. Probably closer to Andy Rooney than Al Bundy, because it would have taken some time for the news, even news like this, to travel. There would have been business to attend to in the woods, staking out the scene with yellow caution tape, photographing the pools of blood, sliding the body into a useless ambulance and bagging the gun—there was a universal logic to such things, if TV had it right, a script to follow that would get even our sorry Keystone Kops past the hurdle of touching a corpse, seeing and smelling whatever happened to a body after three days and nights in the woods. From there, who knew how it worked, officially: where they took the body, who was tasked with calling the parents, how they extracted the bullet, what they did with the gun, the note. Unofficially, it did what bad news did best: spread. My father always liked to say you couldn't shit your own bed in Battle Creek without your neighbor showing up to wipe your ass, and though he said it largely to get a rise out of my mother, it had the whiff of truth.

It was always my mother who answered the phone. "They found him, that boy from your school," she said, once the show had gone to commercial. We were all facing carefully away from one another, toward the giant Coke bottles dancing across the screen.

She said they'd found him in the woods, found him dead. That he'd done it to himself. She asked if he'd been my friend, and my father said that I'd answered that already when the boy went missing, and that I barely knew him, and that I was fine, and my mother said, *Let her speak for herself*, and my father said, *Who's stopping her*, and my mother said, *Do you want to talk about it*, and my father said, *Does she look like she wants to talk about it.*

I did not want to talk about it. I told them I might later, which was a lie, and that I wanted to be alone, which was the truth, and that they shouldn't worry about me, because I was fine. Which was less true or false than it was necessary.

"We're sorry about this, kid," my father said as I made my escape, and these were the last words spoken in my house on the subject of Craig Ellison and the thing he did to himself in the woods.

He wasn't my friend. He was nothing to me, or less than. Alive, Craig was Big Johnson shirts and stupidly baggy jeans that showed off boxers and a hint of crack. He was basketball in the winter and lacrosse in the spring and a dumb blond with a cruel streak all year round, technically a classmate of mine since kindergarten but, in every way that counted, the occupant of some alternate dimension where people cheered at high school sporting events and spent their Saturday nights drinking and jerking off to Color Me Badd instead of sitting at home, watching *The Golden Girls*. Alive, Craig was arguably just a little less than the sum of his meathead parts, and on the few times our paths crossed and he deigned to notice my existence, he could usually be counted on to drop a polite witticism along the lines of *Move it, bee-yotch* as he muscled past.

Dead, though, he was transformed: martyr, wonder, victim, cautionary tale. By Monday morning, his locker was a clutter of paper hearts, teddy bears, and basketball pennants, at least until the janitorial staff were instructed to clear it all away amid fears that making too much of a fuss might inspire the trend chasers among us to follow. A school-wide memorial was scheduled; then, under the same paranoid logic, canceled; then scheduled again, until compromise finally took the form of an hour of weepy testaments and a slideshow scored to Bette Midler instrumentals and the flutter of informational pamphlets from a national suicide hotline.

I didn't cry; it didn't seem like my place.

All of us in the junior class were required to meet at least once with the school counselor. My appointment came a few weeks after his death, in one of the slots reserved for nonentities, and was perfunctory: *Was I having nightmares. Was I unable to stop crying. Was I in need of intervention. Was I happy.*

No, no, no, I said, and because there was no upshot to being honest, *yes.*

The counselor sponged off his pits and asked what disturbed me most about Craig Ellison's death. No one used the word *suicide* that year unless absolutely necessary.

"He was out there in the woods for three days," I said, "just waiting for someone to find him." I imagined it like a time-lapse video of blooming flowers, the body wheezing out its final gaseous waste, flesh rotting, deer pawing, ants marching. The tree line was only a couple blocks from my house, and I wondered, if the wind had been right, what it might have carried.

The thought of the corpse wasn't what disturbed me most, not even close. What disturbed me most was the revelation that someone like Craig Ellison had secrets—that he had actual, human emotions not altogether dissimilar from mine. Deeper, apparently, because when I had a bad day, I watched cartoons and hoovered up a bag of Doritos, whereas Craig took his father's gun into the woods and blew a hole through the back of his head. I'd had a guinea pig once that did nothing but eat and sleep and poop, and if I'd found out the guinea pig's inner turmoil was stormier than mine, that would have disturbed me, too.

Weirdly, then, the counselor shifted gears and asked whether I knew anything about the three churches that had been vandalized on Halloween, blood-red upside-down crosses painted across their wooden doors. "Of course not," I said, though what I knew was what everybody knew, which was that a trio of stoners had taken to wearing black nail polish and five-pointed stars, and had spent the week before Halloween bragging how they would put the devil back into the devil's night.

"Do you think *Craig* knew anything about it?" he asked.

"Wasn't that the same night he ... you know?"

The counselor nodded.

"Then I'm guessing, not so much."

He looked less disappointed than personally affronted, like I'd just ruined his *Murder, She Wrote* moment: *Insightful bystander unveils dark truth behind hideous crime.*

Even to people who gave Craig more credit than I did— maybe especially to them—the suicide was a puzzle to be solved. He'd been a good boy, and everyone knew good boys didn't do bad things like that. He'd been a high school point guard with a winning record and a blow-job-amenable girl-friend: Logic dictated joy. There must have been extenuating circumstances, people said. Drugs, maybe, the kind that made you run for a plate glass window, imagining you could fly. A game of Russian roulette gone wrong; a romantic suicide pact reneged; the summons of darkness, some blood magic that seduced its victims on the devil's night. Even the ones who accepted it as a straightforward suicide acted like it was less personal decision than communicative disease, something Craig had accidentally caught and might now pass on to the rest of us, like chlamydia.

All my life, Battle Creek had reliably been a place where nothing happened. The strange thing that year wasn't that something finally did. It was that, as if the town shared some primordial lizard brain capable of divining the future, we all held our breath waiting for something to happen next.

Thanks to some ambiguous causal link the school administration drew between depression and godlessness, a new postmortem policy dictated that we spend three minutes of every homeroom in silent prayer. Craig had been in my homeroom, seated diagonally to my right, at a desk we all now knew better than to look at directly. Years before, during a solar eclipse, we'd all made little cardboard viewing boxes to stare up into the dark, having been warned that an unobscured view would burn our retinas. The physics of it never made sense to me, but the poetry did, the need to trick yourself into looking at something without really seeing it. That's what I did now, letting myself look at the desk only during those three minutes of silent prayer, when the rest of the class had their eyes closed and their heads bowed, as if secret looking somehow didn't count.

This had been going on for a couple months when something—nothing so bold as a noise, more like an invisible tap on the shoulder, an unspoken whisper promising *this way lies fate*—pulled my eyes away from the lacquered surface scuffed by Craig's many etchings of cocks and balls, and toward the girl in the very opposite corner of the room, the girl I still thought of as new even though she'd been with us since September. Her eyes were wide open and fixed on Craig's desk, until they weren't anymore. They were on me. She watched me like she was waiting for a performance to begin, and it wasn't until she rolled her eyes skyward and opportunity slipped away that I realized it was opportunity I'd been waiting for. Then her middle finger ratcheted up, pointing to the ceiling, to the clouds—unmistakably, to the Lord Our God in Heaven—and when her eyes dropped to meet mine again, my finger rose of its own accord in identical salute. She smiled. By the time our teacher called, *Time's up*, her hands were folded politely together on the desk again ... until she raised one to propose that school prayer, even the silent kind, was illegal.

Lacey Champlain had a stripper's name and a trucker's wardrobe, all flannel shirts and clomping boots that—stranded as we were in what Lacey later called *the butt crack of western Pennsylvania*—we didn't yet recognize as a pledge of allegiance to grunge. The new kid in a school that hadn't had a new kid in four years, she defied categorization. There was a fierceness about her that also defied attack, and so she'd become the two-legged version of Craig's desk, best glimpsed only from the corner of your eye. I looked at her head-on now, curious how she managed to weather Mr. Callahan's infamously fearsome glare.

"You have some problem with God?" he said. Callahan was also our history teacher, and had been known to skip over entire decades and wars in favor of explaining how carbon dating was nonsense and all the coincidental mutations in history couldn't account for the evolution of the human eye.

"I have a problem with you asking me that question in a building funded by public taxes." Lacey Champlain had dark hair, almost true black, that curled over her face and bobbed at her chin flapper-style. Pale skin and blood-red lips, like she didn't have to bother dressing goth because she came by it naturally, vampire by birthright. Her nails were the same color as her lips, as were her boots, which laced up her calves and looked made for stomping. Where I had a misshapen assemblage of lumps and craters, she had what could reasonably be called a figure, peaks and valleys all of appropriate size and direction.

"Any other objections from the peanut gallery?" Callahan said, fixing us all with his look one by one, defying us to raise a hand. Callahan's glare wasn't as intimidating as it had been before the morning he officially informed us Craig wasn't coming back, when his face crumbled in on itself and never quite came back together, but it was still grim enough to shut everyone up. Smiling like he'd won a round, he told Lacey that if praying made her uncomfortable, she was welcome to leave.

She did. And, rumor had it, stopped in the library, then headed straight for the principal's office, constitutional law book in one hand, the ACLU's phone number in the other. So ended Battle Creek High's brief flirtation with silent prayer.

I thought something might come of it, that silent second we'd shared. For days afterward, I kept a stalker's eye on her, waiting for some acknowledgment of whatever had passed between us. If she noticed, she showed no sign of it, and when I turned to look, she was never looking back. Eventually I felt stupid about the whole thing, and rather than be the feeble friendless loser who fuses a few bread crumbs of chance encounter into an elaborate fantasy of intimacy, I officially forgot that Lacey Champlain existed.

Not that I was feeble or friendless, certainly not by the Hollywood standards that pegged us all as either busty cheerleaders or lonely geeks. I was always able to find a spot at one table or another at lunch, could rely on a handful of interchangeable girls to swap homework or partner on the occasional group project. Still, I'd filed the dream of a best friend away with my Barbies and the rest of my childish things, and given up expecting Battle Creek to supply me with anything resembling a soul mate. Which is to say, I'd been lonely for so long, I'd forgotten that I was.

That feeling of disconnection, of grief for something I'd never had, of screaming into a void and knowing no one would hear me—I'd forgotten that was anything other than the basic condition of life.

Outside of elementary school earth science illustrations, plateaus aren't unremittingly flat. Even my carefully curated existence of school, homework, TV, and nonintrospection had its peaks and troughs. Gym class was a twice-a-week valley, and that winter, shivering on a softball field in our stupid white skirts every time the temperature rose above fifty degrees, it was more like the valley of the shadow of death, where Craig's girlfriend and her obsequious posse stood manning the bases while I lingered in left field, fearing much evil.

Craig's girlfriend: Referring to Nikki Drummond that way was like referring to Madonna as *Sean Penn's ex-wife*. Despite his MVP trophies, before his memorable closing act, Craig was inconsequential; Nikki Drummond, at least within the limited cosmology of the Battle Creek High School student body, was God. A spit-shined princess with *who, me?* eyes and a cherry-red pout, Nikki floated the halls on a cloud of adoration and dessert-themed perfumes—vanilla or cinnamon or gingerbread—though she gave no indication that she did anything so vulgar as eat. Like the girls who worshipped at her altar, Nikki streaked her bangs with Sun-In and flowered her LA Gear sneakers with felt-tipped markers, red and yellow daisies dancing across immaculate white. The girls she favored, and a number that she didn't, made themselves over in her image, but the chain of command was never in doubt. Nikki commanded; her subjects obeyed.

I was not among them, and most days that still felt like a point of pride.

After Craig's death, Nikki had briefly acquired an aura of sainthood. It must change a person, I'd thought, to be touched by tragedy, and I watched her carefully—in gym class, in homeroom, in the hall by the disappearing, reappearing shrine—wondering what she would become. But Nikki only became more fully Nikki. Not purified but distilled: essence of bitch. I overheard her in the girls' locker room, two weeks after it happened, talking to two of her ladies-in-waiting in a voice designed for overhearing. "Let them think whatever they want," she said, and, impossibly, laughed.

"But they're saying you were cheating on him," Allie Cantor said, theatrically scandalized. "Or that you were . . ." Here her voice went subsonic, but I could fill in the gap because I'd heard the rumors, too. In the wake of inexplicable suicide, sainthood didn't last long. " . . . *pregnant.*"

"So?"

"*So*, they're saying he maybe did it because of *you.*" Kaitlyn Dyer's voice caught on every other word. Nikki's girls had been competing over who could put on the biggest show of pain, though I wondered why they assumed this would earn them favor from a queen who had endured so many days of memorials and so much vile gossip, without a flinch.

"It's kind of flattering, right?" Nikki paused, and something in her voice implied a bubblegum smile. "I mean, I'm not arrogant enough to think anyone would kill himself for me. But I've got to admit it's possible."

Word—especially that word, *flattering*—spread; the whispers stopped. Months later, I still watched Nikki sometimes, especially when she was alone, trying to catch her in a moment of humanity. Maybe I wanted proof that I should feel sorry for her, because it seemed barbaric not to; maybe it was only animal instinct. Even the dumbest prey knows better than to turn its back on a predator.

Most of us, by that point in our educational careers, had

mastered changing into our gym uniforms without revealing an inch more of bare skin than was necessary. Nikki never bothered. Her bra always matched her panties, and when she tired of showing off the flat stomach and perfect curves she tucked into one pastel set of satins after another, she somehow managed to make even the mandated tennis skirt look good. Me, on the other hand, all saggy granny panties and flabby C-cups bulging from stretched-out lace, dingy white uniform that gave my skin a tubercular pallor—the mirror was my enemy. So that day, the first February afternoon warm enough to play outside, I didn't inspect myself on the way out of the locker room, didn't notice until I was on the field and halfway through the first softball inning that all those people laughing were laughing at me, didn't understand until Nikki Drummond sidled over in the dugout and whispered, giggling, that I might want to *stick a tampon up my cunt.*

This was the nightmare with no *and then I woke up.* This was blood. This was stain. I was sticky and leaking, and if Nikki had slipped me a knife I would happily have slit a vein, but instead she just gave me the one word that girls like Nikki weren't supposed to say, the word that guaranteed from now on, whenever anyone looked my way, they would see Hannah Dexter and think *cunt. My cunt. My dripping, bloody, foul cunt.*

I was supposed to shrug, maybe. The kind of girl who could laugh things off was the kind of girl who lived things down. Instead I burned, hot and teary, hands pressed against my splotchy ass as if I could make them all unsee what they'd seen, and Nikki's teeth glowed white as her skirt when she laughed, and then somehow I was in the nurse's office, still crying and still bleeding, while the gym teacher explained to the nurse that there had been an *incident*, that I had *soiled* myself, that I perhaps should be wiped and cleaned and collected by a parent or guardian and taken home.

I locked myself into the handicapped bathroom at the back of the office and *stuck a tampon up my cunt*, then changed into unstained jeans, tied a jacket around my waist, scrubbed the tears off my face, and dry-heaved into the toilet. When I finally came out, Lacey Champlain was there, waiting for the nurse to decide her so-called headache was bullshit and send her back to class, but—at least this was how we told ourselves the story later, when we needed the story of us to be inevitable—at some deeper, subsonic level, waiting for me.

The room smelled like rubbing alcohol. Lacey smelled like Christmas, ginger and cloves. I could hear the nurse on the phone in her inner office, complaining about overtime and how someone somewhere was a total bitch.

Then Lacey was looking at me. "Who was it?"

It was no one; it was me; it was bad timing and heavy flow and the cruel dictates of white cotton, but because *it* was the laughter as much as the stain, the *cunt* as much as its leak, it was also Nikki Drummond—and when I said her name Lacey's lip curled up on one side, her finger playing at her face like it was twirling an invisible mustache, and somehow I knew this was as close as I'd get to a smile.

"You ever think about just doing it? Like he did?" she said.

"Doing what?"

That got me a look I'd see a lot of, later on. It said you'd disappointed her; it said Lacey had expected better, but she would give you one more chance. "Offing yourself."

"Maybe," I said. "Sometimes."

I'd never said it out loud. It was like carrying around a secret disease, and not wanting to let anyone think you were contagious. I half expected Lacey to scrape her chair away.

Instead she held out her left wrist and flipped it over, exposing the veins. "See that?"

I saw milky flesh, spiderwebbed with blue. "What?"

She tapped her finger against the spot, a pale white line, cutting diagonal, the length of a thumbnail. "Hesitation cut," she said. "That's what happens when you lose your nerve."

I wanted to touch it. To feel the raised edges of the scar, and the pulse beating beneath. "Really?"

A sudden spurt of laughter. "Of course not really. It's a paper cut. Come on."

She was making fun of me, or she wasn't. She was like me, or she wasn't.

"That's not how I'd do it, anyway, if I were going to do it," she said. "Not with a knife."

"Then how?"

She shook her head and made an *uh-uh* noise, like I was a kid reaching for a cigarette. "I'll show you mine if you show me yours."

"My what?"

"Your plan, for how you'd do it."

"But I wouldn't—"

"Whether you'd actually do it is beside the point," she said, and I could tell I was running out of chances. "How you would kill yourself is the most personal decision a person can make. It says everything about you. Don't you think?"

Why I said what I said next: because I could see her getting tired of me, and I needed her not to; because I was desperate and tired and could still feel the wet seeping into my jeans; because I was too tired of not saying all the things I thought were true.

"So shooting yourself in the head is Craig-speak for *My girlfriend is a cunt and this is the only way to break up with her for good*?" I said, and then I said, "Might have been the only smart thing he ever did."

She didn't have to tell me, later, that this was the moment I won her heart.

"I'm Lacey," she said, and gave me her wrist again, sideways this time, and we shook hands.

"Hannah."

"No. I hate that name. What's your last name?" She was still holding on.

"Dexter."

She nodded. "Dex. Better. I can work with that."

We cut school. "This is a day that calls for large quantities of sugar and alcohol," she said. "Possibly fries. You in?"

I'd never cut before. Hannah Dexter did not break the rules. Dex, on the other hand, followed Lacey straight out of the school, thinking not about consequences but about *stick a tampon up your cunt* and how, if Lacey had suggested we burn the place down, Dex might just have gone for it.

Her crap Buick got only AM frequencies, but Lacey had stuck an old Barbie tape recorder to the dash. She turned it up as loud as it would go, some screaming maniac trapped in a hell chamber of jackhammers and electroshock, but when I asked what it was, there was a sacred hush in her voice that suggested she'd mistaken it for music.

"Dex, meet Kurt."

She flicked her eyes away from the road, long enough to read my face.

"You've really never heard Nirvana?" It was a brand of fake incredulity I knew too well: *You* really *didn't get invited to Nikki's pool party? You* really *don't have a Swatch? You* really *haven't kissed/jerked off/blown/fucked* anyone? It wasn't the veiled snobbery I minded but the implied pity, that I could fall so unthinkably short. But with Lacey, I didn't mind. I accepted the pity as my due, because I saw now that it *was* unthinkable that I'd never heard Nirvana. I could tell it was making her happy to solidify our roles, she the sculptor and me the clay. In that car, miles opening between us and the school, between Hannah and Dex, between before and after, I wanted nothing more than to make her happy.

"Never," I said, and then, because it was called for, "but it's amazing."

We drove; we listened. Lacey, when the spirit seized her, rolled down a window and screamed lyrics into the sky.

That Buick: ancient and wheezing and spotted with bird shit and, even on that first day, like home. Love at first sight, like I knew already it would be our getaway car. Its glove compartment, with its heap of maps, crusty nail polish bottles, mixtapes, old Burger King wrappers, emergency condoms, dusty pack of candy cigarettes. Its leather seats exhaling cigarette fumes, though Lacey, her grandma dead of lung cancer, refused to smoke. "It belonged to some dead lady," Lacey explained, that first day. "Three full-body details, and the damn thing still stinks of cigarettes and adult diapers." It felt haunted, and I liked it.

Lacey was a driver—I would come to understand that. She was always inventing field trips for us: We drove to a UFO landing site, a Democratic rally where we pretended to be Ross Perot groupies and a Republican rally where we pretended to be Communists, a sixties-style drive-in with roller-skating ushers, and the Big Mac Museum, which was lame. They were, more than anything, excuses to drive. That first day, she invented no destination; we drove in circles. Motion was enough.

There was something deliciously numbing about it, the sameness of the clapboard houses and seamed concrete, the day unspooling behind us as we circled the town. I tried to imagine how it looked to her, determinedly idyllic Battle Creek with its antique stores and its ice cream shoppe, its empty storefronts and rusting foreclosure signs, its chest-thumping pride, every forced smile and flapping flag insisting this was the *real* America, that we were salt of the earth and blood of the heartland, that our flat green corner of Pennsylvania was a walled-off Eden, untouched by the violence and sin endemic to the modern age, that the town mothers worried only over their pie crusts and garden weeds, the town fathers limited themselves to one after-dinner beer and never prowled beneath their secretaries' skirts, the sons and daughters had only sitcom troubles and, despite their hormones and halter tops, knew enough to wait. When something went awry, when a golden child slipped a gun in his mouth and bled brains on damp earth, it could only be evidence of attack or contagion, an incursion of *them*, never a fault line through the heart of *us*. When night came, it was easy to ignore the things the children did in the dark.

It was impossible, seeing home through her eyes, like seeing your own face as a stranger would. This was my greatest fear, that Battle Creek was my mirror. That Lacey would look at one, see the other, and dismiss us both.

"I can't believe you have a car," I said. I didn't even have a license. "If I had one, I'd drive away and never come back."

"Want to?" Lacey said. Like it would be that easy to Thelma-and-Louise ourselves out of Battle Creek for good. Like I could be a different girl, my own opposite, and all it took was saying *yes*.

Maybe it wasn't exactly like that, all revealed to me in a single burst of glaringly obvious light. Maybe it took longer than one car ride to slough off a lifetime of Hannah Dexter—a careful study of the right bands, the slow but steady creep of delinquency, flannel and combat boots, hair dye and

shrooms and the nerve to violate at least a handful of com-
mandments—but that's not how I remember it now. That's
not how it felt then. It felt, right there in that car, like I could
choose to be Dex. Everything after was paperwork.

"We drive straight through, we could make it to Ohio by
midnight," Lacey said. "We'd be at the Rockies in a day or
two."

"We're going west?"

"Of course we're going west."

West, Lacey said, was the frontier. West was the edge of the
world, the place you fled in search of gold or God or freedom;
it was cowboys and movie stars, surfboards and earthquakes
and pitiless desert sun.

"So, you want to?"

Three times that year, like some fairy-tale temptress, Lacey
asked me to leave with her, and every time I refused, imagining I was being prudent, refusing to give in to the temptation
of running wild. Not understanding that the wild was waiting
for me in Battle Creek—the danger was in staying.

That time, I didn't say yes or no. I only laughed, and so
instead of the promised land, she drove us to a lake. Twenty
miles out of town, it had a swimming beach for families, a
dock for fishermen, reeds and shadows for lovers, a muddy bed
of empty beer cans for the rest. That day it was all silence and
space, leafless branches overhanging a gray shore, abandoned
docks where ghosts of children past bounced on invisible
rafts and dove into sparkling blue. Winter had come, and
the lake belonged to us. I'd been there before, though not

often, because my mother hated the beach and my father the water. Building mounds in the sand beside a beach full of kids living in an L.L.Bean ad, shaded by beach umbrellas, tossed from fathers' shoulders into the water, I always felt like the defective half of a *Goofus and Gallant* comic: Gallant builds a castle with a moat; Gallant buries her mother in the sand; Gallant practices her dead man's float and does handstands on the muddy lake bottom. Goofus lies on a towel with a book while her mother pencils through work files and her father opens another beer; Goofus teaches herself to tread water and wonders who would rescue her from drowning, since neither parent knows how to swim.

Lacey shut off the engine and the music, dousing us in awkward silence.

She breathed deep. "I love it here in the winter. Everything dead. It feels like being inside a poem, you know?"

I said I did.

"Do you write?" she asked. "I can tell you're the type. The word type."

I said I did, again, though it had only the most tenuous connection to truth. Somewhere in my room was a pile of abandoned diaries, each filled with a few stilted entries and several hundred blank pages, each a reminder of how little I had to say. I preferred other people's stories. For Lacey, though, I could be a girl who made her own.

"See that!" She was triumphant. "You're a total stranger, but it's like we already know each other. You feel that, too?"

Although almost everything I'd told her since we got

into the car had been a favor-currying lie, it all *felt* true. It did seem like she knew me, or was conjuring a new me into existence, one question at a time, and it made perfect sense for her to know that girl inside and out. Knowledge is a creator's prerogative.

"What number am I thinking of?" I said.

She squinted her eyes, pressed her fingers to her temples. "You're not thinking of any number. You're thinking about what happened at school."

"Am not."

"Bullshit. You're thinking about it, but trying *not* to think about it with everything you've got, because if you let yourself do it, really marinate in it, you'll start crying and screaming and polishing up the brass knuckles, and that would be messy. You hate messy."

It wasn't wholly appealing, being known.

"What are you afraid of, Dex? You get angry, *really* angry, what's the worst that happens? You think you'll make Nikki Drummond's brain leak out of her ears, just by wanting it?"

"I should probably get home," I said.

"God, look at you, all pale and squirmy. It's not a mortal sin, getting fucking *mad*. I swear."

But anger like that, it wasn't smart. There was no upshot to letting myself feel it.

Feeling it hurt.

"*Stick a tampon up your cunt*," I said, because maybe that was the way to exorcise it. Get it out of my head and into the world.

"Excuse me?"

"That's what she said. Nikki. Today."

Lacey whistled. "That's fucked." She started to laugh then, but not at me. I was sure of that. "Little Miss Perfect Pottymouth. Fucking ridiculous." And then, miraculously, we were both laughing.

"You know why I brought you here?" she said, finally, as we sobered up.

"To psychoanalyze me to death?"

She lowered her voice to a serial killer pitch. "Because here, no one can hear you scream."

As I was wondering whether I'd just entered act three of a Lifetime movie, the kind where the heroine accepts a ride with a stranger and ends up floating facedown in the lake, Lacey stepped to the edge of the water, threw her head back, and screamed. It was a beautiful thing, a tide of righteous fury, and I wanted it for my own.

Then it stopped, and she turned to me. "Your turn."

I tried.

I stood where Lacey had stood, my Keds ghosting her boot prints. I looked out at the water, skimmed with patches of ice, something primordial in their shimmer. I watched my breath fog the air and fisted my fingers inside my gloves, for warmth, for power.

I stood at the edge of the water and wanted, so much, to scream for her. To prove her right, that we were the same. What she felt, I felt. What she said, I would do.

Nothing came out.

Lacey took my hand. She leaned against me, touched her head to mine. "We'll work on it."

The next morning, Nikki Drummond found a bloody tampon stuffed through the vent of her locker. She cornered me in the girls' bathroom that afternoon, hissing *what the fuck is wrong with you* as we washed our hands and tried not to look at each other in the mirror.

"Today, Nikki?" And then I did look at her, the Gorgon of Battle Creek, and I didn't turn to stone. "Not a single fucking thing."

LACEY

Me Before You

If you really want to know everything, Dex—and for what it's worth, I'm pretty fucking sure your eyes are bigger than your stomach on that one—you should know that, before it all started, I was like you. Maybe not exactly like, not so willfully oblivious that I'd forgotten what I was trying to ignore, but close enough.

We lived by the beach.

No, that's another of those pretty lies, the kind I tell you, the kind real estate developers and sleazy travel agents shill to gullible cheapskates, the kind the local founding fathers sold themselves on when they named their shit sprawl of gas stations and strip malls Shore Village, even though it was a twenty-minute drive from Jersey's least attractive beach. We lived by a Blockbuster and an off-brand burger joint and a vacant lot that drunks used on Sunday mornings to puke up their Saturday nights. We lived alone, just the two of us, except it was mostly just the one of us. Between waitressing and groupie-ing, boozing and fucking, Loretta didn't have much time left for mothering, and once I was old enough to fry my own eggs, she started leaving me home with the cat. Then the cat ran away; she didn't notice.

Poor Lacey, you're thinking. Poor, unloved Lacey, with her trash mother and deadbeat dad, and this is why I don't tell you these things, because for you everything is a fairy tale or a Lifetime movie, Technicolor or black-and-white, and I don't need you imagining me in some sulfurous pit of trailer-trash hell. I don't need your *Oh, Lacey, that must have been so hard for you* or *Oh, Lacey, what do food stamps look like and how does neglect smell* or, worst of all, *Oh, Lacey, don't worry, I understand, I have my pretty little house and my father knows best and my picture-perfect fucking sitcom life, but deep down we're totally the same.*

I made do with what I had, and what I had was the smell of the ocean when the wind was right, and the beach itself, when I could thumb a ride. I think you grow up different, by the water. You grow up knowing there's a way out.

Mine was a nineteen-year-old dropout with greaser hair and a James Dean jacket, squatting in the empty apartment beneath ours, because his mother was the super and had given him the key. He read Kerouac, of course. Or maybe he didn't actually read it; maybe he just strategically spread it across his lap while he napped in one of the crappy metal chairs he'd set up in the vacant lot, his own personal tanning zone. He definitely didn't read Rilke or Nietzsche or Goethe or any of the other moldy paperbacks we passed back and forth while I coughed down his cherry vodka and he taught me how to smoke. He was too lazy to make it past the first chapters of most of them, but I can believe he made it through the Kerouac, because Jack spoke his language, his druggy, pretentious, wastrel nympho native tongue.

His name was Henry Schafer, but he had me call him Shay, and don't get me wrong, Dex, even then, fifteen and swoony, I didn't think it was love. Love was the stack of books piling up in my room, maybe, and the bootlegs he brought me; it was sailing down the Schuylkill in his beat-up Chevy, Philly on the horizon; it was South Street and head shops and smoky nights in a shitty back room listening to slam poetry; it was the heat of flesh the first time I dropped acid, salty skin when I licked my own palm. Love was not what Shay had me do to him in my mother's bedroom while she was off trying to fuck Metallica; it wasn't a sticky glob of him in my mouth or the pain of a finger up my ass; it certainly wasn't finding him with his tongue in his girlfriend's ear and then pretending, the next night, that I'd assumed a girlfriend all along, that of course I'd understood what this was and wasn't, that there was no harm and no foul and no reason he couldn't keep using me to kill time while she was busy, and yes, I *should* be grateful that he'd always used a condom, what other proof did I need that he was thinking of me.

This isn't what you want to hear. You don't want to hear that I studied those books, at least at first, to impress him. That I listened to Jane's Addiction and the Stone Roses because he told me that's what people like us should do, and when he asked me whether the baby's breath of hair on his upper lip looked cool, I told him it did, even though I thought his girlfriend was right, that it made his mouth look like a peripubescent pussy. He spent that night with me and not her, and that's what mattered, and still, Dex, that doesn't mean I thought it was love.

I liked him best when he was sleeping. When the lights were out and he was curled into me, kissing my neck in his dreams. Bodies can be anyone, in the dark.

That was before I turned sixteen, before my mother's season of rebirth, born again into the loving arms of AA and then again into the Bastard and his Lord. That was the year I discovered no one gave a shit about how many classes I skipped as long as I still scraped through tests with a C-plus and, when I did bother to show, did so in tank tops that erred on the side of boobalicious, a tactic that also proved effective when my mother would put on a Bon Jovi album, spin the dial up to ear-shattering, sing and twirl and drink along until our landlord showed up to whine about volume and rent. That was also the year he started slapping my ass instead of hers, and she stopped noticing me, except for the nights she would sneak home late, sticky with someone else's sweat, crawl into my bed and whisper that I was all she had and she was all I needed, and I would pretend to be asleep.

Life with Shay was better, if only marginally. I thought maybe we would run away together. Fuck his girlfriend. We would be Kerouac and Cassady, dance wild across the heartland, sip the Pacific, drive for the sake of driving. I believed we both understood that there, *any* there, would always be better than here, just like I believed that he'd dropped out of high school because true intelligence can't be contained, that he let his parents support him because he was writing a novel and true art demanded sacrifice. I showed him some crap poetry, and I believed him when he said it was good.

Shay doesn't matter. Shay was a gateway drug, a cheap glue-sniffing high on the pathway to transcendence. Shay was like something ordered out of a catalog: Of course he quoted Allen Ginsberg, of course he got stoned to the Smiths, of course he smoked cloves and wore black eyeliner and had a glass-blowing girlfriend named Willow who'd made him a Valentine's Day bong. Shay only matters because of the day we camped out in his friend's attic studio a block from the Schuylkill, and after we got good and stoned, someone turned off the Phillies game and turned on 91.7 and there he was.

Kurt.

Kurt screaming, Kurt raging, Kurt in agony, Kurt in bliss. "Fucking pseudo-punk poseurs," Shay said, and reached over to turn it off, and when I said, "Don't, please," he only laughed. It took me another week to find the song again and then steal a copy of *Bleach* and another few weeks after that to fumigate Shay out of my life, but that was the moment he went from mattering a little to not at all.

After that, it was like they say about love: Falling. A gravitational inevitability. Even Shitbag Village had one decent record store, with a giant bin of discounts and bootlegs, and it only took thirty bucks and some tongue wrestling with the walking zit behind the counter to get what I needed. Then I closed myself into my room and, except for periodic forays back to the record store and one very inconvenient move to the middle of nowhere, spent that year and the next one catching up: the Melvins, because that was Kurt's favorite band, and Sonic Youth, because they're the ones who got Kurt his big deal; the Pixies, because once you knew anything about grunge, you knew that was where it all came from; Daniel Johnston, because Kurt said so and because the guy was in a mental hospital so I figured he could use the royalties; and of course bootleg Bikini Kill, for some righteous riot grrrl rage, and Hole, because you got the feeling that if you didn't, Courtney would come to your house and fuck you up.

Then, like Kurt knew exactly what I'd need when I needed it, there was *Nevermind*. I barricaded myself in until I knew every note, beat, and silence—cut school for the purposes of a higher education.

I loved it. Loved it like Shakespearean sonnets and Hallmark cards and all that shit, like I wanted to buy it flowers and light it candles and fuck it gently with a chainsaw.

I'm not saying I go around doodling *Mrs. Kurt Cobain* on my notebooks or that I, like, ohmygod, imagine myself showing up on his doorstep in black lace panties and a trench coat. For one thing, Courtney would gouge my eyes out with barbed wire. For another, I know what's real and what's not, and real is not me fucking Kurt Cobain.

But: Kurt. Kurt with his watery blue eyes and his angel hair, the halo of stubble and the way the rub of it would burn. Kurt, who sleeps in striped pajamas with a teddy bear to keep him company, who frenched Krist on national TV to fuck with the rednecks back home and wore a dress on *Headbangers Ball* just because he could, who has enough money to buy and smash a hundred top-line guitars but likes a Fender Mustang because it's a cheap piece of crap you have to abuse as much as you love if you want it to play nice. Rock god, sex god, angel, saint: Kurt, who always looks at you from the side, from beneath that golden curtain of hair, looks at you like he knows all the bad things scuttling around inside. Kurt's voice, and how it hurts. I could live and die inside that voice, Dex. I wanted to crawl inside it, soft and razor raw at the same time, his voice cutting me bloody, warm and slippery and alive. I don't need Kurt—the real living, breathing Courtney-screwing Kurt—to throw me down on the bed and brush his hair out of his eyes and lay his naked body on mine, miles of translucent skin glowing white. I don't need that Kurt, because I have his voice. I have the part of him that matters. That Kurt, I own. Like he owns me.

I know you don't like him, Dex. It's cute how you try to fake it, but I see you glaring at his poster, like some jealous boyfriend. Which is ironic. And unnecessary. Because the way I felt when I found Kurt? That's how it felt when I found you.

DEX

Story of Us

The boots were sturdy black leather, rubber heel, yellow-threaded sole, eight eyelets with ragged laces, classic Docs exactly like Lacey's, except these were mine.

"Really?" I was afraid to touch them. "Not really."

"Really." She looked like she'd shot me a bear, slinging it over her shoulder and carrying it single-handedly back to our cave to roast and feed on, and that was how it felt. Like sustenance. "Try them on."

After two weeks, I knew Lacey well enough not to ask where they'd come from. She was prone to liberation, as she called it, a redistribution of goods to wherever they most wanted to belong. These boots, she said, wanted to belong to me. To Dex.

Here, then, was Dex: frizzy hair chopped short and sprung free, beige streaked with blue, neck ringed by black leather choker, thrift store glasses with Buddy Holly frames, flannel shirts preowned and a size too big layered over checkered baby-doll dresses and scarlet tights and now, perfectly, black combat stomping boots. Dex knew about grunge and Seattle and Kurt and Courtney, and what she didn't know, she could fake. Dex cut class, drank wine coolers, ignored homework in favor of Lacey-work—studying guitar riffs, deciphering philosophy and poetry; waiting, always waiting, for Lacey to realize her mistake. Hannah Dexter wanted to follow the rules. Never lied to her parents because she had no need. Was afraid of what people thought of her; didn't *want* people to think of her, lest they register her big nose, her weak chin, her gut her hips her brows her thighs her chewed nails her flat ass her alternately oozing and flaking and ever-erupting skin. Hannah wanted to be invisible. Dex wanted to be seen. Dex was a rule breaker, a liar, a secret keeper; Dex was wild, or wanted to be. Hannah Dexter had believed in right and wrong, an ordered world of justice. Dex would make her own justice. Lacey would show her how.

It wasn't transformation, Lacey told me. It was revelation. I was no good at masks, Lacey told me. I wasn't built for a world that insisted I hide who I really was. I'd been hiding so long I'd forgotten where to look for myself. Lacey would find me, she promised. *Ready or not, here I come.*

"I know, you're thinking I'm the most magnanimous person you've ever met," Lacey said as I laced up the boots. "You're thinking how lucky you are that I deign to share my impeccable taste with you."

"It's like I won the friendship sweepstakes," I said, sarcasm being the safest route to truth. "I fall asleep every night whispering my thanks to the universe."

This was the first time she'd been to my house. I would happily have postponed it indefinitely, not because there was anything so revealing but because there wasn't. Our house was lush and half-assed, stuffed with all the leftovers my father'd grown tired of: an unfinished jungle gym, stacks of unframed photos and unread books, unused appliances bought on midnight infomercial whims, unhung "native masks" from an ill-advised sojourn in anthropological sculpting. My mother's detritus was devoted to self-discipline and improvement, calendars and double-underlined Post-it notes, forgotten to-do lists, meditation and relaxation pamphlets, aerobics videos. Home was two homes in one, bridged by a sea of unclaimed clutter, ashtrays no one had used since my grandfather died, needlepoint throw pillows, tacky souvenirs from trips we barely remembered taking, all of it enclosed by a moat of browning weeds and an eyesore of an overgrown vegetable garden whose inception each of my parents blamed on the other. Beige-and-tan-striped wallpaper, my grandparents' hand-me-down coffee table layered with Time-Life books, posters of exotic landscapes we'd never seen. Through Lacey's eyes, I could see the house for what it was: a generic split-level of quiet desperation, ground zero for a family with no particular passion for anything but living as much as possible like the people they saw on TV.

Lacey had told me of quantum incompatibilities, qualities so opposed to each other that the very existence of one eliminated all possibility of the other. I didn't understand it any better than the other brain-knotting theories she liked to regurgitate, convinced that knowing the universe in all its weird particularity was key to rising above what she called *our middlebrow zombie hell*, but I could recognize Lacey's presence in my bedroom as its ultimate illustration, Lacey's combat boots crushing my turquoise shag carpeting, her eyes alighting briefly on the stuffed turtle I still kept tucked between my pillows, Hannah Dexter's past and future in a doomed collision, matter and antimatter collapsing into a black hole that would consume us both. Translation: I was pretty sure that once Lacey saw me in my natural habitat, she would disappear.

"Your parents have a liquor cabinet, right?" she said. "Let's check it out."

There was no lock on it, of course. There was no question that I could be trusted around my parents' dusty quantities of brandy, scotch, and cheap wine. Maybe it was the boots that gave me the courage to clomp downstairs and show Lacey the dark crevice behind the abandoned board games and unread Time-Life books where the bottles lived.

"Scotch or rum?" I asked, and hoped it sounded like I knew the difference.

"Little from column A, little from column B." She showed me how to pour out an inch or two from each bottle, replacing the liquid with water. We mixed a little of everything together in a single glass, then, one at a time, took a foul swig.

"Juice of the gods," Lacey managed when she'd finished choking.

I swallowed again. It was the good kind of burn.

The carpet in the family room was a harsh orange-and-brown-striped shag that, until Lacey settled onto it, stretching into a snow angel and pronouncing it *not bad*, I'd found repulsive. Now, with her approval and a boozy, warm buzz, it seemed almost luxurious. I lay beside her, arms stretched till our fingertips touched, and marinated in the juice of the gods and the hot air gushing from the heating vent. The dissonant chords of Lacey's latest bootleg washed over us, and I tried to hear in it what she did, the foghorn promise of a ship that would carry us both away.

"We should start a club," Lacey said.

"But clubs are lame." I said it like a question.

"Exactly!"

"So . . ."

"I'm not talking about a chess club, Dex. Or, like, some kind of *Let's read to old people so we can get into college* thing. I'm talking a *club* club. You know, like in books. Tree houses and secret codes and shit."

"Like in *Bridge to Terabithia!*"

"Let's pretend I know what that is and say . . . yes."

"But without someone dying."

"Yes, Dex, without someone dying. Well . . . at least not someone in the club."

"*Lacey.*"

"Joke! Think blood oath, not blood sacrifice."

"So what would we do? A club has to do something."

"Other than sacrifice virgins, you mean."

"Lacey!"

"Clubs are stupid because they're not about anything that matters. But ours would be. We'd be ... the ontology club."

"A club to study the nature of existence?"

"See, Dex, this is why I love you. Think there's a single other person in this crap town who knows what *ontology* means?"

"Statistically?"

"Come on, Dex, you can say it. It's not going to hurt."

"Say what?"

"That's why you love me, too."

"That's why I ... "

"Love me, too."

"Love you, too."

"Clearly I'll be club president. You can be vice, and secretary, and treasurer."

"And no other members."

"Obviously. Think about it, Dex. We could read Nietzsche together, and Kant, and Kerouac, and figure out why people do what they do and why the universe has something instead of nothing and whether there's a god, and sneak into the woods and blast Kurt as loud as we can and close our eyes and try to, I don't know, connect with the life force or whatever. Bonus points if it pisses people off."

"So basically, keep doing what we're doing?"

"Basically."

"No regular meetings or anything."

"Nope."

"And no tree house."

"Do *you* know how to build a tree house?"

"And the blood-oath thing?"

"Hello, AIDS?"

"I don't think you can actually—"

"The blood oath is a metaphor, Dex. Keep up."

"So not an actual club, then."

"No, Dex, not an actual club. That would be lame."

If we had started a club for real, ontology would have taken a backseat to Lacey's preferred activity: dissecting the evil exploits of our shared enemy, Nikki Drummond. For years I'd hated her on principle, but after the *incident*—which was how we spoke of it, the better to forget words like *stain* and *blood* and *cunt*—I hated her in concrete particulars that Lacey was eager to help me parse. "What kind of person needs a reason to hate the devil?" she liked to say, when I asked what had put Nikki in her sights in the first place, and I was left to conclude that Lacey hated Nikki because Nikki so plainly hated me.

"She's a sociopath," Lacey said now, bicycling her feet in the air. "No emotions. Probably kills small animals, just for fun."

"You think she's got her own little pet cemetery in the backyard? Rabbits with their tails pulled out, that kind of thing?"

"Imagine the possibilities," Lacey said. "We could exhume the bodies. Give little Thumper some justice. Show the world what she really is."

This was our recurring theme: If only we could expose

Nikki's rotting heart. If only the world knew the truth. If only we had the ammunition for a frontal assault.

The day before, we'd slouched behind her in the auditorium's ratty seats, enduring an assembly about satanic cults, the third so far that year. No one in Battle Creek had been foolish enough to invoke the Antichrist since Craig's death—that is, at least not since the November morning when a gang of grieving jocks jumped Jesse Gorin, Mark Troslop, and Dylan Asp and strung them up by their ankles in a tree. I'd seen them up there, dangling over the school parking lot, we all had, three scrawny stoners stripped to socks and boxers, shivering in the snow. Punishment for satanizing half the churches in town on the same night Craig Ellison died; punishment for trying so hard to scare people, or for succeeding. A sacrificial offering to Nikki, their grieving goddess, and—even if the rumors were wrong, even if she hadn't commanded it—she'd accepted it in kind. *A thing like that in a place like this*, people kept saying after they found Craig's body in the woods, like it was impossible that anything so ugly could happen in our pretty backyard. But ugly things happened all the time in Battle Creek: Boys beat other boys bloody and tied them to branches while girls like Nikki pointed and laughed.

After that, Jesse, Mark, and Dylan stopped chalking pentagrams on their shirts. They stopped bragging about how dangerous they were, stopped breaking into the bio lab to steal fetal pigs. A couple towns west of us, though, a few cows were found slaughtered under "ritualistic" circumstances; in another town to the east, a girl our age washed up on a riverbank, naked and blue and, in some way no one was willing to specify, defiled; here at home, Craig was still dead. Something was wrong with the children, the latest guest speaker said from the stage, and by *the children* he meant us. Something was wrong with the children, and so here we were, and here Nikki Drummond was, perched directly in front of us, shiny, pink-scrunchied ponytail defying anyone to suggest the *something wrong* might be her.

"Did you hear she fucked Micah Cross in the teachers' lounge?" Lacey whispered, just loud enough. Then looked at me, expectant.

"I heard . . . it was Andy Smith." This was the best I could come up with, and a clumsy lie—if Andy were any more obviously in the closet he'd be a pair of shoes—but Lacey nodded in approval.

"That was the girls' locker room," she whispered.

"Right. Hard to keep track."

"Imagine how she feels."

"Hard to imagine she feels at all." It was easier with Lacey there, finding the right thing to say—and doing so in the moment, not days later in the shower, when there was no one to appreciate it but the mildewed tiles and the face in the mirror.

"Not that I think there's anything wrong with a healthy sex life," Lacey whispered.

"Of course not."

"But personally, I think it's kind of sad to try to fuck your way to popularity." She was so good at it, acting cold-blooded.

The secret of pretending to be someone else, she'd told me, was that you didn't pretend. You transformed. To defeat a monster, you had to embody one.

"Tragic," I said.

"What's tragic is trying to fuck yourself into forgetting you're a miserable bitch."

The perfect head never moved. Nikki Drummond wasn't the kind of girl who flinched. It only added to the fun of trying to make her.

That afternoon at my house, exactly drunk enough, we lay on the carpet and fantasized about using hidden cameras to make undercover recordings that would expose Nikki's sins to her doting parents and adoring teachers and every drooling moron lined up to take Craig's place in her pants. Between that and Kurt and the way the ceiling spun when I stared at it too hard, I didn't notice the car pull into the driveway or the front door slam or my father's loafers padding across the rug or much of anything until he leaned over us and spoke.

"Something wrong with the couch, kids?" He took off his sunglasses and squinted down at us. My father blamed allergies for his sensitive, red-rimmed eyes; my mother blamed hangovers. I thought he just liked how well the knockoff Ray-Bans paired with his goatee. "No, let me guess, you've fallen and you can't get up."

"You're not supposed to be home."

I sat up too fast and had to immediately lie down, and that was when the panic crept in, because my father was here and Lacey was here and we were drunk, or at least I was drunk, and he would certainly notice, and there would be a scene, the kind of ugly, uncool scene that would mark me as too much trouble and drive Lacey away for good.

But somewhere beneath that, secret and still, animal eyes glowing in the dark: I was drunk, and it was good, and if anyone didn't like it, fuck them.

My father took Lacey's hand and hauled her to her feet. "I'm guessing you're the Pied Piper?"

"What?" I said.

Lacey repossessed her hand and blushed.

"That's you, isn't it? Leading my daughter astray in the musical wilds?"

"What?" I said, again.

"I'd like to think my purposes are less nefarious," Lacey said, past me, to him. "And my taste in music significantly more impressive."

My father grinned. "If you can call it music." And just like that, they were off, Lacey leaping to the defense of her god, my father throwing out phrases like *new wave*, *post-punk pop avant-garde*, the two of them batting names back and forth I'd never heard, Ian Curtis and Debbie Harry and Robert Smith.

"Joey Ramone couldn't lick Kurt Cobain's shoes."

"You wouldn't say that if you'd seen him live."

Her eyes popped. "You saw the Ramones live?"

"What?" I said again, and fought the sudden urge to climb onto my father's lap, wheeze whiskey breath in his face, force him to see me.

"Saw them?" He gave Lacey a patented Jimmy Dexter smile. "I opened for them."

"You were in a band?" I said. No one was listening. No one was offering me a gallant hand, either, so I pulled myself upright, and tried not to puke.

"You opened for the *Ramones*?" That was Lacey's *Kurt* voice; that was awe.

"Well ... not technically." Another smile, an *aw shucks* shrug. "We played in the parking lot before the Ravers, and *they* opened for the Ramones. It got us into the after-party, though. Did a shot with Johnny."

"Lacey was in a band," I said. Lacey had told me all about it, the Pussycats, like the cartoon, all girls, guitar straps slung over their shoulders, Lacey tonguing the mic, sweaty hair matted to her face, crowd-surfing on a wave of love. Never again, she'd told me, never here in Battle Creek, never anywhere. "The fact that we've even heard of grunge all the way out here in the middle of nowhere?" Lacey had said. "It's like those stars, the ones that explode so far away that by the time you get the news, they've been dead for a million years. We're too late. We missed it. Only the truly pathetic pretend to be artists by making something that's already made. And I do not intend to be pathetic."

I was jealous of Lacey's band, of those girls who'd been her Pussycats, but glad, too, because I couldn't be in any band, obviously, and if she'd started a new one it would have carried her away from me.

"Tell him about your band, Lacey."

But she didn't want to tell him, or didn't hear me. "What was he *like*?" she said. Breathed the name. *"Johnny Ramone."*

"Drunk. And he smelled like dog shit, but man, he gave me one of his guitar picks and I thought I'd build a shrine to that thing."

"Can I see it?" Lacey asked.

My father reddened, slightly. "Lost it on the way home."

I cleared my throat. "When were you in a *band*? And how did I not know this?"

He shrugged. "Long time ago, kid. Different life."

My mother listened to music only in the car, and then only to Rod Stewart, Michael Bolton, and, if she was feeling frisky, the Eagles. My father, when he drove, alternated between sports radio and silence. We had a stereo no one ever used and a box of records in the basement so warped with damp they'd been deemed unfit for the previous year's yard sale. For the Dexter family, music was a nonissue. Except that now my father was talking about it the way Lacey did, like music was his religion, and it turned him into a stranger.

"How did a guy like you spawn someone so musically illiterate?" she asked.

"I ask myself that every day," he said.

"No, I don't buy it. You see what this means, Dex? It's in you somewhere. You just needed me to help you get it out."

It was a generous assessment. Everyone knew I took after my mother: the beige and blotchy coloring, the stick up the ass. But if Lacey saw him in me, there must have been something to see.

"Dex? That supposed to be you, kid?" My father examined me, looking for evidence of her.

"No offense, Mr. Dexter, but Hannah's a shit name," Lacey said.

"Call me Jimmy. And no offense taken. It was her mother's idea. I always thought it sounded like a little old lady."

Lacey laughed. "Exactly."

That my father never liked my name: This was another thing I hadn't known. I'd thought he called me *kid* because he wanted to claim a piece of me no one else could.

"But Dex? Yeah, I like that," he said.

Dex was supposed to be our secret, a code name for the thing that was growing between us and the person she was shaping me to be. But if Lacey was ready to introduce her to the world, I thought, she must have her reasons.

"That's right," I said. "Dex. Spread the word."

"Your mother's going to love this," he murmured, and it was clear the thought of it pleased him as much as the name itself.

"So, Jimmy, maybe you'd like to hear some real music," Lacey said. "Dex has a copy of *Bleach* around here somewhere. At least she'd better."

He looked at me, clearly trying to read the stay or go in my face, but I couldn't send a message I didn't have.

"Another time," he said finally, slipping his sunglasses back on. "*The Ten Thousand Dollar Pyramid* is calling my name." He paused on his way up the stairs. "Oh, and *Dex*, you might want to wash out that glass before your mother comes home."

So he had noticed, after all. And he was still on my side.

"You didn't tell me your dad was *cool*," Lacey said once he was gone. It was like a benediction, and most of me was proud.

Afternoons at my place became, at Lacey's instigation, a regular thing, and it was only a matter of time before my mother insisted we have "this Lacey" over for dinner, so she could see for herself this miracle worker who had her husband digging through the attic for his guitar and her daughter into what appeared to be a trucker's castoff wardrobe.

"Mom's going to be all weird, isn't she?" I said, as my father and I sorted through the stack of Publishers Clearing House stickers. My father was the family's designated dreamer, the buyer of lottery tickets and keeper of an ever-growing list of inventions he'd never build. It was, he always said, why he'd never taken what my mother called a real job. Only make-your-own-hours employment—like his current gig managing Battle Creek's only movie theater—afforded him the free time he needed to fulfill his yen for get-rich-quick scheming.

This particular scheme had been our shared private ritual for years, since the days when I thought carefully licking those stamps and sealing the envelope with a lucky kiss might actually summon the oversized million-dollar check to our doorstep. I'd long since lost the slip of paper carefully inscribed with all the treasures I'd buy when I was rich, but I liked the mint chocolate chip ice cream that came along with the tradition, and the way my mother wasn't part of it. There was music playing now, which wasn't part of it, either, but my father said that the Cure was a universal cure for what ailed us. Wait till Lacey gets here, he said. She gets it.

She was due in an hour. My mother had made lasagna, the one thing she knew how to cook.

"Go easy on your mother, kid. I think one thing we can agree she's not is *weird*."

He was right: Normal was her religion. She'd never implied that she wanted me to be popular—the impossibility of that probably spoke for itself—but she encouraged me, at every turn, to fit in, to be careful, to save my mistakes for later. "You'll have more to lose when you're older, but at least then you'll have something left when you lose it," she told me once while we were flipping through photo albums, old ones that showed her awkwardly jutting into adolescence, bulging in all the wrong places, only a single page turn between apple-cheeked college freshman and bleary-eyed mother with an infant on her caftanned hip, as if all the pages that should have been between had fallen out, and maybe that was how she felt about her life, that something had gone missing. "The younger you are, the easier it is to give everything away."

Dinner was a fright show. The four of us in the wood-paneled dining room huddled at one lonely corner of the long table we never used, pushing around burnt lasagna on chipped Kmart plates, my mother scowling every time a mist of garlic bread crumbs floated from Lacey's mouth onto the plastic tablecloth, Lacey pretending not to notice, too busy fielding rapid-fire questions about her mother's job and her stepfather's church and her nonexistent college plans, each of them more excruciatingly conventional than the last, all of them humiliating enough—but nothing compared to the withering look on my mother's face when I volunteered that I'd also been thinking about taking a year off after graduation, because, like Lacey said, college had been co-opted by a capitalist system only invested in producing more drones for its financial machine, and my mother said, "Stop showing off."

I wondered if mortification qualified as an excuse for justifiable homicide.

Lacey said *yes* and *no* and *please* and *thanks so much* for the delicious and not at all overcooked and underseasoned food. Lacey said that small towns bred small-minded people and she was waging a one-woman war against shrinkage—twowoman now that she'd rallied me to her side. Lacey said she never accompanied her stepfather to church because religion was a destructive influence on impressionable masses and she refused to support any institution with a commitment to intellectual oppression, and when my mother, semiapostate granddaughter of a minister, suggested that it was the arrogant moral cowardice of youth that led us to dismiss things we didn't understand, Lacey said, *And when thou prayest, thou shalt not be as the hypocrites are*, then said that accusing your enemies of ignorance was the coward's way out of honest argument, which made my father laugh, at which point I began to seriously doubt whether any of us would make it out alive.

"So how did you two crazy kids meet?" Lacey asked. "You

seem like the type to have a good story." Which was how I knew that Lacey, too, sensed things were running off the rails, because if there was anything my mother didn't seem like, it was the type with a good story.

Except that, of course, she did have one—and it was this one. Love at first sight, a story I'd always loved to hear, less because of the details than because of the way they liked to tell it together, and the way they looked at each other when they did, as if they were suddenly remembering that this was a life they'd chosen.

My mother smiled. "It was shortly after college, and I was filling in, temporarily, at a subsidiary of my employer, an auto repair facility in town."

This was Julia Dexter-speak for dropping out of college when the financial aid ran dry and taking a crap paper-shuffling job that was supposed to last a summer, not a lifetime. My mother applied the same cardinal rule to autobiography she did to interior design: Accentuate the positive and hang a curtain over everything else.

"It had been, to say the least, an unpleasant afternoon. I was looking forward to locking the doors and finishing my book in peace, when in strolls a gang of hooligans, smelling like an ashtray and dressed like they thought they were Bruce Springsteen." She said it fondly, as she always did. "Your father was wearing this silly grin . . ."

Here, always, she paused, so my father could jump in to say he was wasted, and she would then clarify that he wasn't driving drunk, of course, his friend Todd was at the wheel, a teetotaler Christian they'd only befriended because he was always willing to drive. This time, though, my father said nothing.

She finished the story herself, more quickly than usual. "They'd gotten a flat tire on their way to a party, and as you can imagine, they were in quite a mood. All of them making stupid jokes, showing off for me, not even because they cared but because I was the only girl in sight and this, apparently, was their biological imperative."

Let that be a lesson to you, kid, my father usually said, but mercifully not this time.

"All of them but Hannah's father. He was the quiet one, that's what I noticed first. That he wasn't a fool, or at least hadn't proven himself one yet. Then he noticed I was reading Vonnegut, and he pulled a folded paperback out of his coat pocket. Would you believe what it was?"

"Same book?" Lacey asked.

"Same exact book."

This was the part of the story I loved best, the part I wanted Lacey to hear: That their meeting had been fated. That there was something special about them after all and, by extension, about me.

"Well, his friends went off to their party, but Jimmy stayed where he was, somehow talked me into closing early. We spent the night on the roof, talking about Vonnegut and showing each other the constellations, neither of us wanting to admit we were just making them up as we went along. And then, at the perfect moment, sun rising over Battle Creek ..."

"He kissed you?" Lacey guessed.

"You'd think! And, I'll admit, so did I. But instead he only walked me home, shook my hand, and that was it. I waited two days for him to call. When he didn't, I took myself over to the bookstore where he worked, and said, 'You forgot something.' Then I kissed him."

"*Nice*," Lacey said, then shot me a look saying, *Possible your mom is cool, too?*

"That was when he started calling me Hot Lips," she added, a detail I found gruesomely embarrassing, but also perfect. "It took me years to train him out of it."

"Of course, you can guess why I didn't call," my father said, and my ears perked up. This was a coda I'd never heard before.

My mother lost the dreamy smile. "*James.*"

"I was so drunk that by morning I'd forgotten the whole thing," my father said. "Imagine my surprise when some girl shows up claiming to know me, then kisses me before I can tell her any different. I only called her Hot Lips because I'd forgotten her name!"

"James," she said again, over his laughter. Then, just like she'd said to me, but in a very different voice, "Stop showing off."

It wasn't until she said it that I understood it was true.

My father grinned like he'd gotten away with something, and my mother stood, saying she'd forgotten she had to take a work call. "It was very nice to meet you, Lacey."

I waited for my father to follow her out; he didn't.

"What about your parents, Lacey?" he said, like he hadn't noticed the door to the torture chamber had been unlocked and we were all free to slip loose our chains and get the hell out.

"Don't you think we've had enough interrogation for one day?" I said.

"Chill out, Dex." Lacey tapped her nails on the side of her glass, then skimmed a finger around the rim until it whined.

She never talked to me about her parents, or anything else from the time before we'd met. I didn't mind. I liked imagining the past, the before-us, as a void, as if there had been no Lacey-before-Dex as much as there'd been no Dex-before-Lacey. I knew she'd grown up in New Jersey, nearish the ocean but not near enough; I knew she had a stepfather she called the Bastard and a father she'd liked better who was, in some vague but permanent way, gone; I knew we were better together than we were alone, and better still than everyone else, and that was enough.

"My dad took off when I was a kid," she said. "I haven't seen him since."

"I'm sorry," my father said. I said nothing, because what could I? "That's an asshole move."

Lacey raised her eyebrows at his word choice, then shrugged. "I'm thinking he's a pirate. Or a bank robber. Or maybe one of those sixties hippie terrorists who had to go on the run. I could get behind that. Or, you know, he's your typical deadbeat who chose his dick over his daughter and started up a new family on the other side of town." She laughed, hard and insistently, and I tried not to wither and die just because she'd said the word *dick* with my father in the room. "Jesus, your faces! It's no big deal. My mom's got herself a shiny new husband and a baby to match. Fresh start, she says—best thing that ever happened to her. Of course, a real fresh start would slice me out of the picture, too, but life's a compromise, right?"

I'd figured on the absent father. I knew about the Bastard. But not the baby. She'd never said anything about that.

"I'm sorry," my father said again.

"She just told you it's no big deal," I said, because I had to say something.

"I heard what she said." He stood up. "How about some hot chocolate? A Jimmy Dexter Special."

That was our thing, his and mine, hot chocolate on winter nights with a fingerful of pepper stirred in just for the sake of having a secret ingredient.

"I'm full." I hated how much I sounded like my mother, her diet always absenting her from the room whenever chocolate entered the discussion, leaving my father and me another thing to call our own.

"And I should go," Lacey said.

As soon as she did, I wanted to take it back, say yes enthusiastically—*Yes, let's drown ourselves in hot chocolate and gorge ourselves on cookies, whatever you want, whatever will make you stay*—partly because she didn't have a father and I felt evil for even momentarily refusing to share mine, but mostly because she was Lacey, and every time she slipped out of my sight I was worried she'd never reappear.

My father hugged her good-bye. It was a precise copy of the hugs he gave me, solid and all-consuming. I loved him then, for loving her on my behalf. For being not just the kind of dad who would want to hug Lacey but the kind she would deign to hug back. Still, the next day after school, I suggested we go to the lake instead of back to my place, and the day after that her favorite record store, and that weekend, when she asked about sleeping over, I said, knowing she'd hate it but suspecting she'd be too proud to say so, "Let's do it at your place instead."

There are things you need to know," Lacey said.

We'd been sitting in the Buick for twenty minutes, engine off, music silenced, house looming at the end of the driveway. I could say something to let her out of this gracefully, but I wanted to see inside.

She cleared her throat. "The Bastard is . . . "

"A bastard? Got it."

Lacey uncomfortable was a strange sight. I didn't like it, or at least didn't want to.

"I just want to be clear on the fact that I consider everyone in that house an accident of birth and circumstance. Nothing to do with me. Clear?"

"Clear. As far as I'm concerned, we're basically orphans, raising ourselves in the wild."

She snorted. "If only." And then, "Let's do this."

But we didn't, quite, not until she turned the cassette player on again and we listened to one more track, Lacey's eyes closed and her head tipped back as she disappeared into that place only Kurt could take her. When his screams died out, she pressed *stop.* "Follow me."

Lacey's split-level was a mirror image of mine, right down to the shitty aluminum siding and single-car garage, two and a half bedrooms and bathroom down the hall, all of it reversed, like the parallel-dimension version of home.

The house was schizophrenic. Outside was Bastard territory, everything straight lines and sterile surfaces. Precisely trimmed grass, gleaming gutters, an economical distribution of hedges and evenly spaced potted plants. Inside, Loretta land, was wall-to-wall sixties tack, as if an alien had tried to piece together the American homestead by mainlining Nick at Nite. Flowered upholstery was zipped into clear plastic slipcovers; heavy gilt frames showed off motel art of lighthouses and dour livestock; a menagerie of china figurines grinned at me from behind beveled glass. There were lace doilies. Lots of doilies. A heavy wooden cross hung over the fireplace, and a framed copy of the Serenity Prayer was propped up on the mantel. Which made it slightly surprising when Lacey's mother wandered into the room, breath stinking of what, by that point in our friendship, I could recognize as gin.

Lacey looked like she wanted to unlock the glass cabinet and take a sledgehammer to a few porcelain cats. "God, Mom, did you take a bath in it?"

Lacey's mother had long black hair, longer than a mother's was supposed to be, girlishly flippable and ratted at the ends.

She was loaded down with clumpy mascara and cheap gold chains that disappeared into her red camisoled cleavage, and bleary-eyed in a way I would have read as new-baby exhaustion, were it not for the smell.

"And can you cover that up?" Lacey flicked a hand at the sodden circles around her mother's nipples. "It's disgusting."

Lacey's mother pressed a palm to each of the wet spots. It was always unsettling when parents of a certain age produced a new offspring, its existence undeniable evidence of copulation. But Lacey's mother didn't need a baby to broadcast her message: This was a woman who had sex.

"Never get pregnant, girls," she said. "Motherhood turns you into a freaking cow."

"I love you, too," Lacey said dryly. Then, to me, "Upstairs."

"Girls," her mother said. "Girls! Girls!" It was like the word compelled her as much as we did. "*Stay.*" The couch squeaked as she settled her weight. "Sit. Keep an old cow company. Tell her what it is to be young and free."

"No one forced you to procreate at your age," Lacey said.

"The stack of abortion pamphlets you left for me made your position on that very clear, darling." Then Lacey's mother threw back her head and laughed, a laugh so uncannily like Lacey's it was impossible to pretend they weren't related. "But if it weren't for little Jamie, I wouldn't have all this." Her hands flopped to her sides, lazily taking in the house, maybe the town, the life.

"You wouldn't have Big Jamie, either," Lacey said. "The horror."

A boozy stage whisper: "Lacey's a little jealous of her baby brother."

Lacey whispered back, loud. "Lacey can hear you."

"That's the problem with only children," her mother said. "No matter what you do, they end up as spoiled little bitches."

"That's right, Mom, you *spoiled me*. That's my problem."

"See?"

"Upstairs, Dex," Lacey said. "Now."

"*Dex?*" Her mother's voice flew to a heavenly register. "*You're* the famous Dex?"

That she had heard of me; that I was known. That I mattered, this was proof. When she told me again to sit, I obeyed.

Lacey, disgusted; Lacey, reconciled. She sat, too.

"So, what's she told you about me?" her mother asked.

I said nothing, which was true enough.

"Don't worry, I won't be offended. I know how it is with you girls. You think it's your job to hate your mothers."

"Nice work if you can get it," Lacey said.

"Didn't used to be that way, did it, Lace? Kid never wanted to leave my side. Would cry and hang onto my leg if I didn't take her out with me. So what did I do?"

"We're waiting with bated breath," Lacey said.

"Took her with me. Every party, every concert. You should've seen her, swimming in a Metallica T-shirt, bangs sprayed up to *here*," she said, saluting the air a foot over her head. "Even got me backstage a few times. Bouncers couldn't resist."

"Ask her what she did with me then," Lacey said. "Hard

to keep track of a toddler when you're fucking a roadie."

"You shut your mouth," her mother snapped. Then, summoning a full measure of dignity, "I have never in my life fucked a *roadie*."

"Standards," Lacey said.

"She won't admit it now, but she loved it. How do you think she ended up so musical? It's in her blood."

Lacey snorted. "That trash is hardly music."

"How did I raise you to be such a snob?"

"How did I raise you to get knocked up by Jersey's biggest dickhead? Somebody call *Unsolved Mysteries*."

If I'd talked to my mother like that, and it was a gargantuan *if*, I could only assume she'd duct-tape my mouth shut and sell me to the circus. Lacey's mother, on the other hand, smiled fondly. Mother-daughter bonding, Champlain-style.

"She was less whiny then," Lacey's mother confided. "Didn't complain when I let her stay up until two A.M., dancing around the apartment. We were good then, weren't we, Lace?"

Lacey's face softened, almost imperceptibly. Maybe she was even about to say yes, acknowledge a sliver of good, but then the front door rattled, a key turned, and both of them went rigid.

"Shit," Lacey said.

"Shit," her mother agreed. "He's not supposed to be home this early."

Already on her feet, Lacey tossed her mother a pack of gum. "We'll be upstairs," she said, and this time she didn't wait for me to follow.

I bolted up the stairs after her, behind me a steady

murmur—*pull it together, pull it together, pull it together*—as the front door creaked open, horror-movie-style. Lacey tugged me into her room before I could catch sight of the monster.

In the dark, in Lacey's room, with Kurt's voice turned up to drown out whatever was happening below. Her in black lacy pajamas, me in my Snoopy T-shirt and Goodwill boxers. Our sleeping bags kissing, head to toe. Voices in the dark. Orphans, alone together.

"Never?" Lacey said.

"Never," I said.

"Is it *killing* you?"

"It's not like I'm in this huge hurry."

"Oh, God, you're not ... you're not waiting for *marriage*, are you?"

"I'm just not in a hurry. Plus, it's not like there's some guy banging down my door."

"But if there was?"

"What's he like?"

"Who?"

"This guy, Lacey. The one who wants to ravish me."

"Oh, I don't know, he's some guy. Who thinks you're hot."

"Do I love him?"

"How do I know?"

"Does he love me? Is it his first time, too? Does he think that matters? Is he going to notice how I kind of look pregnant from the side—"

· 64 ·

"You do not look pregnant."

"After I eat a lot—"

"Everyone looks pregnant after they eat a lot."

"I'm just saying, what does he think when he sees me naked? And do I know what he's thinking? Can I read his mind when I look in his eyes? Does he—"

"Jesus, I don't know, okay? He's freaking imaginary. But I get it. You're holding out for the fairy tale. Candles, flowers, Prince Charming. Et cetera." She laughed. "It's not like that, Dex. It's weird and gross and awesome and messy," she said, and told me a story about the time some guy's thing had blown its wad when she popped a zit for him, because guys were weird, and you could never overestimate how much. *Blown its wad* was hers, along with *popped its top*, *went Old Faithful*, and *fizzed its whizz*, which made very little sense to me. She was a poet of ejaculation.

"I don't need a fairy tale. Just ... something better than your average Battle Creek doofus jerking off in his father's Oldsmobile. Something better than, like ... "

"Nikki and Craig?"

"Exactly. The most expected people falling into the most expected thing. Like some depressing fairy tale. Boring and the Beast."

"People can surprise you, Dex. You never know what kind of wild, kinky sex they might have been having in that Oldsmobile—"

I cut her off with a pillow to the face, because the last thing I needed to think about was Nikki's naked body writhing in pornographic positions beneath a soon-to-be corpse. "I just think there's got to be something better out there," I said.

"Dex, my friend, for once you have a point."

"Thank you."

"But you've, like, made out with people, right?"

"Obviously." I had not.

"What base?"

"Seriously?"

"Seriously, Dex. What base?"

"I'm not having this conversation."

"Sure, okay, we don't have to talk about this. I'm not some kind of sex-crazed lunatic, I can discuss plenty of other things, you know. Politics. Philosophy. Gardening."

"Good. Pick one."

"So when you're home, alone, do you ever, I don't know, dig out that old Kirk Cameron poster I know you keep hidden at the back of your closet—"

"Do *not*."

"Totally do too, and I bet you stroke his face and stare into those dopey big brown eyes and slide your hand under the covers and—"

"Lacey! God, shut up!"

"What, it's totally normal. Healthy, even."

"I'm not listening to you anymore."

"You're a growing woman, with *womanly urges*—"

"I hate you."

"Oh, you love me."

"You wish."

"Come on, Dex, I'm sorry, you know you love me, you know you do. Say it. Say it."

"I'm not saying it."

"You love me you love me you love me you love me."

"Lacey, get off me."

"Not till you say it."

"And then you'll let go?"

"Never!"

I waited her out, testing the words in my head, on my tongue.

"Fine. I love you. Even though you're a sex-crazed lunatic."

She did not let go.

I knew without asking that I wasn't supposed to leave the room, but Lacey was asleep and the bathroom was down the hall, and there seemed no harm in following the voices, navigating the dark easily enough in this house that mirrored my own. I knew exactly how far down the stairs I could creep without being seen.

The man Lacey called the Bastard stood shorter and skinnier than I'd imagined, with wire-rimmed glasses and a graying military flattop. Lacey's mother knelt before him in a white bra and panties, palms assuming prayer position, eyes on the Bastard's black loafers.

"God forgive me," she said.

"For being a drunk," he prompted.

"For being a drunk. For being weak. For—"

"For giving in to the temptations of my whorish past."

"For giving in to temptations."

He toed her hard in the belly.

"The temptations of my whorish past," she corrected herself.

I felt like I was watching TV.

Lacey's mother was crying. Somewhere beyond me, a baby echoed her.

She tried to stand, but the Bastard pressed two fingers to her shoulder and shook his head. Her knees returned to the tile.

The baby was screaming.

"He needs me," Lacey's mother said.

"Should've thought of that before." The Bastard's voice was so reasonable, as if they were sitting across the table from each other discussing a credit card bill. He was even dressed like an accountant, a pocket protector tucked neatly into his starched white shirt.

"You won't do with my son what you've done with your daughter," he said.

She nodded.

"Say it."

"I'll do better with James Junior."

"You'll have some respect for yourself."

"I'll have respect."

"No more of this garbage."

"No more," she whispered.

The baby cried.

There was a touch on my shoulder, just gentle enough not to startle, or maybe I wasn't startled because I knew, of course, Lacey would be there.

"There's a back way out through the kitchen," Lacey whispered, though she didn't have to: Our houses shared the same floor plan, escape route and all. I went first, sliding through the dark, any noise covered up by the baby's increasingly unhinged screams. I had to tamp down an impulse to turn back for him, carry him and Lacey away, but of course he wasn't my brother and Lacey was the one with car and license. I wasn't in a position to rescue anyone.

She eased the door shut behind us, and said nothing as we got into the car and peeled away. There was no music.

"You want to go home," she said finally, and I knew if I said yes, that's what it would be. Final.

I understood now: This was a test. Maybe the whole night had been a test. With Lacey, it was hard to tell whether events were unspooling of their own accord or under her behind-the-scenes machinations, but, I reminded myself, it was always safest to assume the latter.

I was good at tests. I reached over to the Barbie recorder and hit *play*, feinting a head slam with each of Kurt's downbeats. "Let's go to the lake."

The lake in February, in sleet and starshine. We had it to ourselves. Wind and water and sky and Lacey. Everything I needed.

"Parents are bullshit," I said.

She shrugged.

"Everyone's bullshit but us," I said.

We called it our lake, but it was only ours the way everything was ours: because the world we created between the two of us was secret and wholly owned.

We were creatures of water, she told me, and those don't belong in the woods. It was the only explanation she ever offered for why we needed to stay away. Never the forest, always the lake, and that was fine with me. I couldn't wait for it to get warmer, to watch her swim.

She breathed water, she told me, and I could almost believe it was true.

The sleet was light and oil slick, the kind that made you wonder about acid rain. Lacey preferred storms. A death-black sky, a sizzle in the air, that waiting, breath-holding feeling, like something was about to break. Sometimes we made it to the lake before the storm's first bellow. We raised our faces to the rain, timed the gap between light and sound, *one Mississippi and two and three*. Until we knew the storm well enough to breathe with it, to beat with its rhythm, to know after the sky burned white how long to wait before opening our mouths and screaming into the thunder's roar.

But that was Lacey's time. I liked it better in the quiet. The storm was like another person between us, angrier and more interesting than I could hope to be. It was best when we were alone.

Lacey watched the water. It was different, in the dark.

Fathomless. I imagined eyes glowing in the deep, teeth sharp, hunger and need. *Things* lurking. I imagined a siren song, a call in the night, Lacey and I answering, wading into icy waters, sucked down into the black.

She scooped up a rock and threw it into the lake. "Fuck."

"Fuck," I said, like I agreed, because whatever she meant by it, I did.

I wanted to tell her it didn't matter what her mother and her stepfather did with each other, that I understood they weren't a part of Lacey, and Lacey was no part of them, had sprung fully grown, goddess-style, blooming in a field or melting from the sun. That other people were irrelevant to us; that they existed only for the pleasure of dismissing them, simulacra of consciousness, walking and talking and pretending at an inner life but hollow inside. Nothing like us. Lacey herself had taught me that, when she read us Descartes. You can only know your own insides, Lacey said. The only real, certified and confirmed, is you and me. I wanted to remind her what she'd taught me, that we could leave together, that life was only as cruel as you allowed it to be, that Battle Creek belonged to us by choice and we could choose to abandon it.

I wanted to tell her that nothing I'd seen had scared me, that nothing had changed, but she already knew me well enough to hear a lie in my voice.

I wanted, most of me wanted, to save her.

Beneath that, though, there was a cold, shameful relief. I had come to need Lacey so much that it scared me. But if her life was this broken, if there was nothing beyond our closed circle but ugly mess, then it opened up the unthinkable possibility that Lacey needed something, too. That if I passed her tests, shaped myself to fit against her edges, that something could be me.

"My father loved the water." She found another rock and fired it hard at the lake. "He liked to take me to Atlantic City, when we lived in Jersey. There was this mechanical pony thing by the casino, and he'd leave me with, like, a bucket of quarters. Enough to ride all day."

"That's a lot of pony riding."

"Seemed like heaven to me. You know what they say about girls and horses." I could hear a little of the Lacey I knew peeking through, winking at me. "Also, I was an idiot."

"All six-year-olds are idiots."

"He promised one day he'd take me to ride a real pony. I guess there are these beaches in Virginia where they run wild in the sand? Just ponies everywhere, like you're back in time or something."

"Chincoteague," I said. I'd read *Misty of Chincoteague* eleven times.

"Whatever. I don't know, because we never went."

I could have told her that my father was the king of broken promises, that I knew all about disappointment, but I was afraid she'd tell me I knew fuck-all about anything, and she'd be right. "I've never been to the ocean," I told her, and these were the magic words that brought her back.

Lacey squealed. "Unacceptable!" She pointed at the car. "In."

For six hours, we drove. The Buick bumped and wheezed, the cassette player ate Lacey's third-favorite bootleg, the crumpled AAA maps beaconed our way, and while I hovered over a suspiciously discolored toilet seat and then washed my hands with sickly gray soap, examining myself in the mirror for some clue that I'd become the kind of girl who lit out for the territories, some trucker tried to feel up Lacey in the Roy Rogers parking lot. We drove until the car swerved off the highway and into a parking lot gritty with sand, and there we were.

The ocean was endless.

The ocean beat and beat and beat against the shore.

We held hands and let the Atlantic wash over our bare feet. We breathed in salt and spray under the dawning sky.

It was the biggest thing I had ever seen. Lacey gave that to me.

"This is how I'd do it," Lacey said, almost too quiet to hear under the surf. "I'd come out here at night, when the beach was empty, and I'd take an inflatable raft into the water. Then I'd hold on, and let it carry me out. Far enough that no one would ever find me. That I couldn't change my mind. I'd bring my mother's sleeping pills, and my Walkman, and a safety pin. And when I was out far enough that I couldn't hear the waves breaking anymore, that the raft was just bobbing on the water and there was nothing but me and the stars? I'd do it. In order. The order matters. Pills first, then the safety pin, just a tiny hole in the raft, small enough that it would take some time. Then I'd put on the headphones, and lie down on the raft so I could see the stars and feel the water in my hair, and I'd let Kurt sing me home."

I was supposed to be the one who paid attention, the one who listened to the chaos of the world and understood—that, Lacey said, was the whole joy of me—but so often that year, Lacey talked and I didn't hear her at all.

"I could never go out there in the dark," I said, and didn't tell her how I would do it, even though I had decided, because Lacey said it was important to know. I would jump off something—something high enough that you would break on the way down. There was nothing like that in Battle Creek; there wasn't even anything high enough for me to find out if I was scared of heights. Lacey thought I probably was. She said I seemed like the type.

I didn't want to be up there in the sky, seeing everything at once, not unless it was going to be the last time. Because then I wouldn't be afraid. I would feel powerful, I thought, toes peeking over edge, this most precious thing entirely mine, to protect or destroy. If you did it that way, you'd have power, up to the very end.

If I did it that way, at least before the end I could fly.

We slept in the car, running the heater for as long as we dared, pressed together for warmth. For once Lacey let me pick the music—"within reason," she said. We turned on R.E.M., because I liked the honey in the singer's voice, and I liked that Lacey liked it, too. She curled up in the seat and I put my head on her shoulder. Right there in the parking lot, with the water watching, he sang us to sleep.

When I woke up, the sky was gray and the horizon was on fire. Lacey was asleep. I padded barefoot back to the shoreline and stood in the water, needles of ice biting my ankles. The ocean looked kinder in the light, and I wished for Lacey's raft so we could take it together, float into the sun.

I didn't hear her come up behind me, but I felt her squeeze my hand. I knew she would find me.

"This is everything I need," she said. "You're everything. Just like I'm everything you need, right?" It was an incantation; it sealed us for life.

"Everything," I told her, a fire sale on my soul. Everything must go. I wanted her to swallow me whole.

"Only us," Lacey said.

We would be orphans; we would be ghosts. We would disappear from the mundane world into one of our own making. We would be wild. We would be free. This was the promise we made to each other, and this, if nothing else, we would keep.

LACEY

If I Lied

You say you want to know. But you don't, not really. You like me better as some mythical creature you dreamed up, a fucking forest sprite who only came to life because you closed your eyes and wanted it *so bad*. Maybe I've lied to you, Dex, but when it comes to the important things, I didn't even have to bother because you never think to ask.

Lies I've told you?

The smoking: I do it. Chimney-style, when you're not around, a nicotine camel soaking it up to save for a rainy, Dex-filled day. Why do you think the car always smells like smoke? You think it's the tobacco-stained ghost of the previous owner, breaking in at night just to puff at the windshield and blow smoke signals to the stars? No, either you knew or you didn't want to.

It wasn't a lie the day I told you I didn't smoke, because that day, I didn't. And it wasn't a lie that my grandma died of lung cancer, which is why I quit that day, the way I quit a couple months before that and twice the year before that. It didn't take. Your Lacey, smart and strong, wouldn't have hidden a pack under the mattress for emergencies, and wouldn't, after a cold meat loaf dinner with the Bastard, slip the pack from under the mattress, stick her head out the window, and breathe hot smoke into the winter air. It almost didn't seem to count, that first drag after quitting—it was cold; the smoke looked like a fog of breath. It would be my last one ever.

The first drag is never the last one ever. Maybe I didn't tell you because I liked having a secret. What's mine is yours, that's what we say. But it's mine first.

I smoke, and the scars are real. The one on my wrist I showed you that first day. The thing I said I did, before I took it back. That was real, too.

Also, there was never any band. I was never some guitar-slinging rock goddess falling back from the stage and surfing a sea of blissed-out hands. You need me to be fearless. When you look at me I *am* fearless. But you're not always there.

How I did it, when I did it.

With a knife. Lacey Champlain, in the bathtub, with a knife.

That was after Jersey, after the Bastard, after Battle Creek and Nikki and Craig but still before you. Nikki and Craig, that's more a lie of omission, but you'd probably say it still counts.

I did it in the bathtub with a knife because that's how they do it in the movies: warm bath, warm blood, everything slip-sliding away. I ran the water and took off my clothes and then I cut, but only once, and only shallowly, because what they don't tell you in the movies is that it fucking hurts.

Before Lacey, my dear mother would tell you, life was an all-you-can-eat buffet of bong hits and Pabst hangovers, which is white trash for the Garden of Eden. Just her and my daddy drinking and screwing and shiny-happy-peopling the seventies away, right up until she went and got knocked up. Ever since then, she'd tell you, she's been starving to death. My mother, Battle Creek's very own Joan of fucking Arc. One broken condom; one abortive trip to some dismal clinic where she couldn't even stand to plant her ass on the rusty folding chairs, much less strip down and let the hairy-knuckled doctor scrape her out; one marriage proposal featuring two six-packs and no ring. One peeing, pooping, puking baby who liked screaming better than sleeping. At the wedding, I was a watermelon-sized lump under a cheap lace gown. They married in a park, and because they didn't believe in all that bad-luck bullshit, they stood together before the ceremony, holding hands next to a Dumpster while the rent-a-minister got his crap together and the fifteen people who'd bothered to show up pretended they weren't drunk or high, in deference to the groom's snotty parents, who hadn't even wanted to come. Mother and father-to-be gazed at each other, playing happy and love-struck—"even though I knew he was thinking, *Holy fuck, let's get this over with so I can get plastered,*" she says, "and you were kicking a fucking hole in my stomach so I was just trying not to puke."

It was my favorite story when I was a kid, the story of their wedding, of how I was there without being there, of how I came to be. Because my father told it differently, back when he would sit on the edge of my bed, stroke my hair, spin me fairy tales. "Your mother never looked more beautiful," he told me, "and you know the prettiest part?"

That was my line, and even a four-year-old could remember it: "The watermelon!"

"Damn right. The watermelon. I couldn't help myself. I reached out and rubbed her belly, just like I'm rubbing your head right now, and that frilly dress crinkled against my hand, and that's when I said it."

"Lacy."

"I was talking about the dress. And how beautiful she looked, and how she felt against my hand, and how I wanted— Well, you don't need to know about that. But she thought—"

"You were talking about *me*."

"And that's how you became you, little watermelon. That's how you became Lacey."

When I was ten, my mother told me she pulled my name

from some shitty romance novel. "Lucky you weren't a boy," she said, "or it could have been Fabio."

It was her hobby, telling lies about the past. Making up stories to help her feel better and me feel worse.

Your father left because he didn't love us.

Your father was a useless fuckup and we're better off without him.

Unless she was in one of her other moods: *It ruined everything, a fucking baby, how could it not. No more fucking on the kitchen floor, suddenly it's all diapers and bills and how can I blame him for fucking off. I would've done it myself if I'd thought of it first.*

Before you, he drank, but he was no drunk.

Before you, everything was good.

Back in Jersey, when she was in an especially good mood, she would tell me how they met, both drunk off their asses at a Van Halen show. He worked security, she was a groupie, and she'd fuck anyone if it meant getting backstage.

She didn't talk about it as much with the Bastard around, because he didn't like the reminder that he wasn't her first. But sometimes, when he was out bowling for the Lord or whatever, she'd get drunk and misty and want to play another round of *This Is Your Life. Your daddy gave me a coat hanger for Valentine's Day. I should have used it.*

I know what I know.

Lacey, he said, when he put his hand on my unformed head, only that thin layer of lace and womb between us, and he said it because even then he thought I was beautiful.

I'd stay if I could, he whispered, that last night. *I'll come back for you.*

He did come back for me, four times that year, twice the next one, always when she was at work or asleep, and I never told her, not once. Sometimes he showed up at night and threw pebbles at my window, like we were fucking Romeo and Juliet, and he would climb up the trellis and crawl into my bedroom with a stuffed animal in his mouth, some limp bunny or three-legged cat that he'd found and saved just for me, because he knew I liked them wounded. He'd put his finger to his lips, and I'd zip mine shut, and we would play in the moonlight, quiet as mice, pretending that maybe this one time, the sun would never rise.

When he stopped coming, I knew he had a good reason. I liked to imagine him on a ship somewhere, the merchant marines or maybe cabin boy on some private yacht, my father swinging through the riggings, shouting *Ahoy there!* and *Land ho!*, making his fortune so he could come back for real and take me away.

Except how would he know to find me in Battle Creek? We were doing fine in Jersey, just the two of us, me doing whatever I wanted and my mother letting me. I gave her the same courtesy, pretending to buy her flexible definition of "waitressing" and ignoring the parade of sad, lonely men, the local car dealers and the drunk tourists. Then along came the Bastard, something wicked this way in a velour suit. The Bastard James Troy, and how ironic is it that your real daddy and my fake one have the same name, like how a double-wide trailer and Buckingham Palace are both called a home.

My James acted like he was still in the military, even

though he'd never actually *been* in the military, unless you counted getting dishonorably discharged from the reserves after less than six months. Who needed a Purple Heart when you could be a soldier in the army of God, fighting the good fight by phone-banking for the Christian Coalition? The man's most valuable possession was a framed, signed photo of George Bush. Reagan, even Nixon, maybe I could have respected—but what kind of middle management weenie has a hard-on for George H. W. Bush?

My James, she called him from the beginning: *My James* knows how it is, unlike that bitch sponsor always up her ass about the Xanax, as if she didn't need something to take the edge off without the beer. *My James* will drive; *my James* will make dinner; *my James* says abortion's a sin—*and anyway he's always wanted to be a daddy and you've always wanted to be a big sister and look at the pretty ring.*

People will assume it's mine, I told her. That you're mothering your own grandson for propriety's sake, and she said people knew her better than to believe she did anything for propriety's sake.

She thought she was better with him than without him, and maybe it was true, but just because dog food tastes better than dog shit doesn't mean you want it for dinner. When dog food gets a transfer to corporate headquarters, conveniently located twenty miles past bumblefuck, it doesn't mean you hitch up the U-Haul and speed into the sunset, listening to Barry Manilow and stopping to pee every twenty minutes because little-bro-to-be is kneeing your bladder.

No one should move to Battle Creek in the summer. I mean, obviously, no one should move to Battle Creek at all, but some of us had no choice in the matter, and should at least have been excused from arriving in summer, piling out of the shit-paneled van to get a good look at the shit-paneled house and almost spontaneously combusting before we made it halfway up the driveway.

In the summer, Battle Creek smelled like fried dog shit. No one who lived there seemed to notice, maybe because it's all you'd ever known. Like the so-called lake covered in so much algae you wouldn't know there was water under there unless you stepped in it, which not even one of the native morons would do, because God knew what was living in the toxic sludge underneath. Or the public pool with its sick green water, the color of chlorine mixed with pee. But it was between the pool, or the lake, or the 7-Eleven that reeked of those disgusting meat pockets roasting in the heater case—because in the summer, in Battle Creek, there was literally nothing else to do. Unless I wanted to lock myself in the house for two months, and when it came to a house containing the Bastard and his not-technically-a-bastard fetus, agoraphobia was not an option.

I took to walking. It's not a walking town, not in any weather and especially not in summer, but it was as good a way as any to mark time. If you're embedded in enemy territory, it's safest to know the lay of the land. Not that there was much to know: main street literally called fucking Main Street, the shithole neighborhood to its south and slightly less shithole neighborhood to its north, too many secondhand shops and even more boarded-up storefronts, prison-shaped school and that gas station with the giant hot dog on top. All that walking and I didn't even notice until I looked at a map that the town is shaped like a gun, with the woods curving out like a trigger.

It was a wet-blanket-heat day when I came across Nikki in the woods, air tailpipe hot, both of us slouching toward junior year, both of our tops basically see-through, nipples poking at sweat-stained cotton, though she was in no condition to notice. Come September, we'd be in the same class, which made me her subject and her my queen, but I didn't know it and wouldn't have cared if I did, and maybe it was that unfathomable glimpse of obscurity that got her attention.

Nikki Drummond, drunk at three o'clock on a Tuesday afternoon, Battle Creek princess in disgrace. She'd propped herself up against a tree in the swamp, bottle of vodka in her lap, cigarette in her mouth, and only that overdried blond hair—*literally* brushed a hundred strokes a night, it turns out— clued me in that this was probably, in the sober light of fall, not my kind of people. But fall was two months away, and I was bored, so when Nikki offered me her bottle I sat down beside her and took a slug.

Would it surprise you to know that I walked in the woods all the time back then? There's another pretty lie for you, that I was some mythical creature of the water, constitutionally afraid of trees. The woods weren't just my kind of place, with their shadows and the music of whispers on the breeze; they were *my* place, this green labyrinth I could escape into and spin a little fantasy of my own. The closest path through the trees picked up less than a mile from the house, but inside the green it was dense and silent and felt about a million miles away from the Bastard and his Battle Creek. I could be the last person on earth, everyone and everything scorched away except for me and the trees, the worms and the deer. I liked when the leaves got so thick you couldn't see the sky.

The first day I came across the old train station, I took a breath and wondered whether I'd willed it into existence. Because here was the end of civilization, forgotten station and rusty tracks and a behemoth of a boxcar sleeping in the weeds. You probably would have wasted your time trying to imagine yourself into the past, some booming, bustling era of ladies with parasols and men with briefcases and fedoras and important places to go, but I liked it the way it was, sprayed with fading graffiti, full of broken glass and jagged edges, lost in time. It was the first place I found that felt dangerous—the rotting heart of Battle Creek. This was apocalypse country, and it felt like home.

You can imagine how it felt when I found Nikki trespassing in my story.

"I don't know you," Nikki said, like existing without her awareness was the worst kind of sin. Like *I* was the intruder.

"Don't know you, either." I took one more slug before she stole the bottle back.

"I know everyone."

"Apparently not."

"Everyone. Everything. What are you supposed to do when you've done everything? Huh? What then?" Nikki Drummond slurring her words, baring her existential crisis to the newest trash in town.

"I highly doubt you've done everything. You live *here*."

"I *rule* here," Nikki corrected me.

At that, I laughed. I didn't know her well enough then to realize how drunk she must have been not to claw my eyes out.

"I've done Craig," she said. "I've done him and done him and done him and dull dull dull."

"Whereas I bet he finds you fascinating."

She blinked big blue eyes up at me; she smiled. Nikki stalked the world like a cat, but that afternoon she looked more like the tiger cub dangling from a branch in some lame inspirational poster: *Hang in there!* Clawed, but cuddly.

Lacey Champlain, in the woods, with a knife to your heart, because here's the truth: Before you, there was Nikki Drummond.

We drank; she talked. I got an A-to-Z of the world according to Nikki, what it was like to be perfect and popular, to be Nikki-and-Craig, like Barbie-and-Ken, to be written in the stars, if the stars were a staple-bound yearbook and the ink was semen and beer. She told me they belonged together, and that if she couldn't love him she couldn't love anyone.

"Break up with him," I said.

"Done that, too. It didn't take."

Too lazy and too bored to do anything but get blackout drunk and whine on a Tuesday afternoon. Such a tragedy, right? Where were the inspirational Sally Struthers commercials, the promise that *even you* could pimp out poor Nikki for just pennies a day?

"Sometimes I'm so bored I could fucking die," she said. We were sitting side by side, dangling our legs over the tracks. "You ever feel that way?"

I wanted to be a different person. I wasn't the girl I'd been in Jersey. I wasn't Shay's girl anymore, the kind who followed a foot behind if the wrong people were watching and said *Yes, whatever you want* when the answer was *No fucking way*; I hadn't been Daddy's girl, not in a long time, and my mother had a new kid to screw up. I was Kurt's girl, and I needed that to mean something. So maybe I was the one who crossed the space between us and smeared her pastel gloss, but the way I remember it, she was already there, and our lips and then our tongues and then the rest of us came together like it had been the plan from the beginning.

You're probably picturing something porny, exploding feather-pillow fights and pizza delivery girls who want a taste of your pepperoni. It *felt* like porn, which made it interesting. It felt filthy, literally, rolling around in the dirt, our hair tangled with twigs, our flesh matted with gravel and moss, both of us panting and sweating and moaning, two wild girls raised by wolves.

So that's how it started: by accident, but also not. We made a plan to meet the next day, same time, same place, same bottle of vodka—only this time she showed up with Craig Ellison in tow, Mr. Hot and Boring, as she introduced him. He'd heard about the action and wanted in on it.

"Just to watch," he said, and that first time, it was all he did.

THEM

Dex's mother knew she should be afraid for her daughter. This, she'd been told, was the tragedy of birthing a girl. To live in fear—it was the fate of any parent, maybe, but the special provenance of a mother to a daughter, one woman raising another, knowing too well what could happen. This was what lurked inside the luckiest delivery rooms, the ones whose balloons screamed *It's a girl!*: pink cigars and flowered onesies and fear.

So she'd been told.

Now she was supposed to be more afraid than ever. Now they were all more afraid than ever, the mothers of Battle Creek, because whatever illusions they'd had about their children and their home and the inevitability that the future would unfold as uneventfully as the past had been punctured by the bullet that Ellison boy blew through his brainstem. And Dex's mother *had* been afraid, that first night. She and Jimmy had stood in their daughter's doorway, watching her sleep, dipping a toe in the unimaginable. They'd counted her breaths, the easy rise and fall of her chest, and Dex's mother felt her own lungs sighing in time with her daughter's, breathing for her the way she had when her daughter was a newborn, when she'd sat by the bassinet, fingertips resting lightly on infant chest, because only by feeling the rhythm of breath and the flutter of heartbeat, one moment after the next, could she reassure herself that the baby was still alive.

They'd resolved everything would be different, after the tragedy. Nothing was different, of course, because it wasn't their tragedy, and Dex's mother had little patience for the mothers of Battle Creek who seemed unable to comprehend this basic fact. Boys weren't supposed to be vulnerable; it overturned the natural order of things, a boy falling prey to pain. That was a girl's purview. So maybe it was understandable that they groped for other answers, these mothers, still twittering all these months later about what had "really" happened, about demonic influences and satanic cults, about heavy metal and blood sacrifice, but it infuriated her, all these ginned-up monsters under the bed, as if that would recuse them from worrying about anything that mattered, overdoses and car crashes and AIDS and, especially in the case of those mothers of sons who thought only daughters should be worried for, accidentally raising little proto-rapists who thought wining and dining a girl meant getting her drunk enough that she'd swallow a mouthful of ejaculate without complaint. Dex's mother hadn't known the Ellison boy, but she'd known plenty of boys like him. There had always been boys like him. And she knew whatever trouble he'd gotten into, if there had been trouble, he'd probably brought it on himself. All these mothers, so concerned about the terrible things that could happen to their children—so unwilling to think about the things their children might *make* happen. Maybe this was why Dex's mother never had managed to muster up much fear for her daughter. Her daughter wasn't the type to make things happen.

Dex's mother was well aware that she embarrassed her daughter. But her daughter couldn't know how much she embarrassed her mother. How she, too, often dreamed of some other, prettier, happier daughter, imagined showing her off to an admiring world, *gaze at my lovely creation and marvel at what I have wrought.*

You created a child; you nursed her, bathed her, wiped her, loved her, kept her alive until she grew up; then she grew up. Ugly and sullen and wanting nothing more than to be a motherless child.

Dex's mother, despite claims by her husband and daughter to the contrary, did in fact have a healthy sense of humor. She had for many years, for example, found her life hilarious. That everything she had been and wanted had been whittled away, her edges smoothed into a featureless surface without a name of its own. Hannah Dexter's mother. Jimmy Dexter's wife. *You* when something was needed; *she* when something was not. She felt, at times, that what had seemed like an infinity of choice turned out to be a funnel, life narrowing itself one bad decision at a time, each mistake cutting the options by half, spiraling her ever downward until there was nowhere left to fall but into a small, dark hole that had no bottom.

Choosing a life for yourself, that was the joke. She had

chosen Jimmy Dexter, yes, but only after the state had chosen to yank her scholarship because the governor had chosen to cut educational funding; she had chosen the charming guitar player with the lopsided smile, yes, the one who kept her up all night declaiming Vonnegut and debating Vietnam and allowing her, through a haze of smoke and pseudointellectual acid rants on the doors of perception, to pretend she was still in college—but she had chosen *that* Jimmy, not the one who couldn't understand why he wasn't to play his guitar while the baby slept or why the changing table wasn't an appropriate surface for rolling joints. They'd fallen in love because they both desperately wanted the same thing: Better lives. Bigger lives. It never occurred to her that it should matter how they expected to get there. She believed in work; he believed in hope. Here was the biggest joke: It turned out this wasn't wanting the same thing at all.

They'd hollowed each other out, she and Jimmy, and now they were good for no one but each other. Most days, she thought that was no worse than anyone else had it, that the world was full of empty husks, smiling and following through. Some days, though, the bad ones and the best ones, she thought about running.

Her daughter would leave for college soon. When the time came, Dex's mother thought, she would leave, too. She was almost worried that he'd leave her first, except that if Jimmy still had it in him to leave, she might have found it in herself to love him again, and to stay. She wanted her daughter gone so they could get on with it; she wanted her daughter to stay, wanted to hold on and scream *stop growing stop changing stop leaving*—then Lacey came along and soon there would be nothing left to hold onto, because piece by piece, Lacey was taking her daughter away.

Dex's mother knew what it was to lose herself in someone brighter, to be trapped by the gravitational field of another sun. She knew what happened when it emerged that the sun was only a lightbulb, and what happened when the lightbulb burned out. It didn't seem fair that her mistakes hadn't been genetically encoded in her daughter, that there'd been no evolutionary adaptation, no innate biological resistance to light and charm. It made her shamefully jealous, watching her daughter fall in love, and what else could you call it—jealous and wistful and mindful of younger days, and maybe it even made her a little nostalgic for the strum of Jimmy's guitar and the way his eyes had always found her in a sparse crowd, fixing her with every sorry lyric he sang. But more than anything, it made her feel like the mother of a daughter, like she'd taken Communion and joined a fellowship of women across distance and time, because finally, as had long been promised, Dex's mother was afraid.

US

April–July 1992

DEX

The Devil's Playground

The first time Lacey got me high, nothing much happened. Lacey said the mushrooms were too old, and anyway her mailman's cousin's friend wasn't exactly the most reliable supplier, so who knew what we were getting. I had angled for pot instead; pot was everywhere, and as far as I knew it couldn't turn your brain into scrambled eggs, no matter what the commercials said. But Lacey said pot was for plebes.

The second time Lacey got me high, we went to church.

Nothing local, obviously. We drove to Dickinson, three towns over, and pulled over to the first cross-topped building we could find. We waved at a couple old ladies hobbling across the parking lot, and because they weren't Battle Creek old ladies, they didn't know any better than to wave back. What nice girls, I bet they thought.

We nibbled on the mushrooms. Lacey licked me on the

cheek, which she did sometimes when she was in a good mood, quick and darting, like a cat. "*What you are to do without me, I cannot imagine*," she purred. We'd just read *Pygmalion* in English, and the line delighted her. I liked another one—*I can't turn your soul on. Leave me those feelings; and you can take away the voice and the face. They are not you.*—but it was harder to slip into conversation.

"When do you think it'll start?" I asked her. The last time, we'd chopped up the mushrooms and mixed them in chocolate pudding, to make them go down. This time we were purists. It was like eating a Styrofoam cup.

"Maybe it already did." She laughed. "Maybe I'm not even here, and you're just imagining me."

I gave her the finger, and we went inside.

It had been Lacey's idea to settle into the wooden pews and wait for something to happen. She'd read about some experiment where a bunch of people got high for Easter Mass and had a transcendent religious experience, so we swallowed and closed our eyes and—for purely scientific purposes, she said—waited for transcendence.

Lacey always said that other people's drug trips were almost as boring as other people's dreams, but when it finally kicked in, inside that church, I'd never felt more wildly and indelibly myself. As if the world were re-creating itself especially for me, the walls whispering a sacred message, the minister's voice blue light and warm coffee and slipping down my throat to my secret self, and I was an *I* like no other I had ever been, life was a question and only I knew the answer, and if I closed my eyes, the world outside, the colors and sounds and faces that existed only to please me, would vanish.

Inside that church, I didn't discover a god; I became one.

The minister said the devil walks among you.

The minister said evil is in this town and the wages of sin is death.

The minister said cows were dying and chickens were slaughtered and dead cats were hung from flaming trees, and this is the evidence you need that these are the end times, that hell is upon you, that Satan's cold fingers hold you in their grasp, that here and there and everywhere children are dying and children are killing and children are danger.

The minister reached out across the congregation, reached for *us*, and I could feel his cold fingers on Lacey's lips, because her lips were my lips, because what was hers was mine. The minister said the devil will sing you to hell, but when he raised his hands, the choir sang in Kurt's voice, hoarse and longing, their robes white, their eyes black, and Kurt's voice sang my name, said *you have always belonged to me*. The minister's eyes glowed, and the walls bled, and the people, the good, churchgoing, God-fearing people, they all turned to us, eyes hungry, and then Lacey's hand was hot against my mouth, as if she knew before I did that I was going to scream.

She rested her other hand in my lap, fingers tight in a fist, then blooming open, and there was a flower she'd inked on her palm. I stopped screaming, then. I watched the flower. Its petals leached color from her skin. They glowed green like Lacey eyes and red like Lacey lips and pink like Lacey tongue.

The flower whispered to me with Lacey's voice and told me there was nothing to fear. Believing her was like breathing.

When the service ended, she held my hand tight and led me out of the church. Her lips brushed my ear and she smelled purple, and when she whispered "Having fun yet?" our laughter tasted like candy.

Fun was meant to be beneath us. *Fun* was for Battle Creek, for the losers who dragged their six-packs into the woods and groped each other in the dark. Not for us; we would get high only for a higher purpose, Lacey had decreed. We would be philosophers; we would devote ourselves to all forms of escape. After the service we would retreat to an empty field and spend the hours until we came down groping for Beauty and Truth. We would lie in the grass, search the sky for answers, make art, make something to make ourselves real.

That was the plan before, when everything had seemed clear—but now was after, silvery and strange. And when we went to the field, bumping and sloshing in the back of a pickup, we didn't go alone.

Boys: some of them in church shirts with shiny shoes, some in flannel with jeans and dirty boots. All of them with sticky beer fingers and grubby breath, all of them boys we did not know and would never like, with faces that blurred and shifted, strangers determined to stay strange. I couldn't keep track: Were there many or few? Had we begged them to bring us or did we beg them to let us go? I waited for Lacey to tell me it wasn't happening, but Lacey only complained about tramping through the mud and breathing in the shit, then asked if, until it was time, she could carry the axe.

One of the boys, I saw then, had an axe.

The sky was pinking and the lowing cows breathed fire like fairy-tale beasts, and I heard my voice saying *you can't*.

"You eat burgers, don't you?" a boy said.

I heard Lacey laughing and knew I must be imagining it.

"They're my property," another boy said. "I decide if they live or die. I'm their god."

I knew that wasn't quite right, but the words to prove it were slippery. Before I could snatch them from the fog, an axe whistled through leathery hide, and blood spurted, and with one voice, the beast and I screamed.

Sticky beer, sticky blood. Laughing boys, giving the finger to an imaginary face in the sky. Laughing Lacey, asking to hold the axe. Lacey's hands on the axe and my hands on the axe. What's hers is mine. Someone's voice saying *don't be a pussy*, someone's voice saying *please don't make me*, someone's knees in the dirt, someone's fist in a steaming wound, some-one's bloody fingers inking a five-pointed star across the grass, someone's breath, someone's whisper, someone's tears. Someone's voice pretending to be Lacey, impossible words carving fire across the sky.

"We trade this blood for the blood of our enemies. Let us bring them to ruin."

Then it was dark, and I was in a barn, lying in the hay, and I came back to myself just as a cold hand slid into my pants.

Just say no, they'd said in school, back when we were too small to imagine the need, so now I said it, "No," and pulled the hand out and pushed the body away.

"C'mon," the body said, and nuzzled its snout against my chest. Red hair, I noted, and disliked. Lacey was sandwiched between a checkered-shirt farm boy and a hay bale, stripped down to her bra and combat boots.

Boys from the field, I thought, then shoved the thought away.

I smacked the copperhead and said no again.

"She said you thought I was cute," he whined.

I took him in, freckles and crooked smile, beady eyes and puffy cheeks, and thought: *Maybe.* But cute didn't mean I wanted this animal thing, wet and clumsy, bones and meat. My first kiss had come at the wrong end of a dare, someone else's punishment; the second came in the dark, someone else's mistake. This was lucky number three, and when I stood up, he said, "I never get the hot one," then jerked off in the hay.

"Lacey," I said, and I was crying, probably. "Lacey."

She made a noise. It's hard to talk when your tongue is tracing messages in someone else's mouth.

"Let 'em be." Red had crusty nails and oozing zits, and I knew without checking that I didn't get the hot one, either.

"Lacey, I want to go." And maybe I was making myself cry, because crying was a thing Lacey wouldn't resist.

"Can it wait?" Lacey wasn't looking at me. The flannel boy bent her over the bale and kissed her knobby spine. "Just a little longer?"

He laughed. "You got the long part right." His dirty hands were on her, fingers smudged with motor oil.

Lacey giggled. I couldn't stop smelling blood.

Hot breath on the back of my neck and "Don't worry, babe, I won't let you get bored."

"Lacey," I said. "Lacey. Lacey. Lacey." That did it. A prayer; a summoning. My witching powers, or the hitch in my voice, or just her name, like the lyrics to a favorite song, calling her home.

"Can't you shut her up?" Flannel said, but Lacey slipped through his straddled legs and scooped up her clothes. She touched my cheek. "You really want to go, Dex?"

I nodded.

"Then we go."

Flannel's nose went piggy when he sneered. "And what the hell are we supposed to do?"

"Suck each other off, for all I care," Lacey told them, then took my hand, and together we ran.

"Sorry," I said, when we were safe in the car, windows down, Kurt's raw voice streaming in our wake, the boys and the field and the church and the night shrinking to a story we would tell ourselves and laugh.

"Sorry for what?" Lacey sped up, as she did when she was bored, and I pictured her toes curling on the grimy pedal. She liked driving in bare feet.

We didn't apologize—that was a rule. Not to each other, not for each other. We made our own choices. We did what we did with the boys in the field, what we did in the grass and the blood and the hay. We kept moving, without looking back. The day behind us was fogging up, and I tried to let it. I tried to feel no shame.

We slept outside that night, and woke up damp with dew. I told myself that none of it had happened, not the glint of the axe or the intestines steaming in the moonlight, not the boys in the field or the barn. The way I felt, floating between the cushions of grass and sky, no longer high but not yet grounded, it was easy to believe.

Lacey had promised there'd be no hangover. She didn't tell me it would be more like the opposite—that I would wake up still feeling like I could fly.

I listened to her breathe, and tried to time the rise and fall of my chest to hers. I counted the clouds, and waited for her to wake up—not bored, not afraid, simply alive to the tickle of grass and sigh of wind. It was only when she blinked herself awake, when she saw my face and said, brightly, "Good morning, Lizzie Borden," that I thudded back to earth.

I sat up. "Lacey." I swallowed. "Last night . . . "

She took in my expression. Recalibrated. "Breathe, Dex. No freak-outs before coffee."

"But what we did—"

"Technically, you made us leave before we *did* anything," she said, and laughed. "The look on their idiot faces."

"Not in the barn." I didn't know why I was still talking. If I didn't name it, maybe I could erase it. "Before."

"Yeah, we're going to have to change before anyone sees

us," Lacey said, looking down at herself, and I realized the stains on her shirt were blood. The stains on mine, too.

I shook my head. Everything was shaking.

"No." Lacey stilled my hands with hers. "No, Dex. They'd have done it whether we were there or not."

It was some note of certainty in her voice, maybe, that cued a memory from an assembly past, then half-remembered words from the morning's service, and the pieces jigsawed themselves. "You *knew*," I said, and of course she knew. She always knew. "You picked that town on purpose."

"Of course I did. I was curious. Weren't you?"

I knew the right answer: Curiosity was supposed to be our lifeblood.

"What do you think they do with cows on that farm, Dex?" she said when I didn't give it to her. "This isn't *Charlotte's Web*."

"That was a pig."

"And they were going to butcher it, right?" Lacey said. "That's how farms work. It's not like killing someone's cat or something."

"*Have* they killed someone's cat?"

"Do you want the answer to that?"

Silence between us, then, except for the bugs and the birds and the wind.

"You were having fun," she said, and it felt like an accusation. "You were laughing. You just don't remember."

"No. *No*."

"You do know it was all a bad joke, right?" she said. "Just

a bunch of asshole hicks trying to freak out their parents. No one was actually trying to summon the devil."

"Of course I know that." What I didn't know, at least not with the same degree of certainty, was whether it mattered. The sacrifice was a joke, maybe, but wasn't blood still blood, dead still dead?

"Anyway, it's not some crime against nature to watch stupid people do stupid shit," Lacey said.

"But it was more than watching . . . wasn't it?"

"What do you think?" Lacey laughed. "You think you helped put poor little Bessie out of her misery? *You?*"

I was sitting cross-legged, and Lacey shifted until she faced me in exactly the same pose. The Mirror Game, I'd called it when I was a kid, springing it on my parents without warning. You scratch your nose; I scratch mine. My mother loathed it. My father, who'd learned in some long-ago acting class how to cry on command, always won. If Lacey and I played, I thought, the game could go on forever.

She cupped my hands again. "How much do you remember, Dex? Seriously."

I shrugged. "Enough?"

"I remember how it was my first time. Everything feels kind of like a dream, right? You're not sure what's real, what's not?"

I nodded, slowly. "Not for you?" I said. "Everything's clear for you?"

"Crystal. So I can tell you everything that happened, in graphic detail, or . . . "

"Or."

"Or you trust me that everything is fine. That all the good stuff happened and all the bad stuff was a dream. You let me remember, and you let yourself forget. You trust me, don't you?"

"You know I do."

"Then?"

"Then okay. Yes. Everything is fine."

She smiled—I smiled. That was how the game worked.

"You're not sorry, are you?" Lacey asked, and I knew, because I always knew, what she really meant. Was I sorry not just about the things that happened in the field and the things that didn't happen in the barn, and not just about the church and the mushrooms, but sorry for everything that led up to it, sorry about Lacey and Dex, sorry to be here with her in this field, damp and shaky and stained with blood, sorry to be with her anywhere?

I knew what she needed to hear. "Never be sorry, remember?"

Never be sorry, never be frightened, never be careful—those were the rules of Lacey. Play by the rules, win the game: Never be alone.

We must have gone to class; we must have scribbled down an English paper or two, made small talk with parents and teachers, emptied dishwashers and mowed lawns, nuked frozen pizza for lonely TV dinners, snooze-buttoned our way through six A.M. alarms, waded through all the mundane detritus of high school life, but that's not what I remember. Somewhere out there, line dancing swept the nation, LA exploded over Rodney King, Bill Clinton didn't inhale, George Bush threw up on Japan, a Long Island nutcase shot her boyfriend's wife in the face, a new Europe chewed its way out of the corpse of the USSR, and history officially met its end. None of it penetrated. We were our own world. I remember: riding down the highway in Lacey's Buick, trying to shove her lone Pearl Jam tape into the player, rain pelting my face on stormy nights because the passenger window was stuck halfway down, the two of us one with the car and with the road, Lacey always at the wheel despite daily promises that she would teach me how to drive. We were at our best when we were in motion.

Once, we drove all night, Lacey slugging back Diet Cokes while I searched for exit signs and inscribed our names on the dewy window. When we hit the George Washington Bridge, Lacey stopped the car on the Jersey side, and we watched the city groan into morning. Then we turned around and drove home. Because it wasn't about *going* to New York City, Lacey said. It was about proving we *could*. Actually going to New York, that was another thing for plebes. Too obvious, Lacey said. When we escaped, it would be to Seattle. We would get an apartment near the Crocodile café, where we'd waitress so we could score free booze and sleep with the bands. We would have a beanbag chair and a cat named Ginsberg. We would sell the car to pay the first month's rent, then buy a bottle of wine with whatever was left over and toast to the fact that there was no turning back.

I fell asleep nights thinking about it, imagining highways ribboning across flat brown land, afraid we wouldn't go, afraid she'd go without me. Some mornings I woke with the sun, convinced I'd dreamed her into my life, and called her house just to make sure she was still there.

We didn't try mushrooms again; we never talked about the night in the field. Not directly, at least, and that made it easier for memory to recede into shared dream. But after that night, Lacey had two new fixations: finding out more about what she called *the devil-worship thing* and getting me laid. Both made my skin creep, but when she grabbed me outside the cafeteria to tell me she had two birds and one stone waiting for us in the parking lot, I did as I was told.

"Three birds, if you want to get technical," she said. "Though one of them doesn't believe in showers, so he's out."

Three birds, scuzzy and greased, one with a pube-stache, one with a shaved head, one with "prison tats" he'd meticulously inked up and down his arm: Jesse, Mark, and Dylan. Boys I'd known since they were still boys enough to play with dolls; boys who'd grown into almost-men who wanted to be dangerous and persuaded the wrong people they were.

I didn't think they deserved it, what had been done to them in the fall and the way people acted after—as if the three of them had dragged Craig into the woods and whispered satanic prayers to him till he cracked, then beat themselves up and lofted themselves into that tree as penance. As if whatever happened to them was just, even merciful. But I also didn't want to be out there in the alley with them alone.

Not alone, I reminded myself. With Lacey.

Never alone.

"You want?" Jesse offered Lacey a hit off his dwindling blunt. She waved him away. He didn't ask me.

"You guys know Dex, right?"

Mark snorted. "Yeah. You still crying over that dead Barbie, *Dex*?"

Jesse whacked the back of his head. "You still playing with dolls, *Mark*?"

I'd known the three of them since nursery school, since the days when Mark lit dolls on fire, Dylan collected Garbage Pail Kids, and Jesse took a shit beneath the elementary school seesaw, just to prove he could. Jesse and I had ridden bikes and woven grass jewelry for our mothers on May Day. Then he'd hooked up with Mark and Dylan, and while individually they'd seemed comprehensible and unintimidating and like the type of boy you might one day grow up to kiss, together they went feral, roaming the streets, baring teeth and brandishing sticks. They bashed bats into mailboxes and left dog shit on neighbors' doorsteps and eventually graduated from skateboards to death metal. Before Craig died, they were so proud of their rotting-skull T-shirts and black trench coats, their car stereos blasting lyrics about bleeding eyes and demon hearts. I thought now about all those dolls and trading cards and that sorry lemonade stand, Jesse and me selling twenty-five-cent cups of water stained with yellow dye, and it felt stupid to be wary of them—but then I thought of bloody symbols on church doors and bloody axes in dark fields, and it felt equally stupid not to.

"I like the new look," Jesse said, and scuffed a toe against my boots. "It's dark."

"He means it makes your boobs pop," Mark said.

"Fuck off, asshole."

"You fuck off."

Lacey rolled her eyes, and I tried to check out my cleavage as surreptitiously as possible. No part of me wanted to be in this alley.

"Can you help us or not?" Lacey said.

"Your friend's mental, you know that?" Jesse told me.

"She thinks we're going to teach her how to worship the fucking devil," Dylan said.

Mark traced a cross against his chest and adopted a Transylvanian accent. "I vant to suck your blooooooood."

"She doesn't think we're fucking *vampires*," Jesse said. "She's not a fucking moron."

"Thank you," Lacey said.

"Except you are a fucking moron if you're planning to start messing around with that shit. Not in this town. And if anyone asks, you tell them we've got nothing to do with that anymore."

It had been half a year since golden boy Craig turned up in the woods, brains leaking into the dirt, and five months since Jesse and the others had discovered exactly how much

Battle Creek wanted to believe in the devil. Battle Creek still watched us closely, like we were walking grenades, hands hovering recklessly close to the pin. *Us* as in all of us, anyone under the age of eighteen automatically under suspicion; *us* as in them, most of all, the Dumpster Row boys, because Craig Ellison was dead when he shouldn't have been and that demanded a rational explanation, even if rational, according to the pamphleteers in the Woolworth's parking lot and the Concerned Parents League, who'd cornered the market on op-eds, meant *teen football star falls prey to satanic cult blood orgy.*

Lacey knew all this—she had to. But I understood her now. I understood that it only made it more tempting, that anything that frightened the plebes this much merited further investigation. That anyone stupid enough to be scared deserved it. I understood that I was supposed to know better.

"I know what you say." Lacey reached forward and tapped Jesse's chest, at the spot where blood gushed from Ozzy Osbourne's silkscreened face. It amazed me, how she didn't hesitate to touch him. "And I know what I see."

"It's just *music*, get it?" Jesse sounded weary. "Slayer, Megadeth, Black Sabbath, they're all putting on a show."

"First off, there's no such thing as *just music*," Lacey said. "Second, *that's* not music. Biting the head off a live bat isn't music, it's a pathetic plea for attention."

"What is this shit?" Dylan said. "You come to our house to talk this kind of shit?"

"Your house?" Lacey echoed, glancing at the nearest Dumpster. "Nice furniture."

I grabbed her, tugged. "Let's just go."

"I got some *Headbangers Ball* on tape," Jesse said. "Back at my place. You guys want to watch, I'll show what you're missing. But no animal sacrifice. No matter how hard you beg."

I thought: *Enough*. "That's okay, we're not—"

"We'd love to," Lacey said.

In the car, bumping along toward the house I hadn't been in since third grade, Lacey said she was pretty sure Jesse wanted to get in my pants and that I should let it happen—*let it happen*, that's how she put it, like sex was a force of nature and I simply needed to get out of its way.

I thought about it, on the couch in the wood-paneled basement, everything the same as it had been years before. Mark and Dylan rolled joints, riveted to their Megadeth videos. Lacey stretched herself out in the leather armchair, closest to the speakers, and fixed on the screen, her *Kurt* face on, waiting for enlightenment. Jesse was next to me, his arm millimeters from mine, and much hairier than the last time I'd seen it.

"Remember *Kids Incorporated*?" I said, because that's what we'd watched when I came over after school. It had been my idea, because I didn't have the Disney Channel at my place, but he was the one who'd taught me the choreography so we could dance along.

Jesse grunted. This, I thought, was not *letting it happen*.

He had a square head. Greasy lips, and those stupid fake tattoos. I could maybe, almost, imagine kissing him. If it were dark and I could, immediately after, dematerialize. I was turning seventeen that summer; such things were supposed to appeal.

There was a look my mother had given me when some neighbor was over, complaining about lesbian jokes on TV, and since then I'd been wondering what she thought but, more than that, wondering if she'd recognized something in me I couldn't see for myself. I said as much once, to Lacey, who crossed her eyes. "Do girls turn you on?" she said, and when I said I didn't think so, she shrugged. "Then you're probably not gay. I hear that's a prerequisite."

Nothing turned me on, as far as I could tell. Lacey thought there was probably something wrong with me, and I thought she was probably right.

Now I think it wasn't my fault, that my younger self can be excused for reading phrases like *fire in my loins* and stumbling over the idea of pleasurable burning. But then it shamed me, the ease with which Lacey could spider her fingers down her stomach, across her thighs, into the dark space that remained a sticky mystery to me, and instinctively know how to feel. When, under duress, I'd locked myself in the bathroom and played around with the showerhead while Lacey cheered me on from the other side of the door, I had felt only ridiculous.

"You still got my He-Man?" Jesse asked, and I smiled because it meant he remembered how he used to bring his action figures over to play with my Barbies, and also because, somewhere at the back of my closet, I did.

"You still pretending you didn't steal my She-Ra?"

In my peripheral vision, I could see him blushing.

"Hey, she was sexy. Metal bikini, Hannah. *Metal bikini.*"

On-screen, a brunette in a spiked leather corset fellated a drumstick. Now I was blushing.

"Her name is Dex," Lacey said, without looking away from the screen.

"Sorry." He elbowed me, gently. "*Dex.*"

"It's okay. Whatever."

"I kind of liked it," he said. "Your name. But Dex is cool, too."

Here is how I imagined things might go, if I *let it happen*: Jesse Gorin would inch his hand across the couch toward mine, ever so casually link our pinkies together, then turn my hand over and tap a message into my palm, in the Morse code we'd taught ourselves one rainy summer week before third grade. It would say: *I remember you.* It would say: *We are still the people we used to be.* And when he said he wanted to make some popcorn and did I want to help, I would follow him up to the kitchen, and while I was grabbing the air popper from the cabinet where it used to be, he would slip up behind me, whisper something suitably romantic in my ear, or maybe just my name, maybe just *Hannah*, then kiss the back of my neck, and when I turned around, I would be in his arms, hair dangling over the sink, lips perfectly parted and tongue knowing what to do. And even though we would return to the basement like nothing had happened, the taste of each other rubbed away by popcorn butter, we would bite down on the inside of our cheeks to prevent secret smiles, and silently understand that something had begun.

That was before Lacey asked Jesse to show her where the bathroom was and they disappeared upstairs together for the rest of the show. When they came back, Jesse's ballpoint tattoos were bleary with sweat and Lacey's shirt was on inside out, which she could only have done to prove a point.

"So, you're welcome," Lacey told me in the car on the way home.

"For what?"

She seemed surprised I had to ask. "Didn't you notice the way that skeezer was eyeing you? If I hadn't gotten it out of his system, I don't know what would have happened."

"I thought that's what you wanted," I said. "I thought I was supposed to *let it happen*."

"With him? God, Dex, learn to recognize a joke." She pulled up in front of my house. "You deserve so much better."

I opened the car door, but she grabbed my wrist before I could get out.

"So?" she prompted.

"So?"

"Magic words, please. A little polite recognition for my sacrifice."

"Right. Thank you."

Lacey decided to find me a more satisfactory dick. That's how she put it when she presented me with a flimsy fake

· 118 ·

ID and a black lace corset. "Amanda Potter"—born Long Island, 1969, Sagittarius, details I repeated to myself over and over again as we stood in line waiting for the bouncer—"is getting some tonight," Lacey told me, but didn't tell me how she'd found this club, a grim concrete block beside the highway, or why it promised to be my sexual salvation. "No argument allowed."

Her corset was purple, and seemed, at least from where I stood, to offer slightly more room to breathe. She wore a silver pentagram around her neck, another thrift store acquisition to go with the *Satanic Bible* she'd finally dug up in the basement of some used bookstore along the highway. She loved the way people looked at her when she wore it, the same way I looked at her when she showed me the book for the first time. It didn't look like any Bible I'd ever seen. It was black, with a red five-pointed star etched onto the cover, and even the author's name gave me the creeps: *Anton Szandor LaVey*. It sounded deliberately fake, like a name the devil himself would choose. Lacey had already highlighted several passages.

Man's carnal nature will out no matter how much it is purged or scoured by any white-light religion.

There is nothing inherently sacred about moral codes.

Blessed are the destroyers of false hope, for they are the true Messiahs.

"You really don't want to let anyone see that you have this," I'd told her, when she showed off her purchases, then pressed the pentagram necklace back into her hand. "And you *really* don't want to be wearing this." She still didn't get it, the rules of a place like Battle Creek. It was one thing being a metal-head with a corpse on his T-shirt and a fetish for black nail polish; it was another thing altogether to be a girl wearing a pentagram. It was always another thing, being a girl.

"The hilarious thing is, they've got it all wrong," Lacey had told me. "Turns out actual satanism's just about freethinking and being yourself. Stuart Smalley could've written this."

"Can we not talk about this now?"

"You say now, but you mean ever."

I did.

"You should read it," Lacey said. "You'll see. There's good stuff in here."

"Please tell me you're joking."

"I'm joking," she said, and it was easiest to assume it was true.

The club was called Beast, and the bouncer, more interested in my cleavage than my birthdate, waved us both in.

"I see you smiling," Lacey said, sidling us up to the bar. She tugged at the laces of my corset. "You're going mad with power." I could barely hear her over the music, was already losing myself to noise and strobe light and the foul taste of the beer she poured down my throat, and somehow these all seemed like good things. Maybe because she was right; I did love the power of it, my chest, squeezed sausage tight, suddenly capable of miracles. I was used to people looking at Lacey. That night, they looked at me.

Maybe it was the corset, maybe it was the shot, maybe it was Lacey pushing me into the single-stall bathroom with some guy she thought worked behind the counter in our record store. Whether it really was Greg the Sex God, who we'd spent two Saturdays in a row peeking at from behind the Christian gospel shelf, or just some unknown grunger with a down vest and a hemp bracelet, he followed me in, and when I opened my mouth to say my name or maybe *sorry my lunatic friend just shoved you into a bathroom*, he stuck his tongue in. I let it worm around for a bit, tasting his beer and trying to decide whether the hand squeezing my ass was doing it right. Between that and my mental tally of the bacteria and fecal matter on the bathroom door, I forgot all about our lingual calisthenics, and the distraction must have been obvious, because eventually he stopped.

"Hey," the guy said, lips still practically touching mine.

"Hey."

The floor was spattered with urine, the walls with posters: The Screaming Trees. Skin Yard. The Melvins. Soundgarden. Even Babes in Toyland, who Lacey said sucked.

"You like this?"

I shrugged, thinking it was nice, if a little late, of him to ask. "I don't usually do it in bathrooms, I guess."

"What?"

The music, even in there, was incredibly loud.

"I don't do this in bathrooms!" I said, louder.

"No, I mean the song! You like the song?"

"Oh. Sure."

"It's the new Love Battery!" He stepped back, did a little air guitar. I winced, thinking of what Lacey would think. "It's fly, yeah? You should hear the album, it's like the fucking A-bomb, just a bunch of stuff, and then, *boom*. Takes you to another dimension. You know?"

"Sure."

"It's some *Star Trek*–level shit there, you know? That's what my album's gonna be like."

"You're making an album?"

"Well, not yet, obviously. But, I mean, when the band gets there. It'll happen. Patience, man. That's the secret."

"So you're in a band?"

"I'm telling you, not yet. But I'm working on it. Stuff's in the works. Big stuff."

"That's . . . great."

"You've got great boobs. Can I get in there?"

"Not sure that's physically possible," I said, more pleased than I wanted to be, but he'd already found a way to fit his fingers into the dark crevice of the corset.

"I uh. That's kind of . . . floppier than it looks."

"Oh."

"Don't get me wrong, I mean, that's just how it goes with the big ones. Most of them are floppier. This is pretty good, actually."

"Thanks?"

"Do you, like, feel yourself up all the time?"

"Uh, no."

"That's what I'd do if I was a girl. Especially if I had your . . . you know. All. The. Time."

"That might get in the way of your recording career."

He spent some time trying to work out whether that was a joke, then, "You want to blow me?"

"Not especially."

"Well, you know. A guy's gotta ask."

That was when I pushed my way back into the club and found Lacey. The band was starting, the one she'd heard had once opened for Nirvana, but from the opening chords it was clear these guys had only recently learned how their instruments worked. It didn't matter. Lacey asked me what had happened, whether Mission Fuck had been a success, and instead of answering I threw my arms around her, because the beer buzz was finally heating me up and because I wanted to, simple as that, wanted to be there, with her, sweat-slick bodies swirling around us. I wanted, for the first time in my life, to dance.

"You're drunk!" she shouted when I wove my fingers through hers and dragged her into the mess of bodies.

"Not drunk enough!" I twirled around, arms in the air, finally understanding what it was to feel a need and seize it. I needed to move. I needed to fly. I needed not to think about dicks and tongues and the gritty wrongness of real life. I needed this to be my real life, me and Lacey, in the smoky dark, strobes bouncing over our head, band screaming and shaking sweat into the crowd. The crowd a single organism, all of us, a hundred arms and legs and heads, a single heart beating, beating. All of us thrashing together, wild and fury in our blood. Lacey's laughter in my ear, the smell of her shampoo like a cloud, her hair whipping across my cheek, and then nothing but the ecstasy of motion. Anything, everything possible. No one watching.

She liked to test me, and it was hard to tell the difference sometimes, between game and truth. Kurt was real, that was nonnegotiable. So were we, Dex-and-Lacey. Sacred ground. Boys, though, were for playing and trading, were equivalent to the sum of their parts, tongues and fingers and dicks. God was a bad joke, Satan a usefully pointy stick. She liked people to think she was dangerous. This didn't explain why, one night when we'd been saddled with babysitting the junior Bastard, she had me hold the wriggling baby over the bathroom sink while she used the blood of a raw steak to paint an upside-down cross on his tiny forehead.

"This is disgusting, Lacey." It wasn't the right word, but it was the easiest one.

The baby whimpered and pulled away from her bloody finger, but she shushed him and stroked his tiny ears, and he didn't cry. "Just hold him still."

The blood smeared watery pink across his forehead, running into his eyes. I held him still.

Lacey gently tapped his right shoulder, his left shoulder, his sternum, his forehead, solemn as any priest. "In the name of the Dark Father and the unholy demons, I baptize you into the church of Lucifer."

They were just words, I reminded myself. They had only as much power as we gave them.

Lacey said she couldn't wait to see the look on the Bastard's face when he found out, though she was careful to wipe off every trace of blood before we laid James Jr. to bed for the night. Lacey said the Bastard thought the Battle Creek hysterics were an embarrassing sideshow, blind to the true war for their children's souls, against the modern Cerberus of liberalism, atheism, and sexual revolution. The Bastard didn't believe in satanism, Lacey said, only in Satan, and claimed anyone who thought differently was doing the devil's work.

"I don't want to be anyone's sister but yours," she said, too, which made it okay that, when I left that night, the baby's forehead still smelled like raw meat.

She wanted to spend her birthday in the graveyard, and so we did.

"Scared?" she said as we picked our way through the dark. Narrow lanes wove through rows of tombstones. I saw a stone angel, a spire circled by stone roses, crosses tilting and crumbling, tombs that gleamed in the flashlight beam where names were etched with lacquer and gold.

"Am I supposed to be scared of ghosts, or of you?"

"We both know you're scared shitless of getting caught, Dex."

She held the flashlight beneath her chin, casting her face in ghoul glow. "The only scary thing here is me."

Maybe it was stupid of me not to be scared—if not by her

big plan for the night, then by the intensity with which she'd insisted on it, that we sneak out with our candles and shovels, build a shrine to the Dark Lord, just enough of a show to give the plebes a good scare. "All I want for my birthday is to freak the shit out of Battle Creek," she'd said, and I was prepared to help.

She stopped at a small square tombstone and sat, hard, beside the dead flowers at its base.

"Lacey." It seemed like bad luck, saying her name out loud, like I might alert some predatory spirit to her identity. The stories had always made it very clear: Names were power. You gave yours away at your own risk. "I thought we were looking for a fresh one."

"Look." She aimed her flashlight at the stone.

Craig Ellison, it said, *b. March 15, 1975, d. October 31, 1991*
Beloved son and brother
Go Badgers!

"*Go Badgers?*" I laughed. Then aimed a cheerleader fist pump at the clouds. "God, that's tacky. Can you imagine taking Battle Creek Badger pride to your grave?"

She didn't say anything. I felt judged by her silhouette.

"What if it's not some big joke?" Lacey said then. "Imagine the plebes are right, and there is some devil cult dancing around the woods, faces painted with blood. Acid orgies. If that's what really happened to him."

I tried to picture it, Craig Ellison forming an unholy alliance with the Dumpster Row boys, stripping off his basketball jersey to frolic naked in the woods, Craig Ellison magicked into drawing his own blood. Standing there in the shadow of his gravestone, stone angels judging our trespass, it wasn't nearly as hard as it should have been.

"And what if aliens are secretly running the country?" I said, desperate now to make my voice a flashlight, guide us both back on track. "What if the mayor is a vampire? What if I'm possessed by Satan and I'm about to suck your brains? It's like you always say, anything's possible—"

"—in the woods. Yeah. It is."

That was when I noticed she was crying.

I almost fell beside her. Lacey wasn't the kind of girl who cried. "What is it?" I put my hand on her shoulder. Took it off again. "*What?*"

"You love me, right?" Her voice was flattened, dead.

"Of course."

"And you're a good person."

"Well, not since I met you." The joke didn't land. Her nails dug into my arm.

"Never say that again."

"Okay. Okay, Lacey, it's fine." Panic. We were in a graveyard and she was freaking out, needing something I didn't know how to give her because Lacey wasn't supposed to need anything. "Of course I love you. And of course I'm a good person. And can you just tell me what's going on so we can get the hell out of here?" I was crying, too. It was a reflex, like contagious yawning or throwing up at the smell of vomit.

"If I tell you to do something, and you do it, whose fault is that?" she asked.

"Depends on what you want me to do, doesn't it?"

"It shouldn't depend. Circumstances shouldn't matter. If it's my idea, it's my fault. Your idea, yours."

"Except it would be *my* idea to do what you told me to do. I get to decide that. I'm not your puppet."

"No? No. I guess not."

I rapped softly at her head, the safest way I could think to touch her. "What's going on in there, Lacey? I know it sucks that he's dead, even if he is *Craig*, but it's not like he meant something to you." As I said it, I was wondering whether it was true. Maybe it all made sense in some seedy, beneath-her kind of way, the fervent and unfounded hatred of Nikki, the unprompted tears for a Neanderthal, the words that seemed snagged in her throat, unsaid, unsayable. "Was he cheating on her with you? You can tell me. I get it, I swear." I didn't get it, not a guy like him, his meaty hands fumbling at her bootlaces, but love was meant to be strange. "You can't think it's your fault, what happened. Even if he felt guilty, or you dumped him and he freaked out, or whatever it was, it wouldn't be—" I thought about what it would be like to do something and not be able to take it back. "Even if you told him you wanted him to die or something, that wouldn't make it your fault that he went and did it. You didn't put the gun in his hand. You didn't pull the trigger. Nothing is your fault."

She looked up at me, face tipping into shadow, and smiled. "You think Craig was cheating on Nikki? With *me*?" She laughed, then, so beautifully, and I don't know whether I was more relieved that we'd escaped the moment together or that

I'd so plainly been wrong. Then she kissed my cheek. "You always know what to say to cheer me up."

If not that, then what? I wanted to say, but couldn't, not when she was happy again, not when she'd taken my hand in hers and pulled us both off the ground, sent us spinning, like the grave was a meadow and the moon was bright summer sun. "I can't believe you thought I could love him." Her laugh was a witch's cackle, our dance a ritual that didn't need spells, only hot blood rising in our cheeks and burning through our veins, an invocation of the gods of love, of whatever force pressed our palms together and whispered on the night wind, *You are one.*

And then we went too far.

"It's what Kurt would do," Lacey whispered, and there was no argument to that.

We eased open her window and dropped down to the bushes below. The car was too noisy, so for the first block we pushed it, gear in neutral and shoulders bruising against the trunk. When it was safe, Lacey gunned it, and I jittered in the passenger seat, cans of spray paint slippery in sweaty palms.

Kurt once got arrested for spray painting *homosexual sex rules* on the side of a bank, Lacey said, up there big and bright for all the rednecks to see, at least the ones who could read well enough to sound out the words. He grew up in an old logging town, Lacey said, full of assholes, their puny brains filled with all the things Kurt smashed with his guitar. Before the guitar, there was spray paint, and there were words. "We have those," Lacey said. "That's enough."

"If we get arrested," I said, "I swear I *will* kill you."

All brick and stone, squat and sad, the Teen Pregnancy Center was deep in last-resort territory. Past the walk-in clinic and the Sunrise rehab center, past the veterans' hall where it was nothing to cadge free donuts from the Alcoholics Anonymous meetings, a mile past even the boarded-up strip club that had survived three months, flush on the town fathers' pay, before the town mothers had driven it to ruin. If it was you that let some greasy animal inside you, and you that hit the devil's jackpot, sperm and egg making their miracle, then it might be you swallowing your panic, flipping through the yellow pages, finding salvation on the highway, in the gray windowless husk just past the Friendly's. You might come from Battle Creek or Marshall Valley or even as far as Salina. You might wonder if it would hurt, or if you'd be sorry; you might be afraid.

You would definitely be surprised when the good people at the Teen Pregnancy Center gave you a pamphlet with Jesus on the cover and set you straight. The Teen Pregnancy Center would speak of miracles and wonders, and show you pictures of a seed they said was a baby and a sin they said was murder. And then, if you weren't careful, they would ferret your name and phone number out of you so that when you got home, your parents would be waiting.

It was evil, Lacey said, and her first idea had been burning it to the ground.

Battle Creek wasn't a sex-ed kind of town. But word got around, in playground diagrams and Sunday school sermons, and by junior high we all knew what to do and that we'd burn in hell for doing it. Just after Easter that year, our health teacher had held two apples before the class, then dropped one on the ground. Picked it up, dropped it again. "Which one would you want to eat?" she asked, finally. "This nice, shiny, clean apple? Or the bruised, dirty, dented one?"

Lacey stole the dirty apple for her lunch that day, and later that month, when Jenny Hallstrom lost it to Brett Koner in a church utility closet, we said she'd dropped her apple. "Guess we know what Brett likes to eat," Lacey said. Jenny was the one who told us what happened inside the Teen Pregnancy Center. That was before she got sent away; we heard her kid was due by Christmas.

Word always got around. That was the rule of Battle Creek, and maybe that was why our parents spent so much time worrying who was shoving what into where in the backseat of whose car. Because we'd be the ones to burn in hell, but they were the ones who'd have to hear about it in church.

Now we tiptoed toward the Jesus freaks' evil lair and hoped they were too cheap for security guards. I wore a fleece hoodie; Lacey was in cat burglar drag, all black with a bloody smear of lipstick that was the same color as our spray paint. She shook the can like she'd done this before, and showed me how to hold it and what to press. I waited for her to go first, to see how she did it, her hand steady and her letters smooth. I waited for an alarm, or a siren, or the men in uniforms who would drag us off into the night, but there was only the hiss of paint and Lacey's cool laughter as the first of our messages glittered under sodium lights.

Fake Abortion Clinic. Beware.

We had written the messages together, ahead of time, while Lacey's mother was downstairs getting drunk and her stepfather was out bowling for Jesus.

Get your politics out of our pussy.

God is dead. Lacey had insisted on that one.

God is dead, I wrote, because it was the shortest. The letters wiggled and the *G* looked more like an *o*, but I wrote it. I pressed my finger against the nozzle and turned brown stone red and Hannah Dexter into a criminal. Magic.

We couldn't go home yet, not feeling like that. We drove nowhere; we drove nowhere fast, because speed was what mattered. Speed and music, *Nevermind* in the player, Kurt's screams tearing up his voice and our screams even louder. I shouted along with Kurt and didn't care that according to my father my voice was like a raccoon screech or that according to Lacey I had the lyrics all wrong. I sang like it sounded to me, because those words sounded right: *I loved you I'm not going back I killed you I'm not going back.*

We drove with the windows up so we could scream as loud as we wanted, and it was easy to imagine we might never go home; we might drive off a cliff or over the rainbow. We might tear across the country, fire and ruin blazing in our wake. Lacey and Dex, like Bonnie and Clyde, like Kurt and Courtney, high on our own madness, burning holes in the night. "We should do this again!" I screamed. "We should do this always!"

"What? Be outlaws?"

"*Yes.*"

I'm not going back, I shouted, and that night, only that night, I loved Kurt like Lacey loved Kurt, loved Kurt like I loved Lacey.

I'm not going back.

I'm not going back.

LACEY

Good Intentions

This is not a cautionary tale about too much—or the wrong kind—of fucking. This is not a story of bad things happening to bad girls. I say this because I know you, Dex, and I know how you think.

I'm going to tell you a story, and this time it will be the truth.

Girl meets girl. Girl loves girl, maybe. Girl wants girl, definitely. Girls drink, girls dance, girls fuck, girls link fingers on a dark night and whisper their secret selves, girls swear a blood oath of loyalty and silence. Girl betrays girl, girl loses girl, girl leaves girl alone. It's a story you won't like, Dex, because this is not the story of us.

"Just to watch," Craig said, that first time he came to our place in the woods.

I'd already started thinking of it like that. *Our place.*

He brought along his mother's picnic blanket, a puffy synthetic with lace stitching at the edges—he was, it turned out later, almost pathologically fastidious. It was a pointless effort, trying to make what happened between us clean. But the ground was hard and sparkled with broken glass, and the blanket was silky against bare skin, so we only mocked him a little.

When he said he'd watch, he didn't say he'd jerk off while we were tangled up in each other, but he was a sixteen-year-old guy, so maybe that was implied. It was equal parts disgusting and hot. Disgusting because *obviously*. Hot because it's one thing to get a guy off with your hand or your mouth, the slippery-when-wet mechanics of skin on skin; it's another to do so without even touching him. That's power.

Maybe it freaked him out, because it was a while before he came back. Or maybe Nikki didn't want him back. Maybe she wanted me to herself.

It was different, with a girl. Not as different as you'd expect, not softer, because there was nothing soft about Nikki Drummond. It was still skin and sweat, and I was still her secret, just like I'd been Shay's secret. I was still the shameful thing, and I was good at that.

Two weeks before Craig came back again. Two weeks, just the two of us, every day, in the woods, rolling in the weeds. Not inside the hollowed-out station, where we might have sunk into the old couch, generations of fluids staining its molding cushions. Not inside the rusting boxcar, where Nikki said she could hear the walls plotting to close in. We stayed in the open, beneath the sky's prying eyes, putting on a show for the sun and the stars. I didn't talk to her about Kurt; she didn't talk to me about prom. We didn't talk much at all, wink wink nudge bleh, but when she asked me questions, I told the truth, and that made things different, too.

I liked the taste of her, Dex. I liked spelling my name inside her with my tongue. Like I was branding her where no one could see. *Mine.*

I got good at getting her off, and then I must have gotten too good, because the day before the first day of school, I made her scream, and then she rolled away from me, curled fetal, and started to cry.

"What?" I ran my knuckles down her spine. It always made her shiver. "What is it?"

Nikki didn't cry. We were the same that way.

She didn't cry, but she was crying, and when I touched her again, brushed her hair out of her face, because that seemed like the kind of thing to do when you were naked and crying together, she sat up, shook me off along with the mood, found her clothes and her vodka, and we got drunk. The next day she brought Craig with her again, and said it was only fair we let him play.

Both of us or neither of us, that was the implied deal, and I thought: Kurt would do it, Kurt would be proud of me for doing it; the Bastard would keel over and die. I thought she needed me, they needed me, and it was good to be needed.

I thought: Why the fuck not?

Craig was never sweet, but he could look it, with a kid's cowlick and a practiced sidelong glance through those long

· 136 ·

lashes that were criminally wasted on a guy. Bulky for a basketball player, with a neck like a gangster. But he could smile like everything was exactly as easy as you let it be. He knew how to make people love him, when he cared to. He and Nikki had that in common, I guess, but Nikki had to make an effort, transform herself into whatever kind of girl was needed. Craig only had to act intensely himself, more the guy everyone imagined him to be.

He couldn't get hard at first, not with me there watching, and not with the condom, which he'd given up on back when Nikki got herself on the pill. We were shy, then, or at least he was, and though I heard him talking to it while he rubbed, whispering sweet nothings into its flaccid flap of skin, he never would tell me what he was saying. Nikki gave it a few soft kisses, which didn't help; then she gave me a few soft kisses, which did. It didn't take long, watching us go at it, before he wanted into the mix, and then, with Nikki gasping in my ear as his fingers did their work, he was inside me, and maybe I was shy, too, because that first time, it hurt. It was messy, then, and confusing. Bodies are supposed to come in twos, ark-like.

Six legs, six arms, thirty fingers, eight holes, the math was tough to contend with, but we did our best, and when Nikki chomped down on my nipple and Craig crushed my fingers under his ass, I didn't complain—it was all too interesting, too new, to stop.

You never like the bare facts, Dex, not when it comes to this. You like to forget that you're an animal, too, that you burp and fart and shit and every month you bleed. You think it's not nice to talk about those things, and not much nicer to do them, except in the dark where no one can see. So you probably don't want to know that Craig was hairy like a gorilla, at least until he let us shave it all off, just to see how it would feel. You might want to know how he looked in Nikki's lace panties, but you don't want to hear that his dick curved ever so slightly to the left and his sac had an old man's complexion. Or that he apologized as soon as he shoved it in, and again when he took it out, like he thought I was going to cry or cry rape, like he literally couldn't believe this was playing out as it seemed.

We were acting out our parts, that first time, waiting for the soundtrack to kick in and for things to go slow and romantically blurry instead of herky-jerky ugly real. We were waiting for sepia tones and candlelight, but eventually we got used to sticky clothes and awkward pokes and the *pock* sound Nikki's thighs made when they slapped together too hard, that and the sound of grunting, and mingled laughter.

Don't feel stupid. You couldn't have known. No one knew, and when school finally started, Nikki and Craig wouldn't speak to me in public. I liked that they were ashamed of it. The secret was part of the fun. I liked it when Nikki prowled past me in the hall, like she didn't know that I could ruin her life with one well-placed rumor. I liked her snot-faced, nose-up public self, because I was the only one who knew how that face looked when Craig's fingers were inside her, plying their clumsy magic.

By then, they were doing that in front of me; turned out we all liked to watch. Sometimes it was watching I liked best. There's something about two people fucking, the way they forget to hide their secret selves. Even after all this time, Nikki and Craig were putting on a show for each other, Nikki playing "excited!" and "turned on!" or "boooooored," depending on her mood, but never straying too far from "granting you the greatest favor of your life," Craig doing "gettin' me some" every time. But there was always a moment. She'd forget to suck in her stomach; he'd forget to gaze lovingly in her eyes; they would each forget the other was there, and the sex became masturbatory, the alien body incidental, just another tool to abuse. I liked turning transparent and immaterial, watching them lose control.

Nikki liked to watch, too, but not for watching's sake. It brought out her inner Mussolini. She didn't watch; she commanded, directing us in her own private puppet show, bossing us into positions meant more for her pleasure than ours.

I don't know what Craig liked the best, especially once the novelty of two girls going at it wore off, which it did surprisingly quickly. Sometimes I don't think he liked much of anything.

We all took a turn; sometimes, instead, we just drank and talked. The abandoned station was a magic place, a sacred one, where secrets were swallowed by the trees. We were different people in the woods; we were our own shadow selves. Nikki told us about the time her inbred cousin raped her at a Thanksgiving dinner, squashing her against her grandma's lace-doily quilt and tasting of sweet potatoes and gravy when he forced his mouth against hers to shut her up, as if she would have screamed. I told them how the Bastard wanted to send me away once the baby was born, that I'd read it in the letter he wrote to his pastor back in Jersey, some Billy Graham wannabe with a local radio show. I told them how I'd also intercepted the pastor's response, godly advice on how to erase me from the family picture for the good of the Bastard's reputation and spawn—then, because we'd sworn an oath of secrecy, not truth, I told them I didn't care. Craig told us about the time in junior high he got a blow job from some poor guy on his JV basketball team, then got so freaked out that he spread word that the kid had been sneaking peeks of the other guys in the locker room and had tried to cop a feel during a wrestling bout. After they gave the guy his third beat-down, he transferred to a school in another county.

"Didn't even feel guilty about it," Craig said. "Does that make me, like, a psychopath?"

"Probably," I said. Nikki laughed and laughed.

He's dead now. It's strange, isn't it? He was here, he was *inside* me, he was sweaty and obnoxious and maybe, like, a psychopath, and now he's just a corpse. Less than that, soon enough: bones and dust and worms. Not a ghost, certainly. If he were a ghost, I'd know, because he'd never leave me the fuck alone.

I know how he died; I know why, unless you want to get all existential *why, God, why* about it, in which case who knows anything, but I can't say I ever knew Craig. He had a little sister, it turned out, some gap-toothed goofball in pigtails who worshipped him for teaching her to shoot free throws and punch out the playground bully. But I didn't know that until her gap-toothed eulogy, and by then I couldn't afford to let myself listen. He was like our doll sometimes, an animatronic jock for us to pose. He was a slobbery kisser and an angry drunk, and he loved Nikki enough to get jealous but not enough, or at least not well enough, to make her love him back.

Sometimes we still met up without him, and that's when she told me all the things even he didn't know, like her secret early-morning runs, which she'd started back when she was fourteen and anorexic, but kept up because she liked the vacant dark of five A.M. Everyone knew that Nikki's mother had spent a year screwing her father's racquetball partner, but no one knew how pathetic Nikki thought her for coming back and begging forgiveness, much less for staying with a husband who now stuck it to her every chance he got. Everyone knew Nikki was good at being popular, but only I knew how little she cared. She fucked with people and built her little kingdom because it came easy, and because it was more fun than the alternative, but it didn't make life any less mind-numbing, or the future any more bearable. She liked to watch people bow and scrape before her for the same reason little kids light anthills on fire. Not because it gave her life meaning, but because sometimes you need to spice up an afternoon.

Everyone knew she and Craig Ellison were destiny, their love mandated by the laws of royal courtship, and everyone was probably right. Craig was seventh-grade Nikki's first kiss, Nikki was Craig's first trip to second base, but there's nothing sexy about inevitability, or at least nothing as sexy as a nameless eighth grader who'll jerk you off in a roller rink bathroom, and so it wasn't until sophomore year that they got together for real—fucking each other and fucking each other over, fucking and fighting and then fucking again. No wonder they were bored.

Craig, somehow, still had his secrets: He could get us anything. We tried heroin—horse, that's what Craig called it, because he didn't know how not to be an ass—but only once. People aren't meant to feel that good, or be that happy. Coke was better. It made the sex better. It made everything better. It was easier to get and substantially harder to screw up, as opposed to the heroin, with which I almost set Nikki's hair on fire. It was easy to laugh about things back then.

That's it, all we did. Watch and fuck and snort and talk, rinse and repeat. Until Craig was dead, and it was all over. I didn't go back. I couldn't. Not to the station, not to the woods. It was desecrated. Not haunted—I told you, I don't believe in that—just ruined.

No one would know unless Nikki or I told them, and we swore ourselves silent. One last sacred promise, and—stupid me—I assumed it would bind us together for life, but that was the last I saw of her, too. Maybe I was her woods, desecrated and ruined. But you know what I think? I think I was wrong from the start, suckering myself into believing that I'd peeled off Nikki's mask and glimpsed her true face, when, in fact, there was nothing underneath but more masks. Masks on top of masks, with a hollow space at the center where some higher power forgot to shove in a soul. All animal instinct, no higher function. No capacity for pain.

She blamed me.
She blamed *me*.
I don't blame myself.
I refuse.
I did nothing wrong.
Pinky swear, Dex. Cross my heart and hope to join Craig on the big basketball court in the sky, nothing is my fucking fault.
No one is my puppet.
You promised me that.

Alone again, after. Alone, in the dark, with a secret, alone with the nightmares and the ghost of their skin, waking up with him inside me, her crawling down my body, invisible fingers and tongues dissolving into nothing with the dawn light. Alone with my mother and the Bastard and of course the precious fucking baby, who wouldn't stop crying, the two of them keeping me away from him as if I had some contagious disease, as if I would want to touch or hold or big-sister their screaming, shit-stained midlife crisis, and who could blame me for taking the knife into the bathtub?

Rhetorical question. The Bastard blamed me for being a drama queen, and my mother blamed me for getting the Bastard riled up, and the cheap-ass therapist blamed me for not wanting to honestly face up to my problems, not wanting to rip the bandage off the seeping wound, but at least he gave me a prescription, and then I didn't give a shit who blamed me for what, even Nikki Drummond. Especially Nikki Drummond.

Those were the cloud days. I floated. I played Kurt loud where I could, and quiet, in my head, where I had to. I could have floated forever, Dex; you should know that.

It's important you know that I didn't go looking for you.

I thought about it sometimes: how she would hate it, seeing me with someone else, watching me lace my arm around a waist or lean close to whisper a secret. It would hurt, and I wanted, more than anything, to make her hurt. I admit that. I could have picked anyone, any of those sad little girls dancing down the hall in their identical denim jackets and neon stirrup pants, bopping to New Kids or maybe Sir Mix-A-Lot because that's what their boyfriends told them to listen to, saying *please* and *thank you* to their teachers and *not so hard* and *fuck me* to the boys they'd only be seen with in the woods, sad girls with big bangs and little dreams. I watched them, and I thought about it.

Then *you* came to me.

It wouldn't surprise you that Nikki told me about you. It would surprise you what she said, something like, "Who, her? That loser's always glaring at me like I drowned her puppy," and forgive me, Dex, but I said, "Probably in love with you," and Nikki said, "Who isn't?" and then, I'm sure, drunk and high, we both laughed.

Truth, Dex: She never gave a shit about you. All that energy you put into hating her, and still you were nothing to her. Not until I made you something. You've never thanked me for that, either.

I watched you. Billow of hair like your very own storm cloud. Interchangeable Kmart T-shirts, always a size too big, like you'd never clued into your best asset, or wanted to make sure no one else did. Always with a book, thick glasses and middling sulk, that smirk you gave people when they said something stupid. I don't even think you know you're doing it, slitting your eyes and raising your lip, like the morons cause you physical pain. You told me once that, before me, you wasted half your time wondering why people didn't like you more, obsessing about your glasses or your hair or the way you rolled the cuffs of your jeans, precisely how tight and how high. I didn't have the heart to tell you that none of it would have helped. People like to believe they're beautiful and smart and funny—*special*. They'll never like the person whose face reveals the truth.

What I saw in your face was the truth of Nikki. She was as ugly to you as she was to me. You wanted to make her hurt. And I helped you do it, even if you didn't realize it. You're welcome for that, too.

I knew you before you knew yourself. Imagine if you'd

marched through high school and college and a lifetime of diaper changes and mind-numbing jobs and garden clubs and PTA bake sales, and never known yourself, so tough and so, so angry. You were afraid to let yourself feel it, but I could feel it for you, simmering. I could hear the pot lid, that clatter of metal like a rattlesnake warning: *Stand back, shit's about to explode.*

So fucking what if that's why we started, if you hating her was the thing I loved most, if I held on so tight because I could feel her fury that she'd been replaced—by a nonentity. So Nikki brought us together. So what?

What matters isn't how we found each other, Dex, or why. It's that we did, and what happened next. Smash the right two particles together in the right way and you get a bomb. That's us, Dex. Accidental fusion.

Origin stories are irrelevant. Nothing matters less than how you were born. What matters is how you die, and how you live. We live for each other, so anything that got us to that point must have been right.

DEX

Urge Overkill

There was a security camera. Two shadows caught on-screen, faces indistinct, ages readable enough that—the very morning after our graffiti triumph—two cops muscled their way into the principal's office. By noon, word had gotten around that they were looking for two girls in possession of spray paint, with possible connections to a dark underground, two girls with dangerous intent. *God is dead*, we had written—I had written—and not realized this would magic us into something to fear. Midway through English class, the PA buzzed, and the principal came on to issue dire warnings: that new evidence suggested agitators in our midst, that we should all be vigilant, that all of us—the misguided perpetrators most of all—were at risk. The rumor mill was delighted, giddy speculation quickly drowning out any buzz about the next big party and Hayley Green's bulimia-induced laxative incident.

Two nameless girls heeding the call of the dark; I could feel people watching us.

We met by the Dumpsters, one of us ice-cold and the other freaking out, three guesses which was which. This wasn't the year to be a juvenile delinquent. "Worst case, it's vandalism, that's got to be a misdemeanor," Lacey said, every word a shrug, and I wanted to shake reality into her.

"A *misdemeanor*? They still arrest you for those, Lacey. We're so fucked."

The refrain had been beating in my head since I saw the cop car pull up to the curb through my homeroom window. So fucked. So fucked. So totally, absurdly, screwed grounded arrested fucked. Lacey pretending otherwise didn't fix anything.

"No one's getting arrested. No one even knows it was us. Stop acting like a crazy person, and they never will."

But the way I acted wasn't the problem. It was Lacey. People knew enough about her to suspect the truth—at least, Nikki Drummond would.

And it turned out she did.

"Let me guess: her idea," Nikki said, snaring me in the second-floor girls' bathroom, where I'd taken to going ever since she'd cornered me in the one on the ground floor. "She promised no way would you get caught. No consequences."

"Do you have some obsession with hearing me pee?"

"It's always her idea, but you're the one who's going to get screwed. She'll find some way to make sure of that."

· 148 ·

"Seriously, are you bathroom stalking me? Because that's significantly weird."

"She's bad news, Hannah."

"What are you, an after-school movie?" I washed my hands, then smeared on some ChapStick, just to show her my hands weren't shaking. "One more time: I don't know what you're talking about. No idea."

"Trust me, I believe that."

"Fuck off," I said, and banged out the door. Not my cleverest comeback, but I hated to give her the last word.

She seized it anyway. When I got to my locker that afternoon, the vice principal was waiting for me, with a cop and a pair of pliers and an "anonymous" tip.

I was crying before they got the door open, even knowing there'd be nothing to find, because even amateur, self-righteous vandals weren't dumb enough to stash their spray paint at school, but it was still humiliating and there was a *cop* forcing open my locker and how the fuck had my life turned into this movie—and in the seconds before they deemed the locker inoffensive and sent me on my way, incriminating tears or not, I cursed Lacey, and thought, if only for a second, *Nikki was right.*

Lacey was ebullient when she scooped me up in the parking lot. We'd officially gotten away with it. "Bonnie and Clyde, right?"

"Bonnie and Clyde ended up dead."

"What crawled up your ass?"

I couldn't explain that I'd turned on her, however briefly,

that I didn't deserve her or the celebration she proposed, and instead I made her drop me off at home. If I could make it to my room before I started to cry, I thought, I would be safe. The day could end and tomorrow everything would be erased.

My father was waiting behind the door. "Your mother's in your room," he said. His face was doom.

"What? Why's she not at work?"

"Just go up there."

"What's wrong?" It seemed likely someone was dead, or at least on the way there. I could see no other reason for my mother to leave work in the middle of the afternoon, no other end for this shitty, decompensating day.

He shook his head. "I promised her I'd give her first shot. But ... let's just say, officially, I'm very disappointed. Unofficially?" He winked.

So fucked.

"Any chance we can pretend I never came home?"

He pointed at the stairs. "Go. And, kid?"

"Yeah?"

"Gird your loins."

What she'd found: Two cans of spray paint, which Lacey had insisted we not throw out (but that she not keep). Rolling papers and a glass pipe I'd never used. Condoms, equally unused, extra-large and strawberry-flavored at Lacey's insistence. Lipstick, too ugly to wear but shoplifted from

Woolworth's just because. Dusty bottles filched from the liquor cabinet. A Polaroid of Lacey's boobs that had served us some ridiculous purpose I couldn't remember.

How she knew to find it: A call to her office from a nameless "concerned friend" who was obviously Nikki Drummond, concerned only about ruining my life.

What she said: *You are a disappointment. You are a disgrace. You are, it goes without saying, grounded.*

You are not the daughter I raised.

You are lucky I'm not calling the cops.

You will never see that Lacey again.

I didn't cry. I didn't betray Lacey, not this time, not out loud. I admitted what I'd done, said I'd done it on my own, and if my own mother wanted to turn me in to the police, I'd be happy to tell them exactly the same thing. I told her that she couldn't keep me away from Lacey, that the only bad influence here was sitting on my bed, holding two cans of spray paint like they were live grenades. I told her I didn't need anyone, especially Lacey, to give me ideas or bully me into standing up for what was right. I was an adult, and if I wanted to fuck the Man, that was my business.

She sighed. "This isn't you, Hannah. I know you better than that."

"The name is *Dex*," I said, and it was the last thing I would say to her that night or the two that followed. The silent treatment was still the only real weapon I could muster.

I must have seemed ridiculous. At least as ridiculous to her as my father seemed to me, cheering me on behind my mother's back and making the occasional frontal assault with vague references to their shared posthippie past, invoking long-lost good causes and heroic stands, though my mother shut him down every time, in a way guaranteed to make both of us feel like shit. "She doesn't care about feminist politics any more than you do, Jimmy," I heard her say, after I'd tossed my burnt meat loaf and returned to my room. "She's simply infatuated. You should know the feeling."

She'd unplugged my phone and was monitoring the ones downstairs.

"No, Hannah *can't* come to the phone," I heard her say that Saturday morning. "Please stop calling."

Lacey, I knew, would never stop calling.

Maybe this was it, the catalyst we needed to escape. Maybe I could finally shake off my suburban shackles, fuck high school and college and my permanent record, climb into Lacey's Buick, slam my fist on the dashboard, and grant the permission I'd withheld for so long, say *Go west, young man*, and chart a course to freedom.

When I packed for school that Monday, I slipped my escape fund, all $237 of it, into my backpack, along with my copy of *Stranger in a Strange Land* and the first mix Lacey had made me, the one with *HOW TO BE DEX* scribbled across it in permanent marker—all the essentials, just in case. I waited for her in the parking lot, desperate for proof that she existed, and as I waited, I composed revenge plans in my head, a gift for Lacey, because before we escaped we'd need to avenge ourselves against the enemy. We would sneak through Nikki's window and shave her head; we would slit the seams of her prom dress, just enough that the gown would dissolve as they placed the crown on her perfectly coiffed head; we would frame her for cheating; we would find someone to break her heart.

They were lame schemes, cribbed from Sweet Valley High books and half-remembered teen movies, but evidence of my will. Lacey would supply the way.

Except that when Lacey finally showed up—not a half hour early, as I had, bouncing with eagerness and certain she was feeling the same way, but twenty minutes after the start of homeroom—and I cornered her in the parking lot, she didn't want to hear about my revenge schemes, and she wasn't full of sympathy for my weekend of torment. She didn't, in fact, seem particularly concerned about my problems at all.

"How worried do I have to be?" she said. "Is your mother the kind who's going to call mine?"

"Depends whether she thinks it'll torture me or not."

"Fuck, this is serious, Dex. You have to ask her if she's planning to tell. Get her not to."

"That's going to be hard when I'm not speaking to her."

"So fucking *speak* to her. What is wrong with you?"

"I don't know, Lacey, maybe being a prisoner in my own home has driven me crazy? Maybe it's been a little *difficult*, having my own mother look at me like I'm some criminal who's going to shiv her in the night? Maybe I'm a little worried that she's forbidden me from seeing my best friend, and I thought my best friend might be a little worried about that, too."

"You're seeing me right now." She sounded distracted, as if there could be anything more important to think about.

"How are you not getting this?"

"How are *you* not getting it, Dex? I can't have the Bastard finding out about this. I can't."

"Oh, but it's totally fine when *I* get caught?"

"That's not what I meant. But, okay, yeah. You seem pretty fine to me."

"Oh, I'm awesome, Lacey. Everything is fantastic."

"You don't get it—"

"I get that it's okay for me to get in trouble as long as *you* don't get in trouble. Even though this whole fucking thing was your idea."

"Can you for one millisecond entertain the hypothesis that not everything is about you, Dex?"

I heard myself spit out the world's ugliest laugh. "Tell me you're fucking kidding me."

She didn't say anything. I willed her to. *Say something; say anything. Fix this.*

"Well?" I said. "Really? Nothing?"

"Please ask your mother not to tell mine."

"That's it?"

"That's it."

School hurt without Lacey there, even more because she *was* there, just no longer mine.

I was the angry one. I was the righteous one. I was the one

· 154 ·

avoiding her in the halls and getting on the bus after school instead of waiting for her car. So why did it feel like she'd abandoned me?

Temporary, I told myself. She would apologize, I would forgive, all would be the same. But when I saw Nikki, I couldn't say anything. It felt different, not having Lacey at my back. All the things I wanted to say, all the *fuck you, how dare you, what gives you the right* curdled in my throat, and I knew how they would come out if I tried.

You won.

I did speak to my mother that week, just once, just to ask her not to tell Lacey's parents what she suspected. Because there was no evidence Lacey had done anything, I reminded her, and being my mother only gave her the right to ruin *my* life.

I didn't speak to Lacey.

I didn't call anyone, for that matter; I didn't go anywhere. I came straight home after school and watched TV until it was time for bed. Life grounded was a lot like life before Lacey, and it terrified me.

"Like old times, right?" my father said, during a commercial, while we waited to see which inbred family would win their feud. And my face must have revealed what I thought of that, because he added, "I know. I miss her, too."

This did not help.

What did: Friday afternoon the phone rang, and after he answered it, he handed it to me. My mother was down at the

Y, tapping into her inner artist at a pottery class—and the customary liquor-fueled wallow that followed—that would reliably keep her occupied through midnight. We were alone in the house. No one to stop him from breaking her rules; no one to stop me from saying, cautiously, *hello*, and finally breathing again when I heard her voice.

"I'm sorry."

I wanted to wait for her to say it first, but I was too puppy dog eager, and so we chimed together, overlapping, desperate, both of us so, so sorry, both of us so quick to dismiss and fast-forward, whatever, it was nothing, ancient history, stupid, inessential, inconsequential to the epic and never-ending story of us.

"I have it, Dex," she finally said. "The perfect revenge."

"Nikki?"

"Of course, Nikki. You think we let her do this to you and get away with it?"

"So, what's this perfect plan?"

"Not now. Tonight. You heard about the foreclosure party, right?"

Everyone had heard about the foreclosure party. An abandoned house at the edge of a half-built development, guaranteed empty, out of the way, and equipped with ample bedrooms. Nikki's father worked at the villainous bank, and every month or two she managed to snag an address and a key. Lacey and I were supposed to be above such things.

"I'm grounded," I told her, even as my father mouthed, *It's okay*, and nodded.

"Sneak out. I promise, it'll be worth it."

It's not that I didn't want to see her. I didn't know what it was. "Lacey—"

"Pick you up at nine." She hung up before I could answer.

"I don't want to know where you're going," my father said. The dial tone was still droning in my ear. "Plausible deniability. Just be back before your mother."

So I was going to a party.

By nine P.M., I had laced myself into the black corset, which I hadn't worn since the night of the Beast. Lacey said it made me into a warrior, ready for battle. It did; I was. She didn't show. I sat on the porch steps, waiting, lipstick congealing, hair wilting in the humidity, time ticking, heart beating, cars passing and never stopping, none of them her. I'd poured some of my parents' scotch into a water bottle—our own private pre-party, or that was the plan.

I drank most of it myself.

Nine, nine thirty, ten—no Lacey. No answer at her house when I called. No fucking way I was going back inside, changing into pajamas, explaining to my father why I'd chosen rules over rebellion, staring at the ceiling, wondering why Lacey had flaked. The party was only a couple miles away, and I had a bike.

Because I was angry. Because I was tired. Because I was sick of being the tagalong, the one things were decided for. Because I had something to prove. Because I was curious. Because I looked hot, and I knew it. Because I'd seen enough movies where the mousy girl goes to a party and changes her life. Because I hated Nikki and thought if I drank enough beer maybe I'd be able to buzz up the courage to spit in her face. Because Lacey would hate it, or maybe she would love it, or maybe I should stop fucking caring one way or another what Lacey would think. Because I was embarrassed, and sad, and that made me angry all over again, and the rage felt good against the pedals, pumping through the dark, toward a strobing shadow, toward what felt that night, with the wind in my ears and my parents' ancient scotch burning in my throat, like destiny. Because anything, because who knows, because it wasn't a night or a week or a year for because, no *why*, only *who what when where*:

Me.

A mistake.

After I should have known better.

Here. The husk of a McMansion, bodies moving across windows lit by the flicker of candlelight. On the grandiose porch, two guys in low-slung jeans taking a final slug of beer before going inside.

"Yo, let's get stupid."

"You damn right, son."

"You know it, son."

It was the thing, that year, for the whitest of boys to talk like they weren't, to sling awkward slang and let their pants sag like the rappers they saw on TV, and they were going where I was going, and that could have been my cue to get back on my bike and ride home, but instead I took the water bottle out of my bag and finished the scotch. I was a delinquent, I reminded myself. The cops were after me. I was grounded and sneaking out—albeit with paternal permission. I was dangerous.

The more I drank, the easier this was to believe.

It would have been the nicest house I had ever been in if it hadn't been so clearly left behind. Left in a hurry, it looked like, couches and tables and rugs all in place, which, despite the mass of bodies gyrating to bad music on stained carpet, gave the house a whiff of Pompeii. Someone lived here, once, and fled in a hurry, set down breakfast spoon and morning paper, ran out the door and didn't stop until far enough away to be safe from the thing that was coming. The bad thing.

Nikki Drummond was waiting in the foyer as if she were the grand dame of the estate. "Seriously? Hannah Dexter? Gracing us with her presence."

"Seriously. Present."

"I figured you'd be shipped off to a military academy by now. Or at least grounded."

I wasn't yet drunk enough to spit on her, so I shifted my attention to the jock drooling beside her, Marco Speck, who'd been Craig's shadow and was apparently now looking to be his replacement. "I think you should watch out," I said. "The last guy had to put a bullet in his head to get away from her."

Marco looked at me like I'd just sucker punched her. "Jesus, Dexter. That was cold."

I felt cold.

Nikki only smiled and handed me a shot, which I tipped back without hesitation, thinking maybe it was enough and we were even. Then she pushed Marco at me, saying we deserved each other, and if I wanted to embarrass myself she wasn't going to stop me. When he said he barely recognized me in those boobs, and also *dude, whoa*, I let one hand play at my cleavage and the other wrap itself in his, because Nikki was watching. Maybe Lacey would have said, *Don't be one of them*, but then again she'd also said *What's the big deal* and *What are you waiting for* and *Don't be so fucking precious about fucking*, and anyway she wasn't there. The shot tasted like lemon and sugar and fire. Marco tasted like peanuts. His breath in my ear was like the wind on my bike, like coasting downhill in a whoosh of summer. Like *letting it happen*. Broken glass crunched beneath our feet, everything gritty and sticky and layered with filth, and it smelled like sex to me, sex as I imagined it, smoke and dried beer and rotting fruit. There was music pounding, hard-core rap; there was a crush of strangers doing the things strangers did in the dark. Marco sucked my neck. Marco's hands were in my hands, and then in my pants, Marco was grinding against me, chest to chest, groin to groin, what passed for dancing, and I could feel him hard against me and almost believed I could do this on my own, without Lacey, I could be what the night demanded, push myself into its live and beating heart.

What the fuck are you doing?

I thought I heard her voice in my head, and I answered out loud, "*Shut up.*"

"Not a chance." That wasn't my head. That was Lacey, really her, standing behind me, hands on my waist, pulling me away from Marco and his hot sweat, pushing me through the bodies, up the stairs, into a child's bedroom, a sad parade of zoo animals peeling off its wall.

"What the fuck, Dex?"

She wasn't dressed for a party. White wifebeater and gym shorts, she wasn't dressed for anything. No makeup. No boots. That was the weirdest part. Lacey in sneakers.

"I didn't even know you owned sneakers," I said.

"Are you *drunk*?"

"Started without you." Then I was hugging her, hugging her and saying how much she sucked for flaking out on me, but now she was here, and sneakers or not, *everybody dance now*—I sang it, took her wrists in my hands and waved her arms in the air.

She shook me. "Sober up, Dex. What the hell were you thinking?"

"You love me drunk."

"When you drink with me. When I can watch you."

"You're late," I said, and we shook each other off. "And in the wrong place."

"And you're sticking your tongue in Marco Speck. We're both having off nights."

"Lacey. *Laaaaaaaaaaaacey*. Lighten up. It's a party."

"I have to fucking talk to you."

"Right. Revenge," I said, open for business. "Vengeance. *Monte Cristo*–style. Bring it on. What've you got?"

"What?"

"Nikki Drummond. You said you had the perfect plan. So, go on. Make this worth it."

"Because you've got better places to be? Like in Marco Speck's pants? Like I'd let that happen."

I would have gone back down to the party then, maybe not to fuck Marco Speck but at least to make a good effort, if she hadn't stepped in front of the door.

"Fine," she said. "You want revenge? Here's the plan. We burn the fucking house down. Right now." She pulled out a lighter. I didn't know why she would have a lighter, or why she was lighting it, taking one of the kids' pillows and setting it on fire, both of us staring, mesmerized, at the flames.

"Jesus Christ!" I knocked it out of her hands, stomped on the fire, hard, desperate, *stop, drop, and roll* spinning through my head, and all those panicked nights I'd spent in fourth grade after Jamie Fulton's house burned down and the school sent home a checklist of clothes the family needed in the aftermath, including girls' underpants, size small. If my house burned down and my clothes turned to ash and the other kids in school had it confirmed in black-and-white that I required their spare *girls' underpants, size small* , , , better to die in a fire, I'd thought.

The flames went out. Docs were good for stomping.

"Are you trying to kill us?"

"The house burns down and what do you think will happen? Nikki's party, Nikki's fault, and everyone will know it," Lacey said, something wild on her face, like she would

· 162 ·

have actually done it, like she would still do it, if only I said yes. "It'd be all over for her. And think of the fire, Dex. Flames in the night. Magic."

"Since when did you turn into a fucking pyro?"

"That's the plan, Dex. In or out?"

"Either you've gone truly insane, or you think this is all a big joke, and either way, fuck you." I snatched the lighter out of her hands. "This stays with me."

There was a feeble laugh. "I wasn't actually going to do it. Jesus, Dex, learn to take a joke."

I believed her; I didn't believe her. I was tired of trying to figure it out.

"Just making sure there's still a little Hannah in my Dex," she said. "Where would I be without that little voice telling me, *No, don't do that, Lacey, that's* dangerous?" It was the sorry, pinched way she said it, like a bank teller rejecting a loan.

"I'm not your fucking conscience."

She must have seen it then, how angry I was, how drunk and how done. "Come on, Dex. Come on, it was a joke, I'm sorry. Look, this was a mistake. This party. This week. Everything. Let's erase it. Start again. For real this time. Burn our lives to the ground—" She held up a hand to silence me before I could object. "*Metaphorically.* Let's really do it this time, Dex. Get away. Go west, like we planned."

"Now?"

"Why not now?"

"I'm grounded," I reminded her.

"Exactly. You'll be grounded for life when your mother

figures out you were here. Fuck her. Fuck all of them. Let's go, Dex. I mean it."

"Tonight."

"This minute. Please."

For a heartbeat, I believed her, and I thought about it. To jump into the Buick, aim ourselves at the horizon. To begin again. Could I be the girl who dropped everything and walked away? Could I be Dex, finally, forever?

Could I be free?

One heartbeat, and then in the thump of the next, I hated her for making me believe it could happen, because what could this be but another test, some wild dare I was supposed to shoot down, because—hadn't she just said it?—that was my job, the wet blanket on her fire.

"Enough bullshit," I said. "I'm going back to the party."

She shook her head, hard. "No. Dex. We have to *go*."

"If you want speed off into the sunset, you do it, Lacey. I'm not going to stop you. I'm going to have another drink. I'm going to have *fun*."

"You don't have to decide about leaving for good, not in the next thirty seconds, I'm sorry, that was crazy." She took my wrist, squeezed hard. "But at least let's get out of here. Please."

It was the second time she'd said it to me in one night, and possibly in all the time I'd known her. It shouldn't have felt so good to shrug her off. "I'm staying. You go."

"I'm not leaving you here by yourself."

That was when I understood. She didn't want me to be

Dex, untamed and magnificent. That was her job. I was to be the sidekick. I was to keep my mouth shut and do as I was told, spin and leap and do tricks like a trained seal. I was to obey and applaud when appropriate. I was to be molded, not into her image but into something less-than.

Could I be the girl who walked away?

"Please. Go," I said.

"It's not my job to watch out for you," I said, "and vice versa."

"I don't care what happens next," I said. Maybe, finally, I was the one administering the test—maybe I was lying and maybe I wasn't.

Lacey believed me.

She left.

How to dance like no one is watching. Or dance like everyone is watching, pale flesh jiggling as you grind against denim and polyester and lacrosse muscles and twitching dicks. Writhe in your Docs and jerk to the beat beat beat of the hip-hop blast, and let a hand find its way past a thin cotton waistband and stick its finger into your warm and wet. Wrap your arms around the closest body, press lips to neck and nape and groin, laugh along with and louder than, and if it feels good, do it. Put your hands on yourself, and rub and stroke, let yourself moan. Think, look at these faces, my friends, look at their love and look at me shine. Don't think. Straddle something, a chair or a body, lower your weight onto it, ride 'em cowboy, ride it hard while they pour beer on your head and you raise your face to the stream and your tongue to the sour splash, then, because they call for it, lick it off yourself, and off the body, and off the ground. Note the heat of skin, the fire that courses beneath, the salt of sweat and tears. Slice your palm on the splintered edge of a broken glass and smear yourself with blood. Let the floor fall away and the horizon spin. Suck at flesh and whirl in place and throw your hands up in the air. This is how to party like you just don't care.

Look at yourself, Lacey had said, the first time she laced me into the corset, turned me to the mirror, made me see. *It's like you were born to wear it.*

Do you see now, Dex? she had said.

I saw: A girl's face, made up with drastic colors and lips pursed in mock defiance. Romance-novel cleavage and black lace. Hair with streaks of icy blue and leather cuff bracelets that whispered *tie me up, hold me down*.

Look at yourself, Lacey had said, but myself was gone.

I thought: *I look like someone else, and she is beautiful.*

You. Girl. Wake up."

I did what I did best and followed orders, waking up slow and in pain, fuzzy mouth and throbbing head and a cavernous feeling like I hadn't eaten in days, though the thought of food made every organ want to fling itself from my body into a putrid puddle at my feet. I woke up cursing and squinting, wishing someone would turn out the sun. Weeds beneath me, jeans and shirt damp with dew. Strange shirt; a stranger's shirt.

An alien landscape: Stretch of overgrown lawn, drained pool, fringe of trees. Dingy white siding, broken windows, stained patio, crushed cans of beer.

A man, his foot nudging my thigh, his face in shadow, gold badge glinting in the dawn.

"That's it. Get up now."

When he touched me, I screamed.

The effort of it nearly made me pass out again, as did the tilt of the world as he dragged me vertical. Then the noise of his words, *security guard* and *trespassing* and, he kept saying, *trash, trash, trash*, but it wouldn't come clear, whether he meant the empty cans and the broken glass and the used condoms or simply me.

The party was long over; everyone was gone. They'd left me alone. They'd left me out with the garbage.

Standing set my insides to sloshing. Thinking was hard, like a toddler unsteady on chubby feet.

"Get in," he said, and there was a door with a sedan attached to it and a leather backseat and the thought of a moving car made me want to die.

"I have my bike," I said.

He laughed like a dog.

"Are you a cop?" I said. "Am I under arrest?"

"Just give me your address."

Don't get into cars with strange men, I thought, and asked

if he at least had any candy, and then I was the one laughing.

Maybe I was still drunk.

Lacey would have said: Skip the name, rank, serial number. No identification, no address, no consequences. He would have to dump me by the side of the road, and then I could sleep.

I couldn't remember the night.

I couldn't remember enough of the night.

I remembered hands gathering me up, I remembered floating in strange arms, chandeliers overhead and then stars, and laughter that wasn't mine. I remembered fingers tugging at zippers and lace, a voice saying *leave her over there*, another saying *turn her over so she doesn't drown in her own puke*, all the voices chanting *puke puke puke* and my trained-seal pride when I performed on command.

I ached everywhere, but hurt nowhere specific. That seemed important.

"Learn to have a little pride in yourself," the man said after I gave him my address, after he led me through the front yard, pausing to let me vomit up everything left inside. "You keep acting like a whore, people will keep treating you like one."

He deposited me at the door, which flew open at the bell, like my parents had been waiting. Of course, I thought, slowly, they had been waiting. The sun was up. I'd been missing. I felt like I still was.

The cop was a security guard for the housing development. The development would not be pressing charges. "Next time, though, we won't be so generous."

My mother was steel. "There won't be a next time."

"You sure you don't want to take me to jail?" I asked the not-cop, brain kicked into gear enough to smile. "Might be easier on me."

Then I heaved again. There was nothing left.

Once he was gone, my parents closed the door behind us, and there was a long stint of hugging. I tried to speak—probably it seemed like I wanted to explain myself, when I only wanted to say *please be gentle* and *can someone turn out the lights*—but my mother said *no*, firmly enough that it was the end of it, then held on tight, and then it was my father's turn, and for endless time I was closed in by their love, and it was almost enough to keep me on my feet.

Then, "Go get yourself cleaned up. You smell like the town dump," my mother said.

"Sleep," my father said. "Then we'll talk."

I lurched up the stairs. I'd been hungover before, but this was like some New Coke version of a hangover, different and deeply wrong. I closed myself into the bathroom, turned on the shower, waited for the water to heat, for the night to return to me.

I wanted to be clean; I wanted to sleep. Ahead of me, I knew, was the grueling interrogation by my parents, lectures and scolding, that I'd stayed out all night, made them worry, lost their trust all over again, and I'd have to sit through it while knowing my father was desperately hoping I wouldn't give him up, that if I kept quiet about him letting me go to the party he'd find a way to compensate. No matter what, I'd be grounded all over again. Grounding, of course, wouldn't extend to school, and I'd have to face all those faces who'd seen me lose control, who knew what I did, whatever it was. There would be whispers and rumors I would have to ignore; there would be stories of what and who, and I would, against my will, pay attention, try to piece together the night. I would be the story; I would be the joke; I would be the thing they'd left outside with the trash. All of that I knew.

I couldn't know about the letter to the editor some Officially Concerned old woman would publish in the local paper, about girls gone wild and the corrupting modern moral climate as encapsulated by the drunk sex fiend who'd been found passed out half naked outside the old Foster place, or that even though the girl went unnamed in the letter, my kindly security guard would spread my name to his nearest and dearest until half the town was calling me a whore, parents fish-eyeing my parents, their kids, chafing under draconian new curfews and rules, blaming me for all the ways in which they'd gotten screwed, that even my teachers would look at me differently, like they'd seen me naked. I couldn't know that I would be famous, the Mary Magdalene of Battle Creek, without my own personal savior, without anyone to rescue me from my own inequities except the judgment of the town, *for my own good*.

I couldn't know that I would go through it on my own. That when I called Lacey to tell her what had happened, to apologize or let her apologize or simply sit on the phone until I unclenched enough to let the tears fall, she wouldn't be there. That she'd packed up in the middle of the night, just like she'd told me she would. That I was on my own now, because I'd told Lacey to go and Lacey was gone.

I didn't know.

So when I stripped naked in the bathroom and saw myself—saw the words that had been Sharpie'd all over my body, the things someone had written across my stomach and breasts and ass, the labels that wouldn't come off no matter how hard I scrubbed, in handwriting I didn't recognize, but could recognize as the work of more than one person, *slut* and *whore* and *skank* and, graffitied neatly just below my belly button with an arrow pointing straight down, *we wuz here*—I thought: *Lacey*.

Lacey will save me.

Lacey will avenge me.

Lacey will hold me and whisper the magic words that will make all of this okay.

I climbed into the shower and sagged against the wall and watched the words shine in the water, the words strange hands had inscribed on bare skin while I slept. Strange hands redressing me, pulling underpants over my thighs, snapping strapless bra in place, lacing corset. Before that, strange hands doing things. Strange lips, strange fingers, strange dicks, all of them, I tried, hot water streaming over me, to remember what I had done, what I had let them do, who I had become in the night. The water burned and my skin burned, and still, I believed I could endure it, because soon I would have Lacey, and I would not be alone.

LACEY

Blood Ties

The Bastard burned it all. In a fucking fire. Like a Nazi.

"Heil fucking Hitler," I told him, which stopped him just long enough to slap me across the face, a nice sharp blow to make my ears sing but which we both knew wouldn't leave a mark. Then Herr Bastard went back to his bonfire, and I spat and screamed and choked on the smell of Kurt melting in the flames. Plastic cases warping with heat, fire eating through Kurt's eyes, Nietzsche and Sartre going up in smoke. It would have been cool—very Seattle, very Kurt—if it hadn't been my whole life disintegrating while the Bastard splashed gasoline. And my mother. Hiding out in the kitchen, probably rustling up some marshmallows and graham crackers so the Bastard could make s'mores over the ruins of the world.

That's why I was late picking you up for the party, Dex. My oh-so-unforgiveable crime. The Bastard found my *Satanic*

Bible and lost his fucking shit. Which looks nothing like what you're imagining, I can assure you. In your G-rated imagination, I'm sure, parents rant and rage and ground you for a week and then everyone has spaghetti for dinner and goes to bed.

Let me paint you a picture, Dex. Life according to Lacey. There's me, bedhead and short shorts, nipples standing at attention, and he wasn't even looking, that's how hypnotized he was by his precious fire. I couldn't stop watching it, either, the fire consuming every song, every page, every piece of me, everything that carried me away from this shit life. Is that how you felt that night, Dex, when your mother found those stupid cans of paint, when she yelled at you, poor baby, and took away your phone privileges? Did you go cold inside, like the night was an ice-covered pond, and you knew if you weren't careful, the surface would crack open and you'd sink into the deep? Were you disgusted by it, by the way your body betrayed you with its goose-bumped shuddering and the sad little croaks and moans you made instead of words? Did you think: *I'm better than this*? Did you think: *Now I am empty*? *Now I have nothing left*?

You didn't. You did have something left. You had me.

The day the music died. It's supposed to be a metaphor. Not a live show in my backyard, the Bastard's bloated face red in reflected light, miniature flames dancing in his eyes, hands stinking of gasoline, the devil in penny loafers and a polyester suit. I thought about those wailing widows in India, the ones who throw themselves onto the funeral pyre, because what's left to live for when the thing you're living for is a column of smoke? Think about that, skin flayed away, bare muscle and pearly bone, flesh fused with plastic, all of us ash together.

"You've got the devil in you," the Bastard said when he shoved me into the corner of my bedroom and made me watch while he tore it apart. "We're going to burn it out of this house, and then we're going to burn it out of you."

We each have our James. My fake dad and your real one. Except that *fake dad* is what you call the kind of guy who bribes you with imitation pearls and Amy Grant CDs, who won't shut up about *How was your day?* and *Who are your favorite teachers?* and *Won't you just give me a chance to prove I can love you?*

The Bastard pretended to be nice to me for precisely as long as it took to get into my mother's pants. Your James, on the other hand. Your Jimmy Dexter. Your *dear old dad*.

That's a different story, isn't it?

Sometimes I keep things from you to protect you, Dex. But this is truth: I never meant for it to happen. Cliché, but accurate: Kick a football, then ask it whether it meant to fly. All action demands an equal and opposite reaction. You can't blame an object battered by inertial forces; you can't blame me, bouncing through the pinball machine of life.

You buying any of this?

Okay, try this one: My mother and the Bastard are right,

I'm the harlot of Battle Creek. I've got the devil in me. I've done terrible things, but this is not one of them.

Here's another cliché for you: Nothing happened. That should count for something.

The first time. Early spring, one of those perfect mornings that fool you into believing that winter never happened and summer might not suck. The door opened as soon as I took my finger off the bell. Like he'd been waiting for me. "Can Dex come out and play?"

"Dex isn't here right now." That was the first thing I liked about your father, the way he called you Dex. Not like your mother, who was always throwing around *Hannah this* and *Hannah that* in that pinched voice, like what she really wanted to say was *She's mine and you can't have her.* "Her mother took her outlet shopping. Blazing-hot clearance sales, I hear."

"Sounds thrilling," I said.

"I begged them to bring me along."

"Who wouldn't?"

He grinned. Like we were friends. "Story of my life, always left out in the cold."

"It's a cruel world."

"Cutthroat." He was wearing a Cosby sweater and dad jeans, and his hair was a black scruff of weeds, like he'd just woken up, even though it was noon. Stubble inching down his chin, a little crud in the corner of one eye. I was wearing cutoffs over black leggings, the ones you said gave me buns of steel, and a tank that cut my boobs about a centimeter above the nipple. He could have gotten some show, if he'd bothered to look. But he wasn't that kind of dad.

"Guess I should go," I said.

"Don't get into trouble out there." He reconsidered. "Not too much, at least."

"The thing is . . . ," I said, and maybe I took a deep breath and held it, because I kind of wanted him to look.

The thing was, I couldn't go home.

The thing was, the Bastard had found my condoms.

That's why I came looking for you, Dex. So we could go to the lake, and I could sink into the icy water until it hurt enough to make me forget. It's not my fault you weren't there when I needed you.

"The thing is?" your father said when I didn't.

"The thing is . . ." I wasn't crying or anything. I was just doing me, leaning against the doorway, one hand slipped into the back pocket of my cutoffs, cupping my ass, eyes on his dad shoes. Ugly blue sneakers, both unlaced. That was the thing that got me, the laces. Like he had no one to save him from falling. "Your shoes are untied."

He shrugged. "I like 'em that way." He stepped out of the doorway, opening a space for me. "Want to come in? Have something to drink?"

We had hot chocolate. No whiskey in it, not that time.

The mugs steamed. We watched each other. He smiled. Dad smile.

"So, what's the verdict, Blondie?"

If you'd ever heard him call me that, you would have looked cluelessly at me, at my black hair, and I would have had to explain about Debbie Harry at the microphone and "Heart of Glass" and how I was really more of a Runaways girl, but what kind of nickname is *Joan*, and anyway, that didn't matter as much as the fact that he could see the kind of girl I was, the kind who should have a mic to tongue and a guitar to smash and a stage to light on fire, that he looked at me and understood. But I didn't have to explain, because we both knew, without saying, that this wasn't for you.

The nickname: That was our first secret, and another thing we had in common. We liked to give things their secret names. We knew there was power in that.

"How are you liking our little town?"

"It sucks," I said.

"Ha." It wasn't a laugh, more like an acknowledgment that a laugh might be called for.

"I like Dex, though," I said.

"Smart girl. Beauty *and* brains. I approve."

If he'd been someone else, just a *guy* rather than a *dad*, or even if he'd been most dads, I would have taken that as my cue, offered up my serpent smile, sipped my drink, and wiped away the chocolate mustache with one slow lick.

"Thanks, Mr. Dexter," I said.

"You should know you've broken my heart." He pressed a hand to his chest. "Dex finally discovers music, thanks to you, and—"

"And you're welcome."

"*And*, thanks to you, she's developing some seriously shitty taste."

"Better watch out, old man, you're starting to sound your age."

He jerked to his feet, the chair screeched, and I thought that was it. Too far. Especially when he stalked out of the room and left me there alone to wonder whether I was supposed to see myself out, thinking at least he trusted me to do so without stealing the silver.

Then he came back, record in hand. He'd also changed his shirt. "I don't do tapes," he said. "No tonal fidelity." He handed me the album. "Call me old again and you're out on your ass." He looked so proud of himself for cursing, like a toddler showing off a turd.

"The Dead Kennedys?"

"You know them?"

I shrugged. I learned that much from Shay. Never admit you don't know.

"Take it home. Listen to it—at least twice. That's an order."

"Really?" I know music guys and their record collections, Dex. They don't hand their precious goods off to just anyone.

"Really," he said. "Bring me one of yours next time. We'll pretend it's an even trade."

Next time.

That's how it went, Dex, and it kept going. We talked about music. We talked about *him*.

Did you know that when he was sixteen, he ditched the guitar for a year and taught himself to play the drums? He wanted to be Ringo Starr. Not because he thought Ringo was the best Beatle or anything, but because you couldn't wish or will yourself into being a genius—Lennons and McCartneys are born. Ringos, according to your dad, are made, by luck and circumstance and practice in their parents' garage. I thought that was sweet, that he'd dream of being fourth best.

I stayed until there was nothing left in my mug but cold milk and soggy chunks of Swiss Miss, then shook his hand. "Thanks for the hot chocolate, Mr. Dexter."

"Just keep doing what you're doing for our Dex." *Our* Dex, like you were a secret we shared. He walked me to the door. "And you better listen to that album, young lady. I'm waiting on your report."

I saluted. "Yes, sir, Mr. Dexter."

"My friends call me Jimmy." Not Jim but Jimmy, which he probably thought lent him boyish charm but actually made him sound like he needed to live under adult supervision.

"Are we friends now?"

"Any friend of Dex's," he said. "You know the rest."

It was just talk. There's nothing wrong with that.

Sometimes I cut school without you. Your dad was home a lot during the day. More than he should have been, you and your mom would probably say. Even the first time, he didn't ask what I was doing there. Neither of us bothered to pretend I was looking for you.

"Hot chocolate?" he said.

"How about a smoke?" I tossed him a pack of Winston Lights.

We took them into the backyard. I liked puffing the smoke into the cold, watching it fog the air. It was like breathing, only better.

I'd spotted the stains on his fingers, the way he kept tapping his spoon against his mouth. The tiny hole at his knee where the denim had burned away. Secret smokers recognize each other. There's a whiff of unfulfilled need about us, of unspoken desire. You want my opinion, I don't even think he likes smoking. I think he just does it because he's not allowed to.

"God," he sighed, blowing it out. "God, that's good."

The first draw is always the best.

He taught me to puff a smoke ring. I reminded him—later, when we knew each other better—how to roll a joint.

That day, though, we smoked our cigarettes standing up, leaning against the back wall. The shitty patio furniture seemed like your mother's territory, all those vinyl flowers and pastel pillows.

"Can I ask you something, Blondie?" He liked to play with the cigarette, carving up the air with its glowing tip. I liked to watch. He has man hands, your dad. Big enough to curl his fingertips over mine when we pressed palm to palm, crooked like they're still trying to curl around an invisible guitar. "It's probably inappropriate."

"I think we're past that, Mr. Dexter."

"Jimmy."

"Jimmy." I liked to make him tell me again.

"Does Dex have ... I mean, she's never brought a boy home, but that doesn't mean ... I was wondering—"

"Why, Jimmy, are you asking me if your daughter has a boyfriend?" I said.

"Well ... "

"Or if she's a dyke?"

"That's not what I—"

"Or are you just concerned with the state of her cherry, whatever drink it's in?"

"You're, uh, mixing your metaphors there, Blondie." It was cute the way he tried to play it cool, pretend like his skin wasn't crawling off his bones.

"Don't ask me about Dex."

This was the week after that night at Beast, when you went a little nuts with the tequila and decided you should put on your own personal bartop strip show. You didn't even remember it in the morning. What you did or what you wanted, or how you cursed at me for dragging you out of there, so you can't appreciate that I took you back to my place, tucked you up tight under my covers, rather than dumping you off on your parents' porch, a drunk, drooling, half-naked and half-catatonic mess for them to clean up. Sometimes I lie to protect you, Dex, so you can keep lying to yourself. You didn't want to know how you went wild in Beast, just like you didn't want to know how, in that field with those idiot farm boys, you were jonesing to get your hands on the axe. You don't want to know that you swung it high and hard and laughed at the blood.

I kept your secrets for you—*from* you. I wasn't about to spill any to him.

"You don't want to know whether I have a boyfriend?" I said. "Or whether I've been in love, any of that crap?"

"That crap's none of my business, Blondie."

"They're all idiots. Guys my age."

"Not just your age," he said.

"So now you're suggesting *I* should look into the lesbian thing?"

We weren't looking at each other. We usually didn't. He preferred leaning against the house, hiding behind his sunglasses and watching the back lawn like he was scanning for movement, that caveman stare, *this land is mine and I will protect it*. Wild boars, deer, errant mailmen—he was prepared. I focused on the same middle distance and snuck glances at him when I could. Sometimes we caught each other out. I liked it when he blushed.

"The thing to know about men is that they're pigs," he said. "*Especially* when a pretty girl comes along."

"Are you calling me pretty, Jimmy?"

"Shoe fits, Blondie."

"You don't have to worry about me," I told him. "I have a dad of my own, you know."

"I know." He did look at me then. "It must be hard, not having him around."

"It's not like he's dead."

"Of course not." He looked like he wanted to put his hand on my shoulder. Don't ask how I knew; I know what it looks like when a man wants to lay hands on me.

"He didn't leave because of me, if that's what you were thinking."

"It wasn't."

"My mother made him think he was worthless. Tell someone that enough and they start to believe it."

He drew on the cigarette, breathed out a puff of smoke.

"I hope you don't believe it, Jimmy."

"Excuse me?"

"You shouldn't let her make you feel worthless."

I was doing you a favor. He needed someone to remind him that he existed, that he wasn't just a figment of your mother's imagination. Let someone start believing they're not real and, *poof*, one day they disappear. You wouldn't want that, Dex.

We both know the last thing you want is to be like me.

"Mrs. Dexter has a lot on her plate these days," he said. "And I'm not making things any easier."

That was when I knew I'd said something wrong, "Mrs. Dexter." Because usually he called her Julia, as in *Julia hates it when I . . .* or *Julia would have a cow if she knew I . . .*

"Maybe I should go," I said.

"Maybe you should, Lacey."

I didn't mind that he said it. Only a screwup lets some strange girl insult his wife. I could be generous, because it didn't change the truth: I was his secret, and he kept it. He lied to you, and he lied to your mother. I was his truth. I'm not saying that meant he loved me best. But it has to mean something.

My father is never coming back. I know that. And my resulting daddy issues are not subtle. I didn't need a therapist to tell me I was looking for paternal replacements, that the "inappropriate" encounter with my band teacher or the time I let that McDonald's fry guy feel me up beside the Dumpster was all about filling a hole. Pun unintended, guttermind.

But I don't need a father, Dex, so don't think I was trying to steal yours. Just borrowing him for a bit, just chipping away a little for my own.

"I'll probably get fired soon," your dad told me once when I asked why he was around so much during the day. Not like the movie theater does such big business in the afternoon, and not like managing the place qualified as actual work, but still. "Though if you want to know a secret—"

"Always."

He leaned in, and the whisper floated on a trail of smoke. "I'm thinking I might quit."

He dreamed big: inventions he didn't know how to build and franchises he didn't have the cash to open, dreams of starting up his band again or winning the lottery or getting salad bar botulism and suing his way into a fortune. He's the one who made you a dreamer, Dex, and maybe that's why your mother never seemed to like you very much, either.

I told him he should go for it. That I would.

"Yeah, well, you don't have a mortgage." He sighed. "Or a wife."

I was starting to think it wouldn't be long before he didn't have a wife, either.

"I shouldn't have told you all that," he said. "You can't tell Dex. We good on that?"

It was insulting. Had I told you any of the other things you weren't supposed to know? Like how he'd proposed to your mom because he thought she was pregnant, and when their bundle of despair turned out to be a stomach virus, he went through with it anyway. He wasn't an alcoholic, but he was trying his best. He'd gambled away your minuscule college fund on some stock scam before you were old enough to notice, and that was the last time your mom let him touch the checkbook. He liked the stillness of two A.M., when the house slept and he could imagine what it would be like if you were all gone. Sometimes he stayed awake till dawn, imagining himself into that emptier life, the songs he would write, the coke he would snort, the roar of his engine on the open road.

"They make me take these pills," I told him, to prove myself: a secret for a secret.

"What?"

I didn't tell him how it started, after my mother found me in the bathtub, the water pink. "You know how it is, you do one thing people don't understand, and they freak out and drug you up like you're some kind of crazy person having daily chats with Jesus and the man in the moon."

"Were you?"

"I don't fucking see things that aren't fucking there," I said.

"I meant, were you some kind of crazy person?"

Then I had to smile. "You're not supposed to say *crazy*. It's offensive."

He held up his hands, like *excuuuuuuse me*. "So sorry. Were you nuts?"

"Wouldn't you go a little fucking nuts if everyone you knew was calling you crazy?"

It must have been lonely for him in that house, without anyone who knew how to make him laugh.

"So they put me on these pills," I said. "One a day to keep the little dark uglies away."

"Do they help?"

I shrugged. They didn't stop the nightmares. They didn't make it any easier to breathe when I thought about the woods.

"Dex doesn't know," I said.

He slipped a finger across his lips, then X-ed it over his heart. "Hope to die," he said.

"You're not going to ... You won't try to keep me away from Dex, now that you know I'm totally fucked-up?"

"I think maybe it's good for Dex to be around some fucked-up people," he said.

No one had ever said I'd be good for someone. "You really think that?"

He sucked down the last drops of whiskey. "I have to, don't I?"

I reached out.

I took his hand.

For a few seconds, he let me.

"Lacey," he said.

"Jimmy," I said.

He let go.

"I shouldn't have done that," he said.

"*I* did it," I said.

It's just something dads do, right? They hold your hand. They hug you and let you lean against their chest and breathe in their dad smell and tickle your nose against the dad hairs poking out from the hole in their ratty dad shirt. There's nothing fucked-up about wanting that.

So there I was, that last night, everything I loved gone to ash in the backyard, the Bastard praying for my immortal soul, and when I got the hell out of there and came to find you, there was no you there to find. You'd left without me, and the only one home was your father, beered up and dreaming in the still of the night.

He came out to the car, wanted to know what I was doing there, where you were if you weren't with me, and that's how I discovered that you didn't sneak out; you just asked permission. Good girl to the bitter end. *He* was the one who'd broken the rules.

I would have left then—come for you—but he said, "You okay, Blondie?" and he looked so worried, so *dad*-like, that I couldn't lie.

We sat on the curb.

"Tell me," he said, and said again, and I couldn't, because I don't believe in breaking the fucking dam.

I wouldn't have told you, either, probably, but only because if I'd told you about the Bastard, how I felt like Kurt was dead, like I was dead, hollow inside and just fucking done, there would have been a scene and you would have fallen apart; I would have had to be the tough one, all *It's okay, don't cry, squeeze my hand as much as it hurts*, and you would have been the one to feel better.

I'm not blaming you, Dex—you are what you are.

You are not the strong one. So I have to be.

"I can't go back there," I said.

"Home? What happened? You want me to call someone?"

"God, no! Maybe—maybe I can just live here with Dex." I laughed, like it was a joke. He looked like I'd asked him to fuck me.

"Kidding," I said.

"Let's call your mom," he said. "We'll talk it all through. Figure it out."

"No! Please."

"Okay ..." Maybe if we hadn't been sitting out on the street, in front of everyone, he would have rubbed my back, like dads do. "Let's go inside, then. I'll call Julia. She'll know what to do."

"Your *wife*? The one who hates me?"

"She doesn't—"

"Dex is forbidden to see me. Or did you forget?"

"She's upset," he said. "She'll cool off."

"Oh, yeah, I'm sure she'll be real cool when she finds out her husband's been palling around with the town slut."

"Don't call yourself that."

"You know what I mean."

"Lacey—"

"Face it, your wife hates me. And that's before she even knows about this."

"This what?"

"*This.*" Like I was going to spell it out.

"Lacey."

"Jimmy." I said his name the same way he said mine, heavy and patronizing.

"Lacey, what, exactly, do you think is going on here?"

I snorted.

"This"—he wagged a finger back and forth between us: me, him, me—"is not a secret. Dex's mother is the one who thought you might need—"

"What? A new daddy? A good fuck?"

He cleared his throat. "Someone to talk to."

I was on my feet then. Fuck him fuck them fuck you fuck middle-aged middle-class self-satisfied judgmental oh-so-proud of their charity to the less-fortunate fuckfaces.

"So she put you up to it? What, did she bribe you? How many blow jobs is an hour with me worth?"

"Whoa. Blondie. Sit down. Chill."

Like he could just choose when to be a responsible grown-up. Like he cared about anything but making sure the neighbors didn't hear. When I didn't sit down like a good little dog, he stood up, but he couldn't look me in the eye, not now that he'd admitted it—that I was some kind of *chore* for him, a way to get out of cleaning the gutters.

"I guess this is good-bye, Jimmy," I said.

"Look, I'm obviously not handling this very well, but if you'd just come inside—"

"I can say good-bye right out here, no problem," I said, and when I opened my arms and he came in for the hug, I put my hands on his shoulders, rose on my tiptoes, tilted my head, and kissed him.

I don't care that he pushed me away, hard, or that he didn't say anything after that, just shook his head and went back into the house and locked the door between us, that when he finally saw the real me he ran away. I don't give a shit about any of it, but you might, because before he did all that? Before he remembered who he was supposed to be and what he was supposed to do? He kissed me back.

I came to find you.

I came to find you and take you away, because I couldn't go home again, and after I'd done what I'd done, I couldn't very well let you go home again, either.

I couldn't go without you.

That was always the plan, that we would go, and we would go together. We were supposed to be two parts of the same whole. Conjoined twins without the freak factor, one mind and one soul.

I would have told you everything. Once we were safe on our way, the past gnashing its teeth at our backs. Once we'd driven far enough to hit tomorrow, I would have told you my story, because I would know you'd chosen me, you'd chosen us, and you could be trusted with the truth.

Maybe I shouldn't have left you there. *Definitely* I shouldn't have left you there alone, in enemy territory, all boozed up and no place to go, thinking you could hold your liquor when all along it's been me holding you up, holding you back, holding your hair and mopping your puke and letting you believe you could handle things on your own. Maybe I shouldn't have left you. But you shouldn't have asked me to.

Girl meets girl, girl loves girl, girl saves girl. *This* is the story of us, Dex. The only story that matters.

The story of us: That night at Beast, before you went all to liquored-up shit, when we let ourselves float on the arms of the crowd, surfing the love of strangers. Love pulsing with the beat, a wave that lifts you up no matter who you are. The ocean doesn't care. The ocean only wants to slap the shore and then carry you back to the deep.

The story of us: You need me to turn you wild. And I need you. I need you to be my conscience, Dex, just like you need me to be your id. We don't work apart.

Our story ends happily ever after. It has to. We escape Battle Creek, pile into the car, and burn a strip of rubber down the highway. Fly away west, to the promised land. Our rooms will be lit by lava lamps and Christmas lights. Our lives will glow. Consciousnesses will rise and minds will expand, and beautiful boys in flannel shirts will make snow angels on our floor and write love letters on our ceiling with black polish and red lipstick. We will be their muses, and they will strum their guitars beneath our window, calling to us with a siren song, *Come down come away with me*. We will lean out of our tower, our hair swinging like Rapunzel's, and laugh, because nothing will carry us away from each other.

You always tell me there was no *before Lacey*, that you were only you once you met me. Now I'm telling you: *After Dex*, there is no more Lacey. No more Lacey and no more Dex. Only Dex-and-Lacey, only and always. You should have had more faith; you should have known I'd find my way back to you.

I will always come back for you.

THEM

Lacey's mother thought things were supposed to be different this time. Of course, they were supposed to be different last time. Supposed to be. That was pregnancy; that was motherhood; that was the motherfucking joy and promise of bringing a child into this godforsaken world, a lifetime of *supposed-to-be*s.

You were supposed to be healthy; you were supposed to be good. You were supposed to be a person who did not drink, did not smoke, did not snort or shoot up or, God forbid, eat some fucking unpasteurized cheese. You were supposed to be a whale, but not too big a whale. You were supposed to rest your hands on your belly and wait for a kick; you were supposed to have sex, but not too much sex, not so much or so dirty that junior would sense his mother is a whore. You were, above all, supposed to be *happy*. About the hemorrhoids, the swollen feet, the pineapple-sized lump of screaming flesh tearing its way through your vagina like a fist through pearl-pink tissue paper. You were supposed to be glowing with the fucking ecstasy of giving your body over to someone else—not the baby, no, that you could maybe accept, in all its nipple-sucking, spitting, burping, shitting glory, but to anyone and everyone with an opinion on what you were supposed to do and who you were supposed to be. You, who had been no one of consequence, became someone whose every choice counted, whose every mistake verged on crime against the public interest. You became a *mother*, and mothers were *supposed to be*. You were somehow supposed to be happy about even that.

Sometimes, especially at the beginning, Lacey's mother sort of was.

Those nights in the dark, feeling the blast of music from the stage, feeling it inside, where the baby wriggled and kicked, like it wanted to be part of the action, to sweat and spin and scream alongside her—that was when she'd felt it most, the euphoric *yes*, that same *yes* she'd felt when she walked out of the clinic and then, after the date of no return, rarely again. She went to as many concerts as she could in those months—Springsteen, Kiss, Quiet Riot—teased her bangs, pulled her shirt over her swollen belly or, toward the end, let it rise up, the flesh glowing with sweat, because fuck it, she was a married woman now, she was practically of the Lord, be fruitful and multiply, and standing there in the dark, with the beat banging away at her, with the lights flashing and the floor shaking, the thing inside her felt alive, made them both powerful. There was magic there, in the hot blood of those nights, and that was something Lacey would never understand, much less thank her for. Those were the nights, the bands, the songs that *made* her. Fuck the sperm and the egg, fuck biology, fuck the fucking, she'd been conceived in a dark mass of writhing bodies and wild music, a child of black magic forged from heat and noise and lust. Of course she turned out the way she did; she couldn't have been any other way.

If only they could have stayed like that, tethered together, everything would have been fine. She was so easy to love, the tiny package tucked neatly in its ready-made carrying case. Lacey's mother would have freely given of nutrients and blood if Lacey had only stayed inside and let her have more of those black magic nights.

But no.

But then.

You couldn't bring a baby to Madison Square Garden. You couldn't even listen to an album in the comfort of your own home—not all the way through, not without waking the baby. The screaming baby. The shit-stained baby. The puking baby. The baby that your husband, who was only your husband because of the baby, couldn't bring himself to love. The baby who left that gaping hole inside you, who had left you like everyone else, so that even when you dumped her on someone else, when you finally snuck away, back to the music, it wasn't the same. Once you'd heard it with her inside you, it never sounded the same again. There was a hollow space that the music couldn't fill, and it wasn't your fault if you had to look elsewhere for something that did.

The baby was supposed to be enough.

There must be something wrong with her, Lacey's mother thought, because after the baby came, nothing was ever enough.

She loved Lacey. She couldn't help it. That was biology, beyond her control.

You could love something and still understand it had ruined your life. You could love something, something small and pink and helpless and nestled ever so gently in your arms, and still want to ugly-cry and give it back, or press its helpless little lips together and hold its nostrils tight until it stopped struggling. You could love something and still feel that pillow-snuffing impulse so powerfully that you would have to guard yourself against it for the rest of your life, even after the helpless thing was big enough to help itself. You could love something and still hate it for turning you into a person who could feel those things, because you weren't supposed to be a monster.

This time was supposed to be different. This time, she longed for *supposed to be*. James was the living personification of *supposed to be*, and he was supposed to help her be the same.

She would be a magazine cutout, commercial ready. She would wear aprons and wash dishes and say her prayers. She would not take another drink. She would love this man, with his flattop and his polyester pants. She would love him for knowing what was right and teaching her to do it. She would find the serenity to accept the things she could not change. She would not expose this fetus to wild music, nor dance in the dark beneath flashing lights and angry skies. She would not enjoy sex, but would perform it as duty required. She would clip coupons. She would dress for church. She would not drink. She would not drink. She would not drink.

She made these promises, and James ensured she would follow them, and she was supposed to be happy.

She did not drink or smoke or dance. She did place her hands on her belly and beam, and still, when the baby came out, his fingers and toes and little penis so perfectly intact, she hated him for splitting her open and wanted to give him back. She loved him too much and hated him for it, and he was just as angry and shitty and pukey and boring as Lacey had been, and this time she'd done it to herself on purpose. She had no one else to blame.

Lacey's mother was, perhaps, not supposed to be a mother. Some people probably weren't. It was too late to get that kind of clue. Bad mothers abandoned their children, and she was supposed to be a good mother, and so she stayed. And if sometimes she yelled and sometimes she drank and sometimes she fantasized about castrating her husband in his sleep and stuffing the testicles in the baby's mouth until he stopped crying and fellated himself into a silent eternity, then that was the price of her mothering. That was the best she had to give. Some days, she woke up and swore, *I will be better.* Some days, she was.

U S

July–October 1992

DEX

Paper Cuts

Lacey was gone.

Lacey was gone and I was alone.

Lacey would never have left without me, but Lacey had left without me. Left me alone with the things I'd done. The things done to me, or not done to me. Swallowed by the black hole of memory.

I had fragments to piece together: The ink on my skin. The whispers. Slivers of the night—bodies pressed together, music, voices—all in a broken filmstrip. That must have been the worst of it, I told myself. If there'd been worse, my body would remember, would ache or bleed. The worst left a stain, so the worst must not have been.

The worst thing that could happen, I thought, and never gave it a name.

The girl on the other side of the night, the girl I was now:

The girl who'd torn off her shirt and danced on a table. The girl who'd grabbed bulges through jeans and moaned filthy things, who said *dick* and *pussy* and *lick my cunt*.

It was a wonder, that I could do those things. There was a box in the basement where we kept stray jigsaw pieces, all of them parts of different pictures, none of their edges lining up. That was me. A Picasso person. The wrong parts in the wrong places. Lacey would have known how to make them fit. Lacey had named me: *This is who you are, this is who you will be.*

She would have known, but she was gone.

I went to school on Monday, because going to school on Monday was a thing I'd always done.

I didn't go back.

As long as the homework got done, no one objected to me spending the final three weeks of the semester in my room. No one wanted to look at me.

Everyone wanted to look at me.

In my room, in the dark, I understood what I never had before, what no one else seemed to. I understood how a boy could go into the woods with a bullet and a gun and not come out. That there was no conspiracy, no evil influences or secret rituals; that sometimes there was only pain and the need to make it stop.

Lacey said it mattered, how you chose to do it, and now I understood that, too: why you might choose the bullet and the gun, choose ugliness and hurt instead of slipping away sweetly into the black. Some pain dictated violence, bloodshed. Oblivion required obliterating not just the pain but its source. Justice necessitated leaving behind a mess. A scream of blood and bone and rage.

It scared me, how much I understood.

If I had let Lacey set the house on fire. If I had watched it burn. Sometimes I dreamed of the flames and woke up with the smell of charred flesh, and sometimes I woke up smiling.

I tried to dream of Lacey, dream myself into our life in Seattle, but I couldn't get there. Seattle was a ghost, and Lacey was like something conjured from one of my books. If it weren't for Lacey, I wouldn't have been at the party; if it weren't for Lacey, I wouldn't have been so angry and so drunk; if it weren't for Lacey, I would have been safe.

I hated her. I loved her. I wished she'd never come back, and I wished she would. That was how I lived, after: not one thing and not the other. Canceling myself out.

I stayed in my room. Safe territory. My room: fifteen feet wide, thirteen feet short, beige from floor to ceiling, with matted knots in the carpet from where our cat had puked her life away. A twin bed with Strawberry Shortcake sheets, because, according to my mother, sheets were expensive and grown-up was a matter of opinion. Shuttered windows that let through slats of light in the early afternoon and a rusty full-length mirror papered with remnants of Lacey: wrinkled postcards from Paris and California and Istanbul written by people long dead and rescued from yard sale bins; deep thoughts courtesy of deep thinkers, inscribed by Lacey in stern black marker; for Lacey's sake, a cutout of Kurt, his granny cardigan matching his eyes; at the center of it all, a Dex-and-Lacey photo collage that captured none of the important moments, because for those we were always alone, no one to hold the camera. A particleboard bureau stickered with glow-in-the-dark stars that three years of scraping couldn't clear away. Stacks of books pressed up against beige wallpaper, spines stretching to the ceiling, every book an adventure that meant climbing or toppling or ever so gently working one out of the middle of a stack, Jenga for giants. There was a card table desk in the corner, stacked neatly with the year's final papers (failures) and report card ("disappointing"), and buried beneath them, for some future scrapbook of shame, two copies of the local paper—the edition with the letter to the editor telling the story of the wild girl passed out in the ruins of an abandoned party, and the weekend edition with the editorial, with its anonymous but all-knowing first person plural: *We believe* the girls in this town are up to no good, *we believe* modern music and television and drugs and sex and atheism are rotting our youth, *we believe* this girl is as much to blame as her toxic culture and her lax parents, *we can't blame her* but *we can't afford to excuse her*, so it follows that *we must use her* as a warning, lest *we lose another* of our brightest youth, and *we the people of Battle Creek*, the parents and teachers and churchgoers and goodhearted folk, *we must do better.*

I called her line in the middle of the night, after my parents were asleep. Every night. All night, sometimes, just to hear it ring. No one ever answered.

No, her mother finally said, she didn't know where Lacey went. No, I shouldn't call back.

My mother was angry all the time. Not at me, she said. Or not *just* at me.

"I don't care what anyone says," my father said, standing in the doorway of my room a few days after—and maybe not, but he'd never stood like that before, like a trainer at the mouth of a cage, waiting for something wild to make its move. "You'll always be a good girl. Maybe without Lacey around . . . things will settle."

Without Lacey, I was incapable of wildness, that's what he was telling me. When I had Lacey, he had a little piece of her, too, could love me more for the things she saw in me. Now that she was gone, he expected I would revert to form. I would be the good girl, his good girl, boring but safe. He was supposed to want that.

*

I read.

Lacey had always discouraged reading that was, as she put it, beneath us. We should spend our time on mind-expanding pursuits, she said. Our mission, and we were obligated to accept it, was an investigation into the nature of things. The fundamentals. Together we paged through Nietzsche and Kant, pretending to understand. We read Beckett aloud and waited for Godot. Lacey memorized the first six stanzas of "Howl" and shouted it over our lake, casting her voice into the wind. *I saw the best minds of my generation destroyed by madness*, she would scream, and then tell me that Allen Ginsberg was the oldest man she would be willing to fuck. I memorized the opening and closing lines of "The Hollow Men" for her, and I whispered it to myself when the dark closed in.

This is the way the world ends.
This is the way the world ends.
This is the way the world ends.

It sounded like a promise.

Without Lacey, I slid backward. I tessered with Meg Murry; I crept through the wardrobe and nuzzled my face into Aslan's fur. I swept the dust and warmed the fires in Howl's moving castle; I turned half invisible with half magic, drank tea with the Mad Hatter, battled Captain Hook, even, occasionally, hugged the Velveteen Rabbit back to life. I was a stranger in a strange land. I was an orphan, abandoned and found and saved, until I closed the book, and was lost all over again.

I read, and I wrote.

Dear Lacey, I wrote, sometimes, in letters I hid in an old Sears sweater box, just in case. In my terrible handwriting, with smearing ink, unstained by unfallen tears, *I'm sorry*, I wrote. *I should have known better.*

Please come home.

The last Sunday in July, I went outside. Just a ride around the block, on the bike my father had quietly collected from the postparty wreckage. The sun felt good. The air smelled good, like grass and summer. The wind sounded good, that thunder you could hear only when you were in motion. When I was a kid, bike riding was an adventure, bad guys on my tail and the wind rushing through a mountain pass, passageway to enchantment. The bike itself was magic back then, the only thing other than a book that could carry me away. But that was kid logic, the kind that ignored the simple physics of vectors. It didn't matter how fast I pedaled if I was turning in circles. The bike always carried me home.

My father was smoking on the porch steps; he'd started in June, after. The cigarettes made the house smell like a stranger.

I dumped the bike on the lawn, and he stubbed the butt into the cement stair.

"Hannah," he said.

"What?"

"Nothing. I just . . . It's good to see you out."

"Don't get used to it." I said it with my best take-no-shit Lacey front.

He lit up another cigarette. Chain-smoking now. Home in the middle of the day. Probably only a matter of time before he got fired again, or maybe he already had and was afraid to admit it. That used to be the kind of secret we kept. It had seemed romantic, the Don Quixote of it all, his conviction that the present was just prologue to some star-spangled future, but these days he only seemed pathetic. Lacey would have said I was starting to sound like my mother.

"I have to tell you something," he said.

"Okay."

"I don't think she's coming back. Lacey. And I don't want you thinking it's about you, that she left."

Lacey was gone, and he was still trying to claim a piece of her.

"Something happened at her house," he said. When I asked what made him think that, he admitted—and it had the timbre of admission—"She came here, that night. Before she left."

Everything went still.

"What did you say to her?"

"She needed someone to talk to," he said. "We talked sometimes."

What the fuck, the old Dex, the Dex who had Lacey, would have said. *What the fuck are you talking about, what the fuck is wrong with you, what the fuck have you done?*

She is mine, that Dex would have said, and believed it.

"Your friend had some problems," he said.

"Everyone has problems."

"You didn't know everything about her, kid."

"What did you say to her?" I asked again. "What did you say that made her leave?"

"All I know is, something happened at home and it upset her. She didn't want to go back there."

"But you made her." My voice was steady, my face blank; he couldn't have known what he was doing. What was burning away between us.

"No—"

"You told her not to?"

"No . . ."

"So *what did you say*?"

"I don't think there's anything we could have done to stop her. A person has to want to be helped."

"She didn't belong to you." There are things that shouldn't have to be said.

"She didn't belong to you, either, kid. But I know what she meant to you. I would never have made her go."

"But you're glad she's gone."

He shook his head. "She was good for you," he said, then, sounding less certain, "wasn't she?"

I wondered what he thought he knew. Who he thought I'd been before Lacey, and who he thought I'd become in her wake. Who he needed me to be: Daddy's girl, sassy but not skanky, flirting with boys but never fucking them, breaking curfew, breaking laws, breaking everything but my precious hymen, trying to be more like Lacey and less like Lacey at the same time, rebelling, not against him but with him, giving the finger to the Man and to my mother but coming home in time to curl up on the couch and watch *Jeopardy!* I saw, then, what I hadn't seen before, that I wasn't Hannah *or* Dex for him; I was wholly Jimmy Dexter's daughter, reflection of whatever he needed himself to be.

"We could go to the movies sometime, if you want. Just you and me, kid, like we used to?"

He wasn't going to tell me what he'd said to her. *Believe what you want*, people always say. As if it's that easy, as if belief and want could dovetail so effortlessly. As if I didn't *want to believe* that my father loved me and my parents loved each other, that Lacey was coming home, that I would stop burning with humiliation every time I left the house, that life was fair, tomorrow was another day, Nikki Drummond would burn in hell. Why stop there? I wanted to believe in time travel and ESP and aliens and God, in a world that was more magical than it seemed and a future that beelined out of Battle Creek and into the event horizon. Lacey said believing was the hard part. If you could do that, everything else would follow,

"You'll give yourself lung cancer," I told my father, and stepped over him to get to the door.

Lacey had a theory that people have a finite capacity for the enjoyment of their favorite things. Songs, movies, books, food: We're hardwired for specific quantities of pleasure, and once the amount is exceeded, good goes bad. The kicker is, there's no warning when you're approaching the limit; the dopamine just flips off like a switch, and there's one more book for the fire.

Very rarely, Lacey said, you find something for which your brain has infinite capacity, and that, Lacey said, is the thing we call love.

I no longer believed in that. But I did believe in overdoses and disappointment, and I wasn't about to risk either on my favorite books. The house wasn't a safe space anymore—there were no safe spaces anymore—and that made it easier to leave. When I did, I only ever went to the library. I felt twelve again, fresh out of the kids' section, stroking the spines in the grown-up stacks as if I could osmose their words through the bindings. I felt almost normal again.

"God loves you all," promised the woman with the stack of pamphlets who'd planted herself just outside the front door. "But He cannot protect you if you willingly put yourselves in the path of temptation." It was beak-faced Barbara Fuller, who wore her clothes like a hanger, who'd snubbed my mother more than once at a PTA bake sale, suggesting not so subtly that someone who settled for store-bought was no more deserving of the title *mother* than Entenmann's donuts were of the title *food*. Barbara Fuller was the type who wrote letters to the editor about loose morals and garish Christmas lights, and she had a voracious hunger for the failures of others. That day, she didn't seem to care that her audience consisted of a handful of bored retirees and one abashed bald guy who looked like he would gnaw his own arm off if his wife—Barbara Fuller's only avid listener—didn't let go.

"Satanists slaughter fifty thousand children each year."

The bald guy picked something out of his nose.

"This is a national emergency. And don't fool yourselves—there is an active satanic cult operating in this town." She raised her voice. "Your *teenagers* are at risk."

It was a joke, this woman preaching to us about risk—pretending she knew who was in danger, and of what.

I walked quickly, head down, focusing on the slap of my flip-flops against pavement, the gravel beneath some old lady's Chevrolet, the crying cicadas, the pulse of blood flushing my cheeks, the jangle of the bike lock as I fumbled with the key.

"They prey on the vulnerable and confused," she screeched, and I suspected she wasn't just trying to penetrate the old folks' hearing aids. I would not look up to catch her looking at me. "They prey on the fallen."

Summer stretched on. Our house whirred day and night with the apologetic wheezing of fans. They stirred hot air; we endured. More than once I read through Barbara Fuller's pamphlet about satanism, a copy of which I'd liberated from the trash. Written by one Isabelle F. Ford, PhD, and jointly published by Parents Against Satanic Teachings and the Cult Crime Research Institution, it suggested that an underground network of tens of thousands of satanists was diligently pursuing a program of grave robbing and child sacrifice.

If only, I thought, because imagine: If there were such a cabal, veins of dark power threading through Battle Creek. If there were others like me, a coven of girls whose secret selves throbbed with pain, who needed blood to feed their hearts of darkness. I'd always longed for a shadow world, ever since I was a kid, searching out garden sprites and bridge trolls, wishing myself into a faerie changeling waiting for the summons home. Now, a new fantasy: spindly arms carving strange symbols in the night, robed silhouettes against the full moon, a bloody altar and a cloud of incense, ritual and invocation, the promise of power. We *laughed*, Lacey had told me; we hefted an axe in a moonlit field, loomed over something large and vulnerable, and there was joy in power, joy in drawing blood, slashing and slicing and destroying. When I let myself remember, I could almost believe it, that there was, that we did. If only the Barbara Fullers of the world were right and all I had to do was summon the forces of darkness and let them consume me.

I threw the pamphlet back in the trash. One more empty promise.

Lacey never called.

No one called.

Until one night—as if the forces of darkness had materialized after all, in response to my silent request—my mother shouted upstairs to tell me I had a call ... from Nikki

Drummond. When I wouldn't come to the phone, Nikki called again the next night, and the night after.

On the fourth day, she came to the house.

Here was Nikki Drummond, perched prettily on the blue velour couch in my living room, sitting in a spot where I'd peed as a baby, more than once. She was dressed for summer in Battle Creek, which meant straddling the narrow line between socially acceptable and buck naked, somehow making a strapped cotton shell and sweaty cutoffs look both girl-next-door sexy and living-room-small-talk appropriate. Kid-tested, mother-approved. I was dressed nearly the same, but looked like a homeless person.

"So," Nikki said.

Lacey had taught me that the best way to unnerve people was to let them marinate in silence. I watched her, waiting, and she watched me, waiting. I broke first.

"What do you want?"

"Are you mad at me or something?"

"Seriously?" It was strange to talk to someone like everything was the same as it had been, like only I was different.

"Come on, what did I ever do to you, Hannah?"

"For one, you ratted me out to my fucking mother." It felt like forever ago; it felt laughably small, considering. But it was easiest to say out loud.

"That was for your own good." Her voice, sweet as syrup.

Sticky. "She got you to break the law, Hannah. Come on, what kind of friend is that?"

"Dex."

"What?"

"My *name* is *Dex*."

She laughed. I'd never actually punched anyone—growing up an only child had deprived me of the wrestling and black eyes that came with siblings—but I could imagine it, the bite of nails against my palm, the crunch of knuckles against cartilage, the spatter of blood, her wide-eyed surprise, her pain, her awe. That I had it in me to break something. That she could be broken.

She must have seen it, because she swallowed the giggle.

"Sorry. *Dex*."

"Please go."

"Not yet. I came by to see if you were doing okay, and you're not even giving me a chance to ask."

"Lacey's gone," I said. It was the first time I'd said it out loud. "So you don't have to *worry* about me anymore. No more bad influence."

"God, Hannah, I don't give a shit about Lacey, I'm talking about *you*. How are you? After . . . you know?"

I did know, and I didn't. Maybe that was why I'd let Nikki Drummond sit on my couch and scuff her flip-flops into my rug. So she could tell me.

"Fine," I said.

"Yeah, so fine you've been playing hermit all summer. You look like an albino."

I stood up. "You came to the circus, you've seen the freak. Now you can go."

Nikki sighed. "Look, Hannah—"

"Dex."

"Yeah. Whatever. It was my party, sort of. Okay? So I feel responsible for how it ended up. For you." She said it like she was expecting credit.

"How it ended up," I said, slowly. Lacey would say: Show no fear. Lacey would say: *She* should be afraid. "With me dumped out back like garbage?"

"I don't know anything about that," Nikki said. "I left way before then, don't you remember?"

I shrugged.

She leaned forward. "Wait, you don't remember? Oh my God, you totally blacked out!"

What I did remember: How it felt, to want to touch, to be touched. The heat and prickle of it, the fire.

"It must be killing you," Nikki said. "Not knowing."

I said nothing.

"You want my advice?" She said it like she wanted to help, and it was all upside down, Lacey leaving me, Nikki refusing to go away. "Decide nothing happened. Decide you're fine, and you will be."

Believing was the hard part, Lacey always said.

"I told you. I am fine."

"Any of us could have gotten snagged by that rent-a-cop," Nikki said. "Don't think we don't know that. You have more friends than you realize."

"I have enough friends."

She snorted. "Come to my place this weekend. My mom's throwing some god-awful mother–daughter pool party, it'll be a nightmare. You'll love it."

"I would rather jab a hot knife in my eye."

"Too bad for you, then, because your mom already said yes."

LACEY

Endless, Nameless

I blame Jesus. And before you get all uptight about sacrilege, remember that it would be just as easy to blame you.

I should have left without you. I could have: I had the car. Shame on me for giving you more time, for assuming the Bastard would calm himself down. For going home.

Call it a failure of the imagination.

Horizons. That's what the shithole was called. As in *Expand your.* As in *Learn to see Christ on the.* As in *Unless you want to be a brainwashed Jesus-freak head case, better run for the.*

They dumped me off just inside the barbed wire gate, and I knew exactly what kind of place it was once I saw the pony-tailed blonde with the lobotomized smile flanked by two thugs just waiting for a chance to test out their Tasers. I let Thing One and Thing Two frog-march me in to see the man in charge—also blond; they were all fucking blond. He told me to call him Shawn. The people at Horizons said *Shawn* the way Shawn said *Jesus*. This puny, pasty gym-teacher wannabe with the cross-shaped whistle around his neck and the gigantic mahogany desk that said more than he intended about the size of his dick, this was the only guy with the power to send me back to you.

"Welcome to your safe haven," he said, and I wondered how many of the girls he'd fucked, hoping it was a lot, because it's the kind of guy who's in it for other reasons that you really have to worry about.

He issued me a Horizons handbook and my very own teen Bible, complete with a couple neutered blonds frolicking on the cover, bone-white horse teeth testifying to their oneness with the Lord. "We've made a space for you in bunk six, Ecclesiastes. Chastity will take you over there. I'm sure you have many questions—"

"Starting with, are you fucking kidding me that her name is *Chastity*?" I had more questions—did he really believe that a few coils of barbed wire could keep out the devil, how much had the Bastard paid for the privilege of dumping me in this shithole, how long would it be before I could go home—but Shawn's game-show-host grin had gone full jack-o'-lantern.

"—but as you'll learn from your handbook, you haven't yet earned the privilege of asking questions."

"What the hell is that supposed to mean?"

"This is a hard transition process, I know. So I'll give you a pass on the language. But my leniency ends now."

"Is that supposed to scare me?" I said.

He jerked his head at She-Who-Would-Not-Be-Penetrated. "One demerit," he said, shaking his head in what I eventually came to recognize as Shawn's Special Recipe Sorrow, because it hurt him ever so much to hurt us.

One demerit meant one chore, of my counselor's choosing, and my counselor, a mini-Mussolini named Heather, never met a toilet she didn't think needed a good toothbrush-scrub. So that's how I spent my first morning at Horizons: on my knees, bent over the bowl, swallowing bile because I was pretty sure that if I threw up I'd have to clean that, too. As I scrubbed, she walked me through my dos and don'ts: Do love Jesus, do follow the rules, don't think for yourself, don't imagine your life is your own, don't fuck up or you'll be sorry.

For each day of not fucking up, you earned a privilege, and privileges were everything. You needed them to speak to other campers, to leave your cabin without supervision, to send letters, to spend your free time outside rather than sitting at your desk reading the Bible, to go to the bathroom without supervision—"and I don't want to waste any more time than I have to watching you pee," Heather said, "so get it together." No amount of privileges would get you five minutes of any music but Christian rock. You earned privileges by memorizing Bible passages, making your bed with hospital corners, sucking up to your counselor, publicly confessing your sins and taking Jesus into your heart, writing antiabortion letters to your local congressman, and tattling on your fellow campers when they momentarily forgot themselves and started acting like human beings rather than zombies. We lived in bunkhouses named for the books of the Bible, a dozen of us in Ecclesiastes: twelve little girls in two straight lines, call it *Madeline and the Jesus Freaks*.

Mornings were for Bible study, afternoons were for exercise, then the sing-alongs and sharing sessions that comprised mandatory fun. Meals were for watching your back and learning your place. Twelve girls, and I didn't need to learn their names or their stories because I didn't intend to be one of them for long. It was enough to know that the Screamer jerked us all awake at three every morning; that the Sodomite had been caught in flagrante with her soccer team captain; that the Skank was a sex addict, or at least had a diary-reading mother who thought so; that the Virgin had remained so—if only by her own technical definition—by restricting herself to copious amounts of anal sex; that Saint Ann had shipped herself off to Horizons voluntarily, in search of some sinners to save.

The Bastard would have liked the regimented schedule, the drill-sergeant counselors whipping us into shape, a boot camp for the army of God; he would have loved the fact that any trespass was met with flamboyant, Old Testament–style consequences. This wasn't hippie worship, the guitar-playing, turn-the-other-cheek kind of lovefest he detested, and it wasn't the bingo-playing, potlucking, pamphleteering morality play that enraged him in Battle Creek. This was a camp created as if in his own image, complete with brimstone and fire and daily viewings of *The 700 Club*. All I had to do, they told me, was learn respect for authority and for the Lord, and they would send me home.

I tried.

I dedicated my life to Christ. I memorized Bible passages. I sang that my God was an awesome god and learned the hand motions to prove it. When we stood in a circle for Squeeze Prayer, I said my line, "I pray that the Lord helps me fight off the devil and his temptations," then squeezed Skank's hand and pretended to listen while she told her own lie. I dedicated myself to craft projects, because Jesus was a carpenter and handiwork was noble work; I sawed wood and carved soap, and when we practiced tying knots I did my best not to dream of a noose. I confessed to lascivious thoughts and agreed with Heather that I'd squandered my life. I racked up two weeks' worth of privileges, and I didn't let myself think of Battle Creek or of you until I was safe in bed, because that was my reward for making it through each day—that and Kurt, who sang me to sleep. Two weeks, and I scored enough privileges to write two letters. One to the Bastard, promising to be good if he'd let me come home. The other to you.

Dear Dex, I wrote, then stopped.

Dear Dex, I've given up. Dear Dex, Everything I told you about myself was a lie. Dear Dex, Everything I do is so I can come home to you, but I don't deserve you if I come home like this.

No. I needed to be *your* Lacey. Strong. So the next morning, during the dawn service, I stood up in my pew and cursed Jesus Christ my Lord for this season in hell, and our whole bunk got rewarded with an afternoon scrubbing shit out of the toilet bowls. The next day I gave Shawn the finger, and Heather tasked us with mucking out the cow stalls, to remind us what it meant to be befouled by sin. I thought of you, Dex, and I thought of Kurt, and knew I would roll in my own shit before living their vision of salvation.

The next time I fucked up, they tried something new.

There's a hidden track on *Nevermind*. You'd never find it if you didn't know it was there. First "Something in the Way" fades out, with a final soft crash of cymbals and Kurt's dying hum and then nothing.

Nothing for thirteen minutes and fifty-one seconds. What comes next is only for us, the ones who care enough to endure the silence. First the drumbeat, thrumming into the too-quiet like jungle cannibals. Then the lion roars: Kurt's voice, pure and gleaming; Kurt's voice like a knife scything the sky. It's the raging of a man not going gentle into that good night. The silence is part of it, those thirteen minutes of agony, and Kurt's in it with you, muzzled and frenzied as the seconds tick by and the pressure mounts and finally, when he can't bear it any more than you can, he tears off the muzzle and goes fucking *nuts*. Thirteen minutes, fifty-one seconds. It doesn't seem like it would be that long. But time stretches.

Remember what we read about black holes, Dex? How from the outside, from a safe distance away, when you watch someone fall into a black hole, they fall slower and slower, until they seem to freeze at the event horizon? How they'll stay there forever, suspended over the dark, the future always just out of reach?

It's a trick. If you're the one falling, time keeps right on going. You sail past the event horizon; you get sucked into the black. And no one on the outside will ever know.

That's how it was, in the dark place. No boundary between yourself and the dark, past and future, something and nothing. You could scream all you wanted, and the dark would swallow it whole. In the dark place, silence was the same as noise.

In prison they call it the hole, at least if you want to believe prison movies, and if you can't believe the movies, then half of what I know about the world is bullshit. But in prison movies, the hole is just some cell like all the others. At Horizons, it's a fucking hole in the ground.

In the dark place, you tell yourself, *This time I will hold on.* This time you'll keep it together, remember that time passes and there are no monsters hiding in the dark. When the slab creaks open each day and the food drops down, you'll fling it back in their faces, along with fistfuls of your own shit. When they lower the rope and offer to lift you back into the sun, if only you'll apologize and say *thank you*, you'll laugh and tell them to come back later, you were in the middle of a nap. This time the dark place will be your gift, your vacation from the torments of daily life. This time will be *your* time.

Bullshit.

The dark place is always the same.

First it's boring. Then it's lonely. Then the fear washes in, and when that tide ebbs, there's nothing left. Silence fills with all the thoughts you spend your daylight life trying not to think. The bad things you've done. The blue of the sky. The bodies rotting away in coffins, the maggots feasting on skeletal remains. What happened to the body when you left it behind, and whether now is your time to return. Your food is damp with tears. It tastes like shit and piss, because that's all you can smell, that and your rotting sweat and shame. The air is hot and stale, thick with your own breath. When the darkness breaks and a voice cracks the silence, you tell them whatever they want to hear.

No, not *you*. That's cheating. I don't know what you would do, Dex. This is what I did.

"I accept Jesus into my heart."

"I renounce Satan."

"I have sinned and I will sin no more."

I always gave in—and that's something I'll never not know about myself—but at least I held out longer than most. It was because of Kurt. He was down there with me. Down there is where he *lives*. Singing was better than screaming. I sang with him; I remembered you. I lived for you, down in that dark place, and I survived knowing you were somewhere up in the light, living for me.

DEX

About a Girl

You're going," my mother said. "We both are."

I felt ancient, but when it came to my mother, apparently I'd never be too old for *because I said so*. We went. A mother-daughter pool party, awkward purgatory of small talk and cellulite that only a Drummond could dream up.

"It was lovely of them to think of us." My mother navigated our beat-up Olds into a narrow slot between a Mazda and an Audi, tapping the bumpers of each of them once, as if for luck. Nikki's house couldn't have been more than a five-minute drive from mine, but it felt like we'd passed through a portal—or maybe through a TV screen, because the sidewalk maples, the colonnade-lined porches, the impeccably pruned rectangles of green all seemed too perfect to be anything but a set. Tragedy or farce, that was the only question. "And it'll be lovely for you to spend some time with your friends."

Okay, farce.

"How many times do I have to tell you—"

"All right. Girls who could be your friends. If you would only give them the opportunity."

How was it, I wondered, that the mere act of growing older precipitated radical memory loss? Here was my mother, naively expecting not only that a coven of PTA moms who'd snubbed her for a decade would spontaneously open their arms to her unmanicured charm, but also that their daughters would follow suit.

"You really want me to go to a *party*? After what happened the last time." It was a mark of my desperation that I was willing to come so close to explicitly referencing it. "Aren't you afraid of what I'll do?"

For someone with no sense of humor, my mother had an expert wry smile. "Why do you think I came as your chaperone?"

It should have been worth something she was willing to be seen in public with me—but then she was my mother, so that was worth about as much as her telling me I was pretty.

"You can't control what people think of you," she said. "You can only do your best to prove them wrong."

"Guilty until proven innocent? I don't think that's how it's supposed to work."

"Life isn't *LA Law*, dear." She turned off the car. We were actually doing this.

"Lacey's gone," I said, the last-ditch effort worth the pain of saying the words out loud. "No more bad influence. No need to sucker me into making new friends."

She put her hand over mine—then pulled away before I could. "You know, Hannah, my issue with Lacey was never *Lacey*. Not entirely."

"Is that one of those Zen things that make no sense?"

"I know how it feels," she said. "To invest everything you have in another person. But no one's dreams are big enough to be worth giving up yours, Hannah. If you don't figure that out before it's too late, you can wake up inside a life you'd never have chosen for yourself."

"I don't know what any of that has to do with me."

My mother did not talk like this, and she certainly didn't talk like this with me. We weren't equipped for it, either of us.

"You can't dream someone else's dreams forever, Hannah. And when you finally stop, it's no good for anyone." She clapped her hands together, plastic again with a Teflon smile, as if I'd simply imagined that, for a moment, she'd somehow melted into a real person. "Let's get going. We wouldn't want them thinking we're rude."

"Who cares what they think? They treat you like crap."

I didn't say it to hurt her, it didn't occur to me, then, that I could hurt her.

Framed in fake gilt on my mother's bureau was a photo of the girl she'd once been, posing at a ballet recital with her younger sister, who, unlike my mother, was actually built to be a ballerina. The two of them were frozen midpirouette, my aunt's form perfect and her smile beaming, my mother sullen and dumpy with a familiar thicket of frizz—her hair had gone limp after pregnancy, something else to blame me for. If this had been a movie, we would have bonded over our mutual ugly-duckness; of course, in the Hollywood version, my mother would have blossomed into an intimidating swan rather than simply expanding into a slightly taller, substantially thicker duck, one who sometimes didn't seem to like me very much. For which I couldn't blame her: She probably didn't enjoy the daily reminder of her yesterday any more than I wanted the glimpse into my tomorrow.

She climbed out of the car and smoothed down her bathing suit cover-up, a blue terry cloth drape I was sure looked nothing like anything the other mothers were wearing. "Just because you leave high school doesn't mean high school leaves you."

I had to laugh. "That may be the most depressing thing you've ever said to me."

She laughed, too. "Then I suppose I'm doing my job."

"Mother of the year."

I could see it on her face, the moment she decided to press her luck and go for it, a mother-daughter moment. "It's nice to see you smile, Hannah."

"Tell me we can get back in the car and go home. I'll smile like I'm in a toothpaste commercial."

"Tempting," she said, pausing just long enough for me to get my hopes up.

Then we went to the party.

*

Bedecked in full-on Rich Guy leisurewear—Ralph Lauren khakis and a polo shirt—Nikki Drummond's father opened the door and grunted us toward the pool deck. I crossed through the house head down, not wanting to spot some domestic artifact—an ancient finger painting on the fridge or a therapist's appointment on the calendar—that might render Nikki human. We padded across fancy tiles, the kind with barely perceptible swirls that make you feel like you're walking on water, and stopped short in the back doorway, a mother-daughter pair in matched contemplation of their dark fate.

Mothers wore artfully draped sarongs or Esprit tracksuits, nails manicured and hair dutifully bobbed into Hamill-esque mom cuts, like they'd sworn a sacred pact to go frumpy at forty; daughters frolicked in designer cutoffs, tan, coltish legs poking through artfully frayed denim. Pink or purple jellies squished on manicured feet; oversized T-shirts belted low or tied in a knot just above the belly button, except on those girls who—despite the absence of any Y chromosomes to impress—had bothered stripping down to bikinis. Nikki's usual crowd was absent, replaced by scattered clutches of second-tiers dangling their feet in the pool or poking suspiciously at plastic Jell-O cups of shrimp cocktail.

If there's a hell, it smells like suntan lotion and sweaty Benetton cotton, and tastes like warm Coke; it sounds like easy listening and urgent whispers; it feels like being X-rayed, radioactive stares penetrating baggy clothes to the naked flesh beneath. I could feel myself mutating; I was the hideous swamp monster come to crash the soiree, and the Lacey in me wanted to play the part, tear a swath of destruction, give them a reason to stare.

Instead, I drifted toward the closest thing to a safe harbor: Jenna Sterling, Conny Morazan, and Kelly Cho, who styled themselves so aggressively as the Three Musketeers that they'd dressed the part every Halloween since they'd met. They were a self-contained unit, occasionally glomming in lockstep onto creatures a little higher up the food chain but never breaking formation. Jenna, with her Barbie hair and chunky field hockey legs, had once cried when forced to partner with me on some fourth-grade math project—memorably demonstrating the concept of remainders. Able lieutenant Conny was an expert at completing Jenna's sentences when Jenna found herself unable, which was often. And then there was Kelly, who'd appeared in second grade, still learning the English for *recess* and *blackboard* and *weirdo*, suffering the boys who pulled their eyes into slits and spoke in nonsense syllables they called Karate Kid Chinese even after she reminded them, yet again, that she was Korean. Somewhere along the way she'd lost the accent and the baby fat, and now was the only one of the three to consistently have a boyfriend, even if it was usually some youth group kid she'd picked up at church.

They hadn't been at the foreclosure party; girls like these didn't go to parties like those. Whatever they'd heard afterward, they hadn't *seen* it happen.

I'd never quite mastered the art of joining a conversation

in progress, so I stood there creeping on their huddle, waiting for one of them to acknowledge my existence.

"So where did she go, anyway?"

It took me a beat too long to realize the question was directed at me. "Who?"

"She probably has no clue," Jenna said. "She's like ..."

"Clueless," Conny offered, and Jenna nodded her assent.

"So do you or don't you?" Kelly said.

"What do you think?" I said, with a tone that suggested *duh*, of course I did.

Result: eagerness. "So? Where?"

"Juvie, right?" Jenna had a wholesome midwestern look I'd never trusted. She was the kind of girl who brought her field hockey stick to class and experimented with Body Shop perfume combinations until she found the one that made her smell most like apple pie.

Conny snorted. "Mental institution, more like."

"New York City, that's where they all go," Kelly said.

"They who?" I asked.

"You know ..." Less confident now. "Girls like Lacey. Who ..."

" ... run away," Conny supplied. "Like in *Pretty Woman.*"

"*Pretty Woman* is about LA." Nikki had suddenly materialized by my shoulder in her witchy way. "And I highly doubt Lacey ran away to be a prostitute." She hooked a finger around one of my belt loops and tugged me away from the Musketeers. "Hannah Dexter. You want to get out of here?"

It took me a moment to realize this was an invitation, not a command—or maybe that's just a convenient excuse for why, instead of coming up with a clever retort or giving her the finger, I said yes.

I don't know why my mother insists on this crap," Nikki said, monologuing us through the woods. Complaints about finger food and her mother's friends led to the laundry list of adventures for which all Nikki's actual friends had abandoned her: tennis camp, arts camp, Jewish camp, Allie Cantor on a teen tour of the Grand Canyon, Kaitlyn Dyer shopping (and doubtless fucking) her way across the Continent, less Virginia Woolf, more Fergie. (It destabilized my world to hear Nikki Drummond reference Virginia Woolf.) She complained about the humidity and the gnat swarms, the creepy pool cleaner whose gaze always lingered one second too long, the hassle of shaving her bikini line, the tedium of reruns, the gall of her parents to refuse to pay for call-waiting on her personal line. She whined and sipped from an airplane bottle of something brown and illicit, and seemed not nearly as concerned as she should have been about what I might do to her in the woods.

The trees closed around us, dark and lush and whispering. The afternoon had taken on a fairy-tale inexorability: The witch told me where to go, and like a child lost in the woods, I followed. Until, finally, she stopped—walking and talking both, and it hadn't occurred to me that the endless stream of complaint might indicate some jangling of nerves until she abruptly fell silent.

We'd paused at the edge of a clearing, its center occupied by a sagging structure, its walls crayoned with black hearts and bubbled tags, its windows jagged black holes. A few yards away, a rusting freight car tilted on bare axles twisted with weeds, like some ancient mechanical beast had crawled into the forest to die. It was no gingerbread house, but it still felt enchanted.

I knew about the old train station, of course. Everyone did. It had been abandoned since the seventies, and whatever cozy charm the architect had been aiming for with its sculpted iron railings and gabled roof was long lost to history and the encroaching woods. Somewhere in the darkness below the platform were broken and weedy tracks, and rumor had it that there were people living down there, storybook hobos who warmed themselves over trash fires and stabbed one another with iron nails. The station loomed large in Battle Creek childhoods, a landmark for bored and daring kids, easy initiation ritual for secret clubs: Brave the haunted station, return with a talisman, a sliver of glass or torn condom wrapper. Try not to get hepatitis. It was a place of possibility, the threat of shadows or even sentience, like the slouching station might be keeping counsel of its own. It was the kind of sacred place Lacey might have tried to make ours, if not for her thing about the woods.

A trench cut through the clearing, bent and broken track unspooling along its base like a canyon river, and Nikki settled onto its bank, dangling her feet over the edge. "This is where he died, you know."

It didn't exactly make the place feel less haunted.

"That's what they say," she added. "They didn't want to make it public, that this was the place. In case freaks wanted to turn it into some kind of shrine. Or do some copycat thing. But they told me. Obviously."

I didn't know Craig at all, not really, except that I'd known him for sixteen years and knew plenty: that he could burp the alphabet, that he could fit four Legos up his nose, that he'd once cried when he fell off the seesaw and broke his arm. He was a fixture, like the condemned church on Walnut Street I walked past every day for years, never wondering what was inside, until the day it burned down. That was Craig's absence, for me: a vacant lot where one shouldn't have been.

Impossible not to imagine him sitting in the shadow of this abandoned husk, pondering the desiccation of the past, reading existential doom into the graffitied dictates: *fuck ronda*, *suck my cock*. Impossible not to imagine him bloody and still, rotting into the dirt.

It belonged to Nikki now, this place. He'd claimed it for her.

"Your boyfriend killing himself doesn't automatically make you a good person," I said, because it hurt to feel sorry for her.

She looked like she'd had that thought before. "It's funny, isn't it? Because you'd kind of think it would." She offered me the bottle, but I waved it away. I knew what to do when the witch offered you a bite of her apple.

Nikki downed the rest in a single swallow, then fired the bottle into the trench. There was something immensely satisfying in its shatter. She swung her legs back and forth. Somewhere, birds sang. A mosquito lit on my knee, and Nikki slapped it away. She left behind a slick of sweat, which surprised me. The Nikki Drummonds of the world weren't supposed to perspire.

"I don't lie to people here," she said. "So maybe you'll believe me this time. I'm not the enemy. There is no enemy."

"Why do you care so much if I believe you?"

She shrugged. "I thought it was weird, too."

The witch builds her house out of candy to charm stupid children, I reminded myself.

"I can help you fix it, you know," she said.

"Fix what?"

"Well, for one, your sullied reputation. For another ... " She flung her hands in my general direction, as if to suggest *your essential Hannah Dexter–ness.*

"What makes you think I need to be fixed?"

"Do you really want me to answer that?"

"And why would you want to make me your project?"

"Maybe I'm bored." She was looking at her feet, pointing and flexing them together, like we used to do in gymnastics at the Y. "Maybe I'm tired."

"Of summer?"

"Of pretending not to be a bitch," she said. "You've obviously already decided I am. It's relaxing."

"You must think I'm pretty stupid," I said, and maybe I was, because at her admission I felt a strange tingle of something adjacent to pride.

She shrugged again, which I took as a yes. "I don't beg. Come to the mall with me tomorrow. Let the idiots see you not caring what they think. Let them see you with me. It'll help."

"Come to the *mall* with you? Are you high?"

"Marissa is cheating on Austin with Gary Peck. She lets him finger her in the chem lab after school."

Marissa Mackie and Austin Schnitzler had been a couple since junior high and had been Craig and Nikki's prime competition for every sweetheart-related yearbook superlative, not to mention my own personal Most Likely to Make You Vomit. Even money had them engaged within a few months of graduation, earlier if the condom broke. "How do you know?"

"Because people tell me things."

"And why are you telling me?"

"So you'll trust me."

"I'll trust you because you're spreading gossip—"

"It's not gossip if it's true."

"Okay, so your logic is, I'll think you're trustworthy because you're sharing your best friend's darkest secret with your worst enemy?"

"Number one, she's not my best friend. Number two, she has much darker secrets. Number three, you're seriously underestimating my pool of enemies."

"God, you really are a bitch, aren't you?"

Nikki stood. "I told you, I don't beg. Take it or leave it, your call."

"You're absolute crap at being nice, you know that?"

There was something different about her laugh, here, something light and sunny, and it felt good.

"You'll have to pick me up. I don't have a license."

"We'll take care of that, too." This time her laugh was more a cackle. "I do love a project."

I felt that tug of inevitability again, some profound sense that life had come unstuck.

"I have to get back, or my mother will freak," she said. "But you can stay, if you want. Cut straight through on the other side of the station and your place is only about a mile. I'll tell your mom you got sick and I gave you a ride home."

It was less a suggestion than an order. "Nikki—" I didn't turn to face her. I couldn't. "Before you go . . ."

"Yeah?"

It would be so easy for all those storybook heroes to avoid adventure, to save themselves from the sorry fate of leading an interesting life. Don't lean over the well; don't rub the magic lamp. When the voice calls to you from the dark, don't listen.

Don't go into the woods.

"What's the deal with you and Lacey?"

She paused just long enough to make me nervous. "Maybe we were lovers, Hannah." She lingered on the operative word, opening her jaw so wide I could see her tongue pry the *l* from the roof of her mouth. "Hot 'n' heavy lesbo action, and you're just some pawn in our lovers' quarrel. Ever think of that?"

It was like she was too lazy to make an actual joke. She might as well have said *insert crass bullshit here, and fuck you very much for asking.*

"Whatever, Nikki."

"I'm turning over a new leaf. It's called, who gives a fuck about the past? The real issue is *you* and Lacey."

"And what issue is that?"

"I already told you. She was shitty to you. And for you. It was painful to watch."

"Who asked you to watch?"

It was the wrong answer. I should have defended Lacey, and then it was too late.

"Why would she let you get so drunk that night, then leave you there on your own? What kind of 'best friend' does that?" She squeezed her fingers around the phrase.

"I don't need a babysitter."

"She was shit to you that night, and she's been shit all along. It's a power trip for her, you get that, right? Making you think you need her? Poor little Dex, alone and helpless, with big strong Lacey to teach her how life works. You were the only one who couldn't see it."

"Fuck you, Nikki."

"Say I'm wrong. She's the best friend a girl could have. So where is she? You're having the worst fucking time of your life, and she abandons you to go throw her panties at Nirvana? You're lucky, Hannah. She would have ruined you. That's what she does. I'm sorry, but that's the truth."

"Go back to your party, Nikki."

She left me alone in the woods to think through her bullshit, or ignore it and imagine all the people who must have passed through the station back when the trains still chugged through Battle Creek: businessmen in fedoras or smutty-cheeked coal miners or grinning teenagers riding off to war, everyone on the way to somewhere else, waving at the sorry town rooted in its place, and I did my best to imagine all of it, until it got dark and I got tired of being alone.

The mall. Lacey and I never went to the mall, which was thirty minutes down the highway, bedecked with bright red and blue banners over the entrances, like a Renaissance faire sponsored by Macy's and Toys "R" Us. The mall, Lacey said, was brain death. A lobotomy built of fake brass and linoleum. Drones and plebes embalming themselves with fro-yo, middle-aged creepers buying "neck massagers" at the Sharper Image. Lacey believed in small stores tucked into forgotten spaces: attics, garages, a basement where we probably would have been murdered if the guy's bong hadn't set off his smoke detector. The chain stores lining the mall were a colonizing force, Lacey said, infecting the populace with bacteria that would breed and spread. The more people were alike, the more alike they'd want to be. Conformity was a drug, the mall its sidewalk pusher, red eyed and greasy and promising you there was no harm in just a taste.

At the mall, the fro-yo tasted like vanilla-scented shampoo. At the mall they played instrumental versions of Madonna and girls danced along, using moves they'd gleaned from MTV. There were cookies the size of my head and pretzels with chocolate dipping sauce and cream cheese frosting. There was a carousel in the center, where children screamed in circles and bored fathers pretended to watch. Armored knights guarded the exits, fending off toddlers who clung to their shiny limbs. There was a booth selling "mead" at the food court, and beside it a table of scruffy lacrosse guys smashing pizza into gaping maws—"gross but cute," said Nikki.

There was a fountain sparkling with coins. I threw in a penny and didn't wish for Lacey.

I watched Nikki try on long flowered skirts and denim vests, but I refused the pastels she shoved at me. "I don't care what other people think," I said. "I dress for myself."

"I guess it's just a coincidence, then, that you dress exactly like Lacey. The goth Sweet Valley twins."

"We wear what we want," I said. Present tense. Like grammar could shape reality. "Not some kind of"—I dangled a tank top off my finger, its lace threaded with shimmering silver, the delicate sheath suggesting a fragility Nikki might sometimes want to project but never embody—"costume."

Nikki rolled her eyes, slipped on the tank top, and somehow, with a shift of her shoulders and a calculated tilt of the head, became someone brand-new, sweet as the orange-blossom perfume she'd spritzed on us both.

"Sorry, I forgot—those hideous boots are an expression of your soul. And just happen to also be an expression of Lacey's soul, and the souls of every other grunge-girl wannabe Mrs. Cobain. One big flannel-covered coincidence." She'd produced a vintage silver flask at lunch, the kind of beautifully beat-up artifact Lacey would have loved, and added some vodka to her Diet Dr Pepper, which had buzzed her straight into lecture mode. "By this time next year, half of Battle Creek's going to be walking around in your stupid flannel shirts, I guarantee it." She thrust one of her discards at me, a sky blue cashmere sweater I could never afford, even if I might someday decide I wanted to wear something that feminine—something that brought out my eyes, as she pointed out. "Everything's a costume, Hannah. At least be smart enough to know it."

The sweater was whisper soft, and it fit perfectly. I didn't have to tilt my head or shift my posture; between the fairy-tale blue and the cherry-pink gloss Nikki had smeared across my lips with her thumb, I looked like a brand-new person, too.

I didn't remind her to call me Dex, and she didn't bring up Lacey for the rest of the day. We stuck to safe spaces: the many ways our mothers embarrassed us, which of the *Dead Poets Society* boys we'd prefer and in what order, whether the incentive of a real-life Patrick Swayze could teach anyone to dance like Jennifer Grey, whether our ninth-grade biology teacher was sleeping with the principal, whether returning to Battle Creek after college and for the rest of agonizing life should count as tragedy or farce.

It was fun. That was the surprise of it, and the shame. We didn't excavate the truths of the universe or make a political statement; we did nothing daring or difficult. We simply had fun. *She* was fun.

All day, I waited for the punch line, but there were only

L'Oréal counter makeovers and Express denim sales and an hour of hysteria squeezing ourselves into wedding-cake formal dresses, the more rhinestoned, the better. There was a turn in the Sharper Image massage chairs, and a shared pack of chocolate SnackWell's in the car on the way home. It was inexplicable and impossible, and then, with that weird summer temporal distortion where one day seems like ten and a week is enough to turn any alien addition into the familiar furniture of life, it was routine.

I got to know her house and its ways. I stopped waiting for her agenda to emerge.

We spent most of our days outside, floating the pool on inflatable rafts, letting the sun crisp our backs and splashing water at Benetton, Nikki's Labrador retriever. That was what I learned best from Nikki that summer: how to float. To stop drowning, she taught me, I only had to stop fighting. I only had to lie back and decide that no dark shapes swam beneath the surface, that nothing with sharp teeth and insatiable hunger was lurking in the fathomless depths. In the world according to Nikki, there were no depths.

I was already empty; Nikki taught me it was safest to stay that way. That if I pretended hard enough nothing was waiting to claim me, nothing ever would.

She played with my hair and vetoed chunks of wardrobe; one sticky afternoon she brought me to the elementary school parking lot and taught me how to drive. She still refused to call me Dex. "Your name is Hannah," she said. "Who lets some stranger give them a new name? It would be one thing if *you* didn't like it. But seriously, to decide to be someone new just because some weirdo tells you to?"

I did like my name—that was the thing of it. I'd forgotten that: I hadn't known there was anything wrong with Hannah until Lacey told me so.

Nikki was too careful to talk about Lacey. Instead she talked around her, let me creep to my own conclusions. "I don't know why you listen to this shit when you obviously don't even like it," she said when I fast-forwarded through one too many Nirvana songs.

"Of course it matters what people think of you," she said when I told her I didn't need her help repairing my reputation, that my reputation was irrelevant. "Anyone who tells you different is trying to screw you."

"Some people can't help being freaks, so they'll try to drag you into freakhood with them," she said, thrusting an armful of hand-me-downs at me. "But you're different. You've got options."

She talked about herself, and maybe that was the thing that slowly suckered me into trusting her. She was bored, she told me, not just with Battle Creek and her friends and her dysfunctional parents and her perfect brother with his dull college girlfriend and obedient premed life, but with herself, too, with waking up every morning to perform "Nikki Drummond."

"You have no fucking idea, Hannah," she said, in the middle of a rant about the girls who assumed themselves adored members of her royal court. "When I say *shallow*, I don't mean like a sandbar. I mean like a puddle."

"*They're* shallow?" I said, with a pointed look at the issue of *Seventeen* in her lap. She'd just spent the last thirty-seven minutes gaming the "Who's Your Perfect Beach Boyfriend?" quiz to ensure she scored high enough to match with "Golden God."

She threw it at me. "Of course I'm fucking shallow. But I *know* it, that's the difference. Like I know that reading Nietzsche doesn't make you deep."

She pronounced his name correctly, almost pretentiously, with the same faux German accent Lacey had used.

"Everything is crap," Nikki said. "It's the people who don't get it that tire me—the ones who think anything fucking matters, whether it's their nail polish color or the meaning of the fucking universe."

She was buzzed. Nikki, I understood by then, was always just a little buzzed. I'd seen enough Lifetime movies to know this was not a good thing. She talked about having power over people, how it was dull but necessary, because the only other option was letting people have power over you. Sometimes she even talked about Craig.

We did this only when we went to the train station, which we did only when she was in a very particular mood. I didn't like it there. They hadn't told her exactly where they'd found the body, she said, whether it was on the tracks or in the old station office or hanging half in and half out of the boxcar, as if he'd tried at the last minute to flee from himself. We might have been sitting on grass that had been flattened by his body and fed with his blood. I didn't believe in ghosts—even as a child eager to believe in anything, I never had—but I believed in the power of place, and who was to say there wasn't something about the old station, something so sad about the sound of the wind rattling through its broken windows that it had infected Craig, attuned him to his own pain? It was the kind of place that whispered.

Nikki said it hurt to be there, but that sometimes pain was good.

"I miss him," she said once, dangling her legs over the tracks, picking at the dirt under her nails. "I didn't even like him that much, and I fucking miss him. All the time."

I'd learned not to say *I'm sorry*, because it only made her mad. "He should be sorry," she always said. "Plenty of people should be sorry. Not you."

Once she lay down along the edge with her head in my lap, and said that maybe she was to blame. Her hair was softer than I'd imagined. I brushed her bangs off her forehead, smoothed them back. The roots were coming in, dirt brown. I wondered when her hair had gone so dark, whether it had ever really been the color of the sun, or if that was just how I'd needed to remember it.

"Don't be a narcissist," I said. She liked that.

"Do you worry you'll never love anyone again?" I asked her.

"Yes," she said. But then, "I didn't, though. Love him. I thought I did, and then I knew better."

"What happened?" I meant, what happened to make her see, but I meant more than that, too. Like everyone, I wanted to know what happened to make him walk into the woods, what made him bring the gun—and, if she didn't have the answers, I wanted to know how could she stand it, the certainty she never would.

"Did you know that until Allie was seven years old, her mother lied and told her that carob was actually chocolate?" she said. "This poor kid, for years her mother's shoveling this health food crap in her mouth and calling it chocolate, and she's wondering why the whole world makes such a big deal out of something so disgusting. And then you know what happened?"

I shook my head.

"Some babysitter didn't get the memo and brings over some ice cream and a bottle of chocolate syrup. Allie gets one taste and goes fucking nuts. She got up in the middle of the night and drank the whole thing. I think they had to pump her stomach."

"Moral of the story, don't lie to your kids?"

"Who the fuck cares what the moral of the story is? The point is, it's not like she could go back to carob after that, could she? But her mother wasn't about to let her have chocolate again. She was fucked."

Nikki wouldn't say any more, and I was left to use my imagination: What was her chocolate? Some college guy, a friend of her brother's visiting for the weekend? Something more illicit, perhaps—a teacher? A friend of her father's?

Someone who'd given her a taste of something she couldn't have again and couldn't forget. Whoever he was, he was gone: She hadn't dated anyone seriously since Craig had died, never seemed to evince a moment of interest, though it occurred to me that was her way of punishing herself.

Maybe she knew exactly why he did it; maybe the worst of the rumors were true, that he'd done it for her, because of her. It would be better never to know, I thought, than to know something like that.

Instead, she occupied herself with imaginary boyfriends: Luke Perry, Johnny Depp, and Keanu Reeves, whose future wedding she had already imagined in great detail, right down to what she'd be wearing as his bride—not that he would give a shit, because he clearly didn't give a shit about anything. Which, Nikki said, was the key to his appeal.

"Not my type," I admitted, and she shrugged. But imaginary worked for me, too. I'd scrubbed away those words on my skin, but it felt like the ink was in my blood. Never again: I would be a fortress now, impermeable. I contented myself with the Dead Poets boys, sweet and lyrical and easily cowed, and River Phoenix, the kind of boy who would light candles and read you poetry, who would kiss you softly on the lips and then let the night fade to black, who was never angry, only sad, who cared about the earth and refused to eat animals and eschewed drugs and had such lonely eyes.

Then Nikki made me watch *My Own Private Idaho*, and there was my River alongside her Keanu, the two of them sky-high on heroin and fucking for cash, and so much for that.

"I thought you'd like it," she said, halfheartedly, not even trying to disguise the fact that she'd done it on purpose, that she knew it would screw with my head and River-besotted heart, and because I knew, and she knew I knew, somehow that made it all right. I could even laugh.

It wasn't the same, the two of us. There were no midnight dances in the rain, none of those heart-thumping moments when the tide of wildness washed in and I loosed my grip enough to be swept away. But it gave me an excuse to leave the house, and a heated pool.

"Probably I shouldn't," Nikki said one afternoon as we paddled our rafts back and forth across the water. I was wearing a new bikini, courtesy of my mother, who was so happy with the new state of Drummond-related affairs—and her own burgeoning acquaintanceship with Nikki's mother—that she'd been ready to buy out the store. Blood money, I thought, as she passed the credit card to the cashier. My very own thirty pieces of silver, complete with pink stitching and push-up cups. Too bad: I liked how the suit glowed against my tan, and the cloud of chlorine that clung to me through the day, my hair as crispy as my skin.

"Shouldn't what?"

Nikki liked to start conversations in the middle, after she'd already hashed them out in her mind, which made it difficult to know whether I'd zoned out or she'd only just started speaking.

"Cut my bangs like that girl on *The Real World*. You know?"

"Not really."

"You know. *Becky.*"

"I don't have cable."

She bolted upright. "Wait, seriously?"

"Seriously."

We spent the rest of that day in her air-conditioned basement watching *Real World* tapes on her big-screen TV. Nikki had every episode, carefully labeled, and we watched them all, straight through for six hours, until I felt like I, too, was living in a house, having my life taped, no longer being polite but starting to get real. The next day we started again, and the rest of August unspooled to the sounds of Julie's cackle, Kevin's rants, Eric's Jersey-boy bravado, Heather B.'s hip-hop rhyme.

"Imagine if we all stopped pretending there was such a thing as *getting real*," Nikki said. "Imagine the fucking relief."

Real World housemates were required to lock themselves in a closet and spill their secrets into a camera and—miraculously, as if they assumed no one would ever watch—they did.

"Let's do it," Nikki said, and I could see it sparking in her, the flare of an idea that demanded action. It was the one thing she and Lacey had in common, and the thing I most envied about them both.

"I'm not telling you my deepest secrets," I said. "I'm certainly not *recording* them."

"No, we won't be us, we'll be them," she said. We would put on a show, play their parts. It would be practice for her future audition tape; it would be fun.

Her father had a video camera and a tripod. Nikki played Becky with her pointy cardboard boobs and then Eric, with his Guido swagger. I took on Andre and his flannel angst, lounging on the leather couch, gazing at the ceiling, all *woe is me* and *why, God, why*. "The world is pain," I said, in my druggy Andre voice, while Nikki manned the camera and cheered me on, "but, like, the music, yeah, when it, like, pours out of me, man, that's just, you know, that's like my soul on the wind."

Nikki laughed. "I thought you were doing Andre, not Lacey."

Even then, even when it hurt, she was right: It was fun.

I learned to pretend away almost everything, but I couldn't will September out of existence. Summer ended without my permission. I went back to school—I put on a show.

Nikki and I didn't associate with each other publicly; this was an unspoken mutual agreement. But she'd taught me how to perform, and I performed for her. Summer was long, but not long enough for people to forget what had happened. They all looked at me too hard, and I knew what they saw: spotty nipples, tiny sprouts of hair, secret stretches of skin. Boys, especially, watched me like they knew my function and were waiting for me to figure it out. I knew how to act like I didn't care, and if I could be all surface, no depth, then the act would be all that mattered. I would not drown.

It was almost a relief, no longer having to be extraordinary.

To give up on existential questioning and simply abide. To give up on Dex; to be dull, to live a small, safe life.

I went to school. I went home. I slurped spaghetti with my family and tuned out my mother. Funny how she'd been so concerned with my first transformation but was so content with the second; there were no more speeches advising me against losing myself. Maybe some long-dormant maternal instinct kicked in, and she understood that I'd already lost too much to risk giving more away. I learned how not to look at my father. He kept offering to treat me to a movie; I took him up on it only once, for a midnight showing of *Honeymoon in Vegas* that had been sold out for weeks and which my mother had given me special dispensation to see, under my father's guidance of course. Not since Lacey had I been out so late, and I'd missed the quiet of the sleeping town and its stars. My father bought popcorn and settled in beside me, and we sat in silence until the Elvises flew and the credits rolled.

He leaned toward me, awkwardly, like a bad date priming to make his move. "No word from Lacey, kid?" Unlike my mother, my father couldn't stand Nikki.

I shook my head.

"Huh." He cleared his throat. "So that's it."

It had been twenty-two days since I'd last biked past her house, searching her window for signs of life. "Yep. That's it."

He sighed and stretched back, kicking his legs up on the empty seat in front of him. "I love it here, don't you?"

"My shoes are sticking to the floor."

"It's not because of the movie, you know? I dunno—maybe

it's just the dark. Two hours, nothing to do but sit here, let the world settle over you."

You spend your whole life sitting in the dark doing nothing, I could have said. I'd always assumed he loved his sunglasses for how they made him look, but maybe they just gave him a place to hide.

A week later, having survived another school day and a long stretch of homework in the library—anywhere was better than home—I biked home through twilight drizzle, feeling, in the surge of wind and adrenaline, that this was manageable, these two-hundred-some days to be endured before the rest of my life.

I dropped the bike in the driveway and was about to head inside when the horn blasted. I turned to see a car idling at the curb, its high beams flashing an SOS. The horn sounded again, impatient, and the passenger door swung open. Kurt's voice scratched at the night.

Lacey was home.

LACEY

Smells Like Teen Spirit

It took me months to stop thinking about her lips. I liked them smiling, pussy pink and quirked at the corners, but I liked them every way. Pouting. Sucking. Trembling. I told her that the flask made me think of her, spun her some bullshit about flappers and daring girls sucking the marrow out of life, but—truth? I just wanted to see those lips pursed around the silver spout.

That's the kind of thing that came back to me in all those dead hours staring at Jesus, pretending to pray: things I was meant to have forgotten, Nikki's lips and Craig's dead eyes and a canopy of leaves the color of blood and fire. Horizons had no horizon. Some girls got sent home after a couple weeks; others were stuck there for years. Your golden ticket: a letter home saying that Jesus had finally turned the bad seed good. No one knew how you got it. There were demerits and credits and an impenetrable algorithm ranking us on a hierarchy of salvation, but nothing to suggest that surviving one day got you closer to anything but more of the same.

I didn't think about the future. I refused the past, pink lips and the smell of gunpowder. I thought about you.

My own version of prayer, my own religion. The church of Dex and Lacey. Where the only true sin is faithlessness. I would have faith you could forgive me. I knew I could forgive you anything.

They were big on forgiveness at Horizons. Disclosure of past sins was mandatory, the bigger, the better, so we amped them up. The Screamer's occasional toke became a drug addiction; the Skank's ill-advised habit of masturbating to her father's *Soldier of Fortune* collection became oedipal lust; even the time Saint Ann kissed some nerd in her church group so he'd help her with her chemistry homework was a gateway to prostitution. The Sodomite's sins were self-explanatory, and every time she confessed to fantasizing about one of us stripping naked in the outdoor shower, they assigned her to wood-chipper duty and an extra hour of praying away the gay. Imagine if they knew what I'd done in the woods. How good it had felt.

It was fun watching them pretzel-twist themselves trying to forgive our imagined pasts. That was Shawn's mandate: We were all equal here. We were all, once we'd dipped ourselves in the lake and sworn our fealty to God and country and Shawn, *cleansed.*

You tell me, Dex, what kind of a bullshit god doesn't care

what you did or who you hurt as long as you say you're sorry?

Forgiveness for the mistakes of the past, revenge for the trespasses of the present: That was the Horizons way. When you got toilet-toothbrush duty for giving your counselor the finger, or solitary for trying to lubricate your unit with laxatives in the pudding, that wasn't punishment; it was *correction*. Curtsy and say thank you, lest you be corrected some more.

It got easier once I found ways to correct myself. Digging into my wrist scar with a paper clip, just a little—that was enough to clear my head. They wanted us fuzzy. *Pliable.* That's what the skimpy rations and the middle-of-the-night prayer calls were all about. The hours of verse memorization, the time in the dark place—it was CIA-brand torture. Survival was a matter of maintaining control, staying steady.

That's why, about three weeks in, I threw out my pills.

I almost went crazy, in there, without them, until I came up with the game. Or maybe the game *was* me going crazy. Either way, it worked. At Horizons, the devil was everywhere. Any time you cursed, lusted, cried yourself to sleep, forgot to ask permission before taking seconds at dinner, that was the devil getting his claws in you. So I figured, they want it so badly, let 'em have it. Something real to hate. Something to fear: me.

The next time they asked us for confessions, I gave them one to remember. "I killed a boy, once," I said. The Skank and the Sodomite leaned close, like they knew this one was going to be good, even before the punch line: "I fucked him to death."

I'd get it from Heather for that one, later; we all would, the punishment of the one visited on the many, the righteous burning alongside the sinners. But confessions were sacrosanct. Call it my Scheherazade moment, Dex, because I did it to save my own life. "Not literally, of course," I continued, "but it was the fucking that got him into the woods, and kept him there once he realized what we were all about. A boy like him should have run screaming in the other direction once he saw the altar, the poor little cat, the knife. Nice boys like that don't mess with the devil."

The Skank snickered. She would know.

I told them of a sacred clearing where moonlight glinted off shining bark and the scent of mossy earth mingled with sweat and breath and blood. I told them that we whispered terrible oaths, promises to each other and to a dark lord, that we invoked the forces of earth and sky and claimed dominion over the natural world, that we raised storms and whirled madly in the lightning. I told them that we'd needed more power and more blood and an ultimate sacrifice, and so I had played the serpent, slithered into a boy's life and let him slip inside me until he lost all reason and became my plaything, until I could loop a delicate finger around his belt buckle and draw him into the woods, where the girls and I were so hungry, had waited so long, would finally wait no longer to feed.

In the hush after I'd finished speaking, they all tried very hard to laugh, and I tried not to. They pretended not to believe me. Heather aborted the confessional and we spent the rest of the day in the sun, holding buckets of water—which, I know, doesn't exactly sound like the Spanish Inquisition, but don't try this at home. After about an hour it feels like your arms are going to fall off. Then, in the late-summer heat, the thirst kicks in, and your head goes all foggy, black dots creeping across your vision, and still, your hands sweaty and raw, you hold tight, because you know if you let go they'll toss you in the dark place until God knows when. We lasted long enough for Heather—who got off on torture in the name of the Lord—to giggle through *la petite mort*, and for three of us to pass out.

They treated me differently after that. I *felt* different, too. Like I really had fucked a boy to death, and was not sorry.

The rest was easy. I'd read Satan's bible; I knew what to do. A few stupid made-up prayers to the Dark One, some bloody pentagrams on the floor, a lot of crap about how my Lord would rain fire and darkness down upon the whole operation. One afternoon I spotted a dying squirrel writhing in the gutter outside our cabin. It was dead by the time I snuck out in the night to retrieve it, and I'll spare your delicate ears the details. Blood is blood, even if you have to dig your hands into some matted fur and rotting innards to get at it. Once I speared the squirrel with the stick, it was almost like using a paintbrush. No one woke up, not even Heather, when I painted the sign of the Antichrist over her bed, then left the squirrel on her pillow.

The way they all looked at me then, Dex—the girls, the

counselors, even Shawn. Like I was dangerous. Not troubled, just trouble. Eve and Lilith, the serpent in the grass. Down in the dark place I chanted imaginary prayers; in the depths of night I whispered in the girls' ears: the things I would do to them, the things I knew their dark hearts had done.

I promised them we would be prisoners here forever, that Horizons was our birth and death, that as long as I lived among them, the devil would have a home. *Blessed are the destroyers of false hope, for they are the true Messiahs.* This is what *the Satanic Bible* teaches, and this much is true.

Maybe it was the game. Maybe it was something in me that woke up when I stopped taking the pills, opening my mouth pink and wide for inspection every morning, mother's little helper nestled safely in fleshy cheek. Who the fuck knows, maybe it was the devil himself. It's not the why of it that matters; it's the what: It's the dreams.

I dreamed of animals eating my face.

I dreamed of the woods, never lovely, only deep. Dead things rotting. I dreamed of a bird, with inky feathers and a smirking beak, talons perched on my breasts, pecking at my stomach, ripping into my intestines, digging out the thing they call a womb.

I dreamed of a man. He climbed through the bunk's window, slid into my bed, and he held me, and I was a child, but I was not afraid.

Or I was afraid, and I screamed, and he laid his heavy hand

across my mouth and his body across my body and had his way in the dark.

He wore your father's face, or mine; he wore the Bastard's face; he wore Kurt's face, and this was how I liked him best. He was always the same man.

He was no man at all.

I told him what I'd done and what I wanted to do. He told me sleep is where you find the people you've lost, and where the dead come home to you.

In your dreams, it's easy to be a god.

When he wore the face I liked, the Kurt face, I liked to touch the hair, blond as a child's. His eyes were blue like the plastic stone on a gumball-machine ring. I liked to lean my cheek against his stubble. He said I would hurt less if someone else hurt, too, and that I already knew. It was safe to want that; it was safe to want anything, in a dream.

I dreamed of death.

I dreamed of maggots crawling out of Craig's hollow eye sockets, feeding on the raw meat of his brain. I tasted metal in my mouth and felt my finger twitch. I saw three bodies in the dirt, three holes, blood pooling together as it sank into the earth.

I dreamed of things that could have been. Some nights, I dreamed what was. The weight of his body when it went limp on mine, the seconds that passed as the skin cooled, as time did not reverse itself and the rupture in his skull did not heal.

In my dreams, the man with the blue eyes and the angel skin told me I had power, and his voice was the kind that only told the truth. He asked what I wanted, and I said I wanted control, and I wanted pain for my enemies, and I wanted you.

Sometimes, as I was trying to fall asleep or trying not to, listening to the other girls dream, I remembered home and the people who'd driven me away from it. I counted the trespasses of mine enemies.

I made lists.

It's important to remember who your enemies are. What you would do to them if you could.

What would you do if you could do anything? What would you do in the dark if you knew you would never be seen?

What would I do if I got to go home?

Awake, I made lists; in my dreams, I crossed off names. I laid waste to my enemies.

His eyes were always watching.

They approved.

The girls wore pillowcases over their heads when they came for me. Moonlit ghosts closing me into a silent ring, pale arms reaching for me, cold fingers tugging back sheets, grasping for purchase on slick skin, pressing me down, holding me still, nails digging into flesh, hands clamping my jaw shut, teeth slicing tongue, the tang of blood dripping down my throat, and I blinked and writhed and thought foggily that I'd dreamed them into reality, that this was my coven, come to claim me for the dark. I was lofted in their arms and floating into the night before I grasped that the ghosts were watching me through eyeholes cut from cotton. Heather will seriously fuck them up for shredding those sheets, I thought, and that was how I understood: They no longer cared. Fear could no longer stop them.

Then my hands were tied together and my ankles lashed tight, and I was lying on my back in the mud, homemade Klan masks blotting out the stars. No one could exorcise what was inside me; that I was there, down on the ground beneath them, that they so desperately needed me frightened and weak was proof enough of that.

I made this happen, I thought.

I willed it to life with my words and my deeds, I transformed myself into a dangerous creature, and there was almost power in that, and almost comfort.

"O Lord, we beseech you, help us banish this evil," one of them intoned. I knew her by voice: Peppy, a beefy cheerleader from Harrisburg who'd been caught blowing her gym teacher and had about as much respect for the Lord as I did. "Devil, *be gone!*"

"We anoint thee with holy water," said someone who sounded suspiciously like the Skank.

With a ritualistic solemnity, she raised a plastic cup over my head and dumped warm piss all over my face.

"Amen," the others chorused. That part had clearly been rehearsed.

The rest they made up as they went along.

*

Alone and naked in the woods. Curled up against mud and bark, twitching at every whisper and crack of branches. Vision tunneled to the next second, and the one after that. Imagining red eyes in the dark. Waiting for someone to come back. Waiting for dawn.

Flies are drawn to the smell of pee and shit and blood. Mosquitos, too, and squirrels, and rats, and when your hands are tied together, you can't exactly wave them off. All you can do is scream.

A search party of counselors found me, eventually—it took all night and most of the next day, but then, who knows how hard they bothered to look.

They found me with shit smeared across my forehead and lips, with *EVIL* written across my breasts in my own dried blood, with stigmata cut into my palms and feet, sliced by the same scissors used to hack off my hair. The next morning, I signed something saying it never happened, and in return Horizons called and told the Bastard I'd turned over a new leaf, that I was shining with the light of the Lord. They sent me home.

I decided: It never happened. I would not allow it to have happened.

It was erased.

Still, everything leaves a stain.

And if there is such a thing as possession, if I really do have the devil in me, now you know who put it there.

DEX

Negative Creep

You getting in, or what?"

The car was the same; Lacey was different. Her hair had been cropped close to her scalp; from the uneven look of it, she'd done it herself. Her eyes were unlined, her nails flesh-colored. Lacey without makeup looked naked. She'd always been thin, but now she was skinny, almost gaunt, deep hollows carving her face into a skull. Her favorite dress, a blue-and-green-plaid baby doll, hung sack-like, and the leather jacket that had hugged her curves now gave her the look of a kid swimming in her father's coat. Even her voice sounded alien, maybe because it was nothing like the one I'd been ignoring in my head. That Lacey was reptilian cool. Lacey in the flesh was warm-blooded, sweat beading at her collarbone, fingers twitching against the dash. "Now or never, Dex."

I got in the car.

"You're back," I said.

"I'm back."

I hugged her, because it seemed the thing to do. She leaned in at the wrong time; our skulls clunked together. "Sorry," I said.

"Never apologize, remember?"

It had never been awkward between us.

"It's late," I said. "I should probably get inside. Maybe we can hang out tomorrow after school or something?"

Her voice flew to a simpering register. "Maybe we can hang out after school? Or *something*?" A weary sigh. "I thought I'd trained you better than that."

"I'm not your dog." It came out harsher than I meant it—I was the only one who flinched. I saw her see it in my face, the wish that I could take it back. Only then did she smile.

"Let's get out of here," she said.

I didn't argue. *How come you never get to decide anything?* Nikki would have asked. But deciding was what Lacey was for.

"I don't know where," she said, as if I'd asked. "Anywhere. Everywhere. Like we used to."

She rolled down the windows, turned up the volume, launched us into the night. Just like old times.

We went to the lake. Not our lake, but the swampy pond on the east side covered in a layer of algae and golf balls. Lacey had always treated its water as a personal affront.

"Here," she said, picking her way through the weeds to a rotting dock. There were no streetlights there, no moon behind the thinning summer clouds. Without the radio, there was nothing left to fill the space between us.

"You missed me," Lacey said.

"Of course I did."

"You've been counting the days until I came home, marking them on the wall in lipstick like a lovesick convict."

"Not lipstick. Blood."

"Naturally."

It was a game we played, narrating the story of me better than I could do it myself.

"I know you too well to ask," she'd said once. "It would be like asking my elbow, *How do* you *feel?*"

When something's a part of you, she told me, you just know. But I didn't; I had to squint through the dark, searching the shadows of her face, and ask. "Where were you?" Whatever the game, I'd lost. "Why come back?"

There was a plunking splash, then another. She'd kicked off her shoes, blue polka-dotted flip-flops we'd lifted from Woolworth's in the spring. Bare feet settled in my lap. "Don't you know, Dex?" It was strange to hear her say my name. "I'll always come back."

"But where did you go? Why?"

I stopped myself before I could say it: *Why did you leave without me?* Small victories.

The sound of a car streaking past, then another. That was how long it took her to answer.

"God, Dex, why do you think? The Bastard and his joke of a wife sent me away."

This was the one possibility that hadn't occurred to me. That she hadn't betrayed me. That I had betrayed her all the more by not, somehow, knowing it.

"They told me they didn't know where you went."

"Gosh, they *lied* to you? Shocking."

"Sent you away where?"

She snorted. "To the kind of place you send wayward daughters. Think of it as a Club Med. With extra Jesus."

Not Seattle, not New York, not starring in music videos or living on the streets but *this*. I waited to feel something.

"You're thinking, *Oh, no, Lacey, that's horrible! If only I had known, I would have come to rescue you*."

"Was it . . . was it bad?"

"Oh, Dex, your face." She circled my cheeks with her finger and squeezed. "It's adorable when you do that worried thing with your mouth."

I'd forgotten the sound of her laugh.

"You think the Bastard has the power to make me suffer? Please. It was a shitty summer camp with brainwashed sheep. Ten minutes and I was running the place."

"Good. I guess?"

"And you, Dex? What did you do on your summer vacation? Other than miss me desperately?"

I shrugged.

I wanted to tell her everything: the foreclosure party and its fallout, the strangeness of Nikki, the chill at home, my father and me and the space between. At least, I wanted to want to tell her.

"Normal summer," I said. "You know."

Lacey scooped up a clump of dirt and tossed it at the lake.

"Forget the past. Let's talk future. You ready to hear the plan?"

"What plan?"

"You've gotten so *slow*, Dex. We'll have to work on that. What were we doing back in June when we got so rudely interrupted? What was number one on our agenda?"

I shook my head.

"*Revenge*, Dex. Knock the bitch off her throne, pay her back for fucking with us. Who do you think tipped the Bastard off to my stash? Why do you think they sent me away in the first place?"

"I don't think Nikki did that. Would do that."

"You're fucking kidding me, right? It's exactly what she did to you. Now she pays."

"Can we just let it go, Lacey? Start fresh. Forget the past, like you said."

"You, queen of the grudge, want to forget the past?"

"Yeah."

"No."

"Yes. I do."

"No, you don't. *Yes, I do.* No you don't yes I do no you don't yes I do—" She stuck out her tongue. "We're not six, we don't need to play that game. And besides, you know I always win."

I remembered a particularly vicious episode of late-night Twister with vodka for stakes and lubrication. The more I drank, the more I lost, the more I lost, the more I drank. I remembered Lacey shoving the drinks into my hand, cheering me on.

"I don't want to talk about this anymore," I said.

"You can't let her scare you."

"She doesn't scare me. She . . ." To explain Nikki would be to explain what had come before. The long days after the party. The party itself, after Lacey left me alone. She would want details. She would want to peel back the surface, because Lacey only believed in what lay beneath. "She apologized. I accepted. It's over."

Lacey burst into laughter. "Fuck that. She *apologized*? I bet she promised never to screw with you again, cross her heart and hope to die?"

"Pretty much."

"You know who else made a lot of promises like that? Hitler."

"Come on, Lacey. Really?"

"I'm serious, Dex. It's historical fact, look it up. *Appeasement*. They were too chicken to do anything but kiss his ass. You know what happened then?"

"I'm on the edge of my seat."

"He invaded fucking Poland."

"Invoking Hitler isn't exactly the sign of a strong argument, Lacey. And I don't think Nikki Drummond is angling for Poland."

"You can't negotiate with evil."

It had been nice, that summer, not having so many enemies.

Lacey threaded her fingers through mine.

"You know why guys like to hold hands like that," she'd told me once. "Because it's *sex*ual." She drew out the word, like she always did, because she liked to watch me squirm. "Your fingers are basically having intercourse."

"Say it, Dex," she said now, squeezing. "You and me against the world. Everything like before."

"Sure."

We drove home without music. Lacey propped her bare foot on the seat and hung an arm out the window, steering with the fingertips of one hand.

"Pick you up tomorrow morning?" she said when the car stopped in front of my house. "We could drive to the ocean again, see some real water."

"I've got school tomorrow."

"Yeah, and?"

"And I can't cut."

"Because?"

"Because I can't. I've got a math test. And this ... other thing."

"What other thing?"

"I'm going to the mall after school, okay?"

"Whatever, let the mother-daughter fro-yo wait a day."

"It's not my mother—" I was almost tempted to say the name, see what she would do. "I said I'd go with some people, and I *want* to, okay? So I'm going."

There was a noise in the darkness, the sound of someone choking on her own spit. "Funny ha-ha."

"No. Seriously."

"Oh."

I wanted to touch her face, then lay my fingers against her lips and feel what shape they took in surprise.

"Are you coming back to school?" I asked, opening the door.

"Nothing better to do. They gave me a week or two to catch up." The words came slow. "Whatever. I can go to the beach myself. Maybe I'll send you a postcard."

"Fingers crossed."

She pulled the car away from the curb, then stopped and stuck her head out the window. It was still strange, that pale moon of a face without its curtain of black hair. "Hey, Dex, I almost forgot—"

"Yeah?" I was prepared. She would ask me for something, something I couldn't deliver and couldn't refuse. Or she would find the magic words that would bind us together again, some spell to fix what was broken. I would have waited there in the dark forever, except for the part of me that wanted to run.

"Tell your dad I say hello." Then she drove away.

That night, I expected to dream of Lacey. When it didn't happen, I woke up convinced she was gone. Run away for real this time, or banished back into my imagination, like some fairy-tale creature who, once refused, spirits herself away.

I went to school, did my homework, answered my parents

politely, didn't think about Lacey, didn't think about Lacey, didn't think about Lacey.

Sunday, Nikki invited me to church. I sat stiffly at her side, examining the fine grain of the pew while the minister explained about hell, counting the bulbs in the track lighting and trying to remember when it was time to stand up for Jesus. The Lord was a lot less interesting without magic mushrooms. Ladies fanning their Sunday finery, husbands jockeying for usher spots so they could sneak a smoke, ribboned and bow-tied kids who took a sickening pleasure in good behavior dodging spitballs from brats who didn't. The minister spoke on forgiveness, opening your heart to those who had wronged you, but he didn't say how.

There was a time, I thought, when I descended on a place like this as a god.

"There'll be wine at lunch after," Nikki whispered. "We can snag some if we're careful."

I was always careful.

Days passed without sign of Lacey, until I started to think I really had imagined her return. Then, one Monday after school, the Buick pulled into the bus lane and honked, one unrelenting blare of the horn that didn't let up until everyone on the lot had turned to stare.

Lacey poked her head out the window. "In."

Her room was different. The giant poster of Kurt was gone. Everything was gone.

"Spring cleaning." She shrugged. "I'm going for the monk thing."

She'd painted the walls black.

"The Bastard had a fit," she said.

Lacey sat on her bed. I sat on the floor, cross-legged, next to where she'd kept her tapes. They were gone, too. Everything she had left, she kept in her car. A handful of tapes in the glove compartment, everything else in the trunk. "You never know when you'll need a quick getaway."

I'd thought we would go on a drive; we always went on a drive. But Lacey wanted to show me something, she'd said. To tell me many things.

She smiled a fake Lacey smile. "So, how was the mall?"

"Fine. You know. The mall."

"I know you went with Nikki Drummond," she said.

"Are you following me?"

"I notice you're not denying it."

"No, I'm not."

"So, what? You two are friends or something now?"

I shrugged.

"Well, not officially friends, I'm guessing. Not in public, not at school, where people could see."

I didn't answer, but I didn't have to. She put on a real smile once we both concluded she'd won. And then, very quickly, it went away again. "Sorry," she said, and she never said that. "I heard some other crap, too. About that party last spring . . ."

"It's bullshit," I said quickly.

"You know I don't care what you did, Dex."

"I didn't *do* anything. People are fucking liars."

"Okay . . . but if someone did something to you, we can handle it. We'll—"

I needed it to stop. "If someone did something to *me*, I don't see how that's your problem."

"What is it? What did she say to you?" Lacey asked.

"Who?"

"You know who. The bitch. Nikki. She told you something about me. That's what this is."

"No, Lacey. There's no conspiracy."

"Whatever she told you, I can explain."

It was the wrong thing to say; it was an admission.

"Go ahead. Explain."

"First tell me what she said."

"Why don't *you* tell me what you think she said? Or, even better, the fucking truth."

"Language, Dex." She tried another smile. I didn't. "It's complicated."

Fix this, I willed her. *Before you can't.*

"She's using you to get at me," Lacey said. "Tell me you see that, at least."

"Because someone like her would never *actually* want to be friends with someone like me."

"It's not you, it's her! She uses everybody. It's how people like Nikki operate."

"Right. *People like Nikki.*"

"Believe whatever you want about me, Dex, but promise

me you won't believe her. She'll do whatever she can to hurt me."

"And why is that, Lacey? Why would she go to all that trouble?"

It took me a long time to understand that this expression on her face, the one that made her look like a stranger, was fear. "I can't tell you."

"Have you always thought I was this stupid?"

"Can't you just trust me, Dex? Please?"

That would have been so much easier—and so I did it; I tried.

"I see," she said, as if she did, and it hurt. "But you can trust *her*. If it's between me and her, you pick her."

I reminded myself it wasn't her fault that she'd left. That she'd molded me from wet clay, and it was law to honor thy creator. We were Dex and Lacey; we should have been beyond ultimatums. I didn't know how to explain that I didn't have to trust Nikki. That was the most appealing thing about her: She didn't ask that of me. She didn't ask anything.

"It's stupid to be jealous," I said.

"Jealous?" She was a wild thing, suddenly. "Jealous of what? Of *her*? Of *you*? Do you know what a fucking favor I did for you, Dex, turning you into something? If I wanted a charity project, I could have gone and read to old ladies or joined the fucking Peace Corps, but I didn't. I chose you. And you? You choose the fucking *mall*?"

She was the one who'd taught me that words mattered, that words could make worlds, or break them.

"I'm going, Lacey."

"Forget I said that. I shouldn't have said that," she said, talking too fast. "The bitch doesn't matter. *You* matter, Dex. Me and you, like before. That's all I want. Just tell me what I should do."

Tell me what I should do. This was power.

I couldn't say, *Go fuck yourself.*

I couldn't say, *Tell me what I should do. Be the person you were so I can be the person you made me.*

Somewhere below us, the front door opened and closed, hard. A baby screamed, and Lacey's mother shouted her name in a witch's howl; it broke the spell.

"I'm going, Lacey," I said. "I'm done here."

"Yeah."

But I didn't need her permission anymore.

I didn't mean for it to be the end.

Or maybe I did.

She came back to school in head-to-toe black, with a silver pentagram around her neck and a bloody tear painted beneath her eye. We didn't speak. By lunch, rumor had congealed into fact: Lacey had Satan on speed dial. Lacey had snuck into Mrs. Greer's room and turned her contraband cross upside down. Lacey had fallen into a trance on the softball field and started speaking in tongues. Lacey drank pig's blood for breakfast; Lacey kept a bloody rabbit's foot in her pocket for luck; Lacey had joined a death cult.

"She's desperate for attention," Nikki said that night on the phone. "*Your* attention, probably. Don't fall for it."

Nikki didn't ask me what I thought Lacey was up to, but she was the only one. People who hadn't spoken to me since junior high accosted me in the halls, wanting to know whether Lacey really thought she could call Satan's wrath down upon her enemies, whether *I* thought she could. I liked it.

My mother asked me, occasionally, why Lacey never came around—it didn't seem like she was disappointed, more like she thought I was hiding something she needed to know—but I usually mumbled something about being busy and hoped she wouldn't bring it up again. My father pushed harder, told me that whatever Lacey'd done I could forgive, and I wondered what made him think that she was the one at fault. Or why he couldn't decide whether we were better off with or without her. I didn't ask. This was how we conversed, now, my father talking at me while I played a wall. I couldn't remember why I was so angry with him. Because he'd kept things from me; because he hadn't fixed things for me; because in some indefinable way he'd taken Lacey from me, which seemed an even greater sin now that she was back. Because he didn't like the Hannah I'd become, and he couldn't pretend otherwise.

Don't you miss her, he said, and of course I did, and he was also saying without saying, don't you miss me, and of course I did that, too. But it was safer like this, to be a wall. To be Hannah. My father, Lacey—neither of them understood why that mattered, staying safe. They didn't know what it was to wake up on damp ground with a stranger's boot toeing your flesh, to find words on your skin that named your secret self. They didn't still, sometimes in the shower, rub themselves raw, imagining ink seeping into their skin, invisible brands leaving permanent marks. They didn't know what it was not to remember.

It was all mine, the power to tell my story, build myself up again from whatever fairy tale I liked. I liked ordinary. Unexceptional. Safe. A story without dragons, without riddles, without a dark witch in the heart of the woods. A boring story about a girl who turned down the quest, stayed home to watch TV.

Now that I was Hannah again, I stayed in the kitchen after dinners, to help my mother with the dishes. *You're such a comfort to me*, she would say, and I would smile my fake smile. We rinsed and rubbed, and I feigned interest in her latest self-improvement strategies, the Post-it note plan for the fridge, the poem-a-day calendar, the challenge of how to persuade herself to spend yet another evening sweating and stretching in time with Jane Fonda. She filled me in on her dull office politics and asked my advice on how to handle the asshole at reception who was always stealing her lunch. Sometimes she complained about my father, though she tried to pretend it wasn't complaining, just idle speculation: "I wonder if your father likes this job enough to stick with it for a while" or "I wonder if your father will ever get around to cleaning out the gutters like he promised." She was right about him, and I couldn't understand why I still had to bite back the only answers that wanted to come: *Maybe if you didn't nag him all the time he wouldn't hate you so much. Maybe he drinks to drown out the sound of your voice. Maybe you've told him he's a failure so many times that he believes it.*

He was drinking less but smoking more. He was happier. He'd stopped complaining about the movie theater, even taken on some extra shifts, mostly at night. I overheard my mother on the phone joking that he was probably having an affair.

That week, over a chicken potpie he'd uncharacteristically cooked from scratch, he said he was thinking about starting up his band again.

My mother laughed. "Oh, come on, Jimmy," she said when he pulled a sulk. "I'm sorry, but if you're going to have a midlife crisis, does it have to be such a cliché?"

"How about you, kid?" he asked me, as if he'd forgotten we weren't like that anymore; I couldn't be counted on for backup. "I could always use a drummer."

It was pathetic, the idea of him jamming in a garage in some torn-up T-shirt with a tie for a bandana, a sad after-hours Springsteen. I didn't say that. I didn't say anything, though, and he must have known what it meant.

The charm offensive swung back toward my mother. "You know you've always wanted to be my backup singer, Jules."

"Not exactly my heart's fondest desire," she said, but without enough bite for my taste.

"That's not what you said on our third date."

Now she was fighting back a smile. "Jimmy, we agreed we would never—"

"Hot Lips here *insisted* we let her up on stage." He reached for her hand, and she reminded him not to call her that, and said that he'd *pushed* her on stage, but when he pulled her out of her chair now, she pantomimed some unconvincing resistance, then let him swing her around and laughed when he started singing in falsetto. "I'm a good singer, I swear, really, let me at the mic," he said, in his version of my mother's voice, and she leaned her head against his shoulder and they swayed to music I couldn't hear.

"To be fair, I'd had quite a bit to drink." She was, ridiculously, giggling.

"They threw rotten fruit at the stage," my father said.

She smacked him. "They certainly did not."

"Cantaloupe. Pineapple. Who brings pineapple to a concert?"

"Most humiliating experience of my life," she said, fondly.

"You loved it." My father grinned at me over her head. "How about it, kid? We'll do like the Partridge Family. Get a bus and everything."

It should have made me happy, seeing them like that, like they must have been before they forgot how. I made it to the upstairs bathroom before my dinner rose up in my throat, but only barely. I let my cheek fall against the cool porcelain of the toilet rim and tried not to taste what was heaving out of me, waited in dread for one of them to come looking for me, but neither one did.

*

Strange things started to happen. Stranger, I mean, than Lacey prostrating herself at cloven feet. Stranger than me going to school in a borrowed denim vest and baby blue peasant skirt with a lace hem. I missed my flannel; I missed my Docs. I missed caring about the things that mattered and not caring about anything else; I missed being afraid of what I might do instead of what might be done to me.

I missed Dex.

Dex couldn't exist without Lacey—but somehow, impossibly, Lacey soldiered on without Dex. As if, in losing me, she'd lost nothing.

If I could, I would have willed her out of existence. Instead I haunted the hallway by her locker and drifted past her classrooms in case she'd decided not to cut. The less I saw her, the less it would hurt to see her, until it stopped hurting at all. Maybe that's why I couldn't stay away.

It felt like we were the only two real people in the building. That the other bodies were automata, simulacra of life that existed only for our entertainment. I watched them watch Lacey. I watched Lacey. I watched her turn our joke into her religion, watched her slip out the emergency exit and into the parking lot with Jesse, Mark, and Dylan, watched her slip an occasional tongue past Jesse's greasy lips, but I couldn't watch her all the time, and so I wasn't there to see the thing she did to Allie Cantor. The thing that, at least, they said she did to Allie Cantor. Plural trumped singular: Whatever they said became truth.

Allie Cantor was, famously, the first girl in our class to have sex—or at least to admit it. At thirteen, she'd briefly inter-sected with Jim Beech as they moved in opposite directions on the popularity ladder (she now ruled as Nikki Drummond's right hand whenever Melanie Herman fell from favor; he wore a cape to school and smelled like bacon). Allie had math with Lacey, a class for seniors still muddling through long division—Lacey because she couldn't be bothered, Allie because she couldn't remember her own phone number. Her mental energy, as far as I could tell, was expended on teasing her bangs, counting her calories (on her fingers, no doubt), tonguing Jeremy Denner's balls, and boring people on the subject of her two King Charles spaniels, which would have been prize show dogs had their tails not been crooked as her presurgical nose.

Stranger than strange: Lacey stared at Allie from across the classroom for a week, her gaze never wavering, her lips betraying some silent, unceasing chant. "Cursing her," she answered, whenever anyone asked what she was doing. Like it should be obvious.

Even Allie Cantor claimed to find it hilarious, until the day she broke down under the weight of Lacey's gaze, fled the room, and didn't show up again for a week. Some mystery illness, we heard. Many fluids expelled in many unfortunate ways. When Allie did come back to school, she was ten pounds and several shades lighter. She transferred to a different math class.

"Food poisoning," Nikki said on the phone that night. "Coincidence."

We watched Lacey; Lacey watched her targets. Next up

was Melanie Herman. Melanie spent half her time trying to knock Allie Cantor out of contention for Nikki's affections, the other half groping Cash Warner while desperately pretending she didn't want to date him and marry him and have his little Cash babies. Lacey stared, day in, day out. There was no reason to associate it with the way Melanie's hair began to fall out, a few strands here and there, as if someone was plucking her in the night. Patches of skull began to show through, sickeningly pale, and she took to wearing hats. The doctors diagnosed alopecia; Melanie diagnosed Lacey.

Sarah Kaye was tolerated only because her deadbeat cousin was always willing to buy her underage friends beer. She went down in gym class, passed out cold on the soccer field, breaking her wrist in the fall. She said that just before everything went black, Lacey had given her a weird look and murmured something under her breath. Sarah, whose diet consisted of celery and Tic Tacs, got a get-out-of-gym-free pass for the rest of the semester. Lacey got a tattoo, a black, five-pointed star at the nape of her neck.

Kaitlyn Dyer, who'd absorbed the concept of "girl next door" from her mother's amniotic fluid and devoted her life to fulfilling *Seventeen*'s bouncy, adorable, baseball-capped ideal, found a rash spreading up and down her left arm. This, she claimed, after Lacey spit on her in the hall, a spray of saliva patterning her arm precisely where the rash bloomed. Marissa Mackie borrowed a pen from Lacey in history class, only to wake up the next morning with a knife-shaped burn on the curve of her palm. Or so everyone believed, until her little sister revealed that Marissa had paid her twenty bucks to burn her with a curling iron and keep her mouth shut. Everyone agreed this was pathetic.

I thought it was all pathetic. Waking up to a mysterious stomachache or a tingling sensation in your foot had become a badge of honor, an anointment. No one could prove that Paulette Green was faking it when she fainted by her locker, even if she conveniently managed to land in Rob Albert's muscled grasp. No one would suggest out loud that Missy Jordan might have deliberately made herself puke her guts all over her chem lab partner. But by the next week, Paulette and Rob were an official item and Missy was ensconced at Nikki's cafeteria table, because the enemy of mine enemy, et cetera.

Even back when Jesse Gorin was inking pentagrams on his forehead and sacrificing Dumpster rats, it would never have occurred to anyone to believe, even half jokingly, that he'd developed psychic powers. The jocks who'd slung him in a tree were more than willing to believe he worshipped the devil, but no one suggested the devil was returning his calls. Jesse, Mark, Dylan, they were known quantities—as were we all. We'd known one another since preschool, through cooties, boogers, cracking voices, diagnoses. We knew one another like family, by scent and by rote, so wholly that it seemed less knowledge than embodiment. We were a single, self-hating organism. Lacey would always be a foreign body. Capable of anything.

Nikki wouldn't dignify it with speculation. "Do I think she's a fucking witch?" I heard her say to Jess Haines, as they were passing by my locker. "Sure. And I think you're a fucking moron."

Her mask was slipping, I'd noticed. She wasn't as good at playing nice as she used to be; the silky smooth exterior had taken on a certain gritty texture. Sometimes I caught spearmint on her breath, her preferred flavor for covering up the smell of her parents' gin. Lacey—or neuroses and desperate striving—picked off the minions one by one, but Nikki Drummond herself escaped unscathed. People, as they say, began to talk.

This is what they say happened when Nikki caught Lacey outside the orchestra room, just after lunch. That Nikki dared her to do something, then and there, to bring down the wrath of Satan. *Prove* it. Lacey stood by, silent and impassive, watching her melt down.

"Well?" Nikki said, and they say she seemed on the verge of violence, that there was something off-kilter about her. "Go ahead. Do it. None of this rash shit. No fainting. Just ask your friend the devil to strike me down dead, right here."

Lacey said nothing.

"Show them all what you are," Nikki said.

"I know how to hurt you," Nikki said. "Don't forget that."

Then Lacey spoke. And she said this: "*Pleasure and pain, like beauty, are in the eye of the beholder.*" It had the sound of memorized scripture. Then, they say, she smiled. "Don't be so impatient."

*

Parents wrote letters and left messages and raised an alarm, and the school sent Lacey home for inappropriate dress or behavior, and sometimes suspended her, but she always came back, and it would begin again. They tried sending her to the school's counselor, but rumor had it that she spent the whole session in spooky silence, mouthing hexes and sending him home early for the day with a suspicious migraine. After that, they sent me.

He had no office, so we met in the empty gym, dragging two metal folding chairs beneath one of the baskets. It smelled like shoe polish and boy sweat, while Dr. Gill, pit stains seeping through his pink shirt, smelled vaguely of VapoRub.

"I'm told you're very close with Lacey Champlain," he said. He wasn't extraordinarily ugly, not in a Dickensian way—that would have suited me—but ugly enough, his throat wattled, his gut bulging slightly over a pleather belt, a swell of man boob filling out his plaid shirt. "How do you think she's doing?"

I shrugged.

"She seems a bit ... disturbed," he said. "Wouldn't you say?"

"Should you be talking to me about other people's problems? Isn't that illegal or something?"

"Are there problems of your own that you'd rather discuss? I know this last year's been somewhat difficult for you ..."

I imagined filling in his pause. Resting my secrets at his feet one by one. Lacey. Nikki. My father. The party. My body. My beast. Without them weighing me down, I worried I might float away.

"Why would you think anything's been difficult?" I said.

"Your teachers have reported some erratic behavior over the months, and there was that, er, incident in the spring."

I almost wanted to make him spell it out.

"It's natural, at your age, to test out new identities. But when a student goes through radical transformations in such a short period of time, well . . . "

Well, then, that wouldn't be natural—that was the implication. You shouldn't be able to so thoroughly change who you are. Natural was having a shape of your own, not living like Jell-O, conforming to any mold.

"Well, what?" I said.

"Well, then we'd have to start asking whether that student is struggling to draw the boundaries of her personhood, and whether that struggle puts her at risk."

"I'm not on drugs. I don't even *do* drugs."

"I'm not necessarily talking about drugs. Or sex."

Dear God, I thought, please never be talking about sex. He was so solid, so *fleshy*, so thick with decay. It was impossible to imagine the boys I knew someday evolving into this.

"Hannah, has your friend Lacey ever tried to engage you in any . . . *rituals*?"

"Rituals?"

"Anything that might have seemed, strange? Perhaps something involving animals? Or"—he lowered his voice to a profane, almost hopeful whisper—"children?"

I got it then, the temptation she'd succumbed to. I wanted it. To narrow my eyes, make my voice Lacey cool, and say, *Well, there was the time we sacrificed the goats and made the children drink their blood . . . does that count?* To shove his face into his own prurient appetites and watch him feed.

Nikki had taught me better.

"Nothing like that," I said. Polite, composed, good-girl Hannah Dexter. As interesting as a bowl of oatmeal. "Can I go back to class?"

Hannah, have you spoken with her?" There was maternal concern in the question, but there was also judgment. Once again, in my mother's eyes, I'd failed.

I shrugged.

"Have you considered it? I don't know what went on between you—"

"That should be your first clue."

Usually that would be enough to derail her, start an argument about my attitude, land safely in my room. Not this time.

"The girl is obviously troubled. Regardless of your differences, maybe you owe her a little compassion?"

"Aren't you the one who forbid me ever to speak to her again?"

"That was in the heat of anger, Hannah. I was worried about you."

"And now?"

"Now I'm worried about her."

"Fucking unbelievable." I said it under my breath, loud enough for her to hear.

"What was that?"

This time, I enunciated. "*Fucking. Unbelievable.*"

"Hannah! Language."

"I love how when *I* wanted her around, Lacey was basically the devil. And now, when she's *literally worshipping the devil*, you assume that whatever happened between us is my fault. Or, like, forget fault. It's just whatever I decide to do is the wrong thing. By definition. Is that it?"

"I realize that you prefer to see me as a villain when at all possible."

I couldn't stand it, the simpering voice, the affected elocution, every bit of her behavior fake—and that wasn't even the worst of it. I could have forgiven her fancier-than-thou act if she hadn't been so *bad* at it.

"I'm not saying anyone's at fault here, Hannah. I'm just worried about her. She's obviously gotten involved in something she shouldn't have. The things they say . . . I'm worried something terrible might happen."

I could have told her, things didn't just happen to Lacey. If something terrible happened, it would be because Lacey had willed it to. I could have told her, I was the one things happened to.

She'd caught me downstairs on the couch, watching TV, which these days I could only do when my father wasn't hovering. Of course she'd positioned herself squarely in front of the screen. I looked away, at the Sears photo framed on the wall, the most prominent picture of me in the house, if that chunky toddler could be considered in any way contiguous with the lumpen, scowling creature I'd grown up to be. She must have had her doubts sometimes, wondered if I was a changeling, if her perky girl who loved tutus and Parcheesi had been snatched away in the night, an angry monster child slipped into her place. I hated the girl in that photo, because I knew how much easier she was to love, all soft skin and smooth edges. How could my parents not want her back?

"Lacey's fine," I said. "You don't have to worry about her."

"That's patently false. Maybe I should call her mother—"

"No!"

"Well, if you won't talk to her . . . "

"She's worshipping the devil, *Mother.*" I couldn't remember when I'd last said that word because I needed it, because it meant home. "Any other mother in this town would be taking me in for an exorcism or something, just in case."

"Aren't you fortunate, then, that I'm not every other mother?"

"Yeah, I won the lottery."

"I hope this isn't really you, Hannah. It's fine, to put on this little show for me. I understand. But I hope it isn't you." She didn't sound angry, and that somehow made it worse when she gave me what I asked for and left me alone.

LACEY

Something in the Way

What I learned from Kurt: It can be a good thing, people thinking you're bad. When Kurt's neighbors worried they were living next to the devil, Kurt strung up a voodoo doll on a noose and hung it in the window for them to see.

I'm not what you think I am, Kurt says. *I'm worse.*

I won't tell you what I did that first night, after I sent you inside to your happy family: how empty the car felt on the drive home, how I had to turn off the music and endure the quiet you left behind in case, if I listened hard enough, the night could tell me what to do.

I didn't sleep much, not anymore. The dreams came for me, came even when I hid under the covers and tried to stay awake. A ring of clasped hands around the bed, singing their love for Jesus; the nightmare girls closing in, fingers like spiders, creepy-crawling across bare skin. I was always naked. I never struggled, in the dream. I went stiff, corpse-like, made myself into dead weight. They chanted about Christ and I chanted to myself, *light as a feather stiff as a board light as a feather stiff as a board*, magic words from a time when we were all little pagans summoning ghosts.

They carried me away into the night, into the woods. Down the dark path, where the bad things live. They tore out my beating heart, their jaws sticky with my blood, and buried it in wet ground. They knew my secret self, the scarecrow-Lacey built of twigs and mud and bark, the Lacey who was made of forest and would someday be summoned home.

So, fuck you. That's what I thought. Fuck you and your new bitch friend, and don't think I'll be waiting around to mop up the blood when a certain treasonous sociopath stabs you in the back. I could have forgiven you for lying to me—maybe, even, for assuming I was so stupid that I wouldn't clue in to what happened at that party, or at least what people said happened, that the rumors wouldn't trickle down to me and that I couldn't understand all the things you must have been, sad and scared and humiliated and angry at yourself for whatever you'd done and whatever'd been done to you and angry at me for letting it. I could have told you about the things hiding inside you, about the secrets I kept for you, the wild you didn't want to know; I could have held you and remembered with you, and together we would have sworn our revenge and pledged that no one else mattered, that words were only words even when they said *whore* and *slut* and *trash*, that we could endure anything if we did so as *us*. That's what was hard to forgive, Dex. That you forgot how much you needed me. And apparently the other side of the equation never even occurred to you.

So I was angry, and maybe, when I ambushed your father at the movie theater, I was looking for a little vengeance, thinking I could go through with it, could shimmy over in my leather cutoffs and fishnets, let him think it was his idea, make him *beg* for it, crook a finger into his collar, tug him into the projection room, slide his hand down my shorts, let his fingers root around, get good and wet, lick myself off him, lick him up and down in all his flabby glory, rub his hairy back and tug those sagging balls, let him bend me over a desk or shove me up against a wall, fumble with his belt buckle, whip it out, then slip it in, both of us panting and crying and trying not to scream your name.

In his defense, he wasn't happy to see me.

"Aren't you supposed to be in school?" He looked over his shoulder as he said it, like someone would wander into the manager's office to catch us, even though the building was empty, no one but us and a couple blue-hairs who had nothing better to do on a Tuesday afternoon than lose themselves in a movie before slinking home to count the minutes till death.

"Hi, Lacey," I said. "So great to see you again after all this time, Lacey. How did the whole getting-tossed-out-of-the-house-and-sent-away-by-a-crazy-bastard thing work out for you, Lacey?"

"Hi, Lacey." We were past nicknames; this time, only real words, only truth.

"Hi, Jimmy."

"How about you call me Mr. Dexter."

"We wouldn't want to be inappropriate."

I could tell from his twitchy face that he felt guilty, not just about the night he let me kiss him and then threw me out on the street, but also about the fact that he'd kept all of it a secret. I guessed, even before he confessed it, that he felt like shit for shutting his mouth and letting you mope around the house like your dog had gotten chomped up by the lawn mower. He was a liar and a coward, and he'd convinced himself you were better off without me, and once he figured out his mistake it was too late to say anything without revealing himself as a pussy. And here's something to feel good about, Dex: The last thing your father ever wanted to do was that. Every little girl's daddy is a superhero, isn't that right?

"You got your small talk, Lacey. You can go now."

"Please, can we talk for a second? For real?" I let him hear some keening underneath, the dog whistle of desperation. Men are men, Dex, all of them. "Please, Mr. Dexter."

That got him.

I put on a good show. Begged him to make you give me another chance, remember how good I was for you. To do whatever it is that good fathers do to guide their daughters down the righteous path, to guide you back to me.

"I'm sorry, Lacey," he said, and sounded it. "Dex is a big girl now. She picks her own friends."

It was him calling you *Dex* that did it, like even if he couldn't come right out and admit it, he was rooting for us, and the part of you that belonged to me.

Men are predictable. He hugged me. It was a dad hug, and don't think I don't know what that feels like. To feel so small, so safe, to feel a warm body and steady breathing and accept it as an end in itself, not an offer or a promise or a debt. I got snot on his shirt, and neither of us cared, and nothing twitched below his waist. It was a caesura, like the silence before a hidden track, a dark to hide in. The good kind of dark.

"Let's watch a movie," he said when we let go.

"Don't you have to work?"

He shrugged. "I won't tell if you don't."

We slipped into the theater midway through *Sneakers* and watched Robert Redford save the day, then ventured out to the alley and shared a cigarette, and it would have been that easy, just the way I'd wanted it, except I didn't want it anymore, didn't want him for the purpose of hurting you, didn't want him at all.

Wanted you.

Missed *you*.

Took what I could get.

*

There was no place for me in the house anymore. Nature abhorred a vacuum, and while I was gone James Jr. filled up the empty space. Little baby, big lungs. Lots of blue plastic crap, bright with stars and monkeys and terrifying clowns. Unwashed bottles, filthy diapers, the smell of lotion and shit, dried trickles of drool and puke, and, of course, the baby himself, the fucking baby, bright-eyed and apple-cheeked and looking at me like he remembered the time I baptized him into the church of Satan and was just waiting till he was old enough to tattle.

Home sweet home: The house was the Bastard incarnated in brick and vinyl. Fake siding outside and fake wood floors inside, grimy kitchen that never got clean. Wallpaper that looked like little James had puked it up, paisley blotches of half-digested peas and corn. I hated that most of all, because I knew my mother hated it even more but was too lazy and cheap to do anything about it. That wallpaper, Dex, that's everything my life is not going to be.

The Bastard wasn't around as much as he used to be, but when he was home, his mood was foul enough to make up for it. While I was gone he'd apparently discovered the limits of paper pushing. It turned out getting to play Mussolini to an office of stoned telemarketers wasn't as much fun as he'd expected, and his election campaign for an open slot on the school board had—praise be to whatever saint watches over public education—stalled out at the signature-collection stage. Maybe even the dim bulbs of Battle Creek could sense he was a repellent toad; more likely, my reputation preceded him.

Let him rant all he wanted about satanism being a phantom of an overheated imagination, about the devil wearing subtler costumes; he wore his costume and I wore mine, and too bad for him if mine was more effective, because when he called Horizons they told him I was saved and refused to take me back.

Meanwhile, Mother of the Year had started drinking again for real. I kept her secret. I had plenty of practice picking up her slack, though this was the first time the slack was the kind that habitually shit itself. I'm not going to say we bonded, me and baby brother, but helpless things are genetically designed to be cute. Big head, big eyes, some kind of *protect me* phero-mone; there was even the occasional moment when I would bounce him on my shoulder and whisper in his ear and not be tempted to drown him in the tub while Mommy Dearest slept it off.

"You'd be better off," I told him, and then, because no one was watching, kissed that soft little baby head and let him wrap his warm little baby fingers around my thumb. "You don't know what you're in for."

It was James Jr. that did it, in the end. Or maybe it was just me, fucked by habit, the lie slipping out before I had a chance to think. My mother had gotten drunk, left the baby alone, and that's how the Bastard found him, squealing in a soggy diaper in an empty house, and "What kind of mother?" and "I should call the police" and "If you think I'm letting you any-where near my son again" and "How many times do I need to teach you the same fucking lesson" and the Bastard thought cursing was spitting in the face of Jesus—that's how mad he was—what was I supposed to do but say it was my fault?

"I promised I would babysit," I told him. "I thought I could just sneak out for a few minutes and no one would know."

She let me lie for her, and I let his hand crack hard across my cheek, and I guess we both thought it would end there, but when it didn't, when he made her choose, her daughter or his son, she let the lie sit, and so I did as I was told, packed up my shit and left.

"You're an adult now," she said. That's all she said. "You can handle it."

When Kurt's mother kicked him out, he had to live under a fucking bridge. At least I had the Buick. I could shower in the locker rooms before school or, if I felt like it, at Jesse Gorin's house. He didn't even make me suck him for the privilege. Once I caught him jerking off, and he liked *that* so much that occasionally I watched, but it was never a quid pro quo kind of thing. More of a favor, like how I kept him company while he listened to his death metal shit and pretended it didn't make my ears bleed. Sometimes we'd drag the action figures out from the back of the closet and make He-Man blow Skeletor or G.I. Joe take it in the ass, then watch old metal videos until the sun came up.

It wasn't the safest thing for him, for any of them, being seen with me. Considering what people thought they were. Considering what I was trying pretty fucking hard to be.

I even apologized once, if you can believe it. "Sorry," I said—and you'll have an even tougher time believing this, but I actually was—"if I'm bringing down extra shit on you guys."

He shook his head. "Do what you do. They deserve it." Then he showed me the box in the basement where he'd stowed all his old devil crap, the incense and the blades and some cheap polyester hoods, and told me to knock myself out.

Jesse got me a job at the Giant, where they didn't give a shit about devil worship as long as I remembered to double bag. If life were a movie, I would have gotten a job at some down-and-out record store, enlightening losers who were still jonesing for New Kids on the Block and learning valuable life lessons from my grizzled yet sexy boss, who would hold out for a few months, like a gentleman, before hoisting me onto the counter and ringing me up. Instead I got Bart the produce guy, who looked a little like Paul McCartney if you squinted; Linda the meat lady, who was pretty sure she could convert me back to the Lord with a couple pot roast dinners; and Jeremy, our sleaze of a manager, who hit on every double-X chromosome in sight except for me.

Sleep was hard; everything hurt too much. There were noises. Engines and sirens and crickets and planes, nothing to keep out the night. I waited for footsteps, a tap on the glass, a face at the window. When it happened, and sometimes it did, I could rev the engine and go.

I could have gone for good. I stayed for you. The two of us heading west, together, that was always the plan.

If I'd asked, you would have said: *Go.* You would have drawn me a map. Like a little kid crushing her tiny fists together and telling her mommy *I hope you die.* You don't believe a little girl like that. You pat her on the head and wait for the tantrum to pass. That's called faith.

You know I think it's bullshit: faith, superstition, some sixth sense *knowing* that actually means *wishing* or *pretending* or *ignoring.* But you've got to believe in something. I believe gravity will keep me from floating into space and that people came from monkeys. I believe that sixty percent of anything the government says is a lie, and that conspiracy theorists belong in the same nuthouse as alien abductionists and the *Elvis lives* crowd. I believe that Democrats are criminals but Republicans are sociopaths; I believe that space is infinite and consciousness is finite; I believe that my body is my body and rapists should have their balls cut off; I believe that sex is good and the deterministic universe is a quantum illusion; I believe that global warming is increasing and the hole in the ozone is widening and nuclear proliferation is worsening and germ warfare is coming and we are all ultimately fucked. Those are my foundations, Dex, my unquestionables. The gospel of Lacey: I believe in choice and words and genius and Kurt. I believe in you.

I don't believe in Our Dark Lord of the Underworld or the rising of the Antichrist, I don't believe in child sacrifice or wild midnight blood rituals, and I don't believe that I can call on the power of Satan to knock some cheerleader off her pyramid. Wearing black felt safe. Wearing it on my skin, the mark of something vicious, that felt right. All the rest of it, that was crap. But: Sarah, Allie, Paulette, Melanie . . . I wanted them to hurt, and they hurt. That's power, Dex. You don't need magic to make people believe what you want them to believe. Believing can hurt most of all.

"What's with all this Satan shit?" your dad asked me once.

I'd started sneaking off to see him a few times a week. We talked over boring movies in empty theaters, and talked more in the alley, always sharing a cigarette, like smoking half didn't count. He told me about the first time he went to the movies and how back in the dark ages it felt like an occasion, and I told him that his beloved Woody Allen was a hack and if he really wanted art he should try Kurosawa or Antonioni. He looked at me the way you used to look at me, like I knew a secret and if I was nice I might spill. We didn't talk about his wife; we tried not to talk about you. Mostly, we talked about music. I would stick the headphones over his ears and play him snatches of the Melvins or Mudhoney. Never Kurt, though. I saved Kurt for us.

I took a long drag on the Winston. "It's not what people think, pentagrams and blood sacrifice and all that. As religions go, satanism makes a lot of sense."

"Translation: You're desperate for attention." He tossed the butt and ground it out with his heel. "Teenagers."

I liked that he was so sure there could be nothing to it, that I was harmless.

We stayed on the fringes of the day, early matinees or mid-week midnight showings that no one bothered to see, and I made sure never to approach him in the presence of witnesses. It didn't even faze me, the morning I spotted Nikki slumped in the back row. She didn't see anything; your father was shuffling paperwork and I was half napping through *The Last of the Mohicans*. Even if she had noticed me, there was nothing to see. So I didn't tell him about it, and I didn't stop. I thought we were safe. Too bad I wasn't the witch they all thought I was, or I would have known better.

He made me mixtapes from old eight-tracks and tried to convince me that the Doors were rebels. A mixtape's the best kind of love letter, everyone knows that, and I think maybe he loved me a little, or at least he loved who he got to be when he was with me—the old Jimmy Dexter, the one who still had all his hair. He told me all about his band: the time they got fifty bucks to play a wedding, then got so wasted on free wine he puked on the bride's shoes; the time they came *this close* to a record deal but lost out because the bass guitarist got drafted; the many times he'd retreated into his parents' garage with his guitar and tuned out all of existence except the strings, the chords, the music, the joy. I told him he should start it up again, or at least duck into the garage once in a while and turn up the volume on his life—that was for you, Dex. Because music, that's one place where your father's more like me than like you; it's blood and guts for him, and living without it is what makes him pathetic. I thought if he could get it back, maybe you could get him back—the him you never knew. That Jimmy died in childbirth, and he never even held it against you.

Every day, I watched you pant after Nikki. Every day, I watched out for you, waiting for her to make her move. The Halloween decorations came out and forgetting the woods got harder every day and I knew Nikki would be feeling the same jitters, that she'd be feeling the bad things coming and would do anything to stave them off, especially if it meant hurting me. She knew how to hurt me.

We had made our sacred promise, Nikki and I. We had sworn our blood oath. Confessions swallowed, guilt strangled, sins buried in salted ground. We played our games and waged our proxy wars. We bloodied you in the crossfire.

But we had promised. To leave death in the woods, and to forget.

The Spanish Inquisitors, before they tortured, would lay out their instruments, one cruel blade after another, show you what was to come, and this was considered torture in itself. This was my torture: What she knew. What she might tell you.

What you would do.

DEX

Love Buzz

October was a good time for witches. Even a town as frightened of the devil as ours went all out for Halloween. As soon as the sun set on Labor Day, Battle Creek embraced its dark side. Fanged pumpkins grinned from porches, pulpy gap-toothed smiles gleamed in windows, the candles at their hollow center casting every night in brimstone glow. Pale-faced cardboard vampires dangled from lampposts, at least until the raccoons got to them. You'd find them mangled in the street, dappled with rabid blood.

Halloween had been my favorite holiday when I was a little kid. The candy, the masks, the opportunity to disappear into someone else, if only for a night. The possibility that the world held just a little bit of magic, that any door could be a passageway to wonders. That a child could slip into the dark and never be seen again. Things changed once I figured out monsters were real. Battle Creek Halloween wasn't for the weak: The hours between sundown and sunrise were anarchic, roving gangs of teenagers set free from the bounds of civility giving in to their inner brutes. Rotten eggs flew; toilet paper soared; mailboxes burned and cats screamed. November first's crime blotter always overflowed its page: trespassing, vandalism, guns fired into the night, houses and people entered without permission, and those were just the sins that someone had bothered to report.

It had never seemed like a coincidence that Craig Ellison killed himself on Halloween. He'd retreated to a haunted sanctum; its ghosts had claimed him. So maybe it wasn't just Lacey who made October feel like an avalanche, the days rushing all of us toward cliff's edge. Maybe it was the memory of Halloweens past, the glow of pulpy teeth, the haunted Ellisons shuffling through town pale and gaunt as the season crept closer to the anniversary of their nightmare. Even the sticky, hot weather that refused to turn felt like a warning: Bad things were on their way.

Small wonder that, as one golden girl after another dropped, the town went fucking nuts. The thing had a momentum all its own. Girls I was certain Lacey had never met, girls mousier and twitchier than even I'd been in the days before Lacey, fled to the nurse and eventually the newspaper, having woken to discover a suspiciously shaped rash or strange streaks sparking across their vision. Diagnosis: Satan. Three girls struck simultaneously with laryngitis attributed their silence to Lacey's dark powers—until it turned out the student council president had given all three of them a key to the student council office, along with gonorrhea of the throat. A third-string goalie insisted Lacey had offered him a blow job in the woods and, in a devilish bait and switch, dragged him to a satanic coven instead. He made it all the way to the local news, spinning a tale of whirling dervishes, bloodletting, face painting, and an orgy in which he wasn't allowed to take part, that last seeming to be his main complaint. Finally, Battle Creek could put name to its enemy. There was finally something to fight, and fighting was crucial, for if someone didn't do something soon, it was said, surely it was only a matter of time before another Craig.

We didn't actually believe it, of course. We believed it without believing it; we made a joke of it, and the joke made it easier to be afraid. We wanted to be scared, like a kid hiding under the covers, screaming, waiting for Daddy to come in and banish the monster—because it was an excuse to stay awake, because it was fun to scream, because it felt good to have a father strong and sure rest a hand on your forehead, because the closet was deep and shadowed and, in the end, who knew what might be hiding in the dark. We didn't believe it, but we wanted to, we believed it, but we made ourselves laugh it away. It was a joke on Lacey, letting her believe we believed it, a nasty joke on her and on the grown-ups, who didn't understand the nuances of such belief, who saw black lipstick and pentagram tattoos and fainting girls and were convinced.

I say *we*, but of course I mean *they*. After Lacey, I couldn't go back to being one of them. I couldn't believe, or let her suspect I did. I could only wonder. Had she lost it so thoroughly—or was it all a show, maybe even for my benefit? To what end, I couldn't imagine, didn't want to.

"This is what she does," Nikki told me, and while she didn't sound frightened, she didn't sound entirely unfazed, either. "She plays games. She stirs shit up. Notice how she's only careless with *other* people. So that, when the time comes, they're the ones who get hurt. But you know that. Don't you?"

We had yet another assembly, of course. This time, Principal Portnoy warned us that it was a matter of our souls. He called Barbara Fuller to the stage—"concerned parent," though her kid was six—who in turn introduced the great Dr. Isabelle Ford herself, national devil-worship expert, renowned pamphleteer. Probably got her PhD in bullshit, Lacey would have said if she'd been next to me in the back row rather than hiding out by the Dumpsters with her new friends and a joint. Ford and Fuller acted out a skit in which the doctor invited Mrs. Fuller to a coven. Satanism was contagious, they warned, and the eyes of the audience turned to me. "Just say no," the doctor reminded us. Nancy Reagan's magic bullet; it was all they knew, and for all they knew, it worked.

It was two weeks before Halloween when Nikki cornered me in the bathroom and suggested we cut school. The Ides of October. I should have been more careful.

"I'm desperately craving a movie," she said.

"Pretty sure the only thing playing during the day is *The Mighty Ducks*, Nikki."

"I'll endure," she said, and because I had several free coupons tucked into my wallet and those days my father mostly worked nights, I went for it.

It wasn't until the lights went up—on a movie that managed to kill my enervated crush on Emilio Estevez for good—that I saw them. I'd noticed their silhouettes in the front row, but hadn't recognized them, his boxy and hers elfin, the two of them bent together in conversation, her shoulders bouncing with laughter. The credits unspooled. They stood up. They turned around.

It was like walking in on a scene from your own life and realizing the details weren't anything like what you remembered—the seats blue instead of red, the floor sticky with nacho cheese instead of soda, the father older and balder, the girl wearing the wrong face. My father, with the wrong daughter. My father, with a beer in one hand and Lacey in the other.

"Dex," Lacey said, then stopped.

There was a tugging on my arm. I remembered Nikki. Remembered that my legs could move, that I could carry myself away, and so I did, running, not listening to the thud of boots as she came after me or the absence where he didn't, running flat out until I got to Nikki's car, pressed myself against it, home base, all safe, cool metal holding me up, and then somehow I was inside the car and we were driving away.

"God, she is disgusting," Nikki said. "What is *wrong* with her? And him! I mean, God."

I made some kind of noise, something squeaky and mouse-like. Most of me was still back there with them in the dark.

"I'm getting you drunk," Nikki said.

"I don't drink," I said, because I didn't, not anymore—it wasn't safe. Then I remembered that nothing was safe and so what the fuck was the difference.

We went to the train station.

We went to the train station and got drunk off the wine coolers that Nikki had in her trunk, tucked beside her father's video camera, which those days she rarely left home without. We sat on the edge of the tracks and guzzled the wine coolers, letting the ground go wobbly beneath our feet and the world turn fuzzy at its corners. We didn't talk about what my father was doing with Lacey or what Lacey was doing with my father.

I did not think about what they had done when I left, whether they'd parted ways or whether they'd sat down together, were still together, talking about me and what made me so difficult to love. Whether Lacey put her hand over his and assured him he was still a good father; whether my father rubbed her back in slow circles, like he did when I was little and needed to be sick, promising her that everything would be all right, he would always love her, his special girl.

I was sick, straight down into the tracks, which had surely seen worse.

"Gross," Nikki said, and by then we were drunk enough that all we could do was laugh.

We were drunk enough to set up the camera and put on a show.

This time, Nikki played herself. She let me be Craig.

"I killed you." She slung an arm around me, her breath hot on my neck. "And now you're back to haunt me, and I can't blame you, because I fucking killed you."

"I did it to myself," I said, because whatever she thought she'd done, it was physics that sealed the deal: cause and effect, finger on trigger, trigger on bullet, bullet on skull.

"You could never do anything yourself. You made me do it all for you so you could blame me, and now I get to blame myself, thanks a fucking lot, and that's why I hate you. I always fucking hated you."

"I loved you," I said, and she kissed me, and we were slippery and wine-tongued together, and she tasted sweet, and before I could wrap my muddy head around it or touch my palm to her neck or feel her fingers scrape against the fuzz at the back of mine, it was over.

Nikki was beautiful. Nikki had always been beautiful. I'd always known that, but I tried to know it differently now, to take in the specifics of her long eyelashes and the silk of her hair, the pull of her shirt against her skin and the expanses where pale flesh peeked through, soft and warm. I asked myself if I wanted more, if this was, finally, the shape of me.

"You can never tell anyone," Nikki said softly.

"We were acting. It was no big deal." It didn't count when you were playing let's pretend; nothing counted when you were drunk.

"Not the fucking kiss. I mean what I said. That I killed him. This is the secret place. No one can know what happens here."

"You didn't kill him, Nikki. You know that, right? Unless you came here with him and pulled the trigger. Did you do that?"

"I did not pull the trigger. I did not do that. I did not."

"Then you didn't kill him. Say it."

"I didn't kill him."

There wouldn't be another moment, not like this. "What happened here, Nikki? What happened to him?"

I'd never asked her so directly before, and I thought she'd be angry, or at least surprised, but she only looked bored. "Everyone knows what happened, Hannah. Old news. Bang bang, you're dead, et cetera. Next question."

"Why, then?" Which was, of course, the same question. The only question.

She shrugged, elaborately.

"Then why blame yourself?"

"Who the fuck knows, Hannah? Why does anyone blame themselves for anything? Oh, wait—I forgot who I was talking to." She tossed back her head and laughed out a cloud of spittle and fumes.

I punched her. It could be this way between us, today, after what we'd seen. No walls. "What?"

She choked on the words, but I was patient. I waited.

"You. *You*, of all people. Telling me I'm not responsible for what someone else does."

"You're not."

She seized my shoulders. "Real talk, Hannah?"

"Okay." I thought she might kiss me again. I didn't want it, but I didn't not want it, either.

"Kettle, meet black pot. Or, I mean, you're like the kettle calling the pot— Wait."

I giggled. "You're drunk, Nikki."

"*You're* drunk." Which was what a drunk would say, and also true.

"It's pot calling the kettle black."

"Yes! That! You! *You*." She poked me hard, just above my left nipple. "How about *you* take responsibility? Lacey's got you so fucking brainwashed, poor little Dex, can't do anything on her own, needs big bad Lacey to protect her. You ever ask yourself why she'd bother with you if you were that pathetic? Where's the fun in that? What's fun is fooling someone who's strong into forgetting that she is. And it must have been so fucking easy for her. You *want* to forget. You're begging for it."

"I don't get it," I said, because the ground was shifting and the air was blurry and my ears buzzed. It was easier to let the words plunk down, drop by drop, no stream of meaning, just disconnected sounds.

"How about Lacey didn't *make* you do anything, and I never *made* you do anything, and you went to that fucking party and took off your fucking clothes and passed the fuck out all on your own, and stop being a fucking victim all the fucking time because it gets. So. Fucking. Tired."

"Oh."

I was weaving and spinning, and the heartbeat in my head insisted: *Pain, pain, pain.*

"Are you going to cry? Hannah? Hannah Banana?" She shook me. "Say something. Don't cry." Her lower lip jutted out, and even in a pantomime of a pout, she was still pretty. "You said real talk."

"*You* said real talk."

"I did? That's right. I did." And then she was laughing again, and I was laughing, and we were on our backs looking up at twirling sky, and my brain untethered from my body and spiraled up toward the blue. The day fell away, even Lacey fell away, and I was here, in this moment, with myself, and the ground was wet and the air was warm and everything was exactly enough.

"I forgive you," I told her. "I forgive everything and everyone. My heart is as big as the world."

"But not Lacey," she said.

"Never Lacey," I said.

"Your turn."

"My turn what?"

"Your turn real talk," she said. "Harsh truths. Or truth or dare. Or just dare. Whatever the fuck. Your turn."

On our backs, staring at the sky, fingers Michelangelo'd toward each other. I'd missed it, that sense of floating away from myself, everything so easy.

"Okay. Dare you to say something true. Really true."

"I always speak the truth."

"Lie!" I giggled. "Dirty, filthy lie."

Nikki sat up. "We can't all be like you, Hannah, just saying whatever the hell we feel like. No act. No costume. It's hard to be naked all the time."

"I am *never* naked," I said, mustering my dignity. "Except in the shower. Always in the shower."

"What's it like?" she asked.

"What? Showers? How filthy are you?"

"No. I mean being you."

It was truth-telling day. It was the sacred, truth-telling place, that's what she'd said. "Shitty. Scary. Hard."

"That's what I figured."

I sat up. Put an arm around her, which was weird, because we never touched, but not so weird, because we'd already made out. "You should try it more often. Naked. People would like you better."

"No, they wouldn't."

"No, they wouldn't," I agreed. "Screw them."

"Screw them," she said, and guzzled another wine cooler—one, two, three long gulps and it was gone. I wanted to throw up again just watching her.

"You know what you're doing, right?" I meant with the booze; I meant with me; I meant with losing Craig and trying not to lose it entirely and holding her shit together so she could be the Nikki Drummond her whole world needed her to be.

She grinned, kissed me on the forehead, a quick graze of lip and, so quick I might have imagined it, darting cat tongue. It was such a Lacey move that for just a second I lost the thread, closed my eyes and imagined the three of us together—Lacey, Nikki, and me—fingers threaded, eyes glazed, love buzzing through us, this sacred place with its dead trains and its ghosts a chaos engine to drive us all into the impossible.

"I always know what I'm doing," Nikki said, and her voice woke me up.

I had to go home sometime. When I did, my father was waiting up for me. He sat on the porch, mug in his hand, hiding behind his aviators. There was no reflection, in the dark.

"I covered for you with your mother," he said.

"My hero."

"Hannah—" He leaned in. "Are you *drunk*?"

"Jealous?"

"Given the ... circumstances, I won't tell your mother, but—"

"But? But what? I should be better behaved?"

"If you want to talk about what you saw today ... "

"No." I didn't want to talk. I didn't want *him* to talk, certainly.

"I can imagine what you thought. But it wasn't that."

"Oh, really? What is it you imagine I think? Do I think you're fucking her?"

"Hannah!"

"Do you think I've got that picture in my head? You and her, naked in some shitty motel? Or just doing it in the empty movie theater? Like some dirty old man at a porn movie. Except it's in 3D?"

"We can talk in the morning, when you're feeling"—he cleared his throat—"more yourself. But please know, it was nothing like that."

"Of course it was nothing like that. You're a fat old man," I said, thinking, *Hurt. Hurt more.* "You can't think you had a chance there."

"Lacey needed someone to talk to. That's all. Swear to God."

I did believe him. Mostly. Almost entirely. He didn't want to sleep with Lacey; he wanted to father her. He thought that made it better.

I stepped around him. "You don't get us both."

"You, uh . . . You won't mention this to your mother, right, kid?"

I'd loved it, once, when he called me that. I couldn't remember why.

"It never happened," I said, and he must have thought I meant the day, and not everything before it and everything between us, because he looked relieved.

I didn't wait around for Lacey to apologize. *Never apologize*—I remembered that much. I avoided her at school and my father at home. Girls got rashes and dizzy spells. Battle Creek cowered from the devil. October continued apace.

Then, a week before Halloween, the thunderstorm. One

last gasp of summer before the snows set in. The thunder sounded its summons, and even though I did not want to miss her, did not want to see her, did not want to want her, I gave in. The night felt unreal, the landscape lashed with wind and water. Like temporarily we'd slipped into another world, where nothing had to count.

I waited until my parents were asleep, stole the car keys, drove to our lake. How surprised she would be, I thought, when she saw that I'd learned to drive without her.

There was no question she would be there. For the storm, for me. There are irresistible forces, but there are no immoveable objects. The storm called; we always answered.

She looked inhuman, spattered with mud, slick and shiny in the headlights, some wild, watery creature of the night.

"You weren't invited," she said when I reached her. "You're not welcome."

It's a free country, I could have said, like a little kid, but I knew I was trespassing, that everything ours was actually hers. She'd gotten custody of the wild.

I wasn't welcome, but when I sat on the dock, she lowered herself beside me. We sat shoulder to shoulder, close enough that low voices could cross the void. Her cheek shimmered. Rain hung on her lashes. She dropped her head, hiding her eyes, exposing the soft, pale slope of her neck and shoulders. The tattoo was a black smear, ballpoint rivulets tracing dark veins down her spine.

I touched the smudge that had once been a star. "Everything about you is a lie."

She raised her head just enough to show her smile. "I'm rubber, you're glue." Then she rag-dolled down again. "I know what you're thinking. It wasn't like that with him."

"You don't know what I'm thinking. Not anymore."

She only laughed.

"You've got to quit with this devil stuff, Lacey."

"What are you worried about? What are they going to do to me? Drown me in a well? *Exorcise* me?"

"Expel you, for one."

"Ooh, scary."

"And, I don't know. What are you going to do if someone really gets hurt?"

"How could anyone getting hurt be my problem? You don't actually think I'm doing something to them?" Lacey shook herself like a dog. The spray was colder than the rain.

"You know this town, Lacey."

"And this is your problem how?"

She had me there.

"I'd save your worry for yourself," Lacey said.

"I'm fine."

"Something bad is coming."

"Is that supposed to be a prophecy?" I said. "Or, what? A threat?"

"Dex—" She breathed. Our shoulders rose and fell together. In, out. Slow, steady. Breathe, Dex. Breathe, Lacey. "I want you safe, Dex. That's all I want."

Nikki would have said she was jealous. That she needed me to need her, no matter how much it hurt.

"It wasn't about you, this thing with your dad," Lacey said. "And the Nikki thing, that's not about you, either."

"Yeah, of course, it's about whatever mysterious secret conspiracy you can't let me in on. I got that."

"What's between me and Nikki . . . it's about Craig."

"You say that like it means anything. Like I'm supposed to pretend it's an answer when we both know it's not."

I didn't actually expect it would make her explain herself; nothing could make Lacey do what she didn't want to.

She said it quietly. "She thinks it's my fault."

All the little ways Nikki had tried to turn me against Lacey, the way she'd taken a razor blade, ever so carefully, to my faith in her, shaving it away in impossibly thin slices until there was almost nothing left—all that time, she'd said nothing of this.

Maybe, I thought, it was just another lie. But that wasn't Lacey's way. Lacey lied with silence.

"Go ahead." She sounded ancient with exhaustion, like there was nothing left to do but wait for bones to crumble to dust. "Ask me if it was. My fault."

I shivered, and wiped the rain from my forehead. The lake water danced, leaping for the clouds.

"It wasn't all bad, was it, Dex?"

I couldn't lie in a storm. "None of it was bad." I took her hand. There was no thought behind it, just bodily need, to press our slippery skin together. To hang on. "Say it, Lacey. Whatever it is. Make it better." She was the witch, wasn't she? I willed her: *Summon the words.*

She squeezed. "Let's start fresh, Dex. Fuck the past."

I didn't see how she could say it when the past was everything. The past was where Dex and Lacey lived. If she erased that, there would be nothing left of us.

"I never tried to hide you away," Lacey said. "I never kept you a secret." Somehow we were talking about Nikki again. I didn't want her there, between us. "People only keep secrets when they're ashamed."

"You keep plenty of secrets."

"But you were never one of them, Dex."

I couldn't say it made no difference.

"Miss me?" she asked.

"You're right here."

Lacey took my face in her hands. Her fingers were spindlier than I remembered. Everything about Lacey, I realized, had become more angular. Her collarbone jutted out; her shoulders and elbows looked sharp enough to cut.

"You really don't," she said, wonder in her voice.

My chest hurt. I couldn't speak with her fingertips burning against my chin and cheek and lip. When I didn't correct her, she launched herself off the dock and into the lake.

I screamed her name.

Splashes in the dark. The familiar laugh. Thunder. "Come on in!" she shouted. "The water's fine."

"It's a fucking lightning storm!"

"Still a coward," she shouted, and disappeared into the black.

Those long seconds of still water and empty night, nothing but rain and lightning and me, and Lacey somewhere beneath;

seconds and seconds waiting for her to surface, gasping and laughing and alive.

There was time to wonder: Whether she could be trusted to save herself. Whether I could. Dive into dark water, impenetrable as sky. Weightless, kicking down and down, reaching for something limbed and heavy sinking to muddy bottom. Lacey would fight me, that was Lacey's way, pull at my hair, climb up my body, so desperate for surface, for air, for life, that she would drag us both down.

I stood at the edge of the dock, heels on the wood, toes hanging over air, willing myself to jump.

The lake was endless dark. And there she was, floating moon of a face. Another game. Now we both knew who had won, because there she was in the water, and here I was on the shore.

Inside the car it was warm and dry, enough so that I was tempted to curl up in the front seat and sleep. Instead I started the engine and left her there, with her water and her storm, knowing the lightning would never dare strike.

She got in my head. That Friday, when Nikki called me to bitch about the sleepover she'd been suckered into throwing, the tedious effort of putting on a happy face for her supposed friends and said, "I'm tired of all this crap, wish you could just come over and watch bad movies," I broke our unspoken agreement and said, "Well, I *could*."

"Could what?"

"Come over. Watch bad movies, or whatever."

"I told you, I can't get out of this party."

She wasn't so stupid; she was making me spell it out. "No, I mean, I could come to the party."

"Oh, Hannah, you know you would hate that. Like, actively, puke your guts out. You hate those bitches."

"So do you."

"And trust me, if I could run away to your place and let the animals take over the zoo, I would, but my mother would kill me if one of them peed on the carpet."

I was lying on my bed, watching the ceiling, counting the cracks, trying not to care.

"You remember that pool party this summer," she said. "A fucking train wreck."

When I didn't answer, she added, "And the other party."

Now we'd both crossed a line.

There were seventy-two cracks, and also a yellowed patch in the corner where something must have been dripping from a hidden pipe. If the ceiling collapsed, I wondered, would it kill me, a blanket of plaster and dust smothering me in the night? Or would I wake up coated in asbestos, wondering why I could see the sky?

"Why aren't you saying anything, Hannah? Tell me you understand I'm doing you a favor."

"Sure. Thank you."

"You're being weird. Why are you being weird?"

"I'm not being weird."

"Good. Don't. Now you tell me something. What tells of

Hannah Dexter's excellent adventure?" She affected a Keanu drawl. "Did you have a most awesome week? Or totally bogus?"

"I talked to Lacey."

There was a hissing on the line. It was the bad connection, but it was too easy to imagine Nikki herself, reverting to snake. She breathed out the word. "Fuck."

"It was fine."

"No wonder you're being so fucking weird. Please tell me you're not feeling sorry for her."

"She said something about you and her," I said, which was almost true. "And Craig."

The snake uncoiled, struck.

"You talked to Lacey about Craig? You talked to *Lacey* about *Craig*?" She was yelling, and Nikki never yelled. "About what I've told you? Things I've never told anyone? How could you even *think* that was okay?"

"I didn't! I wouldn't!"

I protested; I swore I would never break her confidence, that Lacey had asked nothing and told even less, that it's not like I had anything real to tell. I couldn't ask her, not then, why she would blame Lacey for anything; I could only say I was sorry. She hung up on me.

On TV, this was the moment to throw the phone across the room, and so I did and felt like a fool.

So did she, she said, when she called back an hour later. "That was unfair of me. I'm a little sensitive about ... you know."

"Of course," I said.

"I know you would never tell Lacey anything. Right?"

"Of course I wouldn't."

"And I've been thinking about this sleepover party crap. You should come—I mean, if you really want to. It's going to be totally lame, and you're going to hate me for inviting you, but at least it'll be more fun for me."

"You actually mean it?"

"I don't do things I don't mean, Hannah. Haven't you figured that out by now?"

I got there at nine, as I'd been told, but I was the last to arrive. I'd cobbled together an outfit from the Nikki-approved corner of my closet, sleeveless velour shirt in forest green, black cardigan with flared sleeves, a gray choker. I wore vanilla-scented perfume and Gorilla Grape–flavored Lip Smackers. We would all taste the same in the dark.

Mrs. Drummond fluttered a hand toward the basement. "The girls are downstairs."

The girls: lazy cats sprawled across couches and sleeping bags, all smiles and claws, same as they were at school, same as they'd been since kindergarten, same as I remembered from the party I couldn't remember.

The girls: Paulette Green, who no one much liked but everyone tolerated because her parents had a secret patch of pot in their vegetable garden and enthusiastically believed in pharmaceutically raising the consciousness of their daughter and her friends. Sarah Kaye, whose father had multiple sclerosis and never left the house. Kaitlyn Dyer, the sweetheart everyone loved, even me, because she was short enough to be tossed around, short and bouncy and seemingly harmless, who was such a klepto she'd tried to steal the prom fund, and who'd gotten away with super-secret double probation because when the school tried to expel her, her parents had threatened to sue. Melanie Herman, who was sleeping with her best friend's boyfriend. Allie Cantor, who had herpes, and would forever.

I knew these things about them because Nikki had told me, and because she told me, I trusted her. Forgetting, eventually, that they weren't her secrets. That the girls had trusted her, too.

The girls were laughing at something on TV, and the something was me.

Me, unconscious and drooling in the dark. Shadows, then faces, grainy on the screen, grainy in a way I recognized. That was Nikki's father's video camera, the one she loved so much. That was Melanie and Andy and Micah. That was a voice, in the dark, shrieking "*Weekend at Bernie's!*" as brawny arms hoisted me up, danced me around, floppy and bare.

"Slut," someone said, and a hand reached into the frame, carved a Sharpie across my stomach, *S-L-U-T*, then made a smiley face out of a nipple.

Girls' laughter on the TV; girls' laughter in the basement. Freeze-frame, rewind, fast-forward, play.

"She wants it," a voice said off camera, and on-screen,

Andy Smith lowered himself over the rag doll, ground against her, hip to hip, chest to chest, tongue slurped up her cheek, then down her sternum, then ringing the smiley face, round and round it goes.

"Take off her panties," a voice said.

"Slip in a finger," a voice said. "Make her wet."

"See? She wants it," a voice said. "She's dripping with it."

"Make her suck it," a voice said. "She wants to taste it."

Different hands, different fingers and tongues. But always the same voice. Always obeyed. And the Dex doll did whatever they made it do.

Nikki loved to direct.

"Here comes the gross part!" sweetheart Kaitlyn giggled in the basement as vomit trickled out of the girl on-screen, and that was how I knew they'd watched it before, knew it by heart.

On-screen there were groans and retching sounds, and Melanie said, "There goes the boner," and Nikki's voice said *you can get it back* and *don't be a pussy* and *we can't stop now* and then there was a flashing red battery light and fade to black.

Maybe I made some kind of noise.

Maybe Nikki had always known.

Of course she had known.

Nikki turned. "Oh, no. Hannah. You're here," she said, with no inflection. "Oh dear, I guess you saw everything."

*

Somehow, I got out of there. Somehow, adjusting the mirrors, shifting the gears, signaling the turns, all as Nikki had taught me to do, I got home.

Locked in my room, on the floor.

Burning with cold fire.

What I could say now, if I could speak to her then, that girl on the floor, that girl broken: *This is not your fault; this is not your story. This is not the end. This will someday end.*

What I know now, what I knew then: *This will never stop burning.*

Hannah, burning.

Hannah, burned away, hollowed out, scoured clean, Hannah the victim, Hannah the fool, Hannah the body. Hannah, stupid. Hannah, dead.

Dex, awake.

LACEY

Come As You Are

After she had her little fun making you think I was fucking your father, Nikki came for me. It was over, obviously, whatever it was between him and me, as soon as you knew it existed. You're lucky you ran off as fast as you did so you didn't have to see him cry. "God, what the fuck is wrong with me, what was I doing ..." and on and on, literally ad nauseam, or maybe that's not what made me throw up all over the parking lot, but at least once I did, he shut up. Then he told me to go home and never come back, and I said and did some things I'm not proud of, until he took my shoulders and pushed his arms out, rigid, all that empty space between us, and gave me a pretty little speech about how I should respect myself more and expect more from others, and stop thinking I'm only valuable for sex, and all the while there was that bulge in his pants that both of us had to pretend didn't exist.

Everything as fucked-up as possible, just the way Nikki liked it, so of course that's when she slipped the note into my locker, asking me to meet her at the lake. If it had been the station, any part of the woods, I wouldn't have gone. But of course she wouldn't ask that of herself. The lake seemed okay to me, because even the shitty algae slop that passed for a town lake would remind me of the lake that mattered, yours and mine, clear and blue and ours. Nikki was part of the woods, twisting trails and sinkholes and the smell of rotting bark. You were water.

I showed up early, but she was there already, sitting on the dock. When she saw me, she pulled a bottle of Malibu from her bag. "Split it?"

It was too sweet, and the smell made me sick, but I took a couple shots. Judging from the blurriness around her edges, she'd gotten a head start.

We didn't talk much until we were both safely drunk.

"Satan, huh?" she said.

"Our Dark Lord and Savior. Wanna join up?"

"What the fuck happened to you?"

I took another swig. "Figured out I'm all alone in the world, no one loves me, and oh, yeah, a bunch of Jesus-loving psycho bitches force-fed me shit and left me in the woods to die."

She toasted me with the Malibu. "Once a drama queen, always a drama queen."

"Queen of the underworld now, haven't you heard?"

That's when she started laughing. "You're not actually

fucking Hannah's dad, are you? I'd kill myself before letting someone that old stick it in me."

I went cold. "Don't say her name."

"You really hate me, don't you?" she said.

"Even more than you hate me."

"Not possible."

"Try me."

Then her hand was on my thigh, and she was crawling up me like I was a tree, Nikki Drummond, drunk and hungry, straddling me, grinding me, tonguing my lips and tugging at my hair, saying something about how she hated it so short, then cutting off the thought by taking my fingers in her mouth and sucking, hard. Her breasts felt bigger than I remembered them, looser somehow, and there was a trickle of drool at her mouth.

"Get the fuck off." I pushed her hard enough to hurt and hoped that it did.

"Come on, you know you want to."

You know how they say desperation isn't sexy? Bullshit. An ugly drunk without a shirt, wheezing rum and aiming herself at me like a torpedo of need? Pushing her away felt like kicking a puppy, and I got off on that, too.

"Maybe I'm fucking in love with you," she said, doing that half-laugh, half-cry thing that middle-aged women do in bad movies. "Did you think of that?"

"Frankly? No."

She sat back. "Why the fuck did you even show up, then?"

"I want to know what you want."

"Was I not clear?"

"What you want to stay away from her." I would have given it to her, Dex. Anything.

"You're fucking kidding me. You want me to believe you came here to talk about *Hannah*?"

"Her name is Dex."

"Uh-huh. Keep telling yourself that." She laughed again. She'd amped up her acting skills since the last time we talked. She was nearly approximating human. "I get it, what you were doing. But we don't need her anymore."

"Since when is there a fucking *we*, Nikki?"

"You're not serious." She was touching me again, sweaty hands on hands. "What do you think your precious Dex would say if she actually *knew* you, Lacey? Is that what you really want, someone who can't see you? Someone who thinks all your bullshit is for real?"

"Stop talking."

"It's almost a year," she said.

"We don't talk about that."

"You don't think about him? You don't think about me?"

For a second, she almost had me. The stink of desperation, the sheen of moisture in her eyes, the pressure of her hands: She was so good at playing her part that, even knowing everything I knew, I almost bought it, that she missed me, that all this time she'd been secretly in love or lust, that she'd clawed her way into your life for the same reason I'd hung onto your father, that she didn't hate me anymore for what we knew about each other, that the things we'd done in the woods had meant something, hadn't been a hateful joke. Maybe I did buy it, just long enough to tell her the truth, and tell it almost gently. "Not anymore."

She let go.

"You came here for her," she said, and there, in the flat affect, the vacuum of her expression, was the real Nikki. "To tell me to stay away from *her*."

I nodded.

"But why would I stay away from my good friend Hannah?" She was slurring; it was hard to tell how much was rum and how much was effect. "I'm *protecting* her. Saving her from the big bad wolf." She smeared a hand across her nose and wiped the snot on her jeans. "Like I should have saved Craig. I'm *good* now. I do good works. Like Jesus."

"I need to know what you're going to do, Nikki. Are you going to tell her?"

Laughing again, she wouldn't stop laughing. "Tell who? Tell what?" Then she clapped her hands together. "Oh, I get it! All this crap about staying away from Hannah—that's not about her, that's about *you*."

"No."

"You're not afraid of what I'll do to her. You're afraid of what I'll *tell* her."

"They're the same thing."

"No, Lacey. One is about her. One is about you. Normal people know the difference."

"Don't hurt her just to fuck with me."

"Let's be clear. I don't care about fucking with you any more than I care about fucking you."

"Then why are we here?"

She left without an answer. We both knew the answer.

I made it worse. I tried to warn you, and you didn't listen, and that part's your fault, but the rest of it, that's on me. What she did next. What that made you do. It was all my fault and not my fault at all, same as everything else.

When I was eleven, I threw out my retainer with my lunch. Didn't even notice until it was time to slip it back in my mouth and go to class, and that's when I freaked the fuck out—because I could *see* it, wrapped in a napkin on the corner of my tray so it wouldn't get gummy with French bread pizza. Sliding into the garbage on top of Terrence Clay's leftover spaghetti and the tuna fish salad that Lindsay North, getting the same head start on anorexia she'd gotten on boobs, had tossed out uneaten. You want to know what my life was like before you? It was like, given a choice between going home without the retainer and taking a swim in a Dumpster, I didn't even have to think. The janitor gave me a boost, and then watched me pick through the banana peels and clumps of spaghetti—I've blocked that part out, for the sake of my sanity. What I remember is that I found my retainer. I took it to the bathroom, ran it under some hot water, and—I try not to think about this, because it makes me feel like I've got bugs laying eggs inside my skin—*I put it back in my mouth.*

"Careless," the janitor said after he pulled me out, after I'd finally stopped crying. "Means that much to you, why'd you throw it out in the first place?"

You tell me, Dex. Why would a person do that?

You came for me, like nothing had happened, like we were still Lacey and Dex, you and me forever. I felt more like a witch than usual, because I'd commanded it, *you need me*, and there you were. Needing me. You pretended it was a gift, like you were giving for once instead of taking, but you needed me to tell you what to do next.

You told me what my mother said when you went looking for me at the house: Lacey doesn't live here anymore. But you didn't say how she said it, regretful or worried or relieved. Lacey doesn't live here anymore. Turns out that, even in Battle Creek, some secrets keep—especially when they're about something people would rather not know.

You took her suggestion and came for me in the Giant parking lot, and when you found me, you didn't look at me like I was some charity case, and you didn't ask me stupid questions, you just said, *Lacey, I have a surprise for you, something you're going to like.*

Lacey, trust me.

What would you have done if you'd known the truth, Dex? That when you tapped on my window, you were—for the first time in months—not even a speck on my mind. It was Halloween, and that night, of all nights, I was thinking about Craig, and about Nikki. I was thinking kind thoughts about Nikki and how I'd held her while she cried. I wondered if

· 336 ·

she felt it, on this night, dressed up somewhere in some stupid slutty kitten costume, laughing and drinking and finding someone else to make hurt as much as she did. If she'd been the one to tap at my window that night, I would have let her in, and I would have taken her into my arms and sung her to sleep. I would have given her what I owed her, because I couldn't give her what I'd taken, and maybe she would have done the same for me.

It wasn't her. It was you.

Your face, a ghost materializing on the other side of the glass, that hopeful smile, same as the first time I ever talked to you, like maybe, if you pressed your hand to the window, I would meet it with mine.

You had a surprise for me, you said. That night, of all nights, a surprise in the woods.

Once upon a time, there was a girl who loved the woods, the cool sweep of browning greens, the canopy of leafy sky. Hidden in the trees, she picked flowers and dug for worms, she recited poems, timing the words to the bounce of her feet in the dirt. In the woods she met a monster, and mistook her for a friend. Into the woods they went, deeper and darker, and carved a sacred ring around a secret place, where the monster dug out pieces of the girl and buried them in the ground so that the girl could never truly leave, and never bear to return.

Once upon a time, another time, there was a girl who screamed in the forest of her dreams and woke up to grasping fingers and dead eyes, more monsters to carry her back home, and this is when the girl realized it was her fate, to live under the rotting bark and the molding stones, that she could escape, but always, somehow, the woods would claim her.

That's your kind of story, isn't it, everything tidied up and turned pretty. You wouldn't like to hear that once upon a time there was a girl who got totally fucked up by what happened to her in the woods, that there was blood and piss and shit and death, that the woods were where the girl turned into a killer and a devil and a witch, and that even the thought of going back, especially to that place, on that night, made bile rise up in her throat and she had to rake her nails down her palm so hard she drew blood just to keep from screaming.

Because you asked, I followed you into the woods.

You put a scratchy tape into the Barbie player and turned Kurt all the way up, and smiled at me like this, too, was a gift. I rolled down the window so I could breathe, and pretended I was doing you a favor by letting you drive.

"Are you going to tell me where we're going?" I said when you parked the car and we took off into the trees.

"You'll see," you said, but even then, I knew.

I thought Nikki must have told you the truth after all, because how else would you know about the station, why else would you make me go back?

The station was the same as we'd left it, only more weeds, more rust. You needed me to be strong, and so I was. Your Lacey wouldn't run away; your Lacey would remember to breathe.

There's no such thing as ghosts. No such thing as fate.

But there is justice.

You stopped in front of the boxcar, almost tripping over a rusted bucket brimming with brown rainwater. You rested your hand on a shiny padlock, and in the silence between our breathing, I could hear faint music, and her screams.

"Dex . . . what did you do?"

"Just to be clear, this isn't about what she did to me," you said. Then you told me what she did to you, and I folded you into me and felt you shaking and wanted her to die. "It's about what she did to us. That's what she's paying for."

You spun the combination and opened the lock.

Here was Nikki: crouched in a corner, shaky hands splashing light at the shadows, screaming into the noise. Nikki Drummond, a scared animal in the dark.

Here was you: grinning, proud mama showing off your beautiful baby. This scene, this night that you'd made for me, birthed from idea into fact. Hannah Dexter, in the boxcar, with a knife.

"Dex, why is she naked?"

I wasn't ready to ask you about the knife.

Nikki was on her feet, pressed into a corner, ready to pounce, her body registering something new. Incoherent screaming gave way to words. To: "Lacey."

She was crying.

"Lacey, get me the fuck out of here, she's gone fucking crazy, tell her to *let me the fuck out*."

You were watching her, not me. You weren't waiting for

· 339 ·

me to choose between you; it never occurred to you there was a choice. You believed in us again.

You believed in me again.

"You owe me," Nikki said. "Look where we are. Look what night it is. You fucking *owe* me, and you better fucking deal with this."

It never occurred to Nikki, either—that I might disobey, that I might not choose her, that she might want to say *please*. If she had, I might have done what she wanted. I'd tasted enough blood in these woods, and maybe Nikki had, too.

I wouldn't have given her back her clothes. But I might have helped her, because I don't hurt animals. I might have helped her—if only she hadn't been so fucking certain that I would.

"Lacey, you have to."

I closed her back into the dark.

THEM

Nikki's mother had always pitied other mothers. So many of them were less comfortable, less attractive, less skilled at the intricacies of PTA electioneering and bake sale presentation. They were, in a word, *less*, and it was perhaps no surprise they'd raised lesser daughters. She pitied them all, because they didn't have Nikki and she did. What good fortune, the other mothers were always saying, that you should get one like her. What a blessing, they would say, which was simply a way of reassuring themselves that they'd done nothing to deserve their inferior offspring as she'd done nothing to deserve her golden child; as if they still believed in an indiscriminate stork dropping bundles on doorsteps at random. Nikki's mother smiled gracefully at these women, letting them have their delusions. It would be unseemly to correct them, to point out that her daughter was a culmination of good genes and good breeding, and neither of these came down to luck. That she'd worked hard to ensure she had a daughter worthy of her, and raised Nikki to appreciate that hard work and continue it on her behalf. Seventeen years of approximated perfection: hair, skin, teeth, clothes, friends, boys, everything as it should be.

The *best* of everything, as it should be.

Her daughter couldn't be blamed for what that boy did in the woods—that was his parents' cross to bear, and Nikki's mother hoped they felt suitably guilty for what their second-rate parenting had inflicted on her daughter—but Nikki had endured the episode with dignity, and the small markers of grief, the glossy eyes and the blanching skin, had, if anything, made her even more beautiful. Nikki's mother had encouraged her, after a suitable time passed, to choose some-one else. Life was easier with a solid shoulder to lean on, or seem to, she'd taught her daughter. The world was so much more forgiving of strength when it took on the appearance of weakness. *I don't need another boyfriend*, Nikki snapped after her mother had urged her once too often. *Of course not*, Nikki's mother replied. Need was unseemly; need was itself weakness. The love that you needed was the kind best avoided. No one knew that better than Nikki's mother. Though, of course, she couldn't tell her daughter that.

Nikki was doing fine. Nikki was doing great. Nikki, she told herself, standing in the entryway of her daughter's closet, trying to understand what she'd found there, wasn't the problem.

It was, she suspected, this Hannah girl, the one who had followed her daughter around all summer like a mangy dog. Hannah Dexter, with her bad genes and worse breeding, her ill-fitting clothing and her abominable hair. It had to be Hannah's influence that had Nikki acting so erratically. Talking back to her parents. Canceling her dates. Dyeing her hair, of all things, some cheap drugstore purple that had cost Nikki's mother more than a hundred dollars to dye back to its original color before anyone could see. "She's not up to your standards," Nikki's mother had told her daughter the other night at dinner, and Nikki had actually *laughed*.

"My standards are fucked," Nikki had said. Trashy language, trashy sentiments: This was not the daughter Nikki's mother had raised.

Something was off. A mother always knows.

So Nikki's mother waited until her daughter was at school and prowled through her room. She'd never done it before, never had the need, silently judged those parents who were forced to police their daughters, paw through their diaries for secret rendezvous, search underwear drawers for condom packets. Nikki's mother didn't need forensic evidence. A mother knows.

But: All those empty bottles in the closet. Cheap vodka, some gin, and a few tacky wine coolers. Left behind when they so easily could have been disposed of, almost as if Nikki wanted her to see. And the pictures, beneath her mattress, pages torn from magazines, of women doing ungodly things.

Nikki's mother thought about all those hours Nikki had spent alone with that Dexter girl, imagining the girl pouring vile liquids down her daughter's throat, imagining the girl stripping off her daughter's clothing, climbing up her daughter's body, trying to pervert her daughter into something she was never meant to be.

It was not acceptable, she thought.

"So what did you do?" Kevin asked, stroking his finger along Nikki's mother's bare leg, up and up and, almost unbearably, up.

She had called him in a moment of weakness. She only, always called him in a moment of weakness, and every time was supposed to be the last time, but then there she was again, bedded down in her husband's gym buddy's navy sheets, staring at the photo of him with his wife and children at Disney World, Mickey ears perched on all four heads, while he burrowed his face beneath the blanket and did things to her down there in the dark that she could never understand. He'd asked her, once, if she wanted him to put the photo away, and she lied, saying that wouldn't be appropriate, and that she barely noticed it, when the truth was that the photo was another thing she didn't understand, a necessary part of the process, that she needed his fingers and his lips, but also their faces, Cheri's bovine eyes and the twins' sorry cowlicks, that it was this photo she saw when she closed her eyes and let his tongue guide her over the edge.

"I put it all back," she told him.

"Every girl needs her secrets," he said, and smiled like they shared something together.

In therapy, which had been Steven's condition for taking her back, she had told her husband that the affair meant nothing, the other man couldn't compare to him, which was true. Kevin was smaller in every way. Poorer, uglier, meaner. She couldn't tell him that Kevin was the tool that made Steven bearable, which was how she justified continuing it, even now, even after she'd sworn *never again, this time I mean it.*

"Maybe I should talk to her about it," Nikki's mother said.

"Maybe," Kevin agreed. He was nothing if not agreeable. Sometimes Nikki's mother felt like she was having sex with herself.

"But a mother shouldn't know everything about her daughter," she continued. "I certainly wouldn't want her to know everything about me."

"Certainly not," Kevin agreed, and they stopped talking.

She was sore, driving home, but it was the good kind of sore, the kind that would sustain her through her dinner preparations and the inane small talk of family life, a secret and deeply pleasurable ache that would keep the smile fixed on her face. This was what convinced her: Nikki deserved her secrets, as did they all. Hadn't she taught her daughter that who we are, what we do, is all less important than who we seem to be?

Dinner was meat loaf, and it was polite. Nikki's father didn't ask his wife what she'd done that day. Nikki's mother didn't ask her daughter why she smelled, as usual, of breath mints. Nikki didn't ask her parents why her brother wasn't coming home for Thanksgiving. They discussed Halloween, whether to hand out toothbrushes again and risk getting egged, or capitulate to the inevitable and return to the mini Hershey bars of years past. Nikki's father told a politely funny story about his colleague's toupee. Nikki said she'd be home late the next day because she was giving a friend a ride to the doctor, which was just the kind of thing Nikki was prone to do. Nikki's mother offered her daughter dessert and smiled when Nikki turned down the empty calories. She felt better already. Girls went through phases—everyone knew that. Nikki knew what was needed to survive and excel. She would be fine. That's what Nikki's mother told herself that night as she endured her husband's ministrations and went to sleep, and that's what she told herself the next day when evening darkened into night and the little ghosts and monsters stopped ringing the doorbell and still Nikki didn't come home.

She would be fine.

A mother knows.

US

Halloween

DEX

1992

There had to be consequences. Lacey was always right about that. Maybe freaks stayed freaks and losers stayed losers, maybe sad and weak was forever, but villains only stayed villains until someone stopped them.

And it had been so easy.

Nikki had called to apologize. Again, when I refused to answer, and again, when I didn't show up at school. Fuck my parents, fuck obligation and requirement and life; I stayed in bed, I kept the door closed, I waited to feel better or feel something or die.

She left me a note in an envelope on the front porch, and

it said, *I'm so sorry for everything I've done. Never again. This time I mean it.*

Never again. At that, I did feel something, and it filled the void. It brought me back to life.

I couldn't figure her agenda, why it was so important to make me forgive, but this time I didn't need to understand it. I only had to use it.

I laughed; I called her. I let her apologize to me, blame it on grief, blame it on Craig, on Lacey; she'd wanted to teach me a lesson about who I was allowed to talk to and what I was allowed to ask for, that was the explanation for this party; and as for the last one, that was a mistake, ancient history, terrible but past and she was sorry, so that should be enough. She was trying to be a different person, she said, a better person, that's what all this had been about. She'd been stupid, then. Later, she'd been angry. Now she was just sorry, and couldn't I just believe it.

I told her she could apologize to me if she wanted, but only in person, in the place she could be trusted to tell the truth, and on the night her ghosts would howl the loudest. Even ground: We would both be haunted. I swallowed bile and told her to meet me in the woods, and when she showed up, I was waiting.

She laughed, at first, even when she saw the devil marks I'd painted on the walls of the boxcar, the pentagram I'd smeared on the floor in pig's blood. She laughed even when I showed her the knife.

*

The knife.

I brought it, but I never intended to use it. It was generic Kmart crap, its blade the length of my forearm, its edge sharpened once a season, its hilt a cheap black plastic with a leathery feel. I'd used it to chop potatoes and raw chicken, enjoyed the satisfying *thwack* it made when swung recklessly through the air and into a soft breast or leg or straight into the meat of the cutting board. Before Lacey, the knife was the only recklessness I allowed myself. My mother hated it, but it always made my father laugh when I held the duller edge to my neck and pretended to slit my throat. The knife had always felt like a toy, and that night was no different.

I wasn't the kind of person who would *use* a knife, only the kind who would need one. Without it, Nikki wouldn't have listened. She wouldn't have been afraid, and I needed her to be afraid. I needed her to do what I said, to be *my* puppet. Letting someone else have power over you, Nikki had said, that was the only truly intolerable thing. And so she'd told me exactly how to hurt her without drawing blood.

I had dinner with my parents that night, frozen chicken fingers with frozen broccoli, which I ate without comment, knowing they could tell something was wrong, sure neither would have the nerve to ask. My father assumed everything was about him, that if he pushed too hard I'd tattle to my mother. As if I cared, anymore, what he'd been doing with Lacey; as if he could be anything to Lacey but a distraction, a horsefly buzzing at a stallion. What we had together was too big for distractions—I finally understood that. He would never understand, and maybe it was a mercy that he would never realize how much he didn't. My mother, maybe, had a better guess, but she wouldn't push it, either. I missed her, sometimes, the long-ago mother who was still bold enough to say, *Tell me where it hurts*, but maybe I'd only imagined her along with the faeries who'd once lived in the hedges and the monsters snoring under my bed.

I should have hated them both, I thought, for failing. Then I should have forgiven them, for trying. But I couldn't be bothered. They were cardboard cutouts, *Peanuts* parents *wah-wah-wahhing* in the background, and I couldn't feel anything for them anymore. I couldn't feel anything but hands on my body. Strangers' fingers. Strangers' tongues. I couldn't stop feeling that.

I brought the knife into the woods because I knew it was safe. Because I knew I would never use it the way it was meant to be used—I wasn't the kind of girl who would do a thing like that. However much I might have wished otherwise.

I showed Nikki the knife. I said, "Take off your clothes."

"Why?"

"You don't get to ask that anymore."

"You want to see me naked? Fine. Whatever. I always figured you were a little gay. You and Lacey both, with your perverted little—"

"Shut up. Take off your shirt, take off your pants, and toss them out the door."

· 354 ·

Miraculously, she did. I felt a rush of something—power, euphoria, satisfaction, maybe the simple wonder of speaking a command and seeing the world comply. There was something godlike about it: Let there be obedience, let there be fear.

I watched her strip down to her pink-laced panties. I closed her into the dark, slipped the dead bolt, and listened to her scream. I stood in the night, quiet and still, breathing and listening, palm pressed to the boxcar, picturing her on the other side, alone and naked in the dark with the pig's blood and the death metal, her screams bouncing off the metal walls until her throat burned. Nikki, helpless and afraid, cringing from things creeping through the dark, holding on until she had no choice but to let go, and break.

Then I pulled myself away and went in search of Lacey, to make my offering.

Lacey said we should tie her up, so we tied her up. Or, rather, Lacey did, and I held onto the knife.

Lacey, Lacey, Lacey—she was back. It was hard to concentrate with her name singing through my head. All I wanted to do was cling to her, whisper apologies, make her promise all over again never to let me go.

But first I had to prove myself. So I held the blade steady while Lacey brought Nikki's pale wrists together behind her back, wrapping them tight with the extra laces she had in her trunk. She had everything in her trunk. The laces were strong, made for combat, and Lacey bound Nikki's waist and ankles to a rotting old chair she'd found in the station, using more laces and a bunch of leggings. This is a handcuff knot, Lacey said, twisting in elaborate loops, this is a clove hitch and this is a butterfly, and these knots will hold, Lacey said, inexplicably certain, and even if they didn't, we still had the knife.

Once Nikki was bound up tight, Lacey held out her hand to me, palm up. She didn't have to ask: I gave her the knife, and only after it was gone did I feel like I'd given up something that mattered.

"I have to pee," Nikki said, like pulling out a trump card.

Lacey patted her head. "Go for it."

Nikki spit at her face, and Lacey laughed when she missed. I laughed, too, until the smell hit me, and the flashlight exposed the dark patch spreading across Nikki's lace panties. I expected her to look pleased that she'd called Lacey's bluff, but she just looked like a girl who'd peed her pants and was trying not to cry.

I thought about stopping it, then.

A helpless girl, naked, tied to a chair in a dirty train car with satanic scribbles on the wall. Two wild-eyed girls looming over her, one of them holding a butcher knife. I saw it like I was seeing it onscreen, prom queen brought low, soon to have her throat slashed by monsters of her own creation, audience rooting neither for hero nor villain but only for gore. I saw the Hollywood vision but smelled the urine, half a scent away from comforting, and when I did, the girl wasn't Nikki Drummond but any girl, sorry and afraid, and if I'd been in the audience, I would have wanted her saved.

This is real, I thought. But many things were real. Foggy memories of hands on skin were real. Evidence captured on videotape was real. The swooping lines of black permanent marker I'd scrubbed off my skin, the taste of puke and stranger I'd brushed out of my mouth, the creeping fingers doing exactly as Nikki commanded. Real, real, real.

Surfaces were deceptive. Nikki had taught me that better than anyone. The trappings of evil were for scary movies and school assemblies; the real devil wore pink and smiled with pastel lips. And here, in the dark, we all knew who she was.

"Don't think we're going to feel sorry for you," Lacey said, and she was right.

Real was the hollow space Lacey had left behind, and the lies Nikki had told me in her wake. I'd believed the witch, let her put a curse on Lacey. All those days and weeks she'd spent sleeping in her car. While I was slurping frozen yogurt at the mall and debating whether Aladdin could be fuckable even if he was a cartoon, Lacey had been alone. Because I left her that way; because Nikki had made me.

"I'm thirsty," she said.

Lacey snorted. "You're kidding, right?"

"I've been here for fucking ever!" Nikki shouted. "And I'm thirsty."

"Idea," Lacey said brightly. Lacey loved an idea. "Dex, go get that bucket we saw outside."

I set the bucket before her. It was corroded by what seemed like centuries of rust, filled almost to the brim with brackish rainwater.

Nikki shook her head. "No."

"You're thirsty, right?" Knife in hand, Lacey grabbed her hair and yanked her forward, hard enough that she toppled, chair and all, onto her knees, until her lips were nearly on the bucket rim. "Don't you want a drink?"

"Let go." It was a whisper. "Please don't make me."

"So picky," Lacey said.

Together, we righted her; she was heavy, but she wasn't fighting us anymore. That made it easier.

"You realize this is kidnapping, right?" All the trembly vulnerability was gone from her voice, nothing left beneath the flab but hard, pearly bone. "You're going to be in huge trouble when you let me out of here."

"You're not giving us much incentive," Lacey said.

"What are you going to do, kill me?"

"It's so cute when you pretend to be fearless." Lacey turned to me. "Dex thinks you'll never tell. She thinks you'll be too piss-scared of what people would think. Look how well she knows you."

"Better than she knows you. Not as well as I do."

Lacey closed in. I held the flashlight steady. The beam glinted off the blade.

"I want you to tell her what you did," Lacey said.

Nikki tried to laugh. "I really don't think you do."

"At that stupid party. You tell her what you did, and you apologize."

"How much is that going to mean, Hannah? You going to believe I'm sorry with a knife to my throat?"

The knife wasn't at her throat.

And then it was.

"Lacey," I said.

"It's fine."

It was fine.

"Tell her," Lacey said. "Tell me. Let's hear your confession."

When Nikki swallowed, her throat bulged against the knife. "You want me to talk, step back," she said, barely moving her lips. Keeping her head very, very still.

"I want you to talk carefully," Lacey said.

Nikki swallowed again. "We were just having fun. You remember fun, don't you, Lacey?"

Lacey kept her gaze on Nikki. "Did you have fun at that party, Dex?"

"No, I did not." I'd brought along a bottle of my parents' scotch, for courage, like they said in the movies, and now I took a burning swig. It was cold outside but hot in our boxcar, or I was hot, at least. Fizzing and tingling. Fire licking my throat.

"You let her drink too much," Lacey said.

"She's a grown-up."

"You let her drink too much, and she passed out, and when she did . . . "

Nikki didn't say anything.

I didn't see Lacey's hand move, but Nikki moaned. Then, "When she did, we had a little fun, like I said."

"You took off her clothes."

"I guess."

"You let your idiot friends touch her."

"Yeah."

"Feel her up."

"Yeah."

"Fuck her."

"Lacey—" I said. "Don't."

I wanted to know; I didn't want to know; I couldn't know. I drank more.

"*No*," Nikki said. "I'm not a fucking sociopath. Unlike some people."

"Just a perv," Lacey said, "who filmed the whole thing on her daddy's camera. Tell us how you made them pose her. That's still assault, you realize that, right? That's still called rape."

"Stop," I said.

"I never *touched* her," Nikki said.

"Of course not," Lacey said. "Not yourself. You don't get your hands dirty. You just make things happen."

"Enough," I said. Too much.

"It was harmless," Nikki said. "Look, it was stupid, I know. I'm a bitch, *I know*. But it was harmless."

That word. That she could say it. *Harmless*. It erased me from the picture. Without me, there was no one to be harmed.

"She wants to hear you say you're sorry," Lacey said. "And I suggest you try to sound like you mean it."

I never loved anyone the way I loved Lacey that night. She was like a wild thing, a storm in a bottle, so much rage compressed into a tiny black-eyed body and channeled in my defense. It was glorious. Like watching a sunrise, blazing Crayola pinks birthing a new world, meant only for me.

"I'm sorry," Nikki said, quietly. "And for what it's worth, that's actually true. I am sorry, Hannah."

"Her name is Dex."

"Uh-huh."

"Say it."

"I'm sorry," she said. "Dex."

"You buy that, Dex?" She didn't ask whether it made anything better. What made it better was forcing Nikki to admit what she'd done. And knowing I had the power to make her suffer for it.

I wasn't supposed to be that kind of person. I was a good girl, and good girls weren't supposed to take pleasure in pain. But I did, and I found there was no shame in it.

"I wish everyone could hear what kind of person she really was," I said. "Imagine if they knew."

"They know," Lacey said. "They just don't give a shit."

But they didn't know. It wasn't just Nikki's parents who were fooled, the gullible teachers and women at her church, the kids on the outer fringes who looked unto her as a god. It was her own: They knew she was a carnivore, but didn't understand she was a cannibal. They didn't know how many of their boyfriends she'd screwed, how many of their hearts she'd contrived to break, how many of their secrets she'd handed to me, how many of them she'd hurt just because she was bored, just because she could. There was no leverage in me knowing that—no use in threatening to expose her. She didn't care about them, wouldn't care about alienating them and being left alone; that wasn't what appealed to me about forcing her to confess. It was the prospect of forcing her to do what I wanted. Anything I wanted: Nikki stripped bare, limp and helpless, a marionette under our control.

I knew, when we let her out, that we would be safe. She would keep quiet—not to save herself the embarrassment but to save herself the pity. If I could bend her to my will, force her to speak the words I put in her mouth—if she was powerless, and admitted it—then a part of her would always be powerless. Nikki would never tell anyone what happened here, because if she did, it would mean a part of her never left.

It was my idea first, but Lacey was the one who remembered the Barbie tape recorder, and the stack of cassette tapes, and understood what they could mean. What we did next, we did together.

"You're going to tell us everything," Lacey said when we'd trekked back to the car and retrieved the equipment, once Nikki had come down from being left once again to scream and weep alone in the dark. "Everything terrible you've done, from start to finish. And maybe we'll play it for the world to hear, or maybe we'll just keep it for ourselves, for insurance. You'll never know."

"Think of it as a confessional," I said. "Good practice for your audition tape."

"Why would I ever do that?" It was almost impressive, this skinny, stripped-down girl pretending at defiance. "Because of your stupid knife? What are you going to do, murder me and bury me in the woods?"

"I'm surprised you think that's beyond me," Lacey said, but when Nikki held her gaze, Lacey was the one to look away first.

"I'm not doing it," Nikki said. "You can keep me here as long as you want, but you can't make me *do* anything. You can't."

"I don't know about that." Lacey toed the bucket of water, then bumped shoulders with me. I'd thought we would never do that again, never be so perfectly in sync that we could speak with our bodies instead of our words. "What is it they say about me at school, Dex? Don't they think I'm some kind of witch?"

"I've heard that," I said.

"Me, I think Nikki's the witch."

"Understandable."

"I know a lot about witches these days," Lacey said. "You know how they used to tell if someone was a witch? Back in the bad old days?"

"I do," I said, and I remember feeling clever, and giddy, and not at all afraid. These were moments without consequence; this was a night that would never end.

"How about it, witch?" Lacey lifted the bucket, nasty water sloshing over her hands. "Let's see if you float."

LACEY

1991

It was the day I woke up and smelled winter. No frost, no snow, nothing so dramatic as all that, but you could feel the cold crouching in the wings. It had been summer all week, and according to the overtanned idiot on TV, winter was blowing across the Midwest, the sparkly cardboard snowflake inching toward us one corn state at a time.

Winter was our ticking clock. What were we supposed to do, fumble at zippers with wool mittens and Velcro gloves, kiss with frozen tongues and watch our excretions turn to ice? As a novelty act, maybe, but unless you're Dr. Zhivago, frostbite is a turnoff and fucking outside, much less lying on the ground in two feet of snow, high on pot and pheromones and trying to connect with the sublime, is a testicle-shrinking failure waiting to happen. We didn't have to discuss it to understand the obvious: When the cold came, the thing between us would sheathe its fangs, crawl under a rock, and hibernate the winter away.

We used the heat while we had it, and that day, Halloween, Nikki and I skipped school and met in the woods, dressed in costume as each other, to fuck with Craig's mind. She always loved role-play the best, and she made me promise that when Craig showed up after practice—always after practice, because however much he loved her and us and the fleshly pleasures that came with it, he loved the team more—we would keep to our roles religiously, though of course by the time he did, we were too drunk to bother. Maybe if we had, we would have played an entirely different game, and Craig would still be alive, or one of us would be dead.

That day, we'd finished with each other. We were waiting for Craig and making snow angels in the mud, and Nikki was amusing me by itemizing the defects of our peers, one by one, in alphabetical order, just to show she could. Theresa Abbot had a harelip and talked like a cartoon character, and she'd once tattled on Nikki, unforgivably, for smoking in the girls' bathroom. Scotty Bly would have been cute except for the way he chewed with his mouth open and insisted on letting a worm of a mustache crawl across his upper lip, both of which rendered him unfuckable. I was bored by the time we got to *C*, but also pleased, because nothing got her hot like talking about people she hated. Maybe you already know that.

We went through Shayna Christopher and Alexandra Caldwell, and then, Dex, we got to you.

"You want to know what's wrong with Hannah Dexter?" Nikki asked.

"Not particularly."

Not because I cared about you, Dex, but because I didn't care at all.

"She's such a fucking victim," Nikki said. "It's like she's asking you to screw with her."

"Funny, she's never asked me."

"You know what I mean. Where's the fun in it? It's like playing kickball with a dead skunk."

"It makes you smell?"

"Too easy *and* it makes you smell. Like, yeah, you feel bad for the skunk, but why'd it run into the road in the first place? Like it wanted to get run over, you know? Like that would be easier than just finding a way across and figuring out what the hell to do next."

"That's the worst metaphor I've ever heard," I said.

She wasn't listening. She was on a roll. What does it mean, Dex, that in all the time I'd known her, she'd never mentioned you once? But that day, it's almost like you were there with us, the future ghosting itself onto the past. "And also! She's like . . . oatmeal."

"Beige and lumpy?" I said, and then there was some talk of lumpiness that's better left forgotten.

"No. No! Pudding. Hospital pudding, the kind that comes dry out of a packet and you add water."

"So she's pudding. What do you care?"

"I don't *care*. I . . ."

"What?"

"Give me a second, I'm thinking."

"Slowly."

"Fuck you." She stripped off her shirt, then. It was still warm enough for that. I raised my ass off the ground just enough to shimmy out of my skirt. "Because she doesn't *try*, that's what I hate about her. Because she's nothing, she's blah, and fine if that's what she wants, but she walks around all bitter and sulky that people treat her like she's nothing—"

"People meaning you."

"Sure, whatever. Me. Acting like it's somehow my fault that she's a loser. Like I'm some kind of fucking witch, and I put a curse on her."

"Poof!" I zapped her with my magic finger. "You're pathetic."

"Abracadabra!" She waved her arms, accidentally or not whacking me in the boob. "You're a horny toad."

"All that and she's a horny toad?"

"No, you're a toad," she said. "And I'm horny."

Every time was like the first time.

Even that last day, when we'd already done everything we could think to do, when we knew how to fit our bodies together and how to slide in a third, when she knew how I tasted and I knew where to rub and when to pause and what would make her wet. It never got old, not married-couple old, because it was always dangerous. Anyone could stumble upon us; animals could attack. There were always new positions, new dares—down on the tracks or rolling on the station floor, dodging the broken glass, finding ants and beetles later in places nothing alive should enter. The illicit charge sparked extra bright when it was just the two of us, because Craig got petulant at the thought of us enjoying things without him. It dented his ego to realize that his dick was superfluous, and while he got off on hearing us describe what it was like—the tidal wave of sensation, the seizing muscles and the curled toes, the *Penthouse* reality of the full-body shudder—he never really bought it, that it was the same as what he felt, or what we could be made to feel by him. Girls don't get sex, he always said, not really. It was lucky for us, he said, that we didn't know what we were missing. Lucky for him, we giggled, when he wasn't around, and when the wave rippled through, both of us liked to scream.

I don't know why they did it. Maybe they were bored; maybe I was an escape route; maybe Craig was in love with Nikki and Nikki was in love with me; maybe together the three of us made something, like a poem, like a song, like a band, that was greater than the sum of its parts, and we all wanted to be greater than. I don't know why *I* did it, except that life was small and this seemed huge. They needed me, and no one had ever needed me before. You've got to remember, Dex, I'd just found Kurt; I'd sworn to myself that I would be different, that I would live like he sang, that I wouldn't let anything be easy and experience would be my art. I was brand-new, and there's a reason babies don't do anything but poop and suck teat and pee in their parents' faces. They don't know any better; they can't help themselves.

DEX

1992

The first time, it was almost funny. I couldn't do it myself. I didn't trust myself to grip her hair, hold her head under the water without letting go, long enough to break her but not long enough to drown her, so Lacey did it while I held the knife. She thrashed around a bit, or as much as she could all tied up, and when Lacey finally let her up for air she was soaked and shuddering, filthy water streaking down her face. Once she'd gotten in one or two good breaths, before she could even agree to offer her confession or put up any more fight, Lacey shoved her under again, holding tight as her body spasmed.

I held my breath, too, and when my lungs started to hurt, I said, "It's too long?"

"Trust me," she said.

This time, when Nikki came up, wet and panting, she was

ready to talk. "Whatever the fuck you want, just don't do that again. Please."

Sometimes I tried to drown myself in the bathtub—not seriously, just as an experiment, slipping beneath the waterline and staring through it to the cracked ceiling, lips shut tight against the warm water, daring myself to stay down. If I open my mouth, I would think, if I breathe it in. It would be that simple, and it was nothing I hadn't done by accident a thousand times in a thousand summer pools. But I could never will myself to do it. You can't ask your body to kill itself. You want it dead, you have to murder it.

"Ready?" Lacey said, and when Nikki nodded, her wet hair stuck to her face and sending rivulets down her bare chest, I pressed *record*. Lacey crossed her arms and paced, like a TV lawyer, which felt wrong, somehow. We should be sitting quietly in shadow, I thought, our eyes averted, like priests.

Lacey told her to start at the beginning, and so Nikki told us how in sixth grade she'd gotten bored with her then best friend, Lauren, and convinced all the other girls in their group to ice her out for the rest of the year. I remembered this: I had joined the *I Hate Lauren* club—which never existed as anything more than a membership list circulated to half the class, then left anonymously on Lauren's desk the next morning, just as the *I Hate Hannah* list had the year before— not because I did hate Lauren, but because it seemed to have slipped into the zeitgeist that Lauren was hateable, and it was safer to be against than for. She told us about how she'd dared Allie to accuse Mr. Lourd of feeling her up in the computer lab, but when Allie came crawling back to complain about the subsequent mess—Mr. Lourd getting fired, then getting drunk and trying to throw himself in front of a bus, Allie landing in therapy with a guy who *actually* tried to feel her up—Nikki laughed and claimed she'd never dared her, that Allie was just imagining things, and maybe she should do whatever that therapist wanted because she was clearly losing her mind. It went on and on—the time Sarah Clayborn was arrested for shoplifting because *someone* had slipped a Calvin Klein scarf into her bag; the day Darren Sykes was roughed up by a couple of thugs from Belmont because someone told them he'd screwed their mascot, and the months Darren spent trying to live down the rumor that he'd fucked a goat; the way Jessica Ames dumped Cash Warner without explanation or opportunity for apology because someone had told her he'd cheated with the sexy-for-a-sub replacement math teacher—so many catastrophes, all of them bearing her devil's mark but not her fingerprints.

Midnight came and midnight went.

When the stories trailed off, somewhere toward the end of tenth grade, and she said that was enough, she was hungry, she was bored, she was done, Lacey dunked her again, holding her down longer this time, until the thrashing stopped.

When she came up, she was still breathing, and I had a momentary lapse, wondering if I should stop Lacey before things went too far, whatever that meant. That Nikki could make me feel for her, fear for her, even for that one moment— maybe she really was a witch.

I reminded myself it had to look real. Nikki had to believe we meant to hurt her.

She was dripping wet, and crying too hard to speak.

"I'm going out to pee," Lacey murmured. "Watch her."

And then there were two.

"It'll be a while," Nikki said, tears drying. "She probably needs a smoke."

"Lacey doesn't smoke."

Nikki only smiled, or tried to.

She coughed hard, and spit. I aimed the flashlight at the ground. It was harder to look at her without Lacey there. Harder to remember that we weren't the bad guys.

"You can just untie me before she comes back," Nikki said.

"Why would I do that?"

"If you're scared to piss her off, tell her I got away somehow. She'll believe it."

"I don't need to lie to Lacey," I said. "I'm not the one who should be scared."

"Are you fucking kidding me, Hannah? Look around you! You should be fucking scared out of your mind. She's *nuts*. You think she's ever letting either of us out of here? She's totally lost it. Sane Lacey is gone. Sane Lacey has left the building. Look what she's making you do, for God's sake."

"She's not making me do anything."

"I'll be sure to explain that to the cops."

"What cops? I thought neither of us was ever getting out of here."

"Listen, we were friends, right? We *were* friends, I know

· 372 ·

that was fucked-up of me, I know it, but it was also real. You know me now enough to know I'm just fucked-up enough for that. I felt bad about . . . you know, everything, and I wanted to make sure you didn't remember and, yeah, I wanted to fuck with Lacey, but then, Jesus, turns out I actually liked you." She was talking so fast, the words running together, lying at the speed of light. "You liked me, too, Hannah, you know you did. You can lie to her all you want, but I know that."

"There's something very wrong with you," I told her.

"Fuck." She started crying again. "*Fuck.*"

Come back, Lacey, I thought. I could go to her now, but I couldn't be that girl, not for either of them. I had to be the girl who could hold onto the flashlight and the knife, who could stand guard in the dark, who could fend off all enemies.

This time, I would keep the faith. Lacey was in control; we both were. This night would go only where we wanted it, and no further.

Then Nikki spoke again. "She was mine first, you know. Lacey was mine."

"Shut up." A knife is only as powerful as the person holding it. Even then, she knew the truth of me.

"She used to drive me around in that shit Buick, just like you. She still have those candy cigarettes in the glove compartment? She still like to listen to 'Something in the Way' when she's sad?"

She did.

"Oh, I've been in her car," Nikki said. "And in her room. Watched her make out with that stupid Kurt Cobain poster, kneel in front of it like he's some kind of god. Did you think you were the first to catch her act? Did you think you were special?"

"I said shut up."

"You're not special. You're not even relevant. You're just some sad, clueless deer wandering onto the highway. Roadkill waiting to happen."

"I'm serious, Nikki, stop talking. Or else."

"Or else what, Dex? I'm fucked either way, thanks to your batshit friend out there. And so are you. Don't you want to know who's fucking you?"

Nikki was naked and tied to a chair and somehow she was still beating me. And what if Lacey never came back, I thought. How long, I wondered, would I wait?

I'd learned my lesson. This time, I would wait forever.

"*I* know her," Nikki said, and she was crying again, as if that would make me believe her. She was crying, but her voice was hard, as if her lips didn't know what her eyes were doing, had divorced themselves from the shine of panic and would stand their cruel ground until the end. "I know she runs hot. I know, when she puts her arms around you, it's like curling up against a hot water bottle. It's like she's on fire."

"This is pathetic, Nikki."

"I know what it feels like to have her hands on my body and how she looks when she's getting fucked. This face she makes, the way her eyes go all surprised and you think she's going to scream but she just makes this kind of breathy sigh and then it's over."

Come back, Lacey.

Come back and make her stop.

It didn't make sense, except for how it made *all* the sense—
what else but this, what else could it have been, what else was
there, and where did it leave me.

Come back.

"I know what makes her wet. What she *tastes* like, Hannah.
You know all that, too? No, I don't think you do. I can see it
in your face. What you don't have. What you want."

If the door hadn't creaked open. If Lacey hadn't climbed in,
reeking of smoke. If she hadn't taken the knife from my hand.
If Nikki had kept talking, her garbage piling up between us,
steaming and rotting until I couldn't take it anymore and the
knife had found its way on its own to her gut or her face or
her throat, anything to make it stop. If I'd been left on my
own to decide, I would have stopped her. There would have
been blood.

Instead there was only Lacey, back in time, holding me,
whispering, why was I shaking, then shouting at Nikki, what
did you do?

"What could I have done?" she said, sweetly. Then, "I'm
glad you're back. I'm ready to confess a little bit more. How
about we start with what happened to Craig?"

LACEY

1991

He brought his father's gun. It was Halloween, after all. He was a Goodfella, and he wanted to look the part. That's what he said, at least, because that way he didn't have to say he was giving in to Nikki, who'd been whining about getting her hands on the gun ever since Craig let slip that it existed. You can see, can't you, that it couldn't have been entirely my fault? That Craig was the one who set Chekhov's Law in motion? (And this is a guy who only knew Chekov the *Star Trek* character.) The Bastard would tell me not to speak ill of the dead. But if, hypothetically, someone drifted into the great beyond due to his own ape-headed stupidity, and left the rest of us behind to mop up the blood and wipe away the finger-prints—not to mention zip up his pants—he couldn't exactly resent a little postmortem scorn.

Craig showed me how to shoot. Stood behind me with

his arms around mine, closed his hands over my grip, and together, we raised the gun. He showed me how to sight it, line up the mouth of the gun with the beer can we'd propped on a branch, and I could feel him getting hard as we fingered the trigger. What do you think turned him on? The fact of my body against his, the heft of the gun, the anticipation of the shot, or the power of knowing something I didn't, pulling my strings for once, *pull back, breathe, relax, steady, go*?

The weight of it. The cold metal *realness* of it. The knowing that I could turn it on him, on either of them, pull the trigger, and, simply as that, wipe them from existence. Who wouldn't get hard?

Nikki refused to touch the gun. She just liked watching us shoot it. She always loved to watch.

Craig was the jealous type. Pawing at us when we got too close to each other, sliding in between, his every pore oozing *Look at* me. *Want* me. Craig, with his Égoïste cologne and his crooked front tooth, textbook dim, meathead sure of himself, but somewhere deep beneath the roided-up muscle meat— somewhere in the blood or marrow—he must have sensed the truth. He was an appendage. He was Nikki's Velveteen Rabbit, all of us waiting for him to turn real. She was done with him, bored with him, didn't love him. If I knew it, he must have known it, too.

Sometimes he ignored her and went at me like an octopus, tentacles grasping with a need neither of us actually felt. And always, when he pawed me, he watched her, hoping it would hurt. You could feel him deflate when she cheered him on.

It was supposed to be every guy's dream, two girls, one dick, everyone rooting for a home run. He wasn't allowed to say no. To say, *Too weird, too twisted, too freaky for me.* To say, *I want you to myself in the backseat of a car or the empty locker room or even, on a special occasion, in some honeymoon suite rented by the hour.* He wasn't allowed to say, *I don't want adventure, I want crabs-infested upholstery and a vibrating bed.* So he did as he was told. And maybe he had to drink himself sick or get stoned off his head to deal; maybe he thought there was something wrong with him; maybe we *made* him think there was something wrong with him, teased and flicked him when he couldn't get it up, devised demented games and awarded ourselves points when we pushed him too far, spiked his drink now and then to give ourselves some time alone, enjoying the spectacle of King Jock brought low by his concubines. Maybe there actually *was* something wrong with him, ever think of that?

I liked the sound of the gun when it went off. I liked how you could feel the sound in your fingers, and how it hurt.

Later.

Craig passed out beneath a tree, so it was just the two of us again, me and Nikki, evening spreading out against the sky and all that crap. We lay side by side. I cradled the gun against my chest, wondering if Kurt had a gun, if he loved it as much as I could love this one. I could take it home with me, I thought. Slip it under my pillow, hold it as I was falling asleep, let it follow me into my dreams, where we would be one, we would be all-powerful, we would be safe. I rubbed it, long and slow, like it was Craig and I could feel it harden to my touch, and laughed to think it would stay hard forever. Less trouble, in all ways, than flesh.

"We should trade in men for guns," I told Nikki, and it was late enough, we were high enough, that it felt profound.

"We could *be* men, with guns," she said, and touched it for the first time, took it in her hands like she knew exactly what to do, held it to her crotch, raised its mouth slowly toward sky. "Bang."

Nikki started it. Remember that, even if she never did.

"You ever think about it?" she said. "Having one of these?"

"I dreamed I had a dick once. It was so real I woke up freaked out enough to check."

"When I was a kid, I saw a movie where that happened," Nikki said. "Girl wished she was a boy and woke up with a little something extra in her pants."

"That's fucked-up."

"Scared the crap out of me. Then. But now?"

Craig was slumped against ancient bark, head tipped back, eyes closed. He would have looked deep in thought, but for the drool.

"Now I wonder," Nikki said.

Didn't we all? What it would be like to be one of them. To have power, be seen, be heard, be dudes rather than sluts, be jocks or geeks or bros or nice guys or boys-will-be-boys or whatever we wanted instead of quantum leaping between good girl and whore. To be the default, not the exception. To be in control, to seize control, simply because we happened to have a dick.

"Imagine if it were that easy to get off," Nikki said. "I don't know how they ever get anything done. I'd be jerking off nonstop."

"Not worth it," I said. "You really want something hanging off you that just pops up whenever it feels like?"

"Or doesn't." She giggled. Craig had a tough time getting it up when he was drunk. That October, he was always drunk.

"Or doesn't. Seems very inconvenient."

"Good for peeing, though." She stood up, held the gun tight against her zipper, aimed it at the ground. "I bet I could spell my name. In cursive."

"You'd be a lady-killer."

She grinned, spread her legs wide, threw her shoulders back. Held the gun with one hand and smacked an imaginary ass with the other. It was Craig's favorite pose, though he usually accompanied it with some improvised porn music, *bow chicka wow wow.* "Yo, dude. Check out my package."

"Big and hard," I said. "Just the way I like it."

"Not as big as your rack," she said. If I'd let myself laugh, maybe it would have ended there. But I was still wearing my Nikki costume, I'd slurped a deadly puddle of tequila-spiked Jell-O, and it was Halloween—I wanted to play.

"Oh, Craig," I simpered. "I love your big, hard cock."

He liked that, dirty talk, always wanting us to assure him, *Oh baby you're huge oh baby you feel so good oh baby I'm so wet oh baby*—it said he was strong and we were weak, he was supply and we were demand, he was power and we were need.

"Oh, yeah, baby?" she said. "You want it? You want it bad?"

"I want it so bad," I said. "Because you're the most popular guy in all of school and we're going to look super sexy in our Dreamiest Couple yearbook photos."

"I do not sound like that, bitch."

I let my voice go breathy phone sex operator. "Tell me we're going to be homecoming king and queen, big boy. Tell me how all the peons will gaze at us and we'll crush them under our big, royal feet. Tell me how you'll use that rock-hard cock of yours to pee on their parade."

I raised myself onto my knees and padded toward her, till the gun was in my face. Leaned forward, kissed its cool tip. Tongued the edge, tasted its tang.

She jutted her hips. "You want some of this?"

"I want all of it." Then its mouth was in my mouth, and I was licking my way around its rim. Nikki moaned.

"Ohhhh, Nikki," she said, in his voice.

I pulled my lips away, just long enough to gasp, "Mmm, Craig," then swallowed it again, drew higher up the shaft, cupped her ass in my hands.

"I love you," she said, hand on my head, forcing me down, then up, into a rhythm. "God, I love you."

It was no different than sucking at the real thing, hard and slippery and dangerous.

"I love you," she whispered, nails digging at my scalp. "I love you I love you I love you."

And so it went, until the real Craig woke from his stupor

and realized we were playing without him. There was a manly grunt, a skunk of a burp, and then he lumbered over to us and sealed his own fate in one puff of beery breath: "Step aside, ladies, and make way for a real man."

DEX

1992

"You want to stop talking now," Lacey said, less like a threat than like a hypnotist's command.

Nikki smiled. It was a storybook grin, one that might have been called insouciant in some British story of magic and portals. "No. I don't think I do. Hannah, would you like to hear about the last time Lacey and I came into these woods? Once upon a time, on a night very much like tonight—"

"You really want to find out what happens if you don't stop talking?" Lacey brandished the knife.

"It's getting old, Lace. You want to use it, use it. I'm tired of secrets. That's what all this is about, right? No more secrets."

I wonder, now, if Lacey knew that once it started, it wouldn't stop. A body in motion tends to stay in motion unless acted on by an unbalanced force. Maybe she wanted to tell me, needed Nikki to make her. More games, more marionettes, all of us pulling one another's strings, turtles all the way down.

Neither of them was looking at me.

"There are worse things than death," Lacey said. "Maybe you need another bath." She seized Nikki's hair, rougher than before, shoved her face into the bucket, held her hard and tight as her limbs spasmed, and it went on and on and then on too long and I shouted at her to stop.

She didn't stop.

I screamed it. "Stop!" and "You're going to kill her!" and "Lacey, *please*," and only then did she let go. For a long, terrifying second, Nikki didn't move. Then she coughed up a bubble of water and took a shuddery breath. Lacey did look at me then, hurt painted across her face.

"You still don't trust me, Dex?"

"I trust you."

"Then why do you look so scared?"

"Gosh, I wonder why." Nikki's head was hanging limp, her voice hoarse, mouth wide and sucking air, and still she managed to sound smug.

"This is getting boring," Lacey said. "We got what we wanted. Let's get out of here. Untie her and go home."

Just like that. She said it like a punishment, like I'd been too loud and whiny in the backseat and she'd been forced to turn the car around.

"We have her on tape," Lacey reminded me. "She won't tell anyone. Will you, Nikki?"

Nikki shook her head, dog obedient.

"See? It's over. Let's go."

It could have been that easy. We could have gone home, the three of us, safe and sound and only a little bit fucked up for life by what happened in the woods. Lacey set that before me on a platter, and all I needed to do was reach for it. On the other side of *yes*: the empty highway, our artist's loft in Seattle with its lava lamps and dissipated men, the future we'd promised ourselves. *That easy.*

Nikki looked hopeful, but not only that. She looked satisfied. That's not why I said no.

We couldn't stop, not yet. Because Lacey was too eager; because there were still secrets. Because if I let it be over, I would never know what was true.

Secrets were a claim, and as long as they shared one, they owned each other. I needed Lacey to be only mine. We would stay in this boxcar until everything was said. For Lacey's own good, whether she knew it or not.

"Not yet," I said. The air hissed out of both of them. "One more confession."

"You need a break," Lacey said. "Let's go sit in the car for a while, listen to some music."

"That's right, Saint Kurt will solve all your problems," Nikki said. "And if that doesn't work, you can always knock her out and leave her in the woods to rot."

"Shut up!" Lacey screamed.

I didn't like her losing control. Nikki shouldn't have been able to make her do that. Nikki could have no power over Lacey. I couldn't allow it.

"We should stay here," I said. "We should listen."

Nikki laughed.

"We *promised*," Lacey hissed, and the *we* was them, not us. "You promised."

"And *you* tied me to a fucking chair and tried to drown me," Nikki said. "Pretty sure that means all promises are void. Let her hear what you did."

"What *we* did. You always forget that part."

"I'm done with that. This sad story of how we're both to blame. Fuck that."

"Enough," I said.

"I'm sorry, Hannah, I tried to spare you from finding out that your friend here is a sociopath, but you wouldn't let me. So now you get to hear the whole truth."

"I'll kill you," Lacey said, like a growl. "I actually will."

"Right, because you're so scared that Hannah will find out what you're capable of that you'd kill me right in front of her? That'll convince her you're a good person. Foolproof plan."

Then they were shouting at each other, about who was a monster and who was to blame, and they didn't hear me tell them stop; they didn't see me at all. I thought maybe I was the ghost. Maybe I wasn't there, never had been.

"Tell me the story," I said finally, and these were the words that summoned silence. "Tell me everything."

"Smartest thing you've ever said, Hannah. See, Lacey and I used to come out here—"

"No," Lacey was quiet. "I'll tell."

There was no more yelling. I felt it again, what Nikki had

once told me, that this was a sacred place, haunted by all the ruined futures of the past.

"So you can lie to her? Again?"

I didn't see Lacey's hand move, only the silver blur of the knife. Then there was blood, just a dab of it, on Nikki's collarbone, and a tiny yelp of pain.

"I'll tell," Lacey said, quieter still. "The truth this time, Dex. All of it."

I was not afraid of Lacey.

I would not allow myself to be afraid of Lacey.

She would tell her story, prove her faith in me. I would repay her by finding a way to believe. "Tell me, Lacey. Everything."

"Go ahead then, tell her," Nikki allowed, magnanimous in victory. "Tell her the story of us."

LACEY

1991

Nikki didn't just want to watch; she wanted to conduct. I tried to teach her chaos, but she understood only control. So it had been from the beginning: Nikki leaning against a tree, head cocked, eyes narrowed, ordering us from one position into another, telling Craig to lick my neck or turn me over and drive my face into the ground. It made three more manageable: two bodies and one will.

Craig didn't want to do it, not at first. That's something else to remember. He could never say no to Nikki.

"On your knees, bitch," she said to him, and he dropped.

He should see what it was like, she said. She should get to watch him seeing it.

She hated him, if you want to know what I think.

What I think is, she wanted to take that gun and shove it up his ass and pull the trigger. His punishment for the person she was when they were together, the act she put on that required a Craig by her side. But Nikki Drummond doesn't get her hands dirty.

I held the gun. I held it where a dick would be.

"Not gonna happen," he said, even though he was already on his knees. "That's totally gay."

"It's a gun, not a dick," Nikki said. "How is that gay?"

He grunted.

"You know what's gay, Craig? Two naked girls writhing around together. Panting. Sucking. Sweating. You don't mind that, do you? You ever want to see that again?"

She knew so much, Dex, and yet somehow she hadn't clued in that he really, really didn't.

"You ever want me to touch *your* gun again? Or you want me to tell the whole school it's got warts?"

"Like anyone would believe that."

"Have you met me, sweetie? They believe anything I tell them."

This, for them, was foreplay.

"Do I have to?" Even the question was a sign: He'd given in.

"Take it slow," she advised. "Flick the tip. Tease it a little, it likes that. Remember what you told me, the first time? Just like eating an ice cream cone. You love ice cream, Craig. You *love it*."

She didn't need to talk me into anything. I stood steady, kept the gun erect as Craig closed his mouth over it. Maybe I was curious, too.

Darkness swirled around us, the station hissed with ghosts, and my blood was half vodka. Not an excuse, Dex. Just setting the scene.

He was tentative, at the start, like a girl sucking it for the first time, not sure where to put his hands or his tongue, licking and flicking in sorry, frog-like spurts, then easing his mouth around the barrel and holding it there, like the mere ambiance of his warm, damp cave would get the job done.

"Friction!" Nikki shouted, clapping a steady beat. "Friction and rhythm. Get it together. And mind the teeth."

I started moaning. A gasp here, a pant there, partly to help him along and partly to mock him, all for show, until, somehow, it wasn't anymore. Because it felt *good*, Dex, his head under the palm of my hand, bobbing with my rhythm, his lips finding their pace, his fingers doing their work, one hand wrapped around mine on the gun, the other climbing my thigh and finding its way to where it needed to be, hot against my heat, rubbing in time and pressing hard, harder the louder I moaned, and maybe it was the booze or his fingers or just the fact of the gun, but I'm telling you, Dex, I *felt it*. Felt *him*, against me, sucking hard, swirling his tongue around just so, breathing hot and fast, felt him pulling back, pulling away for the hint of a moment, playing with me like I always played with him, then taking it all in his mouth again, swallowing us whole. And it was me, metal but also somehow flesh, and as it came over me—a full-on flash-bang explosion, zero to sixty to holy shit—I thought, this is some kind of black magic at work, this is science fiction and I am a cyborg of skin and steel, this is how it is for them to look down at us on our knees, but it wasn't just that, one great erotic leap for women everywhere, it was this particular boy on his knees and me on my feet, it was this boy's girl in the shadows, screaming my name, needing me to see her, to forget about him and need her back, it was the game and the show and the love and the gun, it was a split second of wild, muscle-clenching, teeth-rattling, tip-your-head-back-and-howl-at-the-sky pleasure, and then it was over.

I was crying and laughing at the same time when he seized up, went rigid—and if I was thinking of him at all, I was thinking how Nikki would never let it go, that he'd gotten off on it, loved the feel of something hard swelling in his mouth as much as any of us—but then he fell away from me, and only when Nikki stopped screaming my name and started screaming his did I realize that the crack of noise had not been some overload of neural circuitry but an actual, world-shattering sound. That the world had shattered. That the wet beneath my fingers was blood.

You don't want to know what a dead body looks like, Dex. Or the sound a person can make when she sees one.

Craig, of course, was silent.

Craig wasn't there anymore. The thing in his place, the raw, wormy, bloody thing that had just been cupping my ass and fingering my cunt and wrapping his hand over my hand over the gun ... that's the thing that comes after me in my sleep, the thing that kept me out of the woods. That was the reason, later on, that I stopped at one wrist, let the knife drop by the bathtub and the water swirl pink. I don't believe in heaven or hell, but I believe you see something when you die, whether the firing of synapses or some groping hand from the great beyond, and I believe that's what I'll see, Dex. That thing, that face, that hole. I think that's the last thing I'll ever see, and I can never see that again.

"You killed him." That's what she said when she could talk, when I'd slapped her out of her keening and back to reality so we could zip up his pants and deal with the gun. "*You killed him you killed him you killed him.*"

I didn't remind her who'd made him get on his knees. I was trying to be kind.

I wanted to move the body. We both did. Away from our place, deep into the woods. I thought we both wanted to exorcise our station of his ghost so we could return. They say you sober up fast in a crisis, but that hasn't been my experience. I must have been drunk off my ass to imagine the two of us would want to come back.

Moving the body meant touching the body, hoisting the body, dragging the body into the woods. Cleaning the trail of blood and brain bits the body left behind. We couldn't do that. Any of it. We would leave him there in our place; we would leave him behind.

Nikki wiped down the gun; I put it in his hand. This was Battle Creek; this was a disturbed teenager alone in the woods with his father's gun; this was a pretty enough picture, and when Nikki added the note he'd written her the day before, after he'd unforgivably forgotten her half birthday, the note that said, in Craig's painstaking block letters, *I love you and I'm sorry*, the picture was perfect.

"Now what?" Nikki said. "We just leave him here?" She swallowed. "There are animals . . . "

"They'll come looking. They'll find him. Eventually."

"Eventually."

She thought I was the heartless one. Because I kept going, because someone had to. If she was going to be the mess, then I had to be the one who cleaned up. If she was going to cling, then someone had to be clung to, and that was me. I am a rock, Dex, like the song says. I'm a fucking island. I do what I have to do, and that night, I had to hold Nikki Drummond while she cried. I had to collect our clothes, our empties, our cigarette butts, anything that would connect us to the body. I had to sit with her in the car while we sobered up and the body cooled, not so far away.

I wasn't the one who suggested we frame it up like a suicide. We never talked about doing anything else. The truth wasn't an acceptable option. What we did was too obvious, too easy, not to be the way.

That's not how Nikki remembered it.

In her version, I'm Machiavelli. I murder him in cold blood, dupe her into covering it up so she'll seem equally to blame. She's the victim, I'm the devil, he's the corpse.

In every story, he ends up dead.

No one made him get on his knees. And if anyone did make him, it was Nikki.

It was their fault as much as it was mine. I stand by that. I will always stand by that.

Murder requires intent; I know because I looked it up. Legally, killing someone by accident is no worse than hitting a deer with your car. Lots of blood and mess and guilt, but no one's to blame except maybe the deer for being dumb enough to step into the road.

I couldn't have killed him because I wasn't trying to kill him. I didn't want him to die.

Belicve that.

If you believe anything, Dex, believe that.

But.

In the dark.

At night.

When I let myself remember.

I feel it beneath my finger.

The trigger.

And I know.

The gun in his mouth, the gun in my hands: It doesn't matter what I wanted. It doesn't matter why. Accident, purpose, motive, mistake, unconscious wish, muscle contraction: It doesn't matter. What matters is that it was in his mouth, and in my hands. It was my finger on the trigger. It was my finger that moved, just a little, just enough. Then he was gone.

DEX

1992

Before Lacey, I wasn't happy. I wasn't anything. Except that's not possible, is it? I took up space; I was a collection of cells and memories, awkward limbs and clumsy fashion crimes; I was the repository of my parents' expectations and evidence of their disappointments; I was Hannah Dexter, middling everything, on track for an uneventful life and only just sharp enough to care.

A world without Lacey: I would have spent my days doodling and chewing gum to keep from falling asleep in class until I could come home and settle in front of the TV for the night. There would have been a few hundred days to endure, then college, somewhere compatibly middling, *High School: The Sequel*, Battle Creek U. That Hannah Dexter might have gathered up enough spunk to move to Pittsburgh or Philly after graduation, make a go of it in the big city, barhop with her gaggle of young single girls until one by one each scored herself a ring and fled to the suburbs. She would have made an excellent bridesmaid, a bit of a pill at the bachelorette party but always reliable for a sober ride home. She would not have complained; she would have thought it unseemly, thought that pretending to be happy was close enough. She would have returned to Battle Creek rarely, only to endure holidays with her parents and eventually to bury them. She would, perhaps, have run into Nikki Drummond at the drugstore before leaving town, and they would have offered each other the wincing approximation of a smile, as you do when you're too old for grudges but still seething with them. Her real smile would come later, whenever she remembered those extra thirty pounds Nikki wore around her middle and the strip of pale skin on her left ring finger; she would be smugly certain it was better to avoid love than to lose it.

Lacey told me everything. What she'd done—what they'd both done—to Craig Ellison. What they'd done with each other. The ghosts of them in that place. The body they'd left behind in the woods.

It was the body that should have made the difference. Not the thought of them laughing together in the grass; not the reality that they came first, that I was the thing tossed back and forth between them, incidental.

"It doesn't matter how it started," Lacey said. "It was only about Nikki in the beginning. Then it was us. Just *us*."

Lacey was the reason Nikki had tried so hard to hurt me,

but then, that wasn't news. News was, Lacey belonging to her first.

"I did this for you," I said, stretching my arms wide, because it wasn't just the night, the boxcar—it was life. It was *Dex*.

"Dex, you have to understand—"

"No. I have to ... " I stopped. What did I?

"I have to go outside for a minute," I said. "I need air."

I didn't want air. I wanted sky, stars poking through branches, the space to run at the night, the freedom to flee, even if I wasn't planning to, and maybe I was.

"What did I tell you?" It was Nikki, thinking she still mattered. "She can't handle it. You think she's going out for *air*? She's going straight for the cops. You know she is."

"No, she's not," Lacey said, so sure. "She wouldn't do that."

"I wouldn't do that," I repeated. They were just sounds.

"You're fucked and you know it," Nikki said. "Look around you. All this Satan shit—who's taking the fall for that? She couldn't have set you up better if she tried. Maybe she *did* try, Lacey. Think of that? Let me out of here now and we'll take care of it."

"Don't leave, Dex."

"She's going to ruin everything," Nikki said. "Untie me, and we can deal with it together. Make her see that she should keep her mouth shut."

"Stop." I was backing toward the door.

"Don't leave, Dex," Lacey said, and she took a step toward me, and she was raising the knife.

"Look at her!" Nikki crowed. "Jesus, Hannah, look at her,

· 397 ·

she's actually thinking about it. Killing you to shut you up. She's *psychotic*, Hannah. You get it now?"

"Don't leave," Lacey said again, and I didn't leave.

"It's her or us," Nikki said, and I didn't know which *us* she meant. "Only one person killed Craig, and she's the one who's got the most to lose here. Untie me. Untie me and I can protect you."

"Stop talking!" Lacey slashed the air with the knife. "Stop talking. I need to think!"

The blood on Nikki's shoulder had dried into a long brown streak, as if she'd tattooed it to remind herself of past wounds.

We were silent. Three of us, waiting.

It was like living inside one of those logic puzzles they gave us in elementary school, a menagerie of animals needing to be ferried across a river in a specific order so no one would be eaten; a sinking hot air balloon with ballast to be tossed overboard, ballast that would keep you aloft, but only if you chose the right thing to sacrifice. Those puzzles were always bloody; failure invited catastrophe, the bloody shreds of a chicken on the riverbank, broken bodies in a cornfield.

Maybe, I thought, we would stand here together until the sun rose. Light would restore sanity, brush away the wild thoughts you only have at night. But the boxcar had no windows; sunrise or not, we would stay in the dark.

Then Lacey spoke. "Nikki's right. We've gone too far. If people knew ... " She tipped the knife toward Nikki. "We can't trust her. That's obvious. But you, Dex?" The blade swiveled toward me. "Can I trust you?"

I made some kind of noise that didn't sound like anything of mine, more animal than human. Animal in pain.

"I trust you to love me, Dex, but you're a good person. You might think you have some kind of obligation to tell. Unless . . . " She nodded. "Yeah."

I reminded myself to breathe. "Unless what?"

"Unless you had a secret, too."

Nikki got it before I did. "No. No no no no. Hannah, *no*."

"Mutually assured destruction," Lacey said. "And if we've both done something terrible . . . we'll be the *same*, Dex. We'll be in it together."

She offered it to me like a gift—like a promise.

All I had to do was take it.

"We tied her up, Dex. We tied her up and locked her in a fucking train car and tried to drown her. You think she's not going to tell someone? You think you're not getting in trouble for this if we let her out of here?"

"We don't know that."

"She flat out told us she would."

"I was bluffing," Nikki said quickly. "And what I did at the party, and what happened to Craig, I'm fucked if you tell any of it. Mutually assured destruction, right? No one will ever know about this. You have my word."

Lacey laughed. "What's that you said before? All promises are void."

"Hannah, don't," Nikki said. "Don't let her talk you into something you can't take back."

Lacey, somehow, was still laughing. "You see that? She's *still*

· 399 ·

trying to turn you against me. That's what I'm afraid of, Dex. Not getting in trouble. Not what she'll do to me—what she'll do to *us*. She'll break us again. She will."

"That's bullshit and you know it," Nikki said. "This is what she *does*, Hannah. She wants you to believe it, that everything is my fault. Nothing is yours. *You're* the one who walked away from Lacey. *You*. Lacey knows you don't want to see that. She knows you like it better the way she tells it, where you're not responsible. You don't like what you saw on that video? Don't let it happen here. Don't just lie there and let her fuck us both. *Please*."

Lacey smiled. "See? She can't help herself. She hates that we have each other." Lacey wanted me to hear it, because she believed that I believed in us. "This can only end one way, Dex. Take the knife."

"Take it!" Nikki shouted. "Take it and use it, because if you think she's ever letting you out of here, you're as nuts as she is."

Lacey set it down on the floor between us.

"I said I was sorry. But you have to be sorry, too. Then everything can be like it used to be. Better."

Better, because there would be nothing between them anymore. Better, because we would have a secret of our own to protect; because we would be indivisible; because we would, finally, be the same.

"You love me, Dex?"

I couldn't not love her. Even then.

"Then prove it," she said.

That night we did the mushrooms, after we'd looked into the face of God, after the cows in the field and the boys in the barn, Lacey had spirited me away, had parked the car for the night on the side of a deserted road, deciding, with our minds still reeling and eyes still following invisible angels, that would be safer than driving home. I wanted to sleep in the car, but Lacey said it would be better in the grass, under the stars. It was cold and damp, but we weren't in a state to care. I curled up on my side, and she pressed her chest to my back and curved an arm around me, holding on. *Do I belong to you?* she'd whispered into my neck, and I'd said yes, of course, yes. *You won't leave me*, she said then, and it was command, and it was request, and it was truth, and it was prayer.

"Don't make me do this," I said.

"I won't make you do anything," she said, and not enough of me was relieved.

"You pick up that knife, and you do whatever you want with it," Lacey said then. "Your choice, not mine."

"No, Hannah," Nikki said. "You can't do that."

But I could, that was the thing of it. I could do anything. It was simple physics, biology: kneel, pick up the knife, carve. I could make my body perform each of those steps, and inanimate objects—floor, knife, skin—would give way to my will. It would be simple, and then it would be done.

And I would have been the one to do it. That was the thing of it, too.

As simply as picking up the knife, I could have walked to the door and kept going. But where would I go, without

· *401* ·

Lacey, and who would I be when I got there? Lacey thought she knew who I was, deep down, Nikki, too, and I couldn't see how it was so easy for them to believe there was such a thing, a me without them, a deep down where no one was watching. That I wasn't just Lacey's friend, Nikki's enemy, my father's daughter; that somewhere, floating in the void, was a real Hannah Dexter, an absolute, with things she could or could not do. As if I was either the girl who would pick up the knife or the girl who would not; the girl who would turn on one or turn on the other, or turn and run. Light is both a particle and a wave, Lacey taught me, and also it's neither. But only when no one is watching. Once you measure it, it has to choose. It's the act of witnessing that turns nothing into something, collapses possibility clouds into concrete and irrevocable truth. I'd only pretended to understand before, but I understood now: When no one was watching, I was a cloud. I was all possibilities.

This was collapse.

THEM

They had all been girls, once upon a time. If they were afraid now, of their girls, it was only because they remembered what it was like. Girls grew up; girls grew wild. Girls didn't know themselves and the sharp-toothed needs breeding within, and it was a mother's job not to let them.

Girls today thought they didn't need their mothers, thought their mothers didn't understand, when their mothers understood too well. Girls today didn't know what it was to march through crowded streets hoisting signs and screaming slogans, to kiss boys off to war, to watch the news and see boys burn, to lie in browning weeds and weave a crown of thorns, to wrinkle and bloat and sag, to watch doors close, life narrow, circumstances harden, to hate the girl you were for the life she chose for you, to want her back. Girls today wanted to believe they were different, that girls like them could never grow up into mothers like these.

They let their girls believe this was true.

They lied to their girls, and taught their girls how to lie to themselves.

Girls today had to be made to believe. Not just in a higher

power, a permanent record, someone always watching—girls had to believe that the world was hungry and waited to consume them. They had to believe in depravity and fragility, in longing as a force that acted upon them, a force to be resisted. They had to believe that they were the fairer, the weaker, the vulnerable, that they could only be good girls or bad, and that the choice, once made, could never be revoked. They had to believe in the consequence of incursion. Girls had to believe there were limits on what a girl could be, and that trespass would lead to punishment. They had to believe they could find themselves in a doctor's office with scalpel and suction, or in an alley with panties at their ankles, or in a plastic bag tossed out with the trash; they had to believe that life was danger, and that it was their own responsibility to stay safe, and that nothing they did could guarantee that they would. If they believed this, they would build fortresses, they would wall themselves in, they would endure.

Girls had to believe in everything but their own power, because if girls knew what they could do, imagine what they might.

They told themselves that this was for the girls' own good. Sometimes they resented the responsibility; sometimes they resented the girls.

Girls today thought they could do anything. Girls burned bright, knew what they wanted, imagined they could take it, and it was glorious and it was terrifying.

They couldn't remember ever burning so bright.

Or they did remember, and remembering made things worse.

They wanted, for their girls. They wanted for their girls more than they wanted for themselves; this was the sacrifice they'd made. They wanted their girls to be safe. To do what they had to do to conform, to defer, to survive, to grow up. They wanted their girls never to grow up. Never to stop burning. They wanted their girls to say fuck it, to see through the lies, to know their own strength. They wanted their girls to believe things could be different this time, and they wanted it to be true.

They wondered, sometimes, if they'd made a mistake. If it was dangerous, taming the wild, stealing away the words a girl might use to name her secret self. They wondered at the consequence of teaching a girl she was weak instead of warning her she was strong. They wondered, if knowing was power, what happened to power that refused to know itself; they wondered what happened to need that couldn't be satisfied, to pain that couldn't be felt, to rage that couldn't be spoken. They wondered most about that girl, a good girl, who'd nonetheless carried herself away to some secret place, taken knife to pale flesh, drawn blood. They wondered about that girl, what she'd known and what she'd discovered, what story she'd been told or told herself that could only end this way, with a girl alone in the dark, with a knife, in the woods.

US

After

US

Best Friends Forever

Three girls went into the woods; two came out.

It sounds like the start of a joke, or a riddle. But it was only, would ever after be, the rest of our life.

We thought about dumping the body in the lake. It would have been comforting, having it gone, bloated and rotting in the deep. But imagine if they'd dredged the lake or some unlucky fisherman had dragged a corpse to shore.

It had to look like a suicide. And, after all, one of us knew how that was done.

We wiped the prints off the knife. We curled her fingers

around it and untied the corpse. The deepest of cuts ran from her wrist nearly to her elbow, *down the road, not across the tracks*. As for the shallower cuts, the bloody slashes that bounced up and down her forearms, they would be read as hesitation cuts, we hoped, aborted attempts by a girl new to pain. We burned our bloody clothes; we erased the night.

The pieces fit. It was one year after her boyfriend had given himself to the woods. The note beside her body was written in her own hand.

I'm so sorry for everything I've done. Never again. This time I mean it.

The girl was troubled; the girl was trouble. As all girls were troubled, as all girls were trouble. They wanted to believe it, and so they did.

Sometimes we wake up screaming. Sometimes we swallow our cries and lie alone, staring at the ceiling, reminding ourselves that we were all innocent, and we were all to blame, and that included Nikki Drummond.

We never say her name.

While we were arranging the body and wiping fingerprints off the knife, the pope was busy pardoning Galileo. We were unimpressed. We doubted that the maggoty dust of Galileo's four-hundred-year-old corpse much cared that the church had finally gotten a clue. But we tried to celebrate the triumph of reason, ventured into an empty field where we could see the stars, passed a bottle of wine back and forth, scanned the sky for the rings of Saturn and listened to the Indigo Girls sing his elegy. The night was hollow and cold, the grass damp. Wine no longer made us pleasantly blurry, no matter how much we drank.

Out there, in the unimaginable world beyond Battle Creek, the army of reason marched on. We knew it was true, because we saw it on TV. Up with the separation of church and state; down with supply-side economics. Up with sex and drugs and the saxophonic approximation of rock and roll; down with the death penalty and "gay cancer" and Dan "Potatoe" Quayle. Our Democrat took the White House, a hippie boomer with his finger on the button. We were all living in Satan's America now, at least according to Pat Buchanan. We'd always liked Clinton, the man with the honeyed voice and the McDonald's jowls who worshipped at the altar of indulgence. He was our kind, we thought once, but not anymore, because he still believed in a place called hope.

We went to the funeral, obviously. People stared. Nikki killed herself—everyone believed that—but she'd done it on Halloween, the devil's night; she'd done it in a boxcar scribbled with satanic symbols; she'd done in it the same season one of her fellow seniors had turned satanist and cursed half the class. The devil's fingerprints were all over. Only Nikki's parents and brother didn't stare. They sat in the front row with their heads down. Her father cried. We wanted to, but we didn't.

Maybe, deep down, we liked it. They were afraid of us, and there was always pleasure in that.

We saw that they liked it, too. You could hear it in the curbside sermons, the barely concealed pride of being proven right. If Battle Creek did have an underground cabal, it was a cabal of shameful joy, and these were its members: the ministers, the principal, the guy who kept writing all those editorials in the local paper, the cops, the experts brought in from Harrisburg to advise on cults, everyone who got to be on TV. We heard that after Geraldo came to town, Kaitlyn Dyer's mother had a viewing party, with seven-layer dip, like it was the Fourth of July. We weren't invited.

We shared a bedroom, marking time till graduation, until we could leave without drawing suspicion. All of our parents had been accommodating; in the days after Nikki, no one liked the idea of a girl living on the streets. We slept side by side. We smelled of the same conditioner and toothpaste; we wore each other's clothes. We couldn't stand the sight of each other, but we had to stay in sight. We had to make sure our secrets would stay locked up, which meant watching each other, always. We dreamed with our eyes open, remembering the noise she'd made as the blood was spilling out of her, the whale song of pain.

We still drove, in those endless days. Never toward

something. Always away. We would drive into emptiness, then set out a blanket, lie down in the middle of a dead sunflower field. A yellowing void we could scan from horizon to horizon, wizened stalks swaying in the breeze.

The buzz and chitter of insects. Our goose-bumped skin. Spring on its way, all too slowly. Seconds ticking by, measured and loud. Life inside a grandfather clock.

We talked about the devil, and whether there was such a thing. Once we had speculated that God and the devil were the same, that they were contained in the holy sound of Kurt's voice, but we didn't need them anymore, our god or our devil. We understood now what we were meant to be, a church of two, worshipping only each other.

When the time was right, we left. Exactly as we'd planned, in the dark of night, bags piled into the trunk, car pointed west. We didn't go to Seattle. Seattle wasn't ours anymore. But we paid attention, and we saw what became of it.

Seattle was a commercial. Seattle was a movie set and a Gap ad. Grunge was ascendant; the revolution was televised. Seattle took over the world, all its possibility and promise made manifest, and didn't survive it.

Neither did Kurt. We didn't cry. We wondered, for a moment, at the rumors about Courtney, because we knew how easy it was to make one thing look like another, to take a cold hand and curl it around a gun. But deep down, we knew: It was Kurt. His finger. His trigger. He owned his death, and it turned out the death of a god was like any other. It was not rage or sorrow or love; it was neither beautiful nor deep. It was the one thing Kurt had never been: pointless noise, pointless silence.

There was no place to go but LA, where you could live on the surface and get lost beneath it, all at once. We found an apartment in the shadow of a freeway and jobs that made our feet hurt and our hair smell of smoke; we paid rent and taught ourselves to surf, trying to pretend we were having fun.

This is what we wanted, we told ourselves, and also, we will be okay, and also, I still love you.

We liked how we looked with platinum hair, and even more we liked how we looked like everyone else. Sometimes we even liked how much we looked like each other, like sisters, people said for the first time. LA was a place to lose yourself and be reborn. It was as far as we could get from Battle Creek without drowning ourselves in the Pacific, and we waited, we wait, for the tide to carry Nikki into the past.

LA doesn't believe in the past any more than it believes in the future, and so neither do we. We pretend away the days to come, when our skin will loosen, our breasts will sag, our eyes will be rimmed by lines and hollows that makeup can't disguise, when we will no longer be girls who've done something terrible but women atoning for the sins of the strangers they used to be. We will never go back; we will search for ourselves on milk cartons and miss the home we were so desperate to escape. We will be waitresses and receptionists and the chirpy voice on the end of the line thanking you for your time and telling you *have a nice day.* We will worship the girls we used to be. We will never have children; we will never have daughters. Someday, maybe, one of us will walk into the sea, and the other will finally be alone.

Not yet. We refuse the future. We hang onto our moment, freeze ourselves in this time, when we are still girls, when we still know pain and its pleasures. We walk in the ocean and dig our toes into sand that comes from far away, from ages past. We scan the horizon for pirate ships and glass bottles, for unlikely miracles washing to shore. We have no secrets from each other; we are two parts of a whole. We have everything we wanted; we have only each other, and we can only trust the girls we used to be, who whisper to us from the past and promise that will be enough.

Acknowledgments

Thanks to the dream team: Meredith Kaffel Simonoff understood what this story wanted to be and somehow bamboozled me into believing I could write it. Cal Morgan's wisdom, insight, persistence, and refusal to let a single semicolon pass without careful consideration and occasional debate made the revision process a terrifying joy. There's not enough gourmet chocolate in the world to repay my debt to either of them, but I'm working on it. I also owe a substantial amount of chocolate—and maybe some tea scones—to Clare Smith, for her transatlantic encouragement, support, and razor-sharp editorial insight.

Thanks also to Jennifer Barth for the extraordinary enthusiasm with which she guided this book into the world, and to the wonderful Jonathan Burnham, Robin Bilardello, Stephanie Cooper, Lydia Weaver, Katherine Beitner, Laura Brown, Erin Wicks, and everyone at HarperCollins; to the indefatigable Poppy Stimpson, Rachel Wilkie, and everyone at Little Brown UK; and to all the amazing cheerleaders at DeFiore and Company, especially Colin Farstad.

Leigh Bardugo, Holly Black, Sarah Rees Brennan, Erin

Downing, Barry Goldblatt, Jo Knowles, E. Lockhart, Ilana Manaster, Mark Sundeen, and Adam Wilson all took the time and effort to read stacks of pages, helping me figure out which ones not to light on fire. They, and so many others, kept me afloat while I was kicking and flailing my way through this book: Dan Dine, Brendan Duffy, Leslie Jamison, Anica Rissi, Lynn Weingarten—thank you, a million times over, for keeping me well stocked in ideas, motivation, ambition, love, hope, and baked goods.

Finally, thank you to the MacDowell Colony, for giving me such a beautiful space in which to finish this book—and to the Park Slope coffee shop where, one rainy morning in a different life, I began it.